The Monastery

by Edwin E. Mier

A Psi-Fi Mystery

ISBN-13: 978-0615840666
ISBN-10: 0615840663

Dedication

Sincere thanks to Linda, Davy,
Loree and Vince – the pit crew
who kept this thing going,
in the right direction,
and over the finish line.

Preface

Few among us will argue that there is something we possess, or can tap, which gives us incredible – albeit inexplicable – insight. It may be sensing that someone nearby is watching you, or knowing that a loved one has died. Some claim they can see and share the thoughts of others, or communicate with the dear departed, or view remote places. And there are even more incredible, and dubious, accounts – visualizing events that haven't happened yet, psychic healing, or moving things or causing other physical phenomena through mental thought alone.

In researching this book I interviewed, or reviewed the work of, scientists, engineers, psychics, medical doctors, clairvoyants, spiritualists, even members of the clergy. Indeed, while the characters and storyline in this book are fictional, the multi-disciplinary efforts depicted here to quantify this energy – or force, or capability – are real.

Psychic phenomena are increasingly well documented and more meticulously scrutinized. But since the scientific community still can't explain them, this whatever-it-is has been relegated to the back burner, shut away in the closet labeled 'Maybe someday we'll figure this out.'

To be sure, these phenomena are seldom consistently repeatable or controllable. Still, engineers and scientists can be somewhat brittle in their thinking. If this 'energy' cannot be explained within the confines of the currently known laws of physics – and it probably can't – they are likely to never acknowledge it and remain content to live in denial. We still do not have even a workable theory of the mechanism that enables the concurrent sharing of information over long distances, defying space and the boundaries of time.

The Monastery

For centuries stargazers and physicists noted unusual, inexplicable astronomical phenomena. But it was not until a brilliant fellow named Einstein came up with a ground-breaking theory – with the radical notions of 'space-time' and 'relativity' – that a credible explanation was offered. Many still couldn't, or wouldn't, accept it. But in the course of time experiment after experiment have proved his space- and mind-bending theory correct.

Fast forward to today and the bold new frontier of psi-ence. As the growing caseload of psychic phenomena undergoes more and better scientific analysis, it's only a matter of time before a break-through discovery – and a credible theory – emerges. It will happen.

Edwin E. Mier
The Pocono Mountains
June 2013

Contents

Chapter I: Long ago, in the Carpathians......................7

Chapter II: Desert warrior 34

Chapter III: Reassignment 58

Chapter IV: The Project 85

Chapter V: The Players and the Team....................128

Chapter VI: The 25-cent tour 160

Chapter VII: Teamwork 194

Chapter VIII: Filling in the blanks 246

Chapter IX: On the road 294

Chapter X: Crisis 346

Chapter XI: The Shades of Eastern Europe 381

Chapter XII: Now and again 423

Chapter XIII: Reflections...462

Chapter I: Long ago, in the Carpathians
I: Tracks in the snow

A nearly full moon punctuated the cloudy night sky, painting the mountainside with streaks of bright moonlight. It had begun to snow, the first snow of the fall … a wispy, powdery precipitate that glistened and swirled in the cold air.

Huge primordial firs covered the mountains. Snow had begun collecting on the canopy of the high outstretched branches. Some sifted through, mixing with the ambient moonlight, to create an eerie, surreal miasma below.

A solitary hooded figure moved furtively over the craggy ground. The figure abruptly stopped, and a gloved hand reached up and threw back the hood. A shake of the head loosened long dark hair. Her labored breathing pierced the silence, each exhale hanging suspended for a moment in the frosty air. She stopped to get her bearings, she told herself, but she also had to catch her breath. It was an arduous climb and she knew the worst was yet to come. The path grew steeper and steeper the further up the mountain she progressed.

Even in the dark she recognized where she was. She reckoned she had covered about half the distance up from the village … still a ways to go. She had made the trip a dozen times – the first when she was just a child, with her parents. But every time was different. Tonight she was ascending, in the dark. And she was alone.

It was late winter when she last made the trip, she recalled. The Magyars had just arrived, rampaging their way down from the northeast. The horde had encamped on the eastern slope, and scouts reported their tribal chieftains had set up headquarters in Suceava, over the mountains to the east. It had taken her nearly ten days to get back here, after sneaking out of the Magyar camp in the middle of the night. Thinking back, she sighed.

A chill and shiver startled her back to the mountainside. A dusting of snow now covered her hair and shoulders and was settling into every fold and crevice. She brushed off, shook her head and pulled her hood back up.

She peered up ahead at the winding path. It was supposed to be a secret, unknown to outsiders. It led to a place never to be found by invaders. But tonight, the light coating of snow drew attention to the well-worn path. The stone steps and walkway, normally disguised amid the surrounding woods and rocks, stood out in the dark woods like a meandering white stairway.

She tugged at her collar, pulling it tight, and started off, proceeding carefully step by step. Getting to safety and warmth was foremost on her mind – not the tracks she was leaving in the freshly fallen snow behind her.

* - * - *

I: Child of the prince

She had to stop and rest a few more times along the way. Finally, rounding the last curve, she found herself standing in a small clearing. On the other side a set of narrow, rock-hewn steps rose, some 30 feet. Covered now in unblemished snow, the stone stairway looked formal, imposing. Along either side of the steps were massive boulders and sheer rock faces. If anyone were to ascend beyond here, they had to go this way.

She felt she was being watched. Indeed, she thought she'd been under surveillance for some time. She was right on both counts. Cautiously she approached the steps.

"Hold," a voice boomed from up the steps. She stopped, flipped back her hood and looked up to where the voice came from. But she saw no one.

From behind a rock face a large figure stepped out into view. He wore a black bear fur coat, which matched his beard, and deer leather pants and boots. A fur band encircled the guard's metal helmet, covering the tips of his ears. His right hand grasped his conspicuous, but still sheathed, sword – a subtle way of showing he didn't expect a fight, but was ready for one.

His left arm wielded the heavy shield of a Dacian guardsman – a large black iron ring, encircling a slab of thick oak. In the center a carved caricature of a wolf's head – the ancient symbol of Dacia –was painted black.

"Get your captain of the guard," she hollered to him in the ancient Dacian dialect. Her voice quivered, in part due to the cold, in part from her near exhaustion, but also from the excitement of nearing the end of her journey. "Go, and tell him Ilinca has returned."

The guard turned his head, looking up over his shoulder to the top of the steps. Standing there – all the while, it seemed –

was another guard, thinner and similarly dressed, but wielding a bow instead of a shield. The first guard gestured to him. The bowman nodded, turned and disappeared from sight. Not a word spoken between the two.

The guard then turned back to Ilinca. "Are you alone?" he queried.

"Yes," she replied. He seemed relieved at the answer. He stepped out of sight for a moment and then returned, this time without his shield. She waited. He waited. She began shivering.

The bowman finally reappeared. Another tacit exchange: The bowman nodded down to the guard, who silently acknowledged, and then turned back to Ilinca.

"Come up, please," he said, gesturing. Ilinca dashed ahead. As she neared the top of the narrow passageway the bowman stepped aside. There, walking quickly towards her was a familiar and friendly face.

"Mihai!" she exclaimed. She ran to him and they embraced. She clutched him tightly, and he reciprocated, his heavy shield pressing against her back. Mihai, the commander of the guard, was a ruggedly handsome man, a little taller than her and a few years her senior. His shield featured a shiny bronze metal ring rather than the guard's black iron, denoting his rank.

Her head nestled snugly in the crook of his neck, and she savored the familiar warmth and safety she felt in his arms. "My love," she said softly, looking into his eyes, "I have succeeded."

He broke their embrace and grasped her shoulders.

"You have?" he responded excitedly, a wide-eyed look of exhilaration on his handsome face. He looked her up and down as he held her firmly. "You are sure?"

Her gloved hands went to her abdomen.

"Yes, I am sure," she said reassuringly, her head dropping. "I carry the child of Istvan, the prince of the Magyars."

"Istvan?"

"I learned about them from our people in Cacica, just before I arrived at their camp in Suceava," she said. "There are seven Magyar tribes, all encamped around Suceava. The heads of all the tribes convened and they selected a chieftain named Arpad, the strongest of them all, as their leader. On a blood oath they pledged that Arpad, and his male descendants, would forever rule the Magyar nation."

"And Istvan?" Mihai asked.

"The eldest and strongest son of Arpad," she said. "He is a fierce warrior. He would be gone leading raiding parties for weeks at a time. His tribe usually is the first to venture into new areas. Many of our people fell under his sword. It took me two months to finally get to meet him," she paused, "Then, on his return one night, I was called to his bed."

"Just you? By yourself?"

"Not at first, no, there were several of us. After a while, though, I learned which ones I could trust. They cooperated and kept quiet. And through the spring and summer I ended up alone with Istvan most of the time. He became quite fond of me, actually," she said, smiling coyly at him.

"By midsummer it was done," she said, glancing down at her abdomen, "I was carrying his child."

"I stayed another month. Then late one night I slipped out of their camp. Our people in Cacica kept me safe and hid me there for a few days. They told me that Istvan sent his most trusted men to find me and bring me back, so I hid in the woods during the day. I made my way back slowly from there, traveling mostly at night from village to village."

Mihai gazed at her, his expression showing that he comprehended all she had been through.

"You must be exhausted," he said. "Come," he grabbed her arm and began walking with her. "You'll stay here in the Monastery from now on."

"Captain!" The guard's chilling scream came from down below. Mihai let go of Ilinca and ran to the edge of the stone stairway, where the bowman was kneeling. She followed. They saw the large guard pointing to the clearing below.

No one was in sight yet, but an arrow shot up and struck the guard, still pointing, solidly in the chest. With lightning speed the bowman next to Mihai loaded an arrow and drew his bow.

As the first intruder appeared in the clearing he let his arrow fly. It struck its mark, lodging in his neck. Even before he fell, the bowman had already reloaded another arrow. He shot again, and then reloaded and fired twice more as the intruders entered the clearing. All found their marks, and one after the other they fell.

Then Mihai grabbed the bowman's shoulder, stopping him as he reached for yet another arrow.

"No, Vlach," Mihai said to him, softly but firmly. "I need **you** to make sure **she** gets safely inside the Monastery," he said, nodding to Ilinca. "Nothing must be allowed to happen to her now."

The bowman halted and glanced skeptically at Mihai.

"Yes," Mihai assured him, drawing his sword. "I will hold them; you make sure she gets to safety. Go, now, the both of you!" he yelled to them. "Quickly now! Go while you can!"

"No!" Ilinca screamed, "Come with us, Mihai. I will not leave you here!"

Mihai nodded to the bowman and then turned back towards the intruders, his sword and bronze-encircled shield at the ready. They were gathering in the clearing below. A dozen or more, Mihai estimated. It was Istvan's search party. They had tracked Ilinca up from Arcobadera, the village below. He had seen Magyar warriors before, but these seemed even larger and more imposing than the ones he remembered.

The bowman obediently leapt into action, grabbing Ilinca's arm and charging off with her, running back towards the Monastery. She staggered along, reluctantly, glancing back over her shoulder at Mihai.

The snow had stopped; the sky was clear. The Monastery now was bathed in moonlight. It stood alone, ominously, in the middle of the flat open mountain plateau. Behind it were sheer mountain faces, soaring hundreds of feet. Around the front was a semi-circle of massive boulders – like huge stone soldiers, forever shielding the plateau and the Monastery from the rest of the world.

They had a hundred yards of flat, open ground to cover to get to safety. The stark, snow-covered fields surrounding the Monastery made it look like an island in a quiet mountain lake.

"Open! Quickly! Attackers are coming!" the bowman yelled as they approached the imposing structure. "We must get the girl inside! Quickly!"

By the time they reached the massive wooden front doors Ilinca was near collapse, gasping for breath. She looked back and saw the trail of their footprints in the snow, leading back to the stone steps, and her Mihai.

In the moonlight she saw him fighting off in the distance, occasionally catching a glint of light reflected off a sword or Mihai's bronze-ringed shield. He deflected blow after blow. He was quick and wiry, compared to the large Magyar warriors. His sword found its mark time and again, and one by one the attackers fell backward down the stone steps, blocking the ascent of the others. But there were too many of them …

Behind Ilinca the large wooden door creaked open and warm yellow torchlight radiated out into the cold, moonlit night. The bowman grabbed Ilinca and spun her around, pushing her towards the opening door. She strained to look back, just once more, as they pulled her inside.

It was too far and too dark to see Mihai glance over his shoulder, just for a second, and see that she had reached the safety of the Monastery. Then a pounding blow from a Magyar axe sent the shield flying from his arm. As the large wooden door of the Monastery pulled shut, and cross beams secured and locked it in place, Mihai fell.

* - * - *

"Seven dead, four wounded," the Magyar warrior reported. "And two of those will not make it back to camp."

Sandor barely acknowledged him. He stood looking down on Mihai, his body lying lifeless between his sword and bronze-ringed shield. "This was a warrior. He knew the fight was lost, but he fought on, delaying us. We could use a dozen like him," he said, adding: "Now the girl has slipped from our grasp again, Lazar."

"Probably in there," Lazar replied, nodding toward the Monastery. Sandor, in command of the search party, looked over. He spotted the trail of footprints and started off in their direction. Lazar, his next in command, followed. It had started snowing lightly again. The moon disappeared behind a cloud, darkening the whole mountain plateau.

The Monastery

"What kind of place is this?" Sandor asked, speaking mainly to himself. "If it were a fortress, it would have been built atop one of those cliffs, hard to get at … not in the middle of a large open field. It can be attacked … from any side. There's no defensive positions. No battlements," he observed, "Looks like we have just that wooden front gate to get through."

They got nearer and Sandor pointed to the main front wall. An errant beam of moonlight shone on a prominent white stone cross above the entrance gateway. "What does that mean, Lazar?" They stopped.

Lazar looked over at it. "I do not know," he replied. But his attention was elsewhere. He looked around warily. "Take heed of their archers, though," he cautioned the commander, "They are deadly shots. They could be hiding out of sight, waiting for us to get close enough."

"I do not think **we** have much to fear," Sandor said. He gestured towards the structure. "They have retreated into … that strange place. And they have nowhere else to go now."

The Magyar leader finished his assessment. It was time to act. "Go and bring up the rest, but leave the wounded," he directed Lazar, adding: "Send a couple men to circle all the way around – carefully – and see if there is another, maybe easier way to get in. We have, what, Lazar, two or three battleaxes? Have the men sharpen them. It may be a long night." Lazar nodded, turned and left.

* _ * _ *

I: Seven Sisters

She was laid to bed, but her rest was uneasy. She was too tired, the result of her condition, the long arduous trip, over-exhaustion, and the horrid events of the evening. Oh, Mihai ... her beloved Mihai. Her mind recalled their simpler times together.

"Come on, it is not far from here," the young Ilinca said. Mihai feigned reluctance as she dragged him by the hand through the forest. They emerged into a round clearing. He looked around. It was uncanny, he thought – a near perfect circle, with luscious thick grass. The midday sun shone brightly through the tree tops, directly onto this spot. She led him to the center.

They stood facing each other, her hands holding his strong arms, his hands on her waist.

"You see the big oak trees that make up the circle?" she asked. He looked about and nodded. "There are seven of them," she said, "They are the same. They are sisters. We stand on the grave of their father, a strong and powerful tree that lived for hundreds of years. Now the sisters look on his grave and remember, and the forest remembers. No other trees dare stand between them. It is said to be a holy place."

He looked into her eyes. She was young, vibrant and exciting, more beautiful than the late spring afternoon. Her arms slowly slid under his, her head rested gently on his chest.

"Father says I am being considered for the heritage mission," she said softly to him, looking into his eyes. "I will be sent out someday to bring back the strength and blood of our enemy, and add it to ours," she proudly announced. Mihai nodded.

"Then I dare not despoil you," he responded, with a righteous expression, "You will need to save yourself." She pouted.

He saw the dreamy look in her eyes. And she saw longing in his.

"Maybe once would not hurt though, Mihai," she said softly to him. They kissed and embraced. But after a few moments he reluctantly pulled away.

"I feel like we are being watched, by your seven fat old sisters," he said, looking about. She giggled and they kissed again, deeply.

Mihai thought of simply falling with her onto the soft grass. He had so wanted to consummate their love, and this setting could not have been more perfect. But he would not be the one to deflower her. Not now. She was to be part of a much grander design.

* - * - *

I: Bittersweet homecoming

"Sister. Sister Ilinca," the young boy's voice said softly,
gently touching her shoulder. She opened her eyes. By the
side of the bunk knelt a young man with short black hair,
wearing the robe of a novice. He was twelve, maybe thirteen;
still a boy.

She sat up slowly and saw she was in one of the small, stark,
Monastery dorm rooms. A single candle cast a flickering
yellowish hue. There was an air of familiarity; it was her old
room.

"You collapsed as we got you inside," he said. "My name is
Radu. Father Bogdan sent me to see to your needs. I brought
you a clean habit, some food and water," he nodded to the
clothing and provisions by her bedside. "Father asks after
you have rested and changed, that you join us in the
sanctuary."

Radu had come to the Monastery some months before, shortly
after Ilinca had departed on her dangerous mission. He was a
gift from his parents: In return for blessing their home and
tiny farm, they gave Radu, their second son, to the Monastery
for a life in God's hands.

"Thank you, Radu," she said, sincerely. She was still
exhausted, and only half awake. She began recalling the
events earlier that evening, and then remembered Mihai.
Tears welled in her eyes. She sighed deeply in despair.

"What of the invaders?" she asked.

Radu's clean-shaven, boyish face looked down. It was not
good news, she could tell.

"They are at the front gate," he said, dejectedly. "Our
bowmen got a couple of them, but there are still a dozen or
more. Our guardsmen fear more may be on the way."

Having spent months among the Magyars, Ilinca knew how tenuous their situation was. Istvan, who she had come to know intimately, was among their most aggressive and tenacious leaders.

The Magyars were a nomadic, warring and rampaging people. But they were also pragmatic. She learned that those who submitted completely would in most cases be left alive, their villages left more or less intact. They would take what they needed and wanted, but usually then they would move on.

But those who resisted, those who cost them Magyar blood and lives – were condemned to suffer their full fury. She tried not to show her dread to the boy.

"Thank you, again, Radu," she told him. Their eyes met for just a moment. She saw innocence, concern, and fear in his. And she knew she could not hide the despair and dread in hers.

"I feel a little better now," she told him, looking away. "Please go and tell Father Bogdan I will join you shortly." He nodded and left. The single candle flickered, nearly going out.

The way to the sanctuary through the dormitory wing was labyrinthine, but Ilinca remembered it well. Sconces on the ancient stone walls lit the way, casting eerie shadows as she made a series of turns and then descended a long winding stairway. Nearing the sanctuary Ilinca could faintly hear someone speaking. Getting closer she could make out a droning soliloquy, which she recognized as Latin.

* - * - *

Centuries earlier, the Roman Empire had advanced to the southern foothills of the Carpathians here in southeastern Europe. It was the doorstep of ancient Dacia. The Romans and Dacians fought for years with no clear victor; the resulting stalemate and uneasy peace lasted for decades.

Then Rome's new Emperor Trajan vowed to settle the matter once and for all. Years of fierce fighting ensued and finally, in the year 106, with the capture of the Dacian capital after a long siege, the Romans declared victory.

But over the centuries the Dacians had become accustomed to migratory invaders, long before the Romans arrived. To survive as a people they adopted a pragmatic strategy: They would fight when threatened, but if facing certain defeat, they would withdraw into forest enclaves and mountain hideouts, and patiently watch and wait – until the invaders eventually, and inevitably, moved on. In some cases it took years, or decades, and in some cases more than a century.

And so it was with the Romans. The area that Rome subjugated was actually just the southern edge of Dacia. Life continued normally for many Dacians in the rural villages and towns in the forested, mountainous expanses to the north. The Romans never ventured there. Dacians who stayed and lived among the occupying Romans learned their language, skills and ways – including a new religion that was unofficially pervading the empire – Christianity.

The Roman occupation lasted nearly two centuries. It marked the furthest that the Roman Empire would reach. Ironically, in the year 271, it was this territory that Rome first abandoned as the empire began consolidating … and collapsing. Rome's legions withdrew, but many other Romans, including retired military officers, had settled the area and remained. And with the passage of time, the patient Dacians subtly added this invader's knowledge, religion, and the blood of their leaders, to their own.

* _ * _ *

I: Sanctuary

"Emitte lucem tuam, Deus, et veritatem tuam: Ipsa me deduxerunt," Ilinca heard as they neared the sanctuary.

"Send forth your light, God, and your truth: They have led me," Ilinca translated to herself. She nondescriptly entered the sanctuary through the concealed entry behind the altar. She saw it was the Monastery's lector and senior presbyter, Brother Grigore, reciting. Grigore was second in charge and, most agreed, likely to be the successor to the aging abbot, Father Bogdan.

Ilinca was a deacon – a senior position, with nearly full priestly authority – and a role most uncommon for a woman to hold. Brought to the Monastery as a young orphan, she adjusted well and grew to love the ancient, foreboding place, adjusting to a simple life of chores, prayer, learning and quiet contemplation. She was charming and erudite, and demonstrated a flair for languages – learning Latin and Greek fluently by the time she was fifteen.

"… Et introibo ad altare Dei, in montem sanctum tuum, et in tabernacula tua," Brother Grigore droned on, reciting eloquently. "Confiteor vobis, fraters, et Deo omnipotenti …"

"… And I will go to the altar of God, to your holy mountain, and to your tabernacle," she again translated, to herself, "I confess to you, Brothers, and to almighty God …" She recognized the passage, from the Dacian version of the Latin mass.

Rows of stark wooden benches were arranged in a semi-circle before the altar. Ilinca walked around the huge altar stone to the far side of the sanctuary, and sat down alone on the last bench at the back.

The altar consisted of a large, ovoid, reddish-brown stone, which, in the flickering lamplight of the sanctuary, seemed to exude an iridescence of its own. Then there were five huge upright stones, also roughly hewn, which encircled the sanctuary. The largest one stood behind the altar, obscuring the entrance Ilinca had used. Two others, not quite as large, stood like sentinels on either side of the altar stone. The last two, slightly smaller, guarded the main entranceway to the altar stone.

The stones had fascinated Ilinca since childhood. They were unlike all the other stone used in building the Monastery – finely dressed light gray granite, quarried from the local mountains. Ilinca concluded that these stones were special, and comprised the heart of this ancient place. For whatever reason, the Monastery was built here, around them, she reasoned.

She looked around. The atmosphere in the sanctuary was one of frantic despair. Kneeling at the altar, bowed in fervent prayer, was Father Bogdan. Kneeling behind him were the novices and acolytes, including Brother Radu, all emulating the old Abbot and seemingly deep in prayer. The other deacons and the elders had coalesced into their own small groups, nattering among themselves. The din of a dozen overlapping conversations, and Grigore's incessant Latin monotone, filled the air.

Then a loud boom sounded, followed shortly by a second. A few seconds later came a third and fourth, in rapid succession. The thunderous peals were coming from the front gate, down the narrow entrance tunnel, reverberating off the stone walls of the sanctuary.
The sanctuary went silent. All heads had turned towards the tunnel entrance. No words were needed: The Magyars were chopping at the massive wooden front gate with battleaxes.

"Boom! Boom!" And again, "Boom! Boom!" The echoes resounded in the ears, the bones, and the hearts of the congregation, sending chills up their spines.

Behind Ilinca the guards were assembling in the entrance tunnel, planning their defense. Conspicuously missing was the captain of the guard, Mihai. For a moment her eyes welled.

Father Bogdan looked up at Brother Grigore, who was now standing motionless, silent, staring straight ahead, a look of terror on his face. The old abbot got up and went around the altar to him. He summoned a novice to come around and help guide Brother Grigore to a seat.

Father Bogdan, alone behind the altar, bowed his head, as if in prayer.

"Boom! Boom!" The pounding continued. "Boom! Boom!" Again, and again. Ilinca got up and went to the sergeant of the guard, who was busily directing his men.

She interrupted: "I am sorry about your commander. I knew Mihai well."

The sergeant broke off his conversation and looked at her, emotionless. "I know," he said.

"How long do you think we have?" she asked. The sergeant considered her question. Some of his men, wondering the same thing, turned around to listen.

"It depends, Sister," he said, "Maybe a couple of hours. Maybe less." He had every right to look scared, or at least annoyed at her untimely interruption, but he did not. He saw the dread in her face, and tried to offer some comfort, speaking to her and, indirectly, to his men.

"The gate is thick, with heavy metal cross-locks." He added: "If they breach the gate we will strike them as they try to come through. If they advance through the tunnel, they can pass only two at a time. And we will have the advantage."

Ilinca tried to look a little pacified, but she wasn't fooling anybody. "Thank you," she told him sincerely, "and good luck." He nodded and turned back to his men; she turned and headed back towards the altar.

*_*_*

I: Father Bogdan

Anyone meeting Father Bogdan now for the first time would see the humble, aging abbot of a remote monastery. But few knew of his remarkable life – as a warrior, husband, father, traveler, historian, and ultimately, man of the cloth. In his 60-odd years, Bogdan rose from being the youngest of his peasant family's seven sons, to becoming spiritual guide of the Dacian people.

After the brutal death of his wife and children at the hands of the Bulgars – the wave of migratory marauders then invading Dacia – Bogdan became a Dacian soldier to avenge them. He saw battle after battle and killed many of the enemy. Eventually the Bulgars were forced to move on, and Bogdan, finally appeased, and exhausted, returned to his village. He decided to dedicate himself to understanding God's will.

The religious head of the village, recognizing Bogdan's intellect and discipline, recommended that he go to study at the Monastery, many miles away. He did, and, as a strong and bright young man with military experience, he was quickly accepted. He assumed dual roles as sergeant of the guard, and a student of theology and languages.

He was a voracious learner, but after about five years he concluded that the answers he sought would not be found in the Monastery. He was reluctantly allowed to go, with their blessing, and determined to put his learning to use in the world. He first toured dozens of remote Dacian communities, listening to their varied historical accounts, meticulously recording them, and experiencing their spiritual rites. Christianity had broadly permeated Dacia, he observed, but it did not displace the ancient Dacian pagan faith. Rather, in most cases, the two were merged.

Then, on a yearlong trip to the west, Bogdan encountered and was embraced by the Roman church. Fluent in Latin, he was formally ordained a priest and even named Bishop of Dacia. But Dacia was too far removed from the Mediterranean mainstream to come under the control of either Rome, or the Eastern Church in Byzantium. Even so, Bogdan later orchestrated the retention of the Latin mass as a standard throughout Dacia, rejecting the encroaching, competing Slavic and Byzantine Greek Christian rituals. The Bishop of Dacia had repaid Rome.

A deeply spiritual man, and yet one knowledgeable in the ways of the world, Father Bogdan eventually returned to the Monastery. He was graciously accepted and put in charge of Latin instruction and the library, recording the historical accounts and religious observations he had collected on his broad travels. He became the protégé of the abbot, Father Traian. The two would engage in protracted theological conversations, sometimes in public and sometimes in private. These often lasted for days, with neither one even showing up for meals. After Traian's death a few years later, Bogdan assumed full charge of the Monastery … a unique, worldly man of God, with an understanding of Dacia's dark secrets …

"Boom! Boom!" And a few seconds later, "Boom! Boom!" The thunderous hacking at the front gate continued with an unflinching, bone-chilling rhythm.

Father Bogdan stood alone behind the huge stone altar, his head bowed as if in deep prayer. The din of mixed conversations began to intensify.

He lifted his head and slowly gazed about the sanctuary. His voice rang out: "It is time." He raised his hands, bidding the diverse factions to come to order. It worked. All eyes turned to Father Bogdan. His thick silver hair, deep-set dark eyes and expression radiated a certain … confidence.

"Boom! Boom!" The pounding at the front gate shattering the silence. "Boom! Boom!"

"Come closer to the altar, all of you!" Bogdan ordered, waving everyone in. "We need to stand together." Dutifully, the robed figures from throughout the sanctuary converged around the huge altar stone.

"Boom! Boom!" The pounding continued, "Boom! Boom!"

Bogdan gazed upwards, his arms outstretched.

"Almighty God," he began, "For millennia you have watched over us. Since the time of the beginning they have come. Macedonians. Celts. Bastarnae. Romans," he paused, recalling the historical litany, "And then came the Goths, Huns, Gepids, Byzantines, Kitigars, Avars, Slavs," he paused, reflecting a moment, "and the accursed Bulgars." He paused. "Now, in the year of our Lord 888, it is the Magyars."

"Boom! Boom!" On it went. "Boom! Boom!"

Bogdan continued, louder: "For millennia we have faced the invaders, and yet, through all the centuries, You have given us the ways and the wisdom to survive – our people and our way of life." He paused, then added: "On this night, we again beseech you."

He lowered his arms and eyed the assemblage.

"Closer. Come closer, all of you," he instructed. They stepped forward. "Lower your cowls; I need to see your eyes." They did. Ilinca saw that it was Radu standing next to her. She glanced momentarily at him and feigned a smile.

"Boom! Boom!" the resonance echoed from the front gate, and again, "Boom! Boom!"

Most of the elders and deacons knew Bogdan well, and had stood with him in various crises over the years. Sometimes they did not understand him. But nevertheless they all trusted and believed deeply in him. They drew comfort and strength from Father Bogdan, from this place, and from being together with their brethren. If they were to die this night, most had accepted, then that would be their fate.

A few of the novices and acolytes, however, were nearly frantic – not knowing what to expect, or what they would do when the time came. They looked to their brethren for leadership, and to Father Bogdan.

"Boom! Boom!" And again, "Boom! Boom!"

"Brethren," Bogdan said, speaking calmly, yet firmly, "Faith is difficult at times like this. But understand that your faith, the belief of every one of us here, is crucial to our salvation."

Many looked at each other, confused.

"A mortal enemy is upon us," Bogdan said, choosing his words carefully: "They have come to destroy us, and you should be filled with fear." He paused, letting that thought sink in, then added: "But know this, too. Deliverance is at hand."

"We have been infused over the many centuries with the will to survive, and the means," he continued. "God has plans for us. And to fulfill our destiny, His will, we must survive." The assemblage hung onto Father Bogdan's every word.

"Boom! Boom!" And again, "Boom! Boom!"

"You must **believe** in our survival. **Each** of you," he told them intently, slowly scanning the group and pausing to look each in the eyes. Death is at the front gate, and you must each know in your heart and mind that we have a future in this world. Concentrate deeply on that belief – our future. Pray. Pray intensely. And concentrate on your prayer."

"Now, all of you, take each other's hand," he directed. The assemblage complied. Ilinca felt Radu's hand slip into hers. His hand was shaking. She looked down at him and feigned a smile. He looked dolefully up at her, comforted by her strength.

Bogdan scanned the group once more, then slowly nodded, approvingly. All eyes watched him intently, eyes rife with fear and anxiety.

Bogdan again raised his head and arms. His voice resounded, picking up where he earlier left off: "Almighty God, we beseech you. You are the Creator. You are life eternal. Our time here, in your service, is but the blink of an eye. Yet we are yours forever."

"Boom! Boom!" And again, "Boom! Boom!"

He continued, louder: "Speaking with the voices of a thousand years, we, your faithful, whom you have blessed, pray for deliverance. We pray to live on … to see our future." He paused. Then, barely audibly, he finished, uttering: "Thy will be done." His head again bowed. All stood silently, reverently.

"Boom! …" Just the one thunderous blow. Everyone noticed immediately. A few seconds passed … and nothing more. They looked around, surprised, at each other. The silence was deafening.

* _ * _ *

I: Dawn

The hacking at the front gate had stopped abruptly. But why? Had the Magyars broken through?

Ilinca spun around and headed to the sanctuary entrance to find out. She saw the sergeant of the guard standing there with another guard.

"What happened? Have they broken through?" she yelled excitedly. The sergeant shrugged, "I do not know." His tone was one of puzzlement; there was no fear in his voice. Then he turned, pulled his sword from its sheath, and headed down the narrow accessway to the front gate. The other guard took off behind him, and Ilinca followed close behind.

In the vaulted tunnel leading to the front gate she saw two teams of bowmen, perched on either side behind bales of hay. In front of them were two teams of swordsmen, with lances and shields at the ready.

The sergeant ran to the front line of swordsmen and stopped abruptly. Ilinca stopped short beside him. All stared ahead dumfounded at the massive wooden gate. A foot-long gash had been hacked through the gate, about chest high, between two of the horizontal iron lock bars. Through the hole poured a beam of bright sunlight, striking the stone floor just in front of Ilinca. No sound was coming from, and neither was there any sign of, the Magyars on the other side of the gate.

"Dawn?" Ilinca asked the sergeant, while still staring straight ahead at the gate. No response. She looked over at the sergeant. He looked back at her and slowly shook his head.

"No," he responded, a puzzled look on his face, "Not for … some time yet." He turned to the nearest swordsman. "Quick, go up top and look around. Look all the way around. See where they went." The swordsman dashed off.

Ilinca stepped into the sunbeam and proceeded slowly walking to the gate. The sergeant reached out to grasp the sleeve of her habit, in a half-hearted attempt to hold her back. She brushed him aside.

"It is alright," she assured him. He followed her, his sword in hand, down at his side. She stepped up to the door and gazed through the hole, looking around in all directions.

"My God," she uttered, and stood aside. The sergeant stepped up and also looked around through the hole. Just then the returning swordsman ran up to him.

"No sign of them … anywhere," he reported, catching his breath. "But something is … wrong."

"Never mind," the sergeant said to him, turning back to the hole, "I can see." After a few moments he stepped back and turned to two other guardsmen.

"Open up," he commanded, his thumb pointing to the gate.

The men removed the heavy iron cross-lock bars, and then the wooden crossbeams and pegs. Finally, the gates were loosened.

"Wait," the sergeant said, just as they were about to pull open the gate. He went and looked once more through the hole, then stepped back, pulled his sword, and gave them a nod.

The two massive gates swung open. A gush of warm air rushed in.

It wasn't dawn. It was mid-morning, nearly noon. And there was no sign of the snow from the night before. Instead, there was knee-high grass, and wildflowers. A clear, beautiful, sunny sky. Comfortably warm. By all appearances a beautiful spring or early summer day.

The sergeant of the guard sheathed his sword, and then carefully examined the gaping hole in the gate from the outside. The damage was considerable. It would not have been much longer before the gate was breached. He heaved a sigh of relief that all around him heard.

"You, Vlach," the sergeant said to a nearby guard. "Go tell Father Bogdan and the others that it is alright, that the invaders are … gone. Tell them … what you see here. Go now."

Ilinca walked out, pulling up the hem of her heavy habit as she walked through a grassy patch. She stopped, puzzled and confused, and crossed her arms. A warm, gentle breeze blew her long dark hair. The warm breeze and sunlight on her face felt good. She looked around, and then out to the edge of the plateau where the stone stairway descended. It looked as she remembered, except …

She headed off to the spot, walking quickly. Most everything looked familiar, but now there was high grass, pleasant warm weather … and a tree – the only one on the whole isolated plain. She headed towards it. A fairly large fir tree. She could **not** have missed it the night before. It was **not** there before, she told herself. But then again, in the dark and the snow, and with attackers on their heels, could she be sure?

The tree was near the stone steps, near where she last saw Mihai, valiantly battling the Magyars. It looked as if it may have been planted there, at that particular spot, on purpose… like some kind of a marker. It was a foot thick at the base. She wondered how long it took a tree to grow that big.

She looked down and saw that the tree, oddly, had grown through a large metal ring. Reaching down she felt the metal, then rubbed it. Beneath a coating of green tarnish it was … shiny. It looked like … bronze. It looked like … no, it was … the metal ring of an officer's battle shield.

Ilinca sat down, exhausted and bewildered, her back against the tree, her hand gently stroking the metal ring. And she began to cry.

* _ * _ *

Chapter II: Desert warrior
II: Babylonian, I think

The radio crackled: "Bad Boy, this is Mighty Mo. Over."
The hulking sergeant strode to the Humvee and picked up the
small black handset, holding it daintily in his powerful hand.
He held it to his ear and pushed the transmit button, cutting
off the radio static.

"Roger, Mighty Mo, Bad Boy here. Over," he responded.

"G'morning, Bad Boy, need a sitrep. Over."

"Wait one," the sergeant responded. Then he called out to the
others, who were settled in the nearby ruins: "Hey,
Lieutenant. HQ checking in. They want a situation report."

Lieutenant Bradley Ozera stood up. His loose desert fatigues
couldn't hide his trim, six-foot, broad-shouldered frame and
muscular arms. He and the others were eating, having arrived
at this remote site late last night. There was an air of
casualness, camaraderie, bravado. You wouldn't know that
they were 50 miles behind enemy lines, sitting between
coalition forces, which invaded Iraq the day before, and
Saddam Hussein's Republican Guard to the north.

"I got it, Sarge," Ozera said, walking over and taking the
handset. "Bad Boy here," he said, "We are at reference point
Delta. Checked in about six hours ago. A quiet night. And a
cool, clear morning. Got an OP out a few miles north; they
report ten-mile visibility. Nothing yet. Just us and the sand
fleas."

"Roger that, Bad Boy. Be advised, though: satellite just ID'ed
a large armored unit about 75 to 80 miles north of you,
headed your way. They look well equipped and organized.
We think a Republican Guard armored regiment, likely
moving to intercept our guys and counter-attack."

"Thanks for the heads up, Mo," Ozera said. A knot formed in his gut. "Still got close air support standing by, right? Over."

"Roger that. They're just cooling their jets on the flight line, itching for a fire mission. Over."

"Thanks, Mo. We'll see what we can do from here. Keep us posted. This is Bad Boy, out."

He pondered the situation for a moment – an armored regiment, just a couple hours out and headed right for them. Then he turned and headed back to the rest of the team. They got the job because they knew how to operate behind enemy lines. Their mission: to spot any Iraqi units moving through their area that could threaten the American advance, and then call in and direct air strikes against them.

They were all seasoned Special Forces field operatives. They'd taken up position here in the ruins atop this desert hilltop. Two others from the team, in the second Humvee, went ahead to set-up and man an observation post a few miles to the north. The OP would be the first to detect any sizeable enemy movements headed south, towards them.

Ozera looked them over – a burly, surly bunch, warming themselves around a small fire. It was cold this February morning. Master Sergeant Jerry Carpenter, Ozera's comrade in arms and the team's senior enlisted man, was cajoling the others.

"It's true. Our Lieutenant speaks a bunch of languages. Ain't that right, Lieutenant?" Carpenter said teasingly with his subdued southern drawl. He stood up to hand Ozera a coffee. At forty, Carpenter was carrying a few more excess pounds than his wiry companions, and a noticeable midriff paunch.

"Yeah, I can order a Big Mac and a beer in six languages, including English," Ozera fliply responded. They chuckled. "Let's see … I still do pretty well in German, Romanian and Russian, and I can get by in Français and Espanol." They nodded approvingly. Each of them actually had a working knowledge of at least one other language. Ozera knew one spoke Farsi, another Arabic – either language more likely to be useful here in southern Iraq than Russian or French, Ozera thought to himself.

Ozera lifted his cap, revealing his short, curly, dark brown hair, and scratched his head. "Damned fleas," he muttered, adding: "Reminds me of a girl I knew from Paducah," knowing it was Carpenter's hometown. Carpenter grunted obligingly, while busily opening his meal pouch. Ozera smiled his trademark devilish smile, complemented by his black eyes – eyes that reflected wisdom and wickedness.

There was a lot of gypsy in him – the child of Romanian parents who immigrated in the early 1960's, settling in Pennsylvania. He would joke that he and his parents both learned English at the same time. But the household spoke Romanian, as he did from birth.

The team had settled in among ruins of an earlier, long-gone civilization. Waist-high mud-brick walls and a few broken stone columns. Ozera found it intriguing, even tantalizing, having been a student of architecture. He fondly recalled his graduation day at Lehigh University, what seemed like a million years ago, when he got his sheepskin in the morning, and his second-lieutenant gold bars in the afternoon. His appreciation of architecture was taking a back seat these days, though; Ozera now saw the world through military eyes, respecting this site more because it offered good visibility, as well as cover and concealment. Their Humvee was parked in a ditch out of view except for the radio antenna.

"Not to dwell on the unpleasant," he addressed the group, adopting a more serious, sober tone of voice, "But our eye in the sky spotted a large Iraqi armored unit headed this way." Silence. A little theatrical, he supposed, but he had caught their attention.

"How many?" Sergeant Tomlinson sat up and asked.

"A thousand plus, maybe two thousand. HQ reckons it's an armored regiment. They think they're Republican Guard, and probably maneuvering to counter-attack."

"Where?"

"Last seen 75 to 80 miles north of here, but that was a while ago."

"Damn, sir! When were you going to tell **us**?" snarled Carpenter, "That means they could be on top of the OP anytime now. We best get it in gear."

Ozera adopted a more formal, command voice, "Okay, time to earn our pay. Sergeant Carpenter, brief the OP. Remind them to get their butts back here if they spot 'em coming – but not til they've confirmed their strength and direction." He added: "And see if Morris can get an update from the AWACS." While his rank eliminated any uncertainty, Ozera nonetheless had an innate skill: He could get men to do what he wanted.

"Right, sir," Carpenter snapped back. He turned to Staff Sergeant Morris, the team's commo expert. "Come on, Charlie," he said, waving him to follow. The two sergeants got up and headed to the Humvee and the radio. Without saying a word, the last two soldiers systematically put out the fire, grabbed their scopes and took up look-out positions – one facing northeast, the other northwest. Ozera heard the familiar static crackling as Morris got on the radio. He looked over to the Humvee; Carpenter was walking back.

"We should pack up and be ready to split pronto," Ozera told Carpenter, "soon as Gordon and Wilson get back." Sergeant First Class Eddie Gordon and Staff Sergeant Ben Wilson made up the OP team. Ozera watched in the light of the full moon as their Humvee headed off north to set-up the observation post.

"Lieutenant," Morris yelled from the Humvee, "HQ says they're moving south in a column about 20 miles per hour. They should be in sight of our OP pretty soon."

"Thanks, Sarge," Ozera responded, "Go ahead and make sure the OP knows."

Ozera's team was doing long-range recon and acting as a forward observer. They were not expecting to engage the enemy directly, and they were not equipped for it. In Special Forces tradition – what some call bravado, others a false sense of invincibility – they wore neither Kevlar helmets nor body armor – just their desert-camouflaged caps. Weapons: M-16's, 45-cal side arms and a 50-cal machine gun on each Humvee.

"The team travels light," Ozera remembered telling the operations officer when he got the assignment. "And besides, the Humvees will get us out of harm's way at 60 miles per hour," he said, adding his trademark smile.

"Yeah, but anything bigger than an AK-47 will rip right through that thin armor and ruin your day," the captain told him. He was deadly serious. "But it's your call, and your patrol, Lieutenant."

* - * - *

Everything was in place in short order. The Humvee was packed, and everybody was busily doing their job. Carpenter unfolded his maps and pulled out his marker pen. Then he and Ozera sat down … to wait. By U.S. Army convention they were boss and subordinate. But to each other it was more of a partnership arrangement. Still, both knew that it was Ozera who was responsible for the mission's success or failure.

Looking around, as if for the first time, Carpenter asked: "What *is* this place, Lieutenant?" It was little more than small talk to ease the tension and the tedium of waiting. Carpenter was good at that.

Ozera studied the ruins. "Babylonian, I think. Probably too late for Sumerian," he responded seriously, ignoring for a moment the fact that Carpenter hadn't quite finished the ninth grade.

The two had spent over a year in the field together, covering each other's backsides in tight spots in Latin America and then Africa. They first met in the jungle of Costa Rica on the Nicaraguan border. Ozera was new, a "shave tail" second lieutenant. Carpenter befriended him, and the two learned all about each other over the weeks and months to come, mostly during idle hours of such diversionary small talk.

Ozera learned that, two decades earlier, Carpenter was drafted, and in a few months shipped out to Vietnam. By the end of his tour he had a Bronze Star and Purple Heart, from an ambush that wiped out the most of his squad, and sergeant stripes – rare for a draftee. After re-enlisting he was recruited into Special Forces, and since then was sent from one backwoods brouhaha to another. Sometimes the mission was to subdue unrest; in others the job was to cause it. Ozera learned somewhere along the line that Carpenter had gone through two previous wives and had a son and a daughter somewhere.

And Carpenter came to know the dynamic Lieutenant Ozera, who also recently divorced. The two had grown very close. Ozera saw and respected Carpenter as a survivor and a man who showed strength when strength failed most everyone else. Carpenter liked and respected what he saw in Ozera – a smart, educated young officer, who was a resourceful and natural leader.

With nearly 20 years' service under his belt, Carpenter was increasingly threatening to take an early retirement. His oft stated ambition: to open a combination bar and cathouse back home in Kentucky. Anyhow that was the plan – until Saddam invaded Kuwait six months ago. Now here they were, together again, this time behind enemy lines in the Iraqi desert.

"Babylonian, huh?" Carpenter asked. "Been here a while, it looks like." That was obvious.

"Oh, I'd say about four thousand years," Ozera said matter of factly. "The stonework came much later, probably Macedonian – y'know, Alexander the Great. The walls are all mud brick, though."

"Mud, huh?" Carpenter responded, feigning interest, and reaching out to feel the wall he was sitting against.

Ozera continued his under-appreciated historical narrative: "You can tell, though, that people lived here for a long, long time – many centuries. And actually, that's why we're here."

"How's that?" Carpenter queried.

"The mud brick walls," Ozera explained. "Rain dissolves them. But here in the desert, since it doesn't rain much, that takes a long, long time. Anyhow, the old walls would eventually be replaced with new ones, usually in the same place. Over the centuries, all that old mud and clay would build up, forming this rise, and new structures would be built on higher and higher ground. And so here we are today, on top of that hill, because it's a good lookout point." Ozera raised his hands and grinned, denoting the end of the lecture.

Carpenter mulled it over and looked around. "Sir, you are a warehouse of exciting information," he said with a deadpan expression. Ozera smiled.

"Lieutenant!" Morris yelled out from the Humvee, "Gordon and Wilson say they see lots of movement, dust clouds about 10 miles out and closing in."

* - * - *

II: Fire mission

Carpenter got up onto his knees, a felt marker in his hand, looking down at the maps unfolded on the ground before him. In the expanse of the desert it usually took several maps to paint the whole picture. The top map was to plot the estimated location and movement of the enemy column. A compass on the map below marked the location of the observation post. And another map below highlighted their hilltop location amid the ruins.

Morris regularly relayed reports from the OP. "The front of the column is now at an azimuth of two-nine-zero degrees from them," he called out. "Distance estimated at eight miles." Carpenter extended a line from the compass and marked an "X" where the enemy's advance had reached. He would continue the tracking and then provide grid coordinates to Ozera, who was responsible, when the time was right, for calling in the fire mission.

"They estimate 150 to 200 vehicles in all, tanks and trucks," Morris called out. Ozera, with notepad and pen in hand, was taking notes of enemy size and disposition, revising them regularly as updates came in.

"Do they see any infantry on foot?" Ozera yelled. Morris relayed the question. In a moment the response came back.

"Negative, sir. Looks like everybody's riding."

"Can they make out what kind of tanks?" Ozera asked. Morris passed it on.

"All Soviet-made, they believe. T-72s and some T-55s. A mix," came the reply.

"Front edge of the column now at two-seven-zero degrees," Morris called out. "Estimate six miles. Can't see much of the column because of the dust."

Carpenter plotted the latest advance, and then turned to Ozera: "They're headed almost due south, Lieutenant. Maybe 15, 18 miles an hour, it looks like. They'll be passing by us – three, maybe four miles to the west, if they stay on their present course." He called out to the men on look-out. "Check to the northwest, maybe 10 or 12 miles out. Ought to see something soon."

"Latest count is 70 tanks, and about 80 trucks, probably mech infantry," Morris called out.

A plan formed in Ozera's mind. He knelt next to Carpenter. A huddle. "Sarge, they're rolling forward and can't hear or see shit behind them with all the noise and dust. If we can get some 'Hogs' to surprise and strafe them from north to south, they can hit the tanks from the rear and probably take out a lot of 'em." 'Hogs,' or Warthogs, was the affectionate term for special Air Force tank-killer aircraft, formally the A-10 Thunderbolt.

"I think we ought to try to hit them as they pass us to the west. That way we'll have max visibility and be able to best assess the strike," Ozera added.

Carpenter digested it and thought it over. Impressive. A good sound plan. He nodded approvingly, and then added: "If we can stop enough of the tanks and halt their advance, the infantry will stop, too. A lot of troops and big fat trucks in the open. So a few passes with cluster bombs afterwards would be icing on the cake." They both smiled and nodded.

"Sergeant Morris, let's raise fire support," Ozera directed him, still scribbling on his pad. In a few seconds Morris called back.

"Got 'em sir."

"Pass this on, word for word," Ozera commanded. Reading from his notes he dictated: "Fire mission. Fire mission. Authorization Alpha Six." Morris called it in.

Ozera continued: "Target is an enemy armored regiment. Half tanks; half mechanized infantry. Moving from north to south at 20 miles per hour." He looked over Carpenter's shoulder at the maps. "Now at … grid reference 23-58. Will be in grid square 21-53 in about 20 minutes. Target is 70, that is, seven-zero tanks, mix of Soviet T-72s and T-55s, and about 80, that is, eight-zero trucks of mech infantry." He paused, giving Morris the chance to call that in. When Morris finished he continued.

"Recommend 'Hogs' attack from their rear, north to south, and zap the armor with 30-mike-mike cannon. Then a run of cluster bombs, for mech infantry trucks and troops in the open." He glanced over at Carpenter; they both smiled. "We are three to four miles east of the main enemy column, at reference point Delta, and will observe and adjust fire as long as we can," he paused, then added: "Acknowledge."

Ozera waited as Morris finished calling it in. After a few moments he called back: "They got it all, sir."

He looked over at Carpenter. They nodded to each other in tacit acknowledgement. But for the fireworks to come, their job was now largely done. Ozera heaved a sigh of relief.

A few minutes of quiet. Then they could faintly hear the first sounds of the distant clanking and thunder. The look-outs were peering through their scopes to the west. The enemy column, and the enormous cloud of dust, could now be plainly seen, just a few miles away.

A call came in on the radio. Morris took it and then called out: "Our guys spotted a small unit, a few armored vehicles, about a mile away, heading right towards them."

Ozera called back: "Have they been spotted?" Morris relayed it.

"Negative. They don't think so. Not yet. But they think they better boogie."

Ozera decided in a second and responded: "Okay, have 'em saddle up and get back here."

"Roger, sir," Morris replied. He passed it on to Sergeant Wilson, who was manning the Humvee's radio and relaying Gordon's observations. Gordon was still on look-out with his scope. An old Special Forces adage: If you can see the enemy, the enemy can see you. Everything was packed and they were more than ready and willing to take off – just waiting for the word. In 20 seconds the two men had hopped in and the Humvee sped off south.

"They're out of there, sir," Morris reported.

Approaching the OP position was an armored platoon, which was covering the Iraqi column's left flank. Three BMPs – Soviet-made armored troop carriers – each with a half-dozen troops aboard. They hadn't spotted them yet. From just a mile away, though, their commander, through binoculars, spotted the dust cloud left by the speeding Humvee. And he decided to go check it out.

In a few minutes one of the lookouts called to Carpenter: "I see something to the north, Sarge. Probably Gordon and Wilson."

The light, wheeled Humvee easily outruns the armored, tracked BMP. But the BMP far outguns the Humvee. Firepower versus speed. Tortoise versus the hare. It would take the tortoise time to catch up. But the hare's dust and tracks in the sand were easy to follow.

* _ * _ *

II: Hunter and hunted

The telltale dust cloud followed Gordon and Wilson as they drove up the hillside at breakneck speed, slamming on the brakes and parking on a rise. The two sergeants jumped out, rifles in hand, and ran over to rejoin their comrades.

Ozera looked over at their Humvee. Exposed. Silhouetted. He thought to himself: "We ought to stay concealed as long as we can." But on second thought: "Of course, in a few minutes, the enemy's going to have a lot more to worry about than us." He let it go.

The team boisterously renewed acquaintances and then everyone settled down, with a scope or binoculars, awaiting the upcoming fireworks display.

The Iraqi column was clanking and rumbling by, just a few miles west of Ozera's team. Then, as if on cue, twin-engine A-10's appeared, a lot of them. Three at a time they dove sharply from a high altitude and, just as planned, strafed the column from the rear. By all appearances the Iraqi tanks and trucks were caught utterly by surprise.

It was a spectacle to behold. In the first wave three Hogs swooped down. Bursts from their 30-millimeter Gatling-gun cannons ripped open one tank after another, most of them exploding into a billow of black smoke as the explosive rounds ignited their fuel tanks. The vintage Russian-made tanks couldn't stand up to the 50 or 60 armor-piercing cannon rounds that tore into each of them. A single Hog would take out four or five tanks in a pass. When they finally ran out of cannon rounds they would fly off, clearing the way for the next attack wave.

The Iraqis began returning heavy machine gun fire as the second wave descended on them. Through the billowing smoke Ozera and his team saw the tracer rounds as the Iraqi machine guns sprayed the sky, like July 4th sparklers. But the

Hogs, undaunted by the return fire, continued to pound tank after tank.

In the next wave an Iraqi anti-aircraft rocket found its mark, striking one of the A-10's large rear engines. The wounded jet veered off to the west, smoking, and was soon out of sight of the team.

"Sergeant Morris, get air support on the line," Ozera yelled as he walked over to him. Morris set up the call, to an AWACS airborne warning and control flight circling somewhere high overhead. He handed the radio handset to Ozera.

"Bad Boy here," Ozera said, "Your Hogs are giving 'em hell. Hit 'em right in the ass. Estimate you have put half to two-thirds of the armor out of commission. One of your Hogs took a rocket hit to a rear engine, though. Last saw him flying off to the west, smoking. Didn't see him go down, though, and no sign of an ejection from our position. Over."

"Roger, Bad Boy," the Air Force strike controller responded. "We're about out of 30-mike-mike rounds. Ready for some clusters? Over."

"Roger. Let 'em have it," Ozera replied. In a few moments the jets started making passes again, this time dropping cluster bombs. Three jets at a time, flying straight over, the explosions ripping through the trucks and exposed troops on the ground.

Billowing smoke from dozens of burning vehicles was turning the western sky black, obscuring their view. The team was glued to the scene, fixed on the now-stalled enemy column. Their mood was euphoric, congratulating each other for a job well done.

The reverberation of the cluster bombs and the roar of the A-10s eventually subsided. From their vantage point the team could hear intermittent explosions as tank shells exploded, like popcorn in a microwave.

The Monastery

Ozera picked up the handset: "Thanks, guys. A great strike. You stopped 'em in their tracks – pardon the pun. I doubt there are a dozen tanks still running down there. Pass on to our ground troops that they can expect a bunch of POWs when they get near here. For this gang the war is over. Bad Boy, out."

"Oh, shit!" Sergeant Gordon suddenly yelled out. He was staring behind them, off to the northeast. Everyone turned in unison and saw the dust cloud, only a half-mile away. Three BMPs came into view, just as their main guns fired in rapid succession. One round struck a wall right behind them. A 100-millimeter, high-explosive fragmentation cannon round. Two other rounds exploded quite a ways behind them. Everyone hit the ground. They knew more were on the way.

Ozera hastily assessed the situation and yelled, "Let's get the fuck out of Dodge!" Carpenter was lying flat atop his maps. He yelled something back just as another round struck nearby. Ozera couldn't hear but suspected it was probably something very close to: "No shit, Lieutenant!" He scampered over to Carpenter.

"You alright, Sarge?" Ozera asked.

"Yeah, I'm fine. But I don't know about the others," Carpenter replied. He looked at Ozera and implored him: "How about if you, Gordon and Wilson take off in their Humvee? It's a sitting duck out there anyway. So grab them, hop in and get going while you still can!"

"Yeah, okay. But how about you?" Ozera asked. Another shell hit, a little closer than the last one. Ozera's ears were ringing now.

"You go ahead, sir. Get going. I'll grab the maps and scopes and the others and we'll be right behind you." He turned and yelled: "Morris, you're driving! Fire up the Humvee!"

Morris acknowledged, ran around the vehicle and hopped into the driver's seat.

"Come on, Sarge, let's go!" Ozera implored him, looking him sternly in the eye.

"I'm coming, damn it! You get out of here, sir. And remember, the first round's on you tonight," Carpenter said, and then grinned broadly at Ozera. It was his way: Still able to crack a joke while everything around them was going to hell.

Ozera smiled back, then turned and yelled to Gordon and Wilson. They looked back and Ozera pointed to their Humvee. The three of them ran to it, jumped in, and in seconds they had taken off. They had gone just 50 feet when the next shell struck right where the Humvee was parked. Carpenter saw it and smiled. "You're a lucky prick, Lieutenant," he muttered to himself.

Carpenter crammed the maps into a case and got up, crouching, waiting for the next shell. Another one struck a wall just 20 feet to his right. Large chunks of ancient mud brick zipped by his head; small particles stung his face. A thought flashed through his mind that these ancient mud-brick walls actually offered decent protection against this cannon fire. They absorbed the incoming rounds and much of the explosion.

The BMPs were now about 500 yards away and closing fast. Carpenter signaled to the others and they all ran down to the Humvee. Morris was revving the engine. They hopped in and, just as the last one hopped in, Morris hit the gas.

* - * - *

The commander of the BMP unit knew that much of the main regiment had been wiped out. He was livid, desperate and wanted revenge. And he figured, correctly, that this American patrol was at least partly responsible. He saw the first Humvee take off, just missing his cannon fire. Now another one took off, chasing after the first. It was still within range, but he had to act fast.

He radioed the first vehicle, telling them to go on and check out the ruins, and told the other BMP to follow him. They turned and headed for Carpenter's fleeing Humvee.

* - * - *

Ozera scampered up to the mounted 50-cal machine gun and spun it around to face the rear. The other Humvee finally pulled out behind them and he knew they had gotten away, too. Ozera saw the BMPs split up, with two of them in hot pursuit, firing everything they had.

He pulled the bolt on the 50-cal and chambered a round, but didn't fire. Carpenter's Humvee was right in the line of fire, between him and the enemy vehicles. Now the Humvee was zigzagging as streams of Iraqi machine gun fire sprayed them. Then cannon rounds exploded – one to the left and another to the right. They were pulling out ahead of the BMPs, maybe 500 yards now, but the zigzagging was slowing them down. A calculated risk.

Ozera was already a quarter-mile away. Clearly the Iraqis were ignoring him and concentrating instead on the closer target, Carpenter's Humvee. Ozera yelled down to Wilson, who was driving: "Slow it down a little, Sarge. Give them a chance to catch up." With anxious trepidation he looked back at the other Humvee. He was secretly hoping some of the Iraqi's attention would shift to them.

"C'mon, Jerry, floor it!" Ozera muttered to himself.

Then a cannon round exploded just at the rear corner of Carpenter's Humvee. It must have done some damage because the vehicle slowed – still moving but slowing down to maybe half speed. Ozera became frantic. "Stop! Stop!" he yelled down to Wilson.

The next round found its mark, slamming squarely into the back of Carpenter's Humvee, ripping the back off the lightly armored vehicle and knocking it up and over on its side.

"Turn around!" Ozera impulsively directed Wilson, "We've got to go help them!"

Wilson slowed down and glanced over to his senior teammate, Sergeant Gordon, who had seen the other Humvee get blasted, too. He yelled back up to Ozera: "Sir, they got hit pretty bad! I don't think we can help 'em much! The Iraqis will be on them before we could even get back there. And then they'll be on us." He paused a moment and added: "And Sergeant Carpenter wouldn't want us ending up in the same shit."

Ozera saw that Gordon was right and silently nodded his head in acquiescence. The two BMPs were already closing in on the disabled Humvee. His moment of indecision ended when a cannon round exploded just behind Ozera's Humvee, forcing him down into the vehicle from the machine-gun mount.

"Okay, okay!" Ozera dejectedly told his sergeants, "Let's get out of here. Head for home." Wilson immediately floored it, making Ozera fall back. His gut tied in knots, Ozera went back up top, binoculars at the ready, to watch the disabled Humvee … and any sign of the men he was leaving behind … for as long as he could. In just a few moments the Humvee, the BMPs, the hilltop ruins, all of it, were out of sight. But it would never be out of his mind.

* _ * _ *

II: Debriefing

Ozera called in a situation report to headquarters. Most of the trip back was quiet and solemn. The three soldiers said little; there wasn't much to say. It was getting dark by the time they wended their way back – past advancing American units and through the breach zone – back across the border to their base camp in Saudi Arabia.

Ragged and haggard, they grabbed some hot chow at the battalion mess hall. Ozera thanked and bid good night to his comrades, then retired to his quarters – looking forward to a few fingers of bourbon, a shower and a soft bunk. He slept, but it was an unsettling sleep.

He had an early morning debriefing with his boss, Colonel William Burrus. Showered, shaven and in clean desert fatigues, he strutted in, snapped to attention and saluted.

"Lieutenant Ozera reporting, sir."

"At ease, Lieutenant," the colonel said, nonchalantly returning the salute. Ozera detected a softer-than-usual, uncharacteristically compassionate tone in his voice. Colonel Burrus was a sharp, capable commander. He had run a dozen Special Ops units and had seen it all. Word was he passed up a promotion to general just to stay in the field with Special Forces.

"I know you didn't all make it back, but congratulations on a job well done," he began, "That tank regiment could have dealt us a world of hurt. We could have hit them remotely, using just satellite and AWACS intel, but it was your team's eyes on the ground and your fire mission that nailed them."

The colonel referred to a report already in his hands. "Forward elements of the First Cav Division ran into them and cleaned up. They counted 560 enemy dead and 60 Soviet tanks destroyed. Another dozen were barely touched, just abandoned. Some nice, mint condition T-72s, too. They took more than 600 POWs. They saw a few tanks and trucks limping back north towards Baghdad, but not many. Most of them have since been taken out."

"Did they find my other men, sir?" Ozera asked.

"They did," he confirmed. Both knew what was coming. And both knew it wasn't going to be nice. "I got a note late last night from First Cav's second brigade commander, an old West Point classmate of mine. A patrol in his unit came across the Humvee just south of reference point Delta. All were believed dead. I'm sorry, Brad. I knew you and Sergeant Carpenter were close." Ozera closed his eyes a moment and choked back any emotion."

"What happened out there?" the colonel asked.

"During the air strike an Iraqi patrol in three BMPs surprised us, coming in around behind," he related, his voice monotonous, emotionless. "They started shelling us. I took off in one Humvee with Sergeants Gordon and Wilson. Carpenter stayed behind, grabbing the maps. He was supposed to hop in the other Humvee and follow right behind me. They finally pulled out and we were both tearing south, with two of the BMPs on their tail."

"They were a few hundred meters behind me," Ozera continued. "Their Humvee was closer to them, a half kilometer behind us, and they caught a lot of their fire. Then a cannon round hit them square in the rear. Ripped the back off their vehicle, and I saw them flip over." He paused, reflecting, then quietly added: "The Iraqis were right on top of them. We ... I ... didn't have a chance to go back and help. We had to keep going ... or we wouldn't have made it back either."

"I know from your record you've been in sticky situations before. You know by now that it never gets any easier," the colonel said, looking Ozera in the eye. "It looks like two of your boys died in the explosion. We think the other two survived the blast." His tone went soft, emotion in his voice: "But the Iraqis were looking for revenge and it looks like they took it out on them. They were pretty badly mutilated. The First Cav bagged and sent back as much as they could." He paused, adding: "I'm sorry, Brad."

"Do we know whether Sergeant Carpenter ..."

"No," the colonel cut him off, "We're not sure which ones they were." He lied. The report indicated that it looked like Carpenter and Morris were riding in the front of the Humvee and probably survived the blast. Their bodies were unidentifiable but their dog tags were found among the remains. The colonel tried to change the subject. "Your fire mission saved a lot of American lives. I'm putting you in for a Silver Star, Lieutenant."

"Already got one," Ozera quickly responded, with uncharacteristic curtness. He caught himself: "But I appreciate the thought ... sir." The colonel understood. For a 29-year-old Ozera was carrying a lot on his broad shoulders. He knew that Ozera had recently divorced. And now he'd be bearing a huge load of guilt on top of everything else.

"Anything else, sir?" Ozera asked.

"Not right now. Take some time and try to relax. Then come back and see me. Your name came up a couple days ago, right after you left on your patrol. Somebody in HQ asked about you, by name. Let me check on a few things. I'll know more after Washington wakes up and gets to work." He paused, and then added: "Again, I'm sorry about your men."

Emotionless, Ozera came to attention, saluted, about-faced and walked out.

Jerry Carpenter's death was a deep blow. A million what-if's ran through Ozera's mind. He had come to believe that the tough master sergeant was invincible, a survivor who could get himself out of anything.

It wasn't just that he lost a close friend, one of very few he had. Making it worse was the fact **he** was in charge. It was **his** men who died. Could he have done things differently? Would anything have made a difference, and perhaps saved their lives?

Time would help, but the haunt and the hurt would follow him forever.

* _ * _ *

II: Homeward bound

Cleaned up and rested, at least to some degree, Ozera returned late the next afternoon.

"How are you managing, Lieutenant?" the colonel asked.

"I'll get by, sir." He didn't want to talk about it. There wasn't anything that either of them could say or do that would help.

"Well, looks like this is going to be a short war," the colonel told him. "President Bush personally halted our advance, way short of Baghdad. It seems Saddam doesn't have the stomach for a real fight. Word is a cease-fire is in the works. We may all be getting out of this sand trap soon."

"Can you tell me anything more about that situation involving me?" Ozera asked.

"Actually, I'm glad you asked. Here," the colonel handed him some papers. "Orders for your new job. Some highly classified unit, something I've never heard of. And as it turns out, the duty location is not that far from your home of record, somewhere in eastern Pennsylvania."

Ozera scanned the document. One thing caught his eye immediately. "**Captain** Ozera?" he asked.

"Congratulations, **Captain**," the colonel replied, with a hint of a smile. "I got the orders on that last night, too. It seems your new job is a captain's slot. And so presto, you are heretofore promoted to captain. You've done the time; you deserve it."

"What's this all about, sir? Why are you sending me back stateside?"

"**I'm** not sending you anywhere, Brad. I'm just the messenger. I got a query a few days ago, from DA MILPERCEN, asking about your status and availability. A friend of mine there told me **you** had been tapped especially for this job, based on unique qualifications you have."

"What qualifications?" Ozera interrupted.

"I'm sure I don't have a clue, and neither did my friend. He told me they were just following orders, too. But whose orders we don't know. It's all classified crap, way above my pay grade."

The colonel leaned over his desk and spoke softly, as if someone nearby was listening in. "It's some kind of security position, at some kind of research facility, and you have certain skills and a background that match it perfectly. That's all I know," he said, adding: "But I know this too: You've been out in the field for a couple years now, and you deserve a little downtime. So go with the flow and enjoy it. These things happen for a reason."

Ozera saw the sincerity in the colonel's eyes, and was thankful.

"When do I ship out, sir?"

"Take some leave en route, Lieu … er, Captain," the colonel said. "You've got til March 15 to report in. I can get you on a flight back to Bragg whenever you're ready to go. Tomorrow, if you want."

"I'll take it, sir."

"You're a good soldier, Brad, and I'm proud to have had you in my command. That Silver Star will catch up to you. You deserve it. Really. I've got a feeling this new job is going to change your outlook on life. Hopefully you'll have a chance to re-charge your batteries. And besides, this Army isn't all that big. We'll cross paths again."

"I'll look forward to it, sir. And thanks for everything." He came to attention and snapped a salute. Colonel Burrus returned his salute, then stood and held out his hand. A hearty handshake and Ozera walked out. He was tired. And it looked like the curtain on the Gulf War was about to drop right behind him, after just a few days. He didn't know how many American soldiers died in Operation Desert Storm. But four of them were his.

* _ * _ *

Chapter III: Reassignment

III: En route

It was a long flight, but comfortable and uneventful. Captain Brad Ozera arrived just after midnight, but even so, Pope Air Force Base was abuzz with activity. There was the usual endless flow of troops coming and going, but there were also hordes of parents, wives, loved ones, even a TV news crew – all clamoring and hungry for the latest word from the Gulf. It was nice to be back, but he was also glad to finally navigate the crowds and get out of there.

The cold night air struck him as he left the terminal. It was early March, but a late winter cold snap had settled over the East Coast. Ozera took a cab to the Fort Bragg Bachelor Officer Quarters and he checked in for a few days. He figured he had at least one day of business, and would then take a couple of days to check on friends and acquaintances.

The whole next day was spent processing his reassignment through a labyrinth of petty Army bureaucracies – transportation, medical, housing. Surprisingly, though, all seemed uncommonly cooperative. Maybe it was the captain's bars. Maybe it was the Gulf War. Maybe it was his orders: Eyebrows rose on seeing his assignment to an obscure Pennsylvania research facility that nobody ever heard of.

Transportation arranged a new Ford Explorer SUV for him on a two-year lease. He got authorization for temporary-duty, interim living and then approval for reimbursement for apartment or house rental at his new duty station in Pennsylvania.

A last stop was at the Adjutant General, to see what he could do for his soldiers who didn't make it. Their next of kin had been notified, and the AG colonel assured Ozera he would get their names and mailing addresses, so he could send letters. All considered, things went well – surprisingly, refreshingly, and unexpectedly well.

He would have to get some furniture. All of his furnishings went with Kathy – the stunning blond he married three years earlier. It started off as a solid relationship, or so he thought. They made love the night they met, and almost every night afterwards. They talked, they laughed and they loved. Then came his graduation and his marriage proposal to her. She hesitated, then said yes, but insisted they put off the wedding until he completed all his Army training courses – more than a year. He agreed, and during that year they amassed a lifetime's worth of steamy romantic interludes.

Then he learned of his acceptance into Special Forces. And he knew that meant a lot of time away from home – far away, on months-long, classified, usually dangerous, out-of-country operations. He didn't bring it up until after the wedding, and by then it was too late. They went off together to Fort Bragg, for better or, as it turned out, for worse.

Their times together were delightful and mutually satisfying – but too intermittent. Kathy was a wonderful woman, Ozera would tell himself, but there was one serious issue – she could not live being alone on an Army base for months at a time, away from family and close friends. She needed constant companionship, holding and loving, he discovered, too late.

"You're never around anymore, Brad," she lamented, "I don't know when, or even if, you're coming home." She sat teary eyed, her legs crossed, her statuesque figure in a short, tight knit dress. He had come home late the night before, after four months in a camp in sub-Saharan Africa, and could barely keep his eyes open. It was Saturday night and she had plans – her own plans, and they didn't include him. He loved her. But that night he let her go – in more ways than one.

She had moved from their on-post housing right after the divorce, just a month earlier. He had a pretty good idea where she was, but decided to not even try to track her down. He knew when he was overseas that the divorce was coming.

He just signed the papers and sent them back. Now it was over.

Ozera stopped at the Provost Marshall, looking for Lieutenant Phil Lemon, an ROTC buddy from college, who got commissioned in the MPs and then ended up assigned to Fort Bragg. The two were notorious at Lehigh as a pair of incorrigible hell raisers, and Ozera wanted to see and spend a little time with his old friend. More importantly, though, Lemon would be a familiar and friendly face, and someone he could share with – up to a point. Even for old buddies and soldiers, male bonding had its limits. Lemon was a confirmed bachelor and, suiting his name, had the drollest and wriest sense of humor, which Ozera cherished. It would be good to see Phil again, he thought to himself.

But it was not to happen. He learned instead that Lemon had shipped out to the Gulf three months earlier. Hopefully he was out of harm's way. Probably handing out traffic tickets to Saudi camel jockeys, Ozera thought with a chuckle.

So it was off to the Class 6 store, and back to the BOQ with a bottle of Wild Turkey 101. Pretty good hooch, he thought, and now he wouldn't even have to share it. A quiet night, alone …

The next day he checked on two other old acquaintances, but the story was the same. He stopped at the home of his first company commander, Captain Walt Steinmetz, where he and Kathy had many a pleasant evening. But someone else had moved into their government quarters. The freckle-faced girl who answered the door said they'd just moved in a few weeks earlier, and she had no idea where the previous occupants went.

Then he tried Lieutenant Roger Rendell. By a quirk of fate, he and Roger had gone through Ranger and Special Forces schools together. Very tough courses. And both men knew that, were it not for the support and comradeship of the other, neither would have made it. In fatigues and Green Beret,

Ozera leapt up the steps to Roger's apartment. An attractive woman answered – black, shapely and with a pronounced Jamaican accent.

"No, mon," she told him, eyeing him from beret to boots. "Roger's been gone for ..." she had to think, "a month or so. I take care of the place for him when he's gone. You know the score, Captain. Never know where or for how long. I just pray Roger comes home to me."

Ozera nodded, and noticed she wasn't wearing a wedding ring, or any jewelry for that matter. Still it was clear they were close; she spoke with a distinct softness when she mentioned Roger. Ozera had found out that, ironically, Roger had finished several years in a Catholic seminary. It was the topic of endless discussion out in the field, during their hardest times together. He told Ozera he awoke one day and decided that, rather than a priest, he wanted to be a soldier. Go figure.

"Roger's a lucky man," Ozera said with an adoring smile. "Please tell him that Brad Ozera stopped by." He smiled again, then turned and walked away, with much less lilt in his step than when he arrived.

It was Friday night. He decided he'd check out and leave post the next day and head north for Pennsylvania. He still had lots of time before he had to report in. He would spend a few days visiting his parents. But tonight, he'd see what was happening at the Officers' Club. He could have gone in fatigues, and pounded down drinks with the boys at one of the grunt bars. But he decided instead to dress up a little – Class A's: crisp shirt and tie, shined low quarters, captain's bars and brass cleaned and shined, and all the ribbons and decorations he'd earned over the last four years. Tonight he was looking for some good chow, a few drinks, maybe even companionship. Who knows? Maybe he'd get lucky.

Ozera had a light dinner, and along with it most of a bottle of good wine. He sipped an after-dinner cocktail and decided to check out the bar scene. Manhattan in hand, he was feeling rather handsome and beguiling – enhanced by a moderate blood-alcohol level. He slowly cased the joint.

She was sitting alone at a small bar table with her Manhattan. Blond, forty-something, and with a low-cut dress and buxom payload that would catch any man's attention. It worked. And she was looking at him. He smiled and raised his glass. She reciprocated, ever so slightly. He waited a few more minutes, sipped and glanced around, just to be sure she was alone. He concluded she was and walked the length of the bar to her table. He flashed one of his ice-melting smiles and asked if he could sit down. She nodded affirmatively.

"Do you know why a Manhattan is like a woman's breasts?" Ozera asked. It was one of his favorite lines, and he wanted to see if she was put off by the sexual innuendo. She wasn't.

She smiled and obligatorily responded, straight-faced: "No, why?"

"Because one is not enough and three is too many." She laughed out loud. She hadn't heard it before. He had almost forgotten the pleasure of hearing a woman's laugh. It was nice, especially knowing he was the cause.

They mixed two more rounds of Manhattans with some meaningless conversation. Before long he had his arm around her shoulders and she was responding warmly. Her name, at least the name she told him, was Bridgette. It was getting late. She suggested they go back to her place, but they'd have to be quiet and not wake the neighbors. He thought of suggesting the BOQ, but decided not to, figuring that, for whatever reason, she preferred the security of her place. He retrieved their coats; they walked out together and took a cab. Neither was feeling much pain.

On the way she told him, almost matter-of-factly, in a hazy, intoxicated voice: Two days ago, she said, an Army sedan pulled up and a Captain got out. She said she knew why. Her husband, a Special Forces sergeant, had just been killed in Iraq. She hadn't seen him in a year. It was like someone dumped a pail of ice water on Ozera. He looked down and, for the first time, saw she was wearing a wedding ring.

They pulled up to her quarters, in a senior enlisted section of post housing. He pulled his arm from around her, and looked her in the eyes.

"Bridgette, I can't. Not tonight. I will not be very good company," he said.

"Why? What's the matter? What happened?" she asked, confused. Her eyes were imploring him to come in with her, to hold her, love her.

"I can't. I'm sorry for leading you on. It's not you. It's … I … didn't know."

"Well, you son of a bitch," she railed. He just sighed as she continued her verbal assault, and then he calmly reached over her and opened her door. The cab driver turned around and, figuring the hour and the state of his passengers, just turned back to the front.

He sat calmly, accepting her rage. Then abruptly she stopped, apparently realizing it wasn't going to make a difference. So she got out, slammed the cab door and staggered up the walkway to her apartment. He could have looked and seen her last name on the front door, but he didn't want to.

Ozera returned to the BOQ. He got to his room and sat down, in the dark. He didn't know her last name, and he didn't want to know. His mind returned to Iraq, to the hilltop and their desperate escape. He saw the BMP cannon round again hit the Humvee. And again, and again. He started to cry.

* _ * _ *

III: Long road home

The drive from North Carolina was tedious. Virginia went on forever, it seemed, and then 20 miles of stop-and-go traffic around the Washington beltway. As he emerged from the Baltimore tunnel, it began to snow. It was the last days of winter, but it was winter still.

And it was getting dark as Ozera continued northward. The snow had become heavier, and was now covering the shoulder of I-95. He hadn't seen snow in years and he welcomed it. It was an indelible part of his Pennsylvania upbringing and memories.

He passed Aberdeen and the snow was now accumulating on the roadway, too, making things slippery. The long Havre de Grace bridge, skirting the northern edge of the Chesapeake Bay, was freezing. Then Ozera nearly slid into a tractor trailer he was passing. Traffic was light, fortunately, but it left him rattled.

He checked his watch: just after 8 pm. He'd been on the road some eight hours, and it would be dangerous to push on. He'd been away a long time and he wanted very much to get home, but it would have to wait til tomorrow. He decided to pull over at the next exit, find a motel and crash for the night.

It looked like he was the only customer at the motel near Port Deposit, Maryland, a couple miles off the Interstate. His tracks to and from the office were the only ones in the fluffy snow, now covering the otherwise empty parking lot. Nothing fancy – a clean bed and warm shower. Worth the $30. He poured himself a bourbon, undressed and stretched out. It was quiet as a tomb – a deafening quiet, muffled and amplified by the falling snow outside.

In minutes he was deep asleep, and he dreamt. It was a long, long time ago. He was still a soldier, but wearing a fur jacket and deerskin pants and boots. His left arm bore a heavy

The Monastery

shield. He glanced down and saw a sheathed sword on his left hip.

"We haven't got far to go, Brad," came a voice from his right. He looked and saw Roger Rendell, as he remembered him except with long hair and a long brown mustache. He looked like a Viking.

"Where are we going, Roger?" he asked his old field buddy. Roger just smiled and nodded up ahead. He looked around; they were in deep woods. It was twilight and getting dark. Several inches of snow covered the ground. Every step crunched through the snow and the leaves and twigs underneath.

He heard voices behind them and turned and looked around. It was all the men from the patrol –Sergeants Carpenter, Morris, Gordon, Wilson, and the rest. They too wore furs and animal hides, and also bore shields and swords. They were nonchalantly wise-cracking and exchanging barbs with each other as they trudged along behind him. It all seemed very normal, in a surreal sort of way.

They emerged from the woods out onto a large, open field, several acres. He stopped and looked around, and saw he was alone. Roger, all the men, all gone.

"Do you know what you're looking for?" someone asked, in a language Ozera hadn't heard for years. It was Romanian. He turned and saw beside him an old man in a monk's robe, with white hair and deep-set dark eyes, carrying a large walking stick.

It took a moment to re-set his mind for Romanian. *"I'm ... not sure,"* he responded to the old man in Romanian, quite bewildered now by the whole situation.

"Then how will you know when you've found it?" the old man queried, with a smirk.

"Do you know what I'm looking for?" Ozera responded.

"It's what they're all looking for," the old man said. He pointed to the barren, snow-covered field. *"It is here, Captain. It has always been here, and will always be here."* He said with a wink and a smile, *"And find it you will ... when the time is right."* The old man then turned and started walking away.

"Wait!" Ozera yelled to him, " *What are you talking about?! Where are my friends?!"* The old man was now far away, out in the open field, walking away from him. *"Wait!"* he shouted as loud as he could, "*What is this place?!"*

He awoke, and quickly realized his own yelling had awakened him. He lay quietly for a moment then looked around, trying to remember where he was. It was a response he had learned out in the field; awake quietly, be still a moment and get oriented. His mind raced from the hilltop in Iraq, to the base camp in Kuwait, to Fort Bragg and the BOQ. He was here in ... a hotel in Maryland. He had brought his waking mind up to date.

The motel room was quiet and cold, but under the thin blanket he was damp with sweat. He didn't feel ill or fevered, though, and chalked it up to the transition: A few days ago he was in the Kuwaiti desert, 50 degrees warmer and seven time zones away.

The sun was shining brightly, he could tell, through the cheap, light cotton curtains that barely covered the small window by the front door. He got out of bed and shivered with a chill, then walked over and pulled the curtains aside. Bright sun, and the snow was already melting. The road looked clear. Must have been plowed during the night, he concluded.

He showered, shaved and donned his Class A uniform. It wasn't often that he wanted to be seen in clean, dressy Class A's, but he did today. He was going home. He'd been away for years, and he wanted to show he was proud – of himself, of his military service, and truly happy to be going home.

Ozera didn't call to warn his folks he was coming. He wanted it quiet, without a bevy of neighbors or a big welcome-home reception. He figured it would be a surprise. It was Sunday, and he expected his parents wouldn't be home until after church. So he planned to show up noon-ish. With morning chores and church taken care of, they'd be relaxing after a late breakfast.

But he was famished, not having eaten since the previous afternoon. So just before getting on the Pennsylvania turnpike he pulled into a diner for a hearty breakfast. It seemed everyone in the place, all complete strangers, had to stop by and ask about the Gulf War. They wished him well, or derided Saddam Hussein, or asked whether he knew this soldier or that Marine, and on and on. He downed a quick bite when he could, between well-wishers. They wouldn't let him pay, but he nevertheless slipped a few dollars tip under his plate as he left.

By noon he was back in the Poconos, turning off the main road in Eldred and onto the gravel driveway of his family's small dairy farm. He stopped a moment, savoring the experience. It was all exactly as he remembered it. Even the "Farm Fresh Eggs" sign was still on the front fence, although a bit more weathered than he remembered.

His mother, looking just a bit more gray and frail than he remembered, opened the door. Her jaw dropped. "*Oh, my God*," she uttered in her native Romanian. She turned and called out: "*Pietre! Come! It's Bradley! He's here; he's come home!*" Ozera held out his arms and they embraced warmly.

"You're in America, Mom," he told her softly. "You should speak English."

"If it makes my Bradley happy and brings him home to me, then I talk American," she said resolutely, as a tear streamed down her cheek.

Then his father appeared in the doorway – a large, stocky, powerful man, from whom Ozera no doubt inherited his own broad frame.

"Hi, Pop," Ozera said softly. His father smiled, but said nothing. Ozera recalled his father's wisdom – that when you don't talk a lot, people pay more attention when you do. Nothing needed to be said, though. The tears welling in his eyes said it all. The big man stepped in and embraced them both. And for the moment, and for the first time in a long time, Brad Ozera was at peace.

* _ * _ *

III: R & R

It was a few days of much needed rest and recuperation. Ozera felt guilty after sleeping in late the first morning, and was determined to lend a hand and help out around the farm. His father, in his mid-50's, had to run the farm by himself since Ozera's younger siblings were both now away at college.

He was up the next day before dawn, even before his father, tending the cows and cleaning out the barn. In the afternoon he made needed repairs to the chicken coops. The next morning he drove into town and surprised his father by bringing back a truckload of feed for the chickens and cows, noting that the food bins were almost empty. He knew what had to be done and was glad to lend a hand.

Over the next few days he spent more time with his parents than he had in many years – indeed since he left for college, Ozera reflected. He was the firstborn and the apple of his father's eye. Younger sister, Liz, was finishing her last year at Boston College. She would be visiting soon, during spring break, and may even be bringing her new boyfriend, his mother told him with excited anticipation. His younger brother, Pat, had left in the fall and was finishing his first year at his old alma mater, Lehigh University.

"We wanted you all to be good Americans," his mother would always tell them. So she took particular pride in their names. Brad was named for General Omar Bradley. Pat was a shortened version of Patton, and Liz a permutation of Betsy Ross.

Ozera always envisioned his parents huddled in the maternity ward, she nine months pregnant and in labor, frantically thumbing through an American History textbook.

The last night Ozera went out, visiting a few of his old local haunts and watering holes. He came home very late and more than a little drunk, staggering noisily up to his bedroom. He worried that he would be caught by his parents and reprimanded, like the old days. But not a sound came from them. If they knew or suspected his condition, he had already been forgiven this indiscretion.

* - * - *

III: Arrival

The sun was just making its presence known and somewhere a rooster dutifully sounded reveille. But Ozera was already up, shining his shoes and brass. He came down for breakfast in his black-striped trousers, crisp shirt and black tie. He was in more of a somber mood than he'd been in recent days – exacerbated, perhaps, by a moderate hangover and too few hours' sleep. The last few days of regression to earlier, simpler times were therapeutic and restorative, but much too brief. He sighed as he sat down at the kitchen table.

At breakfast he told them he was to report in at a Government research facility, somewhere down along the Delaware River near Upper Black Eddy. They glanced at each other with the same puzzled expression: Neither had seen or even heard of any such facility in the area. Light-heartedly changing subjects, he told them he might even end up living nearby, and warned they'd get tired of seeing him around. But then he added, on a serious note, that in his line of work he never knew for sure where he'd be staying, and that they tended not to keep him in the same place for very long.

Right after breakfast his father got up and, characteristically without a word, left. His mother let the dishes be and stayed with Ozera as he packed up the SUV. Then he turned to leave.

"Where's Pop?" Ozera looked around and asked.

"*Your father said he had a lot to do*," she answered in her native Romanian. "*But between me and you he is sad that you are leaving so soon, and I think he just didn't want you to see him cry. He does, y'know. He wants you to know how proud we are of you, that we love you and we miss you terribly when you are gone.*"

This time it was Ozera whose eyes welled with tears. They embraced.

"*I will see you again soon, Mom,*" he said softly to her in Romanian. It was still quite cold this March morning, but with the warmth they shared neither mother nor son noticed. Ozera checked his watch and it was time to go. He threw his overcoat and beret onto the front passenger's seat, started up and took off down the gravel driveway to the main road.

His orders were to report at 0900 on Friday, 15 March 1991, to "Commander, NEPA Research Facility, Narrows Hill Road, Upper Black Eddy, PA 18007." And so he would.

It was a pleasant drive, winding his way through bucolic Pennsylvania back roads. He wondered about what manner of Government research facility they would tuck away here, up in the hills and cliffs that rose high above the Delaware River. The name didn't reveal much: NEPA was a common local acronym for Northeast Pennsylvania – that part of the state north of Allentown and Bethlehem, to Scranton and the New York border.

He'd been driving an hour and was nearing where he estimated the turn-off from the river road would be. Ozera had driven down this river road dozens of times but never really took note of the occasional side roads that wound their way down through the hills, like mountain streams flowing to the river.

He rounded a corner and a small side road popped into view. Ozera hit the brakes, almost passing it. A weathered road sign read 'Narrows Hill Rd,' which no one would see unless they were looking for it. He turned and accelerated up the incline.

One mile, nearly two. The road, winding through quaint farmland and countryside, would level off for a while, then twist and turn sharply, continuing ever upward. Then Ozera spotted a gravel driveway leading into the woods. Several innocuous, but unquestionably Government-issued signs marked the entrance: 'NEPA Facility,' 'No Trespassing,' and 'Private Property.' "Must be the place," Ozera muttered to himself. He turned in, but then came to sudden stop: A thick log lay across the gravel road, blocking the way.

Not sure what to do next, he got out and looked around. Out of the corner of his eye he caught movement and a sunlight glint. Near the tree line on the right was a nondescript wooden post with a closed-circuit TV camera mounted on top. He was being watched. It moved again, panning him and his SUV. He waited. A few moments later he heard an electronic relay and, surprisingly, the obstructing tree trunk slowly swung away, allowing him to pass. "Now that's something you don't see every day," he mumbled.

Ozera drove ahead on the neat gravel road, around a few sharp bends, still climbing. The road finally leveled off and he arrived at a huge clearing. There were several two-story buildings.

A few people were walking about. All of them, oddly, were clad in long gray robes, like monks' habits, with their hoods up. Slowly he continued on, to a parking lot near the first of the buildings, with a few cars and a couple government-looking, black SUVs. He pulled in and parked.

Ozera got out and, as he was putting on his beret, noticed a robed figure walking towards him. A hand reached up and pulled back the hood, revealing a young woman. She had a pretty face – with short dark hair and high cheekbones. She smiled beguilingly as she neared him.

"Hello, Captain," she said, with a noticeable accent Ozera recognized as eastern European. Either she recognized military rank, he thought to himself, or she was expecting him and it was a lucky guess.

"Hi," he responded, returning a trademark smile. She stopped and eyed his uniform – checking, he guessed, that his nametag read 'Ozera.' "I'm here to meet with the commander," he said.

"Won't you please follow me?" she said and, without waiting for an answer, turned and began walking back to the nearby building she came from. No salute. No "sir." No sign of ID or rank, and a strong foreign accent, Ozera noted. It's doubtful she is military, he concluded.

He looked around as he followed her up a gravel path to the first of four two-story, rectangular buildings, arranged in a row. All looked the same – concrete block, metal-frame windows, entrances on the front and back, and a fairly steep asphalt shingle roof. There was a large concrete pad behind them, and several acres of open field behind that. At the far end of the parking area was a single, one-story concrete-block building, with propane and oil tanks. Probably electric generators and water supply, Ozera reasoned. A high chain-link fence bordered the back of the compound.

They walked up a few steps and in through the front door. There were two desks and chairs, a sort of reception area, it seemed, but no one else in sight. They proceeded down a narrow hallway, stopping at an office door. She knocked on the door and a gravelly male voice said to come in. No sign denoting name, rank or title. But on the wall by the door hung a hand-carved wooden plaque, which read: 'Abandon Hope, All Ye Who Enter Here.' Ozera recognized it from Dante's Inferno – a warning at the entrance to Hell. He smiled. If this was the guy in charge, he was either an ogre to work for, or else had a wry sense of humor.

She opened the door, then politely stepped aside, inviting Ozera to proceed in on his own.

* - * - *

III: The Colonel

The room was spacious but spartanly appointed. Ozera
looked around. Bland, utilitarian. Unadorned, bare walls.
Nondescript fluorescent lights. A well-worn black leather
sofa at one end looked like it had been used more for sleeping
than sitting. There were several book shelves, mostly empty.
In the middle of the room was an oval conference table with a
half-dozen chairs. At the other end was a large desk,
uncluttered except for a few telephones and radio transceivers
and handsets. Ozera recognized one as a basic Army issue,
secure radiophone – range about 20 miles.

Behind the desk sat a stocky man in his late 40's, maybe 50,
wearing the same type of monk's habit. His dark hair,
graying slightly at the temples, was well trimmed and combed
straight back. He had piercing dark eyes, and a goatee, also
well-trimmed and peppered with gray. Likely military, Ozera
figured, and likely Special Forces, since only they allowed
that type of goatee. He decided to find out, and walked
smartly up to the desk. But before Ozera could say or do
anything the man behind the desk casually raised his hand
and forefinger – a clear, silent signal to wait.

Then he turned and dismissed the young woman with a
simple "Thank you, Lisa." She nodded and walked out,
closing the door behind her. He dropped his hand – Ozera's
cue to proceed.

"Captain Ozera, reporting as ordered, sir," he said, coming to
attention and snapping a salute. He didn't wait long; the
salute was smartly returned. So he *is* military, likely a senior
Special Forces officer, and presumably in charge of this
operation, Ozera concluded.

"Please, Captain, relax and pull up a chair," he said, gesturing
to a nearby wooden chair. It was little more than a stool with
a back, and it looked painfully uncomfortable. "Welcome to
the NEPA Research Facility. My name is Smith." Ozera

pulled off his beret and pulled up the chair. He sat down, and in a few moments discovered he was right about the chair.

Smith did not mention rank, but Ozera figured him for a Lieutenant Colonel, maybe even a full Colonel. In either case, just calling him "sir" would suffice. Ozera was in no position to begin asking questions – at least not yet. It was considered bad form. Special Forces would often leave you guessing with unanswered questions. You were expected to make do with whatever you had. For now, Ozera would do the listening; the Colonel would do the talking.

He congratulated Ozera on the success of his last mission during the short-lived ground war in the Gulf, and his recent promotion. No mention of the casualties, but Ozera was sure he knew the whole story. The Colonel, it seemed, kept uncommonly well informed. And he was articulate: His speaking manner was clear and sincere, but without a scintilla of emotion. After a while Ozera sensed his new commander was loosening up with him a bit. Maybe commiserating with a fellow Special Forces officer was something he didn't get to do often here, especially one fresh from the field and combat, Ozera thought.

"I've heard all good things about you, Captain," the Colonel said, "We raked through MILPERCEN records for weeks and I was lucky to find you for this assignment. We are – I am – very glad to have you here. I know you haven't been told many details yet, but we'll get into all that later."

He looked at Ozera's awards and decorations – Combat Infantryman Badge, Ranger tab, Airborne wings, Silver Star. "This will be your last time in that uniform for a while," he told him. "On your way out you'll get your new 'uniform' – same type of habit I'm wearing, comes in summer and winter versions. I don't care what you wear under it; I wear a T-shirt, jeans and sneakers."

"Why the monk's robes, sir?" Ozera asked.

"It's all a cover, of course," he replied, "We don't want to advertise that this is a U.S. military-run facility, and that's appropriate actually since most of the people involved here **are** civilians. That would just invite too many prying eyes," he said, adding: "And then there's keeping up appearances to the locals."

"How's that, sir?" Ozera asked.

"We let it leak out to the locals – state police, neighbors, the bar and restaurant down in town – that a group of Franciscan friars would be leasing the property for meditation and religious study. Now what could be more peaceful and less threatening than that, right?" the Colonel asked rhetorically.

Ozera smiled. "I see there are women here, too, wearing the same habits. Is that consistent with a Franciscan religious retreat?"

"Yeah, well, we're a progressive sect," the Colonel replied, tongue in cheek.

Ozera grinned and nodded, anxious for him to go on.

"We have 600 acres of this mountaintop, about a square mile," the Colonel continued. "It used to be a federal game preserve, which was released in the 50's to Pennsylvania. They made it a State Game Land for hunters. The federal government still owned it, though, and a few years ago it reverted back to federal control, ostensibly to erect an astronomical observation station, a NOAA weather-monitoring facility, and some other bullshit like that."

He paused a moment and went on: "Actually, we **did** do a lot of construction. But more on that later. The first thing I did when we took over here was to post the entire perimeter with 'Private Property,' 'Posted,' and 'No Hunting' signs."

"I like the swinging log down at the entrance," Ozera quipped.

"That was a lot of work," the Colonel said, "It really is a log. They cut down and drilled out the center of a big oak, heavy as hell, and put a big metal bar down the middle. A powerful electric motor, all underground, swings it open and closed." The Colonel was being very candid discussing the facility's security details with him, Ozera noted.

"I saw the closed-circuit TV camera, too."

"You're supposed to," the Colonel said, "And it does work; we checked you over when you pulled in. But we also wanted curiosity seekers to see that they are being watched, and that the place has up-to-date electronic security. There are cameras and motion sensors all over the place outside the fence, so we know when anything or anybody is approaching. Every now and again someone will pull in down there, see the camera and then back out and go away."

"Who runs security, sir?" Ozera asked.

The Colonel smiled, "Well, technically, you will. That's supposed to be your job … soon as you've learned your way around." Ozera figured that might be the case and nodded in acknowledgement, careful not to show any reaction, pro or con.

"Now don't get me wrong," the Colonel quickly added, "Any competent officer could handle security around here. But you've got several other, unique qualifications." Ozera raised an eyebrow, but restrained himself from asking.

"Actually, you don't even have to worry about **local** security," he said. "It pretty much runs itself. A five-man security detail choppers in from Maryland, and rotates in and out every two weeks. Four enlisted men and a senior NCO. Right now we've got one of the best here, a regular, Sergeant First Class Ernie Rivera. Very sharp."

"The security center – all the electronics and gear – is upstairs here," he said, pointing up. "It's where the feeds from all the cameras and detectors go, including that one at the entrance. Besides security control it's also their living quarters – there's a kitchen, dining room, dayroom, latrines, and individual rooms and bunks."

"They have the run of the whole place, of course, but they tend to stay together upstairs when they're not working," the Colonel said. "You may not even notice them, but they're watching all the time. They make sure someone is monitoring all the systems upstairs 24 hours a day, seven days a week. And one of them is usually out patrolling the compound."

Ozera nodded in acknowledgement, and appreciation, raising his eyebrows. This was well organized. Professional security troops, managed by a senior NCO. It all took detailed planning … and a lot of influence and money. This was expensive: the log gate, cameras, wiring, cabling, monitors, motion detectors, round-the-clock monitoring and outside patrols, by a full-time on-site security team, helicoptered in from … God only knows where.

"We have 18 to 20 people on-site here at any given time," the Colonel said. "Most of them – the security detail, the workers – stay and live here. There's a separate barracks building and mess hall for the workers. They pretty much keep to themselves, too."

"The full-time, on-site military contingent consists of me, you now, and the security team. A few other military folks come and go from time to time. For example, there's an AG captain who comes in a few times a month. He handles contracts, logistics and other paperwork stuff. He's sort of my adjutant. I set up an office for him down the hall."

"We've also had a lot of engineers and support troops in and out from Belvoir. Building materials and contractors were coming and going heavily for a few months, but a lot of this was commercial contractor traffic and that's largely subsided now. You can't tell by that puny gravel driveway that a lot of heavy equipment has come and gone that way," he said proudly. "And we may get a few other military visitors from time to time. I'll coordinate those with you."

"Didn't the locals wonder what was up, with all the construction activity?" Ozera asked.

"They did or they didn't. What does it matter? We've put out enough plausible explanations – and conflicting explanations, by the way – that they can pick and choose whatever they want to believe. I started the whole 'Franciscan monk' thing about six months ago. Like I said, we want to de-emphasize military – y'know, uniforms, Humvees."

"Most of our military visitors come and go by chopper, like the security team," he added. "It's fast and private. Nobody sees who's coming and going that way. We can get a chopper here on a few hours' notice. I travel by chopper, too, to get to my meetings and back."

"It seems you've got things well in hand, sir," Ozera said. It was a little patronizing, he knew, but designed to get the Colonel to move on to the meat of the matter.

"Then there's the "Team" – our group of experts," the Colonel said, making quote marks with his fingers. "There are a half-dozen of them, who will be coming here on a regular basis. You'll need to focus your attention on them, as well as our employees here. It's an odd lot, to be sure. You'll need to get to know them all personally. Meet with them, privately, interview them tactfully. Your job is to assess each one, determine their motives, their plans, progress, if any, and their dedication. Most importantly, identify any of them who may pose a risk to the security, or the outcome, of this project."

That raised Ozera's eyebrows. Whatever was going on here apparently could potentially impact national security. His curiosity was heightening.

"I assume you stayed at a nearby hotel last night, Captain?" the Colonel asked.

"Actually no, sir. I stayed at my parents ..."

"Oh, that's right," the Colonel interrupted, "Your home **is** Pennsylvania and, if I recall, not very far from here."

"About an hour or so north, sir."

"Well," he said, cracking a smile for the first time, "Welcome home, soldier." A brief moment of levity ... very brief ... then it was back to business.

"You'll need to find a place to live," he continued. "Department of the Army says I've got you for as long as I need you. You'll need to find a place nearby 'cause you'll need to be close at hand – except when you're traveling of course. You're welcome to crash here for now, until you find a place. We've got some nice rooms over in the barracks building, which we've set up especially for overnight visitors."

"Take some time and get settled in," the Colonel added. "I ask, though, that you don't go exploring until after I've fully briefed you. I'd like to take you around and introduce you personally. Go see Lisa outside – her name actually is Elisabeta – and she'll help get you situated. She's one of our civilian workers, by the way. And keep in mind that, like most of them, she has minimal security clearance."

"I understand, sir," Ozera said. He thought he would probe the Colonel, ever so gently: "Our work here is classified then?" he asked.

"Oh, yes, highly," the Colonel shot back. "I know you're anxious to know what we're up to, and you will. I will brief you tomorrow." Ozera was glad to hear that.

"Just one more thing. For now, please speak only English to the staff here," he could tell by the Colonel's expression he was serious. "This is important. I'm aware you know a bunch of languages, but don't let on to anyone here, okay?" Ozera nodded, curious and confused.

"Now I need to prepare for an off-site meeting tomorrow morning. I won't be back til afternoon, so how about we plan for 1300 tomorrow?" the Colonel said. It was not a question, or open for negotiation. It was clear Ozera would get no more details this afternoon, and that their first meeting was over.

"Right, sir," he said, standing up. The Colonel nodded; Ozera turned and left.

* _ * _ *

III: On the way out

Ozera introduced himself to Lisa and got an armful of monk's habits. Three sizes were available, and she decided on Extra Large for him. They conversed for a while. She was cute, early 20's, and with a cute smile. He saw that she noticed his ring finger – bare but with a well-worn line from where his wedding ring had been. He subconsciously slipped his left hand into his pocket..

She told him she was selected to handle the phone and reception because she spoke better English than most of the others. But there were very few visitors these days and she was bored most of the time. He learned too that she regularly drove one of the vans off-site, mainly to the nearby town to obtain supplies, provisions for the kitchen, shuttle people to the store or doctor, or run other administrative errands. Wearing the habit off the mountain was discouraged, she told him.

Lisa explained the layout of the compound. There were four cement-block "barracks"-type buildings, plus a fifth utility building, which housed the water well, pump and electric generators. They were in the first building, Control Central, with reception, the Colonel's office and a few other offices on the first floor. She told him she knew the second floor was where the security soldiers stayed, but she was told strictly never to go up there.

The second building was the just-completed Conference Center, with several large meeting rooms on the first floor and offices upstairs. The third was the Dormitory Building, where she and most of the other civilian workers stayed. A few guest rooms and private rooms and bathrooms were upstairs; kitchen, dining hall and dayroom were downstairs. And the fourth building was still not finished inside, and used now just for storage, she said.

And then there was the construction "through the woods, up on the hill," which she said she couldn't talk about because she and "the others" weren't allowed to go up there. That caught Ozera's interest, but he tried to act dispassionately – as if he might have known what was going on up there – and didn't pursue it. For now, he would let it go.

Lisa indicated she'd been there about a year, and that she and the others moved in when the dorm building was finished and ready for occupancy. Ozera concluded that the civilian workers were a group, and that they all came to this place together, from somewhere in Eastern Europe.

He didn't have to be back until afternoon tomorrow, so Ozera figured he'd spend one more night with his folks and collect the rest of his meager belongings and gear. He wondered what he would tell them. His new assignment, like most so far in his military career, was a classified operation. Of course it wouldn't be hard to play dumb, he thought to himself with a chuckle, since he really didn't have a clue yet what was going on there or what his job would be.

* _ * _ *

Chapter IV: The Project
IV: Killing time

"So there really is a government installation down there on the river?" his mother queried.

"Well, it's not on the river; it's a few miles inland, up in the mountains. It's pretty remote and hard to find, but it's there. It's only been there a year or so, and construction is still going on. There are just a few buildings and not many people." He fended off the litany of follow-on questions – What went on there? What was his job? How often would he get home?

In the morning Ozera loaded his meager possessions and most of his civilian clothes in the SUV. It was cold, just above freezing, and raining. As he drove down the river road this time he started looking for a place to stay. There wasn't much – just woods and cliffs along the river. He spotted a worn "Room for Rent" sign out front of one farmhouse, but the place looked empty and abandoned and he kept going.

He neared the entrance to his facility at the mountaintop and decided to drive on past, to see what lay on the other side. Just down the road, across from the driveway entrance, was a small farm. He pulled over and scanned it, maybe 50 or 60 acres. A large white farmhouse and a huge red barn with empty paddocks. A small mountain creek meandered and babbled through the field in front. It was peaceful and pastoral, and well taken care of – almost manicured, and inviting.

He slowly drove by and saw a signpost, without signs, out front near the road. Two old wooden signs, painted white with black lettering, had been taken down and were on the ground, leaning against it. One read "Griffiths Bed and Breakfast." On the other he could barely make out "Horseback Riding" from the weather-worn letters.

Ozera made a mental note of it, and drove on. Heavy woods closed in on both sides of the roadway, which began weaving back and forth downhill. The road narrowed in spots, traversing a couple of single-lane bridges that spanned mountain streams, rushing from the earlier rain.

After a while the dark imposing woods started thinning and finally cleared. The roadway leveled and he entered a small town. 'Village of Fern Valley, pop 102' the small sign read. He came to a stop sign at a quiet rural intersection. Across the road was an old stone inn – the Fern Valley Inn, appropriately enough. 'Circa 1830,' the sign said. It looked cozy. He'd have to come back and try dinner there sometime soon.

He spotted a deli down the street and thought how good a hot coffee would be. A short while later he was back on the road again, a coffee and bagel in hand, headed back uphill.

On the way he contemplated his new job. For a soldier with his skills and background it was uncommon good fortune – especially compared to his most recent duty assignments: a steamy guerilla camp in the jungle, and a base in the cold, dry desert of Iraq. Of course it's always a good deal, he thought to himself with a smile, whenever you get a clean dry bunk to sleep in, a toasted bagel with cream cheese, and nobody trying to kill you and your buddies.

It was familiar territory – a quiet and peaceful corner of Pennsylvania, near where he grew up. He didn't know much about the job yet, but his boss seemed glad to have him. All things considered, life couldn't get much better, he concluded.

He pulled into the entrance to the facility, put the SUV in park and stepped out. He slipped off his jacket and pulled on his monk's habit, then grinned as the relay predictably clicked, the motor whirred and the log barrier slowly swung back. He drove up the winding road, pulled into a parking space and then sat a while in the car, looking around the compound: His new home. He sipped his coffee and

The Monastery

munched his bagel, enjoying the mountaintop view and bright, warming sun breaking through the clouds.

Watch check: Just after noon. He hopped out, strode up the front steps and into the control center. Lisa was seated dutifully at the front desk.

"Welcome back, Captain," she said with a radiant smile.

"Hi, Lisa," he responded, "Quiet morning?" She rolled her eyes and nodded in assent.

"Your habit fits well, I see," she said, eyeing him up and down, noting the broad shoulders. "You're a little early. The boss isn't back yet. Would you like a coffee?" she asked. He'd just finished his coffee, but he readily accepted, not wanting to discourage her attentiveness.

She went down the hall and returned in a moment with a steaming black coffee. He took a sip, appreciatively thanked her, and they chatted idly. Curiously, she never asked about creamer.

Then all of a sudden, in mid-sentence, Lisa stopped talking and sat up motionless, her face taking on a blank expression. Ozera set his coffee cup down on her desk, puzzled and concerned. She was staring straight ahead ... at something, it seemed. He looked over; it was just a blank wall.

"He's back," she said, clearly and quietly, to no one in particular. A moment later, as unexpectedly as it started, she seemed to return to ... normal. Her body relaxed and life returned to her face. She looked at Ozera and smiled.

"I must go and get things ready," she said, unapologetically, standing up. She walked around the desk and disappeared into a back room.

He pulled up a chair. Another sip of coffee and he heard it – the faint but unmistakable sound of a distant helicopter. The sound grew louder; it was approaching. He listened carefully as his mind processed it. It was familiar: Likely a single UH-1 – one of the ubiquitous, Vietnam-vintage, 'Huey' Army choppers – he figured.

Curious to see if he was right, Ozera went back out the front door and followed the gravel walkway around the building. He stopped and looked out over the field in the back. A concrete slab out behind the Control Center building was a helipad, with a red circle and 'H' painted on it. Ozera looked skyward. A mile or so out and approaching fast he saw it. As it neared he saw he was right – a Huey, with typical U.S. Army markings.

It came in fast, flying directly in on a fairly steep descent angle. It pulled up at the last minute and gently touched down onto the helipad. This pilot had made this trip before, Ozera could tell. The engine throttled down and the large side door facing him slid open.

There was a single passenger, a burly man wearing a standard-issue Army overcoat and a Green Beret – the Colonel, not unexpectedly. He took off his radio headset and handed it to a crewman, then turned and hopped out onto the helipad, a briefcase in hand. Almost immediately the green door slid shut behind him and the engine revved up. The Colonel bent low and pulled off his beret, rather than lose it in the powerful updraft, and strode hunched over to the edge of the helipad. The chopper lifted off, hovered for a moment, spun around, and then zoomed off, back in the same direction it came from. Total elapsed time on the helipad: not even 30 seconds.

The Colonel stood up straight and Ozera saw the silver eagles on his overcoat shoulders glint in the noonday sun. So he was a **full** colonel, and Special Forces, as Ozera surmised.

Lisa walked out towards the helipad to greet him. They met and walked together back to the building, busily chatting all the way. The Colonel glanced over and saw Ozera standing there watching. A brief moment of eye contact. Ozera checked his watch: still a while before their designated meeting time. He went back to his car to wait.

Lisa returned to her desk and the Colonel went to his office and changed clothes. He pulled on his habit and prepared for the meeting with Ozera.

The Colonel recalled the last time he gave this presentation – two years earlier, at the Pentagon. A roomful of the U.S. intelligence elite – some were in uniform, mostly generals and an admiral; the others wore suits, expensive suits. He didn't know and had never met most of them. And he likely would never know who they were or see them again. When he was done, though, all of them walked out worrying about things they never worried about before.

The presentation this time was for an audience of one – Captain Bradley Ozera.

* _ * _ *

IV: Why am I here, sir?

Ozera patiently marked time in his Ford, giving his new boss time to get situated after his trip. Just before 1 pm he grabbed a notepad and pen and sauntered back in. Lisa looked up and saw him, smiled and waved him on back. He proceeded down the hall and knocked on the open door.

"Come in, Captain," the Colonel said, "and please close the door." He walked in. The atmosphere was much more casual than the day before.

The Colonel pushed a button on the phone on his desk: "I'm with Captain Ozera now. Please insure our privacy for a while." Ozera assumed it was Lisa, but then the Colonel added: "I'll bring him around tomorrow to meet the new team."

"Roger, sir," a male voice on the speakerphone said in response. So he called the security team. Why would he call them to insure their privacy?

The Colonel stood up and came around his desk, gesturing Ozera to the conference table. "It's a lot more comfortable," he said. So he knew how uncomfortable that damned wooden chair was.

They settled in and the Colonel started: "You didn't mention to Lisa that you spoke Romanian, did you?" the Colonel asked.

"No, sir. Just English, like you said." Fluency in Romanian was in his record, along with the formal Army language training he'd received in Russian, German, French and Spanish. But the Colonel asked just about his home-learned Romanian.

"Good. Let's keep that just between us for now. They'll find out about it eventually. We'll get more into that later." He leaned back, presenting a relaxed image. "So, any idea yet where you might end up staying? You know the area pretty well, I guess."

"Well, the area's changed a lot since I left on active duty," Ozera responded. "With your permission I'll crash tonight over in one of the dorm bunks." It was nice to start with a little small talk, and Ozera knew it was a good leadership technique to take an interest in the personal welfare of your subordinates. "I started looking around the area this morning," he continued. "Saw an interesting farm just down the road from the entrance here. Looks like it used to be a Bed-and-Breakfast."

"Actually, it still is," the Colonel said. "I was hoping you'd ask about that. But it's not open to the public anymore."

"I … don't understand," Ozera replied.

"I didn't want strangers and prying eyes there, right outside our front door, so I booked the whole place when we moved in," the Colonel said matter-of-factly. "We're just about a year into a three-year contract. So for a couple more years, it's all ours." Ozera raised an eyebrow. This Colonel had a passion for secrecy – and apparently the high-level approval and budget to pursue it as he saw fit.

"Actually, there are several very nice rooms and suites there," he went on. "I stayed there a while myself when we first got here. It's owned and run by a sweet lady, Mrs. Griffiths, who also serves a great breakfast by the way. She was quick to accept our offer; she gets a nice monthly rent check, whether we put people up there or not."

"So it's just sitting there empty now?" Ozera asked.

"Not quite. One of our senior staff is staying there," the Colonel said. "And I expect some of our team will stay there when we start hosting regular meetings here. It's right across the road and very convenient. Otherwise, it's 12 miles to the nearest motel." He was aware he was sounding like a salesman, so he continued. "Since it's all ours already, there's no paperwork. You'd be close to work, get great breakfasts – and nobody but me would know where you're staying. Somebody at Department of the Army knows you're here, but nobody knows anything else and I'd like to keep it that way. So why not stop in and look around, maybe consider staying there a while?"

He nodded, curious about the security implications. Only the Army bureaucracy would care where he was living and how much it cost. "Okay, sir," he assured him, "I'll check it out."

The Colonel scrawled a phone number on a pad and handed it to him. "Here's the lady's phone number. Call her first and tell her Smith is sending you over."

Ozera tucked the note in his pants pocket, then folded his hands on the table and leaned forward, looking the Colonel in the eyes.

"So why am I here, sir?" he asked.

"You have certain qualifications that make you perfect for this job," the Colonel began. "First, you speak Romanian like a native; your records say you've spoke it from birth. Your parents come from the old country and you've been exposed to the culture. Plus, you know enough Russian to be dangerous."

"The people here are Romanian, then?" Ozera asked. The Colonel nodded. It made sense. He had narrowed Lisa's accent down to one of a few possibilities: Ukrainian, Bulgarian … or Romanian. He didn't discuss it with her, and now he wouldn't need to pursue it.

"For the most part, yes, they're Romanian – although there's been some occasional Russian dialog, too. As it turns out most of them used to work for the Soviets, and that doesn't sit well with me. I've had to record their chatter and conversations and get them translated back at HQ. We desperately needed somebody here who knows the lingo. That's one of the main reasons you're here."

"And my other qualifications, sir?" Ozera queried.

"You majored in architecture," the Colonel said. "I checked your transcript and even went down to the Fine Arts Department at Lehigh. You concentrated in ancient and Middle Ages architecture. I read your undergraduate thesis on early church design. In fact, Professor McFadden credits you with gifted insight in that area." Ozera was a little taken aback, but also impressed, by the depth of the Colonel's checking into his personal background. He tried not to show his slight discomfort at the scrutiny. But it was part of the job and he was used to it.

"But how does that help us here, sir?" Ozera asked.

"Bear with me. It does very much help us. You'll see."

"Any other qualifications?" he asked.

"You're experienced in dark ops, secrecy," the Colonel said, "You're Special Forces, and a field-proven U.S. Army officer, whose loyalty and dedication to our country is beyond question. You're intelligent, innovative. Plus, you're familiar with Pennsylvania and this part of the world." He summarized: "In my estimation, you can help us identify who's an asset to the project, and who's not. You'll meet them all, individually, and check them out, quietly of course – and report back to me."

It took a moment to soak in. The Colonel was giving him a sterling character assessment, but also saddling him with a heavy responsibility – in a role he didn't have that much experience.

"That's a tall order to fill, sir. Do we have any additional staff support?" Ozera asked.

"I'll get you whatever you need," the Colonel told him reassuringly. "You were brought here ostensibly to head security. But like I said yesterday, you really don't have to worry about physical security. The boys upstairs take care of that. The objective of this project is highly classified, with potentially awesome consequences to the U.S. I have the resources of the U.S. Army – and several other agencies – at my disposal. Here, **you** are **my** additional help, **my** staff support. For now it's just you and me. We need to fully share with each other, and back each other up."

Ozera leaned forward, as if sharing a secret, and asked, "So what **is** it we're doing here, sir?

"Okay," the Colonel said, leaning back, "Let's take it from it the top. And keep in mind that everything I'm going to tell you is highly classified."

* _ * _ *

IV: Psi

"We were already winding down in Vietnam when I graduated from the Point," the Colonel began. "But they still needed ground pounders over there. So when I finished Infantry school at Benning, off I went. I did my first six months with the 101, humping up and down the central highlands. Then I got assigned to MACV, Fifth SF Group, in G3, operations. We had a hundred different missions going on, all over Southeast Asia. And I planned quite a few of them."

He paused for a moment, reflecting. "Of course, at the time, we had no idea how it would turn out … that none of it was going to make any difference in the outcome of the war … and we were just wasting a lot of good soldiers." He looked up and continued: "I was one of the lucky Army lieutenants – who came home alive and in one piece."

Ozera was unaware that he was nodding, sympathetically. He could see the Colonel carried many painful memories. Age-wise, they were decades apart, but both were soldiers, and bound by the same experiences. It was a bond others couldn't share or even understand. Looking at the graying man across the table, alone with his memories, Ozera wondered if he was looking at himself in twenty or so years.

"Anyhow," the Colonel cleared his throat and resumed: "They promoted me to captain and I worked out of Bragg for a few years, spending months at a time in shit holes around the world." He looked at Ozera: "You know the routine." Ozera nodded.

"In '78 – I had just been promoted to major – I met a general named Ed Thompson, at a classified briefing at Bragg. He was a top dog with INSCOM, the Intelligence and Security Command, which at the time was out of Fort Meade. They're at Belvoir in Virginia now."

Ozera nodded. He had run into INSCOM before. Their agents were easy to spot: They wore cheesy civilian clothes – mismatched shirts, pants and jackets – but typically telltale Army clip-on black ties and shiny, government-issue, low-quarter black shoes.

They would appear from nowhere and walk right up to you when you were least expecting it. You might be walking down the street, in the motor pool, or getting out of your car at the 7-Eleven. You never knew their rank; they'd flash their ID and then slip it right back in their pocket. They came to Ozera seeking notes, recollections or records he may have had, from operations he was involved in. Nothing was ever in writing. Ozera could never discern what or who they were really after, and never asked. He just complied. And INSCOM knew, after their first couple encounters, that Ozera could be counted on to cooperate. No muss, no fuss. Just the facts. And then they'd go away.

"General Thompson was directed by the Joint Chiefs to develop a program for the Pentagon, similar to one the CIA started some years earlier. They were studying the paranormal capabilities of the human mind – ESP, mind reading, all that creepy stuff."

The Colonel studied Ozera, looking for any discernible response. But Ozera remained emotionless. It's not that Ozera wasn't very interested in where this was going; he was intensely engrossed. He just thought it prudent not to show it.

"Some of the CIA work leaked out. You probably heard or read bits of it – Stargate, remote viewing, that stuff." Ozera slowly nodded. He had heard about it. His initial assessment had been that the Agency had more time and money than it knew what to do with.

"Well," the Colonel went on, "The general asked me to join INSCOM and sign on with him. I did. My first job: to follow up on and check out the legitimate achievements, if any, from the CIA work. We wanted to know what they turned up that deserved further research and investment by DoD, y'know, anything with military applications. They gave me a security clearance at a level I didn't even know existed, and they sent me out to learn and report back the "truth" – the Colonel gestured quotes with his fingers – "in other words, find out and report what was real and what was bullshit."

"The Agency was embarrassed when the 'remote viewing' thing leaked out. So they officially put word out that there wasn't much to it, and that they were getting out of the business. It wasn't true, of course. They still pretty much run our research on remote viewing, at Stanford and Fort Meade."

"But remote viewing was just the tip of the iceberg, it turned out. I later found out that they had their research fingers in even spookier stuff – psychokinesis, even clairvoyance and premonition."

Ozera's eyes widened. He couldn't help it. The Colonel noticed.

"I've got to tell you, Captain, this stuff – what insiders call 'psi' – the collective term for all parapsychological phenomena – is real. I've seen it." He let that sink in and closely observed his protégé's reaction. Intense interest. Ozera was totally engrossed, receptive. That was good … it indicated an open mind. That was important, and hard to find in the mindset of many in the military. It was what he was hoping for.

The Colonel leaned forward, looking Ozera in the eye. "This stuff is potentially more powerful than the H-bomb," he said, adding, with deadly seriousness, "And we can't let the U.S. fall behind in this."

* _ * _ *

IV: Eight-martini results

"We still can't consistently repeat successes under strict scientific conditions," the Colonel continued, "and so we can't prove it to everyone's satisfaction. In my job I was able to see what nobody else did, because I had the clearance and high-level Pentagon influence to go wherever I wanted, through the dozen-plus research centers, walk in any room, ask anybody any question, and expect straight and honest answers."

"So you've been tracking this stuff then for, what, more than a decade?" Ozera asked.

"With INSCOM, yes," he replied, "But the organization, and my role, evolved quite a bit over the last decade. When the CIA put out that they were closing down their psi research, they claimed their remote viewing results were just 15 percent above chance guessing, making it sound like it wasn't consistently successful enough to continue to study. That's what they said publicly, anyhow."

"But the CIA **did** continue to pursue it, and many other psi capabilities. They just moved it into deep secrecy and kept it all dark. I found out that their remote viewing success – with the right subjects, training, and provided with map coordinates of the target – was typically **40** percent accurate."

"I've seen eight-martini results more than a couple times," he continued. "That's what the CIA boys called them – when your grasp of reality is shaken to the point it takes eight martinis to calm down, get a grip and accept what happened."

The colonel sat back, reminiscing: "We had one woman who could sit in Maryland and identify – consistently, and with **90-plus** percent accuracy – which of our silos had operational Minuteman and Titan missiles in them, and which were empty. Now, you don't have to be a genius to realize if we could do it, so could the Soviets."

"Once in Langley I was in a room, looking directly at a perfectly fine printed-circuit board they pulled out of a nuclear missile. A team in Stanford, California was concentrating on rendering it inoperative. The result? Subtle, but unquestionably effective. We didn't see a thing and couldn't tell that anything happened. But when it was plugged back in it no longer worked. It took two days for them to find it – a single, microscopic break in the soldered contact of a key component."

"No … shit …," Ozera uttered, not quite aware of what he'd just said.

The Colonel added: "And although intermittently, we **could** achieve the same result again. When they were successful, the points of failure were different, but it was always just as subtle, and just as effective."

"Are you saying that it's possible to **think** our nukes into … not working?" Ozera asked, cutting to the chase. The Colonel looked over at him and soberly nodded.

"And if **we** can do it to our nukes …" the Colonel posed.

"… then the bad guys can do it, too," Ozera discreetly completed the thought.

"I was a physics major at the Point," the Colonel continued, "Most of my contemporaries got engineering degrees. But that's not where I wanted to go. Engineers accept whatever they are told, as long as their formulas work out. I did not, and ended up doing some graduate study in theoretical physics after I got back from Vietnam."

"Anyhow, it wasn't long in my job with INSCOM before I had an epiphany: None of this – telekinesis, remote viewing, ESP, premonition – can possibly work, according to conventional science. But yet it **does** work. I've seen it. It needed to be explained, and so far we haven't been able to come up with even a theoretical basis for how psi works."

"We haven't come up with anything yet?" Ozera asked.

"Oh, we learned some. But it's really just bits and pieces. It's more tendencies and inclinations than any real understanding or hard, absolute facts. Like, whatever it is comes out of the right side of the human brain. And enclosing something in a vacuum seems to shield it from psychic manipulation or influence. We're like blind men, trying to understand what an elephant is by feeling the different parts."

"It's kind of like gravity was a hundred years ago," he went on. "For thousands of years man has known the **effects** of gravity. And thanks to Newton we even figured out how to calculate it, down to a dozen decimal places. That satisfied the engineers. But nobody, not even Newton, ever knew what gravity really was. Then, seventy-something years ago, this guy Einstein comes along with a breakthrough theory, that gravity is the effect of the curvature of a dimensional structure called space-time. And that has since been proven in spades."

"And we're still waiting for an Einstein to come along and explain psi to us," Ozera said wryly.

"We're not waiting," the Colonel snapped back. "The CIA discovered in the 60's that the Soviets had undertaken an aggressive program to study parapsychological effects. For a few years it was run by academics, but then it came under KGB control. We got wise to them in the mid 70's. That's when the CIA began its own psi research. But by then the Soviets were some 10 to 20 years ahead of us, we estimated."

"One of INSCOM's first real accomplishments was setting up the Russian Institute in Europe," he continued. "It was staffed with linguists, cryptologists, analysts, trainers and all manner of spooks, who amassed volumes of intelligence on our Soviet comrades. I had a hand in it, especially after INSCOM got the Joint Chiefs' mission to start researching psi."

"We learned what the CIA knew, and we shared with them. They ended up focusing more on intelligence gathering – y'know, remote viewing and that stuff. We focused on military aspects and applications. And we weren't the only ones. Pursuing different psi capabilities in different directions were the Air Force's Foreign Technology Division, the DIA's Psychic Center … and other agencies I doubt you've ever heard of."

The Colonel paused, letting it sink in, and watching Ozera's reaction. So far, so good. The captain was a good pick. Smart and receptive, plus all his other qualifications. So now down to brass tacks.

* _ * _ *

IV: Something found ... them

"In '85 the CIA tried something new," the Colonel began, "They set up a team of remote viewers – twelve of them, about half of their entire trained viewer staff – with a single mission: to search for remote viewers on the other side, throughout Eastern Europe and the Soviet Union. They knew of eight Soviet psi research sites, and our people scanned everything and everybody that they could find, from Czechoslovakia to Department 8 in Novosibirsk."

"Within the first week the team made contact with, detected and catalogued **hundreds** of Soviet remote viewers and assorted psychic agents, at nearly two dozen research locations. We only knew of eight of them up to that point. Captain, they had a **battalion** of trained remote viewers and psychics –ten times the number of our trained personnel."

The Colonel paused, looked over at Ozera, and added: "While our team was reaching out to find the Soviet psychics, something in return found *them*." Ozera again raised an eyebrow.

"A week after the project began, the first member of our team died. Heart attack. A guy in his late forties. Smoker. Overweight. Yeah, he was kind of young, but it happens, we all figured," the Colonel said matter-of-factly. "But then, a couple weeks later, another one dropped dead. Heart attack, too. No warning. But he was only 29, and in excellent health." Ozera raised both eyebrows.

"A few months later the cancer deaths began," the Colonel said, "Over the next year five more – all members of that remote viewing team – died of cancer. Two of lung cancer, and one each pancreas, liver, and blood leukemia. And one died of a stroke. Eight in all – two-thirds of the team."

"How about the rest of them?" Ozera asked, "What happened to them?"

"Nothing," he replied. "Not even a cold. It's been six years since then. Two of them have since left the program, but they're still just fine. The other two are still at it. In fact, for the last few months they've been in the gulf, busily trying to locate Saddam's SCUD missile sites."

The Colonel continued: "We did turn up one notable difference between the team members who survived and the ones who died. The four survivors were all 'naturals' – psychics, clairvoyants, mind-readers, who'd demonstrated solid parapsychological talent **before** they signed on with us. That's how we found them. The ones who died had no particular innate psychic abilities, it seems; they were volunteers, all military, who we recruited and trained for remote viewing." He paused, then softly added: "I dunno. We speculate that maybe there's some kind of built-in self-defense mechanism that comes with natural psychic ability."

"Anyhow, in 1987, when word of the attacks – and clearly they were Soviet-launched, psi-based attacks – reached Washington, all hell broke loose. Everyone in charge of our psi research, from all the agencies, was called in and grilled: Who attacked? How did they do it? Is **anyone** susceptible to such an attack? Can we do it? Can we retaliate?"

"We mostly shrugged our collective shoulders," the Colonel said. "We had no answers, only theories and suspicions. Like, we were reasonably sure that it was the same group of trained psychic assassins – a special team – that executed all the attacks. And it seemed they could assault only one target person at a time. So there had to be some cumulative, **concentrated** effort. And that was a significant new realization: that the psychic energy of multiple individuals can be consolidated, under conditions we still don't know. Beyond that, though, we didn't know shit. We couldn't retaliate because we didn't know how. But that was the last time any U.S. psi team ever tried to psychically probe the enemy like that again."

Ozera was astonished at the lethality of the attack, but relieved to hear it had not escalated into a psychic war.

"There was a silver lining to all this, though," the Colonel went on, "Black-budget funding for psi research, especially military applications, including ours, was upped tenfold. INSCOM spawned several new branches – including one to monitor and assess the psi research of the U.S.S.R. and China. It turns out China has an aggressive program, too, but they're not nearly as far along as the Russians were."

"And one of those new INSCOM branches is who I … and now you, too … work for," the Colonel said, as if drawing this part of the story to a close. He put down his pen, stood up, stretched and looked at his watch.

"How about we take a break and grab a coffee?" he said to Ozera. "We have to get our own, though. Lisa made a fresh pot before she left; she's been out since we began."

Ozera checked his watch. It was after four. His mind was swimming from the details revealed in the last few remarkable hours. But he still had to find out what their job was, and what role they played in this bizarre new world.

"Sure, a coffee would be great, sir," he said, "Can we resume then? I'll grab a room here in the dorm tonight, and go see Mrs. what's-her-name down the road in the morning."

"Still haven't had enough?" the Colonel chided him. "Good man. Sure, let's pick it up again in a few."

* _ * _ *

IV: In the middle of nowhere

Two seasoned U.S. Army officers, donned in heavy monk's robes, at a conference table in a secret research site perched atop a mountain in eastern Pennsylvania, assessing parapsychological phenomena that no one could yet explain.

'Is it just me?' Ozera thought to himself, walking back with his coffee, 'or is this all just a little surreal?'

They sat and reconvened. The Colonel took a deep breath, let it out slowly and began anew.

"A few years ago, as part of Gorbachev's glasnost, Soviet scientists – for the first time in decades – were selectively allowed to publish papers on their research and findings. A flurry of articles on previously restricted subjects appeared in Russian journals of psychology, physics and medicine. Our people scarfed them up and began poring through them."

"It turned out that the new openness would be short-lived," he continued. "There was no review bureaucracy in place at the time, and some of Ivan's secrets unintentionally snuck out. So after a couple issues were published, the KGB pulled the plug. And despite Gorbachev's best intentions, a veil of secrecy was again pulled over Soviet science."

"For a few months anyhow, we had a hell of a window into new Soviet scientific research – including psi," the Colonel said, "We saw indications that they were pursuing all kinds of things, shit we never thought of – like psychic testing and training of their cosmonauts, looking at time distortion, gravitational sensitivity, even psychic communication as a back-up to radio electronics."

"Now before I go on, know this: Some of the stuff they published was phony, hokey, planted by the KGB to misinform and misdirect us. We know that; we ran down a couple of them and found they were total shams, dead ends to misdirect us, waste our time and money. Hell, we do the same thing to them." He paused, then added: "But some of what leaked out was legitimate, tipping us off to classified psi research we hadn't heard of. We had to read between the lines and do some investigation and analysis, but we developed some great leads."

The Colonel continued: "There was a 1986 article that made a casual reference to psychokinetic research at a site in northern Romania. It said the facility was near 'Arcobadera,' in the mountains north of Vatra Dornei. It wasn't a city or a town. It turned out to be the ancient name for a very remote area, up in the Carpathian Mountains near the Ukraine border."

"I sent a team to check it out. A month later I got a report back. Damned peculiar. There was indeed a research site there, several wooden buildings high up in the hills. But it was truly in the middle of nowhere. Hell, you had to be a mountain goat to get there. There was no direct access. We figure they built the place from local trees they downed. Other building materials and supplies were probably brought in by chopper."

"It turns out research had been going on there for several years, likely from the mid '80's. Most of the staff and workers were Romanian, but Russians were clearly in charge. The facility was under the command of a GRU colonel – Soviet **Army** Intelligence, not KGB – who reported directly to the Presidium in the Kremlin."

"The technical head was a Dr. Olga Vinogradova," he continued, "a Ruskie, and a noted neuroscientist, who specialized in electrical stimulation of the brain. Like I said, damned peculiar – extremely high-level oversight, but circumventing normal research, budget and review channels. It was clearly very important to the Russians – and so it became important to us."

"Now, you don't put a research site in so remote a place, especially in an unfriendly satellite state like Romania, unless that particular location had significance, right?" the Colonel asked. Ozera thought and then nodded. "It was so out of the way, in fact, that they had virtually no local security. In 1987 one of our people hiked right up to the place."

"So why was it put there, sir?" Ozera asked.

"That's what we wanted to know. We thought at first it was the remoteness – that the Kremlin was up to something so secret they didn't want their own Russian bureaucracy or people to know about. But except for a very thick, old-growth, evergreen tree canopy, which effectively blocked our satellite surveillance, the facts didn't support this. If we found out about it, others knew about it, too. There was no local security, like I said, and it was staffed with native Romanians. Now, of all the communist satellites, nobody hated the Russians more than the fiercely independent Romanians." He added: "No, the Russians didn't put this place there to get **away** from something."

"So something was there they wanted to be close to?" Ozera asked, a tone of impatience in his voice.

"We think so, but there were a couple possibilities. First, the facility was built near a site that is regarded as holy and sacred by the locals. It's somewhere higher up in the hills, on a flat mountain plateau. Oddly, the locals don't want to even talk to strangers about it, and they wouldn't even show or tell us exactly where it's at. Among themselves they call it *Munte Manastirea*."

"Monastery Mountain," Ozera muttered softly.

"That's right," the Colonel said, "I forgot; you know the lingo. Anyhow, our satellites scoured the area for miles around. Besides the research site and a village a mile away there's nothing else up in the mountains for miles around but woods, rocks, cliffs and dirt. There are a couple flat plateaus up in the hills nearby, but all of them are barren. There are no other structures."

"So why would the Russians be researching some holy ground up in the mountains?" Ozera asked, incredulously. "What about that psychokinesis? What's that all about?"

The Colonel held up his hand, a signal to Ozera to please be patient.

"Here's what we found out. This area, a remote part of southeastern Europe, was home to an ancient people called the Dacians, who have long since vanished, or maybe I should say dissipated. But it looks like there are two things the Dacians left behind," the Colonel said, adding: "And that's what this is all about."

Ozera had been weighing heavily everything the Colonel told him so far. But this only heightened his anticipation even more.

* _ * _ *

IV: What the Dacians left behind

It had been dark for hours, and the fluorescent lights in the Colonel's office shed an unnatural white light over the two men huddled at the conference table. The Colonel's day had started long before sunrise that morning and he was getting tired. But he knew the captain couldn't leave, and probably wouldn't leave, without answers to a few key questions.

"It's clear to us now that one of the two main reasons the Russians set up the research facility – there in the sticks of northern Romania – was due to the local residents in that area," the Colonel said. Ozera responded with the puzzled look he expected.

"We found out that, in the mid-70s, the Soviets launched an extensive program to find people with psychic capabilities and potential. Dozens of teams were put together and dispatched to the corners of the Soviet sphere of influence, to test high-school and university students, as well as all their active and reserve military members, for signs of psychic potential. It's kind of hard to hide an undertaking like that."

"So what does that have to do with the research facility they built there in Romania?" Ozera asked, trying to prompt him to the bottom line.

"We didn't know the answer to that until a few years ago," he replied. "Let me explain. We found out that each Soviet screening team included an accomplished psychic. The team would conduct a preliminary two-minute interview, asking seemingly general questions: whether the subject ever experienced precognition, or could feel or sense another person's thoughts, or had a hunch that turned out to be true. That sort of thing."

"The psychic would then conduct his or her own probing. Then they'd hold up a card, and ask the subject whether they could guess the shape on the card, or the color of the object, or the number of objects. And they would record their own assessment. Based on all this they'd rate the subjects with a score of one to five."

He continued: "Those who scored four and five were put on a list for follow-up. Unconfirmed reports indicated that something like two-tenths of one percent – two people in a thousand, on average – scored four or five on the preliminary screening test. In some areas it was over 1 percent who made the list; in other regions no one scored four or five. The difference was chalked up to statistical and test-team variation. Two people per thousand, by the way, is fairly similar to the results of our own psi-screening tests."

"Those on the list would later end up in a protracted hour-long session, which was conducted by a different team. We still don't know much about how they did those advanced sessions, but we know the result was a score from 0 to 100."

"A few years ago, in 1987, the Soviet Union began to unravel – and secrets came on the market. We procured a copy of a report, from 1979, verified authentic, that showed the distribution of the results of the advanced Soviet psi screening. It was … incredible."

Ozera perked up.

"They ended up with 45,000 subjects who rated four or five in the preliminary screening. They were all tested and rated over several years. The average advanced rating: 16.3. We still don't know what the rating scale was, but our analysts believe that 12 or 15 points were awarded for **each** discrete psychic capability that the subject positively exhibited. We believe those included: clairvoyance, ESP, precognition, remote viewing, intuition, and psychokinesis – y'know, causing physical effects through mental and psychic energy alone." Ozera nodded.

"Those were pretty much the psychic capabilities we – or the Soviets – knew about at the time, based on mind readers, fortune tellers and spoon benders. So, if we are reading the numbers right, most of these pre-screened prospects exhibited no solid psychic proclivity whatsoever," the Colonel said, adding: "But many – nearly 9,000 – did."

"Of nearly 1,000 geographic subdivisions across the entire Soviet empire, there were 11 – count 'em, just 11 – locales where the subjects rated abnormally high. By high we mean the average of those undergoing advanced assessment in that region placed well above the global average of 16. In seven of these, subjects who underwent advanced testing rated between 20 and 30, notably above average. These seven areas are scattered, half of them are in central Asia – southern Russia, and in Soviet states that no one ever heard of – Kazakh, Uzbek and Turkmen." The Colonel paused, letting it sink in.

"And then there were **three** hot spots where, inexplicably, the subjects tested rated between 30 and 40. Now that's statistically very significant – more than double the overall average. This is a much tighter shot group. In fact, all three were within a circle with a 200-mile radius – one in Czechoslovakia, another in southern Poland and one in the Ukraine. None was in Russia, interestingly."

"Now here's where it gets interesting," the Colonel continued, "There was one, and only one, spot where the subjects scored **over 40**."

"Let me guess," Ozera uttered reflexively, "Northern Romania, in the Carpathians near the Ukraine border."

"Bingo," the Colonel tersely replied, "It was actually near the center of the other three hot spots. And right in the middle of this area is where the Russians set up their research site." The Colonel paused a moment. "The Russians apparently concluded – based on interviews and genealogical studies – that many of the subjects in this area, those who scored high in advanced testing, were likely direct descendants of those ancient Dacians."

The two sat quietly for a moment. "Yeah, go figure," the Colonel said. Then he added, pleadingly: "And Captain, I'm going to need some more coffee if we're going to go on tonight."

"I'll join you," Ozera said, checking his watch. 8 pm. He was mentally exhausted, and hungry. But he expected that the remarkable briefing would soon be coming to an end.

The Colonel slowly stood up, with a groan. He looked visibly drained and tired. With cups in hand, the two walked down the hall.

* _ * _ *

IV: Monastery Mountain

"Okay," the Colonel started again, as they both settled down with steaming cups of microwaved coffee. "I know I've dropped a lot on you already today. But there's one more piece of the puzzle – the piece de resistance." He chuckled at the unintentional pun. Ozera leaned forward, as he had most of the day, in eager anticipation of what was to come next.

Ozera's notepad laid open on the table before him, a pen by its side. It was customary to take notes during a briefing by one's military superior. But the notepad remained blank – despite the incredible revelations told to him. Ozera just didn't know how any of this applied to his job. And for that matter, he still didn't know what his job was, or what the Colonel and this research facility were up to.

"What I'm about to tell you comes from several sources: our own research; from Russian research records we 'acquired' from that site in northern Romania; from intelligence we collected from Moscow; from various other Soviet officials we bought and paid for; plus our own lucky finds. It's our best assessment of what happened, but we still have a lot of unanswered questions. Please understand that." Ozera nodded.

"We believe this ancient people, the Dacians, have occupied this region of southeastern Europe continuously since Stone Age times. Some even speculate that it may have been these people, or their ancestors, who originally settled Europe from the Middle East, 30,000 to 40,000 years ago. It is right along the path that anthropologists know modern humans entered Europe. We have an anthropologist and historian on the team and you'll be meeting her. She could tell you more about the Dacians than you'd ever want to know."

"Anyhow," he continued, "a mystery is how these people managed to stay and survive in this area for so long. That's because the region has been a corridor for migrating hordes and various barbarians and invaders throughout history. We are talking some tough hombres – Macedonians, Huns, Slavs, Goths, Magyars, Bulgars, even the Romans. But somehow the Dacians did survive there, as a people and a culture, through all this – although it's believed they did eventually die out, sometime in the Dark Ages."

"As it turns out, probably not by coincidence, near where the Russians put their research site was a key spiritual center of these people. It was like a Mecca to them, and that probably accounts for the high percentage of Dacian descendants still living in the area today. We believe this sacred ground is somewhere on an outcropping of a nearby mountain."

"Munte Manastirea," Ozera uttered.

"You got it, m'boy," the Colonel said, pointing at him, like a game show contestant who just got the right answer. "I knew I picked you for this job for a reason." The two exchanged tired smiles.

"But I thought you said we couldn't find anything up in the surrounding mountains," Ozera said with a puzzled look.

"Correct," the Colonel replied. "Whenever we looked, from the ground or by satellite, during the last few years, we found nothing." He paused and then repeated: "But I emphasize, during the last few years."

Ozera looked at him askance, puzzled.

"I'm going to tell you a story," the Colonel said. "It is part legend and partly documented fact. I'm not going to tell you which is which, because frankly we aren't sure."

Ozera considered what he said and returned a puzzled look. "Alright," he hesitantly replied.

The Colonel set the stage: "In a remote part of Eastern Europe, in the Carpathian Mountains of northern Romania, high on a mountaintop ledge, is …," he groped for the right word, "… a Monastery. It is situated on one of the small, naturally hidden plateaus that are hidden away throughout those mountains. It is hard to find, and hard to get to. It is said to have been an imposing structure – reflecting a mix of styles from evolving architectural periods over many centuries."

"It wasn't always a monastery," he continued. "The original structure is believed to pre-date churches, or temples, in the Greek or Roman or Judeo-Christian sense. In fact, no one knows what was first built there, or when or by whom. But to the local people the place is sacred and carries deep spiritual significance. They protect it, and hide it from outsiders."

"Back to the story. It is the darkest of the Dark Ages, around the year 900, and the place is serving as a remote Monastery, loosely following Roman Catholic dogma and practices. There is a contingent of monks, ranging from head abbot to acolytes in training. Interestingly, and ignoring Catholic doctrine, men and women are regarded as equals and serve shoulder to shoulder in all respects."

Ozera sat quietly, hands folded on the conference table, listening politely to what was sounding like a fairytale.

"One day, what the Dacians most feared happened. Invaders – probably Magyars migrating south from the Russian steppes – somehow happened upon the Monastery, and laid siege to it. The structure was not a fortress, but there was a small garrison of defenders – swordsmen, archers. As the story goes, they fought the invaders valiantly, but they were doomed. And they knew it."

The Colonel continued: "Then something very strange happened. This imposing structure, hundreds of tons of stone, the entire Monastery, and everything and everybody inside it, down to the bedrock it was built on … just vanished." He thrust his fingers in the air.

Ozera responded with a clearly incredulous look. "Vanished?" he asked. "More than a thousand years ago? How do we even know that it ever existed?"

"A very good question, Captain," he replied. "Over the millennia, in general, when conquerors laid waste to the stonework of an indigenous people, there would invariably be ruins left. Over time usable building stones would find their way into new structures nearby. Roman aqueducts provided hewn stones for many later churches and cathedrals, and so on. But nowhere in this entire area is there any evidence of ruins, or stones hauled away and reused."

Ozera nodded, then reiterated: "Yes, but again, sir, how do we even know that such a place ever really existed?"

"The story circa 900 A.D. comes from multiple sources," the Colonel continued. "One account is from local legend, which many in the area know and orally pass on to their children. Another is a vague reference from early Magyar history, in a document found in Bratislava, written in the 11th century. Then there is a report to Pope Benedict IV, who ruled from 900 to 903 A.D., that one of our team dug out of the Vatican archives. It was in response to an inquiry initiated by his predecessor, Pope John IX, who died in the year 900 A.D. That document, in Latin, concluded that what happened there is pretty much as I just related to you."

"Alright," Ozera responded, a note of impatience and frustration in his voice. "So what happened to this Monastery? And what does it have to do with us?"

The Colonel got up and walked over to his desk. He opened a file drawer and took out a manila folder. He pulled out some photos as he walked back and put one on the table before Ozera. He uncapped a marker pen and circled an area the size of a coffee cup.

"Here's a satellite shot of the region that includes the area – here – where we think the Monastery may have been," the

Colonel said. Ozera looked over it. He was familiar with satellite photos; the intelligence they provided was often invaluable to his missions' success. The terrain of this one was much more mountainous than the jungle and desert satellite pictures he had seen before.

The Colonel pointed to a spot nearby but outside the circled area on the photo. "Here's where their research site was, not quite a mile away. You can just make out a couple of buildings." Ozera studied it and nodded.

"Okay ...," Ozera was playing along, not knowing where it was leading

"Here, Captain," he placed another photo in front of him. "Here's a shot of the place from the ground." It was a large, crystal clear, well-focused photo of a large, flat plateau. There was no real point of reference but Ozera estimated it was maybe a few hundred yards square. It looked stark, absent vegetation and perfectly flat, with boulders along the sides and an interesting mountain skyline as a backdrop.

"A nice picture, sir," he replied. "So how do we know anything was ever there?" Ozera repeated.

"Another excellent question, Captain," the Colonel replied. With that he got up and went to a door behind his desk and opened it, revealing a walk-in closet. He entered, flipped on a light, and re-emerged in a moment with an armful of items: an old wooden board about the size of a clipboard, a parchment roll and some papers.

"Take a look at this," he said, and placed the board down in front of him. On a very old piece of wood was a painting – a rather crude oil painting, of an unusual structure. It looked somewhat like a church, featuring a prominent stone cross on top of what seemed to be the entrance, with two massive wooden front doors. It was hardly a typical church though, Ozera noted, since the building lacked the usual cross-shaped footprint of a church or basilica.

A hodge-podge of architectural styles comprised the structure. Around the base were huge, hand-hewn, upright stones. He guessed these monoliths were some eight to ten feet wide and 11 or 12 feet high, using as a reference the wooden entranceway doors.

Situated between, and in stark contrast to, the rough monoliths were smooth, Greek-style columns of an early order. Tightly cut and fitted stone walls filled the spaces between the columns and huge monoliths. Above the Greek columns was a colonnade of Roman arches, which encircled the structure and comprised an elegant second level to the outer wall. Yet another level rose inside the outer wall – supported by unseen inside columns, Ozera surmised. Thin cut stones, perhaps slate, covered the intersecting roof planes, in the style of early Christian churches.

"Wow," Ozera uttered to himself. The painting, while clearly very old, captured the architectural elements in exquisite clarity and detail. He dared not touch the painted surface.

"Quite a sight to behold, eh?" the Colonel said, tauntingly.

"So **this** is the Monastery?" Ozera asked. "I could make a career out of studying this. The structural designs and elements cover thousands of years of architectural evolution. Where'd you get it, sir?"

"We found it among the Russian materials at the Romanian research site. It is authentic, genuine pre-Renaissance."

"How do we know this is the missing Monastery?"

The Colonel didn't answer. Rather, he carefully unrolled the parchment and held it down in front of Ozera. It was a beautifully detailed pen and ink sketch. Ozera eyed it carefully. It was a drawing of the same structure as in the wood painting – that was certain because of the unique, eclectic architectural mix. But this drawing was made from a different angle.

"This was found in a vault in the Byzantine cathedral in Vatra Dornei, about 50 miles south of the Romanian research site. The Russians did **not** know about this." He gave Ozera a minute to look it over.

"Now look at the mountain skyline behind the structure." Ozera did, and it looked familiar. "Okay, now compare that with the ground photo I showed you." Ozera pulled out the photo and placed it below the parchment, then carefully compared the two, looking back and forth. The new photo, and the pen and ink drawing on the ancient parchment, were of the exact same location. No question about it.

"Okay, they are the same place," he said, still looking back and forth between the two. "The structure was there when the pen and ink drawing was made," he said, pointing to the parchment. "But it was not there when the photo was taken." Ozera added: "That's not too hard to believe, given that over a millennium transpired from one to the other."

"Well, that's the interesting part," the Colonel teased, "The painting on the board has been dated to the late 12th or early 13th century. And the parchment and drawing have been irrefutably dated to the mid 1500's."

There was silence as Ozera considered it all. After a few moments he looked up at the Colonel.

"But how could … this be … when the Monastery disappeared centuries before?"

"Exactly," the Colonel replied. It had taken the generals and intelligence chiefs at the Pentagon a while longer before they asked the same question.

* - * - *

IV: The mission

For another hour the Colonel laid it out for Ozera, with all the deftness of a good trial lawyer – recorded accounts of other sightings of the monastery over the centuries, giving similar descriptions. And there were references to searches for the monastery, across the same centuries, which turned up nothing but a bare, flat, mountain plateau.

Then they discussed the extent of the Russian research that they've been able to determine. The Colonel related how the head Russian scientist, attending a conference in Venice in 1987, was secretly drugged, snuck away for the night and interrogated – and then reportedly returned to her hotel room with no memory of the session. They learned from her that the Russians were exploring the possibility of a new and unknown form of psychokinesis. They, too, believed the locals' story of a Monastery that seemed to disappear and reappear.

The Russian hypothesis, according to the Colonel, was that somehow, those inside the Monastery, all those many centuries ago, caused themselves and the entire massive structure surrounding them to move from their current reality … but not really disappear, at least not permanently, it seems. Their research, it seemed, was focused on experimenting with – and on – the locals who scored high in their screening tests, especially for any psi ability to affect objects, space … or see across time.

Ozera stood at a window of the office, looking out at the other buildings, the open field, the woods and hillside – all bathed in the light of a rising full moon. The Colonel sat at the conference table. Their conversation went on, the two talking indirectly to each other.

"The high psi ratings of the locals, those likely descended from the Dacians, has to be connected with what happened with the Monastery," Ozera said, still staring out the window.

"That's what we all concluded three years ago," the Colonel responded. "We put two and two together, just as the Russians did. But fortunately, we have more to go on, and more time than they did."

"How's that, sir?" Ozera asked, turning around.

"Sixteen months ago the Berlin Wall came down," he said. "November 2nd, 1989. I was there. Even got my mug on CNN," he chuckled. "But in Romania that just fanned the flames of a bloody revolt against the Russian occupiers – and the communist puppet who the Soviets installed to run the country for them, a slimy despot named Nicolae Ceausescu."

"It was not a good time to be Russian in Romania," the Colonel continued. "For half a century these people had borne the brunt of Soviet repression, corruption, economic stagnation, ecological rape. It wasn't life under the Soviet communists; it was morbid existence." The Colonel paused. "And now it was payback time."

"Within two weeks after the wall came down, the Russians at this research project in northern Romania closed shop and hightailed it back across the Ukrainian border to Moscow. We know they left in a hurry, judging by how much stuff they left behind. Most of the paper records were taken or destroyed, it seems, but almost everything else was just left – including the Romanian staff, workers … and all their test subjects. They probably had to load all the Russians, and whatever they could carry, on a Kasatka chopper and vamoose pronto. Not a lot of room for souvenirs or personal belongings."

"Anyhow, a month later, on Christmas day, a people's tribunal in southern Romania was executing Ceausescu and his wife. On the same day, at the same time, amid the chaos and the holiday, my men were driving two trucks across the Romanian border into Hungary. One was full of Romanians – those who were involved in or working at the Russian research site, who volunteered to go with us. In the other was as much material as they could collect and carry away, by hand, a mile down to the nearest road."

"So that's where these people …," Ozera speculated.

"We made the Romanians an offer: They could stay there in Romania – amid the political chaos, a stagnant economy circling the drain, and likely Russian reprisals. Or they could come to the U.S. and work with us. They would live comfortably, in peace. They would stay with each other, and then, after a couple of years, they could return to Romania, or they'd get permanent green cards to stay in America."

"All of them signed on," the Colonel continued, "from senior research scientist to janitor. Thirteen of 'em. We flew them to a base in Germany, and then on to the states. We put them up initially at Fort Indiantown Gap, an idle Army base over near Harrisburg. I'm sure you know it; it's the same place we housed Vietnamese refugees and boat people in the late '70s after Saigon fell. It is secure and largely empty now. It was the middle of winter, and up there in the Appalachian Mountains it looked to the Romanians just like back in the Carpathians. Real homey," he smiled.

"It was simply not viable for us to resume the research at that site in northern Romania. The political environment in Romania was too chaotic and unsettled. And the Russians were right across the border, although we now expect that the Ukraine will soon withdraw from the Soviet Union altogether and become an independent state. And so will a lot of the other Soviet states. So it was decided to continue the research – but here in the U.S." He looked at Ozera and smiled: "And I got the job."

"We looked at alternatives and settled on this tract, here on this mountaintop in northeast Pennsylvania. As it turns out, the Appalachians around here are very similar to the Carpathians, where the Monastery and research site are. This locale is similar to the Romanian site in altitude, in climate, flora and fauna, even the same types of surrounding stone."

"Construction started here a year ago. We had these buildings up in a few months, and shortly after our Romanian guests moved in from Indiantown Gap. And here we are, Captain," the Colonel concluded.

"Have the Soviets dropped their research, or just moved it back to Mother Russia?" Ozera asked.

"We don't know for sure, but it seems there's little money or budget now for such projects. The Soviet Union, Russia and all its satellites, are now bankrupt. Reagan bankrupted them, with our defense spending, Star Wars and all that. And with our deployment in the Gulf, Bush is carrying the ball further downfield. No, I don't think the Ruskies have the interest, will or resources to continue the research … not at this time anyhow. Plus, we have a lot of their research materials. We know what they were looking for. And among our Romanian refugees we have many of their study subjects. We also have a **lot** more resources to pour into it."

"But we don't have the Monastery, or access to the site where it was … or is," Ozera countered.

"We've been working on that, too, Captain," the Colonel said with a cunning smile. "So what's our job, you asked? Here it is. We need to come up with answers to these key questions." He counted on his fingers: "First, how can a Monastery that disappeared a thousand years ago reappear … from time to time … on that mountain plateau in northern Romania? Second, is there a connection to the abnormally high psi capabilities of local Romanians in the area? Third, is this the result of an as-yet unknown psychic power? And finally, if so, can we recreate, and ideally control it?"

Ozera sat subconsciously nodding as the Colonel counted off his points. Then he looked up with a smile. "Thanks, sir. I needed that. I have no idea where to begin, but you know I'll do everything I can to get the job done, or die trying."

"I know you will, Captain. We both have that mission," he told him. Maybe he was tired – and he had every right to be – but his tone was as a senior manager conversing with a partner, not a subordinate. And he needed assistance.

"Now, I am confident that the Romanian delegation knows more than they've told us, and that's where you come in. We need to find out what they know … every bit of it. Also, we need to make sure our 'expert' team is contributing to the war effort, and that's another part of your job. We've got to crack this thing open. That's my responsibility, but now it's your job, too."

Ozera checked his watch. Midnight. They had been at it since 1 pm, well into the night, and hours without a break. The Colonel was clearly drained.

"Grab a bunk over in the dorm tonight, Captain. Tomorrow we'll look at where we go from here. I've got more to tell you, and I've got some ideas how to proceed."

"See you in the morning then, sir?" Ozera offered.

"Make it afternoon, 1300, okay?" the Colonel subtly directed.

"See you then, sir," Ozera said, picking up his blank notepad and walking out. "I'll go check out that Bed-and-Breakfast first thing then." He was exhausted, and wondered what kept the Colonel going. It seemed very important to the Colonel that he buy into the project. And by all outward appearances to the Colonel, he did.

"Give my best to Mrs. Griffiths," the Colonel said. As Ozera walked out he saw the Colonel pick up the phone. He wondered who he'd be calling at midnight.

* - * - *

IV: To sleep, perchance to dream

The dormitory building was two doors down from the Control Center. All four of the buildings looked identical from the outside – the same concrete block, steel-framed windows that Ozera had seen on many U.S. Army bases, mainly for housing unmarried, enlisted soldiers.

He walked first to his Ford in the parking lot, where he had an overnight bag already packed. It was a cool evening, but not very cold. He took a deep breath. The fresh, moist mountain air felt good in his nose and lungs, especially after the long session in the Colonel's stuffy office. The full moon was now high in the sky, illuminating the compound with an even, mellow glow.

He glanced back at the Control Center building. Most of the lights were still on up in the second floor. Only the Colonel's office was still lit on the first floor. And as he watched the Colonel's light went out. He chuckled, picturing him crashing on the beat-up sofa in his office.

The next building, the Conference Center, was all dark. He walked past it and the Dorm building came into view. A couple of the rooms on the second floor were still lit, revealing curtains on the windows. The first floor was mostly dark. As he approached the front steps and porch, his footsteps crunching on the gravel walkway, he saw a figure standing there. As he neared he could make out a female form. Someone was waiting for him, it seemed. He got closer and finally saw it was Lisa.

"Good evening, Captain," she said. She was wearing pajamas and a housecoat, and looked considerably more relaxed and informal than she did in her monk's habit. She stood with her arms folded, no doubt due to the cool evening air. "The boss asked me to get you settled for the night," she told him. He smiled and put aside any thoughts of a crude response. So it was probably Lisa who the Colonel was calling as he left.

"I'm sorry to keep you up so late," he apologized.

"No problem, really," she responded, "It's all part of the job."
She pointed to the outside stairwell. "The bedrooms are all
upstairs." He went up first. The second floor door was
unlocked; he opened it and walked in.

"First door on the left, Captain," she directed him.

"Do I need any keys?" he asked.

"No," she replied, "We are all very open here. You can lock
your door from the inside."

Ozera opened the door and flipped on the light. A double bed
all made, immaculate. Carpeted. Mirror and chest of
drawers, desk and chair. Curtains on the two windows. Not
too warm, but acceptable. A bit snug, but cozy and
comfortable-looking.

"This room has its own bathroom," she said. Apparently
some of the others shared a bathroom.

"That's great," he said, "I may just move in here for a while.
You stay here, too, I take it?"

She smiled, "Just down the hall." She turned and started
walking away. Then she stopped abruptly and turned: "Oh,
and our kitchen downstairs – coffee is on by five am and
Maria starts cooking at six. She's pretty good."

"Thanks for everything, Lisa. Good night."

"Good night, Captain," she responded, with a smile, then
turned and went back down the hall.

He dropped his bag on the bed, then stood for a moment and
collected his thoughts – everything he'd learned today. No
matter that he was mentally wiped out, he doubted he would
sleep much this night.

In the silence he heard the clock. A white, battery driven military issue clock, on the wall next to the bed. A sweep second hand clicked notably as it ticked off the seconds. Click, click, click – on and on, with perpetual, punctual, painstaking precision. Oh, well. Maybe he'd get used to it.

He doffed his heavy habit, then reached in the bag and pulled out a pint of Wild Turkey. He retrieved a glass from the modest bathroom and poured himself a respectable nightcap. Plopping exhaustedly on the edge of the bed, he looked at the clock and hoisted the glass, as if toasting it. "For medicinal purposes only," he uttered, and deposited the bourbon.

In short order he undressed and climbed under the blankets, and then lay silently. He couldn't discount any of what the Colonel told him, as much as he'd like to. It was just hard to accept that people could **think** other people to death, and from the other side of the world. The power of the mind. Able to bring down a nuclear missile? Was it the same thing that could cause a medieval Monastery to disappear, and then reappear? And if so, where did it go when it disappeared?

Vatra Dornei. The Colonel mentioned it twice. It was the city in Romania near the research site. Why did it sound familiar? He'd heard of it before, but where?

He was at the edge of sleep, and about to step off, when the clock ticking again stirred him. He looked over at it.

"That's enough of that," he yelled. Then, the clock stopped.

"Well, thank God for small miracles," he muttered. He was too tired to give it a second thought, and he fell into a deep, but troubled sleep.

* _ * _ *

Chapter V: The Players and the Team
V: Breakfast in the barracks

He thought he heard a knock at the door, abruptly ending a night of restless sleep. Where was he? Oh, yeah. Ozera didn't expect the dorm to be so quiet in the morning. But no big deal today; he recalled that his next meeting with the boss wasn't until afternoon. He lay quietly for a moment. Flashing through his mind were the remarkable revelations of the previous day. He had to assure himself it wasn't a dream.

Another knock at the door jarred him back to reality. That wasn't a dream, either. What time was it? Just 6:30. He was usually up and at 'em by 6. He leapt to his feet, clad in his matching olive drab boxer shorts and tee-shirt, and went to the door, cracking it open a few inches.

"Oh. Sorry," she said, "You still sleep? I come back clean later." She was a stout, 50-ish woman in an unattractive jumpsuit, with hair so jet black she must have just dyed it. Accompanying her was a cart brimming with cleaning supplies, linen and towels. Her accent, Ozera now knew, was Romanian.

"Geez," he said, looking at his watch, "It's still pretty early. I've got to shower yet. I'll be out of here in a half hour."

"Okay, sleepy head," she smiled at him, "I come back." She began wheeling her cart down the hall. "There is coffee downstairs," she said over her shoulder, walking away from him.

"Oh," Ozera called to her, "Is there a phone in here?"

"Downstairs," she replied, not missing a step.

It was a standard Army barracks design, but Ozera was impressed with how comfortably the room was decorated. Kind of compact, but neat and well appointed, and clean as a hospital operating room. In the shower stall he found a wrapped bar of soap and a small container of shampoo. Just like at the Holiday Inn, he chuckled. A phone and TV would be nice, but hey, he wasn't complaining.

He dressed in jeans and a tan knit pullover, and then packed up his overnight bag. The plan was to try to get re-situated into that Bed-and-Breakfast right down the road.

Ozera stepped out into the hallway and pulled his door shut. He walked the length of the second floor towards the back of the building, passing a dozen or so rooms, plus separate men's and women's bathrooms. A few doors were ajar, revealing neatly made single beds, desks and dressers – like shared rooms in a college dorm. The cleaning lady was busily at work in a room at the far end of the hall.

A doorway at the end of the hallway opened into a stairwell, as he expected. It was the same cookie-cutter layout in all these buildings. He went down and entered the first floor, into what turned out to be the kitchen area. He startled the kitchen crew – two women and a man. Clearly they were not used to strangers walking in. All stopped what they were doing and stood looking at him, not sure what to say or do.

One of the women, in her 30's, was clearly in charge. Her black hair was in a net and she wore too-tight cook's whites. The other two, both in their 20's, wore aprons.

"Coffee?" Ozera asked sheepishly, lifting his fist to his mouth, as if holding an imaginary mug.

"Ah, cafea," the lady in cook's whites responded, smiling at him uncertainly.

"*He is our special guest,*" a voice behind him said in Romanian. He turned around to see Lisa. "*Please be nice to him,*" she said to the cook.

Ozera flashed a particularly charming smile at Lisa, "Oh, I'm saved," he said, remembering that he was not to let on that he spoke and understood Romanian. Lisa smiled her reply.

"Is he the one who stayed here last night, Elisabeta?" the cook asked her.

"Yes," Lisa said to her, in English – an intentional suggestion that she follow suit. "Chef Maria, this is Captain Ozera," she introduced him. "He just arrived here. He works for the Colonel, too."

Maria wiped her right hand on the butt of her whites and then extended it for a handshake. "Da. Hello, Captain," she said to him with a feigned smile, still a little apprehensive. "I am very much happy to meet you." Ozera smiled and graciously reciprocated.

"And these are kitchen assistants, Anton and Helena," Lisa continued with the introduction. Ozera smiled as the young man and young woman each responded in turn with a slight bow and respectful nod. Ozera felt that they were more than just co-workers, perhaps married, or at least lovers. They were close, his instinct told him.

"Please come and join me, Captain," Lisa said to him. As usual she didn't wait for an answer; she just turned and headed toward the kitchen exit. She was wearing jeans and a sweatshirt, but had her monk's habit in hand. Probably getting ready to go to work, he reasoned.

"You try my omelet, okay?" Maria said to Ozera, as he turned to follow Lisa. He looked back and nodded.

"Sure, ham and cheese would be just great," he said to her. She winked back, apparently warming to him. He wasn't sure she understood, but he wasn't going to ask in Romanian. He'd devour whatever she came up with.

Lisa led him out into a cafeteria-like dining room. Like the rooms upstairs it was cozy and similarly spotless. Bright morning sunlight streamed through the curtained windows. There were a half-dozen tables, mostly four-seaters and one larger, round six-seater. Red-and-white checkered cloth tablecloths made it look like a French cafe. Plants and flowers were tastefully placed throughout – artificial, Ozera figured, given that it was still not quite spring.

People at several tables were busily talking, munching, sipping drinks. At one there was an attractive blond woman in a red dress, late-20's, maybe 30, sitting at a window table across from a handsome younger man dressed in neat business attire. They were talking in Romanian – professionally, not personally, it seemed – and sipping coffee, their finished breakfast plates before them. An old man in his 70's, with glorious bushy white hair, sat alone with his coffee. At a corner table a man and woman, both about 30 and dressed in work clothes, were eating assertively, as if they were already 10 minutes late.

Everyone stopped what they doing and looked over when Lisa walked in with Ozera. Lisa casually raised her hand, denoting 'it's alright,' nodded and smiled. And in a moment they all went back to what they were doing.

"Well, *Elisabeta*," Ozera teased, emphasizing her Romanian name, "Can I buy you a coffee?" Lisa was a little surprised that Ozera caught her name from what Maria the cook asked her, in Romanian.

She looked up at him without her characteristic smile, showing a hint of irritation. "Please, just Lisa," she pleaded, a bit too dramatically. They walked to a counter by the wall where there were urns of coffee and hot water, a pitcher of orange juice and glasses. He poured a mug of hot coffee, black, in a few seconds, but then waited patiently as Lisa meticulously prepared a cup of tea, with milk and sugar.

Ozera went to the table where the old man was seated, put down his coffee and gestured, tacitly asking if they could join him.

"Da, va rog," he replied, inviting him with an open hand.

"He says 'Yes, please sit down,'" Lisa said from behind him – although Ozera needed no translation. "Alexandru, this is Captain Ozera," she introduced them, in English.

"Hello, Alexandru. I am pleased to meet you," Ozera said, extending his hand, which the old man accepted. His hand was large and rough, a workman's hand.

Lisa put her monk's habit on a chair and sat down between the two of them. Alexandru and Ozera studied each other for a few moments, quietly sipping their coffee. Then the old man broke the silence.

"You soldier, da?" he asked Ozera, more a statement than a question. Ozera nodded. "I am sorry about you soldiers," Alexandru said.

Ozera wasn't sure what the old man was trying to say in his broken English.

"I'm not sorry to be a soldier," Ozera responded. "Yes, it is a hard job, but it is a respectable profession ..."

"No, no," Alexandru interrupted, "I mean **you** soldiers. I am sorry for the soldiers who die in the desert for **you**." Ozera was stunned. He couldn't mean the men he lost in Iraq. How could he possibly know?

"Alexandru!" Lisa addressed him sharply. She told him sternly in Romanian, *"Don't you have work to do? Please go now."*

"Da, da," he responded, slowing standing up, "Time to go work." With that he nodded politely to Ozera, turned and slowly walked away. Ozera wasn't sure what just transpired. He glanced over at Lisa, who looked a little unsettled…like a school marm who just disciplined a student.

Maria emerged from the kitchen, her arms full of dishes. In front of Ozera she plopped down a large serving dish. His eyes widened. An omelet – had to be four big eggs, and he could see oozing ham and cheese – and beautifully crisped hash browns. On a smaller dish were several slices of buttered bread.

"Fresh bread, I make this morning," she said with pride. She placed the last small dish in front of Lisa – half a toasted English muffin, neatly coated with orange marmalade.

"You eat like bird," Maria berated Lisa, "How you expect to get a man when you just skinny bones?" Maria stood erect, chest out, her ample curves accentuated in her tailored too-tight cook whites. Lisa looked up at her with baleful eyes, as if to say: 'Oh, please. Not again.'

Ozera chuckled. Clearly it was a discussion those two had before. This time it was replayed, in broken English and with Maria's choreography, for Ozera's benefit.

He was starved and it all looked too good to rest on ceremony, so he dug in. It was as delicious as it looked, and Ozera downed most of it in a few minutes. Lisa quietly watched him with feigned indifference, nibbling occasionally on the jellied half-muffin and sipping her tea fastidiously. His plate cleaned off, he sat back for a few slurps of coffee.

"You certainly have a good appetite, Captain," Lisa tactfully observed.

"I was hungry," he tersely replied. He looked around. The blonde in the red dress and her young protégé were gone. The other couple was just getting up to leave. Maria's two kitchen assistants were cleaning up and wiping down.

"Lisa," he casually addressed her, "Is everyone here part of the Romanian group that came over last year?"

"Yes," she replied, "All of us stay here in the dorm, except for the Doctor."

"The Doctor?" he asked.

"Yes. Doctor Lupescu, who lives down the mountain."

"Oh," he said, nodding as if he understood. He wondered how far away it was that 'the Doctor' found a place to live.

"Did you all know each other before you agreed to come to America?"

"Yes," she again replied.

"Did all of you work for the Russians at that research facility?"

She paused a moment before answering, as if wondering how much more he knew. "Yes, in a manner of speaking," she again replied.

"And everyone does the same job here?"

She laughed: "Oh, no. Here we do what needs doing. Old Alexandru, for example. Here he is – how you say? – janitor. He takes care of the Conference Center. Some handle the kitchen and cooking – Maria, Anton, and Helena – who you met. And there is Helga, the housekeeper. The other couple that was sitting over there, Emil and Sonia, handle maintenance and repairs – toilets, heating, carpentry. Another couple handles the grounds – gardening, snow shoveling, and so on. And I am the Colonel's assistant and receptionist. I handle local errands – pick up food, supplies, medical prescriptions, movies, take people to the doctor, get the vehicles fueled and serviced … that sort of thing."

"And the lady in the red dress, with the young man?" he asked.

"Ivonna, always with Stefan," she replied. "They work with the Doctor on the project."

Ozera wondered how much she knew about 'the project," but decided this was not the time or place to probe deeper. "I see," Ozera said, curious about the Doctor's role in all this, but not wanting to sound uninformed.

"What did you all do in Romania?" he asked.

"We did cooking, cleaning and maintenance there, too. But mainly, except for the Doctor, we were – how you say? – guinea rats."

Maria reappeared, this time putting down in front of Lisa a tray and dishes covered with aluminum foil.

She glanced over at Ozera: "And you like Maria's omelet, Captain?"

"It was delicious, Maria. I can't remember an omelet so delicious and juicy," he said, flashing an especially endearing and appreciative smile. Ozera had a special place in his heart for anyone who made food for him. Cooking was not a particularly favorite pastime of his, but eating was.

"Good. You come back again," Maria said, giving him another wink – out of sight of Lisa.

"Thank you, Maria," Lisa said, her voice devoid of sincerity. She stood, unfolded her monk's habit and, in a few seconds, had effortlessly slipped it on.

Ozera stood up, reached in his pocket and pulled out some folded paper money, along with the note the Colonel had given him. Lisa leaned forward and touched his hand, catching his attention. He looked at her and she subtly shook her head. He understood, nodded and slipped the money back in his pocket.

"I must go now, Captain. I need to take this to the Colonel, open the office and get coffee on."

"So what does the boss like for breakfast?" he asked, guessing that this was the Colonel's breakfast.

"It is Friday, so today it is oatmeal with raisins and milk, and well-done rye toast, no butter," she said, matter of factly, like a bored waiter reciting the daily specials from memory. She was an automaton, this one, Ozera concluded, wondering what she was like if she ever really let her hair down.

"Where is the phone here?" he asked.

"In the lounge, right through there," she said, pointing to the room in front of the dining room.

Ozera checked his watch. 8 am. "Thank you for the company, Lisa," he told her, "See you this afternoon." She smiled politely, picked up the tray and left.

Their relationship was evolving. They were co-workers; both worked for the same boss – the Colonel – but in quite different capacities. Yes, Lisa emanated a subtle air of aristocratic aloofness, almost snobbiness – quite the opposite of Ozera. But he found her snooty demeanor cute. Plus, he respected that she was very bright, tactful, clearly a trusted confidante of the Colonel, and apparently also very influential among the Romanian contingent.

She had answered all his questions candidly and, it seemed, honestly. But he wondered how much more she knew.

* _ * _ *

He was the last to leave the dining room. Ozera walked out into what was a day room, looking for the phone. He'd been meaning to check on getting one of the new-generation mobile phones, now they were small enough to slip in your pocket. But he figured it would be years yet before wireless coverage came to this rural and mountainous region of northeast Pennsylvania.

The carpeted day room was cozy and, like the rest of the dorm, immaculate. Two couches and several chairs formed a semi-circle in front of a TV. There was a card table and a small pool table. And on the back wall, a phone.

He expected a payphone, but it turned out to be a regular wall phone. He picked it up, listened, dialed 9 and got the dial tone of an outside line. It was a nice gesture, he thought, allowing these people unrestricted phone calls – certainly local, probably long-distance, too, and maybe even internationally. He punched in the number and, after a couple rings, a woman with a pleasant voice answered.

"Mrs. Griffiths?" he asked.

"Yes?"

"My name is Brad Ozera. A mutual acquaintance of ours, named Smith, recommended I stop over and see you, and maybe I could interest you in putting me up there for a while."

"Oh, that would be delightful," she replied, sounding genuinely pleased that he was interested. The Colonel did say to drop his name.

"Can I stop by in a little while, maybe look around and discuss it with you?"

"Sure. Do you know where I'm at?"

"Yes, I do. See you shortly. G'bye."

Ozera went back up to his room and slipped on his monk's robe. He grabbed his overnight bag and walked out through the front entrance. He was a little tired, not having had much sleep, but his belly was full and that was a good feeling.

The day was warming in the bright sunshine. The morning air on the mountaintop was still moist and fresh and he savored it, breathing deeply. It was nearly spring. It had been a long, hard winter, and a long time since he spent springtime in his native Poconos.

He was walking towards his car when he heard it and stopped abruptly to listen. It was the same distant sound he'd heard the day before: A chopper was coming in. Ozera walked over to the edge of the parking lot and looked out over the open field behind the buildings.

Standing by the helipad was a robed figure – holding a radio and looking around the skies and grounds. In a few moments a black helicopter came above the horizon and into view. Ozera saw it was a Black Hawk, one of the Army's newest combat transport helicopters, and oddly, it was unmarked except for a number. The chopper approached in a quick, sharp descent.

It had barely touched down when the door slid open and five soldiers in standard Army camouflage fatigues hopped off, each with a duffel bag. Crouching to stay clear of the whirling blades, they scurried off the helipad and into the Control Center building, followed by the robed figure. In a few seconds five other men, similarly dressed and carrying duffel bags, ran out and boarded the chopper. The Black Hawk lifted off and banked a sharp right, over the woods and mountaintop, and in a few moments was out of sight. The quiet and solitude of the mountaintop quickly returned. Total elapsed time: maybe two minutes.

The robed figure was the outgoing sergeant in charge of the security detail, Ozera concluded. It was all done professionally, by the book: The replacements move in, take up position, and then relieve the other detail, which slips out quickly and quietly. And security continues uninterrupted.

Ozera thought of the many hours he had logged – on too many missions – aboard Black Hawks. He recalled the Colonel's arrival yesterday in the older Huey helicopter and chuckled: The chopper and the Colonel, ironically, both aging leftovers from Vietnam.

*_*_*

V: Room at the inn

Ozera drove down the half-mile to the exit and, while waiting
for the log gate to swing open, pulled off his monk's habit.
He turned left and the B&B came immediately into view.
Couldn't ask for a shorter commute to work, he told himself
with a smile.

The entrance driveway meandered down to a one-lane arched
bridge over the brook, and then up to the main farmhouse.
He pulled into a parking area, where there was a shiny red
Chevy pick-up truck and a Jeep Comanche. It was still fairly
cool, but Ozera decided to tough it without his jacket. He got
out and looked around.

The heavy slide door to the large red barn was half open. He
went over and peeked inside. His nose caught the aroma of
fresh manure. He heard the whinny of a horse, and saw a
tack room with English and western saddles and assorted
leads and bridles.

He looked over at the main farmhouse: An imposing two-
and-a-half-story structure, with four columns supporting the
roof overhang above the front patio. It was architecturally
reminiscent of an antebellum Southern mansion, with three
well-balanced dormers along the slate roof. Ozera guessed it
was probably built in the late 1800's. It was well-made but
now was in need of some care and attention. Here and there
paint was cracking and peeling.

He strode up the walkway towards the front door. The stone
pathway was neat, bordered by bushes and flower beds,
which would begin budding and blooming in another couple
of weeks. The flagstone front terrace featured a loveseat
swing chair on one side, and a wrought iron table and chairs
on the other. He strode to the front door and rapped the
knocker twice.

The large front door swung open, and a lovely woman stood
before him. Fifty-ish, Ozera guessed, but certainly not past

her prime. Her hair was a tasteful blend of brown and gray, pulled up in a bun. A pretty face that featured sensitive, thoughtful eyes. She had a figure that any younger woman would envy – considerable bosom with a narrow waist, which accentuated her rounded hips. She wore a short dress, revealing shapely legs, and black patent leather Mary-Janes. She had on a small apron, and her left hand held a feather duster. She looked to Ozera like a mix of middle-aged cleaning lady and sexy French maid. He offered her a charming smile.

She was similarly checking him out from head to toe, and apparently liked what she saw. "Oh, my," she uttered without thinking, "Mr. Ozama?" she asked, "I was expecting someone … oriental."

"No, it's Ozera … Brad," he corrected her, "Mrs. Griffiths?"

"Alive and in the flesh," she said with a smile. Her attractive eyes looked right into his. And for a moment, they both wondered what the other was thinking. It was a pleasant thought – for them both – but, for now at least, the moment passed.

"Come in, come in," she said, moving aside and gesturing invitingly. "Any friend of John's is a friend of mine." John Smith? So that was the Colonel's first name. Ozera thought about how much it sounded like an alias. And maybe it was, given his intelligence background. But then again, it just might really be John Smith, he thought.

"Is that for personal protection?" Ozera asked with a deadpan expression, pointing to the feather duster.

"Oh, this," she giggled, "It's saved me for many years." A cute, quick, funny comeback. He smiled.

"How about a look around?" she posed to him, "You might see something you like." He followed her, letting the urge for a wisecrack pass unfulfilled. And she noted his restraint.

She led him through the front sitting room and walked around behind the back of the reception counter, which apparently doubled as a bar, with shelves of assorted liquor on the wall behind her. She pulled out a card and passed it over the counter to Ozera, then held out a pen for him.

"We are technically a hotel, and I need to keep the paperwork straight." It was a 'Guest Registration' card, asking all the usual hotel-guest questions. Ozera started filling it in.

"Where are you from, Bradley?" she asked, apparently adept at reading upside down. She was bold enough to call him by his first name, but hadn't offered him hers.

"The NEPA Facility up the hill," he responded, being intentionally vague.

"Yeah, I figured that," she replied, "I mean, where do you come from?"

"I was actually born and raised here in Pennsylvania," he answered her, "About an hour north of here. But I've been away for years." He finished the card and handed it back. "I'll have to get back to you with my business phone. And I don't know yet how long I'll be staying … I'd say at least a few weeks, maybe a few months."

"Oh, that's okay," she said, scanning his responses. "It'll be nice to have you. Now, I have three rooms you can pick from, on the second and third floors. I live in the back here on the first floor."

"I'm not real fussy, Mrs. Griffiths," he replied, "I'm by myself and all I need is a comfortable bed and a bathroom with shower. Oh, and a nice closet or storage area somewhere nearby would be great; I've got some clothes and a couple boxes of personal belongings."

"I've got just the room," she said, "Come on." She led him up the grand staircase. She was spry and in good shape. If she took care of this whole place by herself, that would do it, he reasoned.

They turned right at the top of the stairs and went to the door at the end of the hall, No. 5. She explained this was her favorite room, because of the view out over the back and beautiful afternoon sun. It had a queen-size canopy bed, with frilly pillows and lace throughout. There was a feminine touch to it all.

She showed him the bathroom – with beautiful tiled floor and walls. Ozera guessed it dated from the early 1920's or 30's, judging from the ornate, black-and-white tile patterns. But there were modern updates, too: a new pedestal sink and faucet, and a large, walk-in, tiled shower with a clear glass door. No tub, but that didn't matter to him.

There was a big walk-in closet, with just some blankets and pillows on a top rack. "That big enough?" she asked him.

"That'll do just fine," he assured her. He looked out the large double-hung windows over the back. It was beautiful – park-like, about 10 acres, with stone-paved and graveled walkways. It would be perfect for jogging early in the morning. The same babbling brook circled around from the front, down a short waterfall and into a small natural retaining pond, from which water overflowed out and down the mountain. He spotted a covered hot tub on the patio below.

"Does the spa work?" he asked.

"It hasn't been used for some time," she replied. "It's been drained and empty. But if you're willing to help me get it running, sure, we can fire it up again. It's a lot of fun."

"You've got a deal, Mrs. Griffiths. The room's perfect. I'll take it."

"Great," she said, handing him the key, "Breakfast is at seven, and I do a pretty good breakfast," she said, hands on her hips in a boasting pose.

"So I heard," he told her. She smiled, and wondered what else he'd been told.

"I change towels twice a week, and sheets on Monday."

"Perfect," he said. "I have my stuff out in the car. I'll just unload and then head off to the office. And I'll be back tonight." He was pleased, especially since he'd be staying so close to work, in a beautiful quiet setting, in a luxurious room with a view, a charming and intriguing landlady … and breakfast no less.

"Happy to have you here," she told him, in a sincere and welcoming voice. "It'll be nice to have a man around." With that she smiled, turned and walked away down the hall, cognizant she was being watched. A sweet gal, vibrant and fun, Ozera thought, though lonely and seeking attention.

He'd made several trips out to the Ford and had most of it unloaded and stowed in the large closet. He stood in the doorway of his room catching his breath, about to go back down. He turned back to scan the room again, pleased, taking it all in one more time.

Then he heard something behind him and spun around. The door to the room at the far other end of the hall opened, pouring morning sunlight into the dark hallway. A female form stepped into the doorway, silhouetted against the bright light. But he could tell she was tall: five-eight, maybe five-nine. And she was shapely. She pulled the door shut, turned around and stopped short – as surprised to see Ozera standing there as he was to see her.

She composed herself and started walking towards the stairway, and him. She moved like a cat, Ozera observed, with smooth strides, her perfectly fitted dress shifting with her steps, accentuating her curves. She was not trying to be seductive, Ozera concluded. She just couldn't help it.

She approached the stairway, halfway down the hall, and Ozera got a better look. She was late 30's, maybe 40, with shoulder-length chestnut hair that also swayed as she walked. A beautiful face with high cheekbones, light complexion, dark blue eyes, inviting lips.

Ozera wanted to say something witty but decided he didn't want to seem forward. Just before she turned to go down the stairs he managed a single word.

"Hi," he said, adding his characteristic smile.

"Hello," she responded, and flashed him an unforgettable smile. He detected a slight foreign accent. He watched her transfixed, as she descended and was gone.

"Wow," Ozera uttered to himself. He walked down towards her room and saw No. 2 on her door. He looked at his watch. Better finish up and get to work. He went back out to his SUV, noticed the Jeep was gone, and brought back up his last load of belongings.

* - * - *

V: Who knows what?

"I just finished moving in over at the B&B," Ozera said as he and the Colonel sat down at the conference table.

"Good," he said, almost ignoring him, as he pored through file folders he had assembled in a pile. "Just consider it government quarters as long as you want to stay there." That meant he wouldn't have to pay to stay there, since housing was available at the Bed-and-Breakfast under a government contract. But neither would he receive a separate housing allowance then.

"That Mrs. Griffiths is quite a gal," Ozera offered.

"Amen," was all the Colonel said, continuing to shuffle through the files. A simple one-word response. Ozera hoped for some elaboration. He wondered how well they knew each other. Did they see each other socially? Maybe even sexually?

"How was breakfast in our dining room?" the Colonel asked.

Figuring he had already gotten the low-down from Lisa, he thought he'd give his perspective.

"I met most of the … Romanians. It's a pretty diverse group, but they seem to get along together pretty well. I think it's great that you've got them all working, and working together. They're proud people and they take pride in their work."

"And they're getting paid," the Colonel interrupted. "They've each got bank accounts down in town, and I think most of them will want to take off on their own when their two-year stint with us ends. That's a deadline we've got to keep in our planning, by the way."

"Right. I was kind of surprised to learn that they were all test subjects at the Russian research site."

The Colonel looked up at him, apparently taken aback. "I didn't know that. **All** of them?"

"Except for the one they call the Doctor."

"No shit. Who'd you get that from?"

"Actually it was Lisa," Ozera said.

"I'll be damned," the Colonel said, "I debriefed her and brought her over. She's worked for me for over a year. Treated her like a daughter. We've talked for hours and hours … and she never told me that. Good work, Captain." He added: "They still don't know you speak Romanian, do they?"

"No, sir," he responded quickly.

"Good," he said. "Be careful about that. They're a smart bunch and they'll get wise to you in no time, I'm sure. But let's see how much you can get out of them before they catch on."

"Right, sir," Ozera responded, "But that raises the question about how much we can discuss and share with them."

"I understand," he replied. "Right now there are only two people on this mountaintop who know the whole story – you and me. And you don't know it all, either. We'll get into that later."

He continued: "Based on hours of debriefings with each of them, here's what we concluded: The Russians set up shop at that site late '83 or '84. As I told you, this is right smack in the middle of the region with the USSR's most psi-intense population, according to their screening data. The best we can tell, their objective was to test local subjects who scored high in their psi screening – and try to find out why them, and why there."

"Most of the subjects either lived nearby or within 50 miles. They were well looked after and taken care of, and no one was harmed." The Colonel paused. "Don't get me wrong; sure, there were injections, electronic stimuli, probes, diodes, meters and all that. But no one was permanently harmed, from what we can tell, and the subjects didn't live in abject fear. Most were more than willing – food, shelter, medical care. We understand the test subjects were supposed to stay there, but they knew the area well and many it seems came and went as they pleased."

"We estimate that over five years some 150 to 200 or so subjects came through the Russian research site – about 20 or so stayed there at a time. We knew that a **few** of our group had been screened by the Ruskies and scored high. But if they were **all** test subjects – as you indicate – then likely most or all of them possess psi capabilities, perhaps significant psi capabilities, and possibly in more than one psi area." The Colonel mulled this over for a moment and smiled. "And all this time we figured most of them were cooks, maintenance and clean-up staff."

Ozera posed his query again: "So how much do these people know about our project, and how much can we share with them going forward?"

"Well, they obviously know what happened to them over in Romania," the Colonel replied. "And they know we want to know whatever the Russians found out, and that we're after the same thing. In interrogation after interrogation, though, we've gotten conflicting stories from them about what exactly went on there – like the screening and testing the Russians conducted."

He continued: "From what we've pieced together, it seems they all know about the Monastery. They know the story. They all seem to regard the area up in those Romanian mountains as holy and sacred – and they seem to want to preserve whatever is there, or was, and keep it from us. It's like I said, Captain: They know more than we know they know. I'd bet my retirement on it."

"But if they already know what we're after ..."

"We aren't really sure what they know and don't know," the Colonel interrupted. "They don't know everything we do. That's a fact. But we probably don't know everything they know, either. So for the record, everything we discussed yesterday – what the U.S. is doing and has done, and what we know about Soviet capabilities – is all Top Secret. Please remember that."

"Yes, sir," Ozera assured him.

"Only one of the Romanians, the Doctor, has been cleared for Confidential. The rest of them have no clearance at all – not even Lisa, who's been my close assistant for the past year. She sees and hears a lot, and she's a smart one," the Colonel paused and then chuckled: "She's smart enough not to ask questions."

"You will need to tread a fine line dealing with these people, Captain," the Colonel said. "They are our guests and we may not do any of them harm. Please remember that. But still, you can and should get out of them whatever you can. Just try not to disclose anything else to them, beyond what they already know."

Ozera nodded. "Understood, sir." Then he asked: "And the Doctor? Who is that?"

"That's what I wanted to brief you on today," he replied. "I have here personnel files of everyone in the "Team" – the so-called specialists we have working with us, working **for** us, on this project."

"I try not to keep classified material here," the Colonel confided, "Most of it is down at headquarters. But you and I are going to need these files going forward, so I had copies made, which the security detail brought up to me this morning. These must be kept under lock and key when they're not in use. There's a couple places you'll be able to secure them." Ozera nodded. "Consider these confidential and do **not** disclose anything in any of them to any member of the Team. You are the only other one here, besides me, who has access to these. I'll update Lisa on your status Monday morning – that you have access to my office, and so on. I gave her the afternoon off." Ozera suspected that the sensitivity of the material they were discussing may have been the not-so-subtle reason.

The Colonel looked down at the files in front of him. "There are six of them. The last team member just came on board a few weeks ago." As before, Ozera was listening intently.

"There are two project heads," he began. "Both are co-directors. One is the Doctor, who really is a medical doctor – as well as a physicist, psychologist and research scientist. The Doctor is Romanian, at least that's what we believe, and was one of only two Romanians who were actually involved in conducting research with the Russians at that site in Romania."

"The other one is a PhD in theoretical physics from Stanford. He was a former SRI researcher – breaking new ground in remote viewing with our colleagues in Langley. He is heavily into ESP and psychokinesis, and has a track record of getting to the bottom of what's really going on in projects like ours."

"Why two co-directors, sir?" Ozera asked.

"I believe hot-shot experts like these two are most likely to achieve results when there's a peer competitor looking over their shoulder day after day. The professional tracks of these two are quite similar: they read the same papers, track many of the same developments and, we believe, conducted actual tests and experiments on a broad base of individuals with bonafide psi talent. I expect quite a bit of contention between them, if for no other reason than one spent years doing for the CIA what other did for the Russians – whether the KGB, Academy of Sciences, or whatever, we're not even sure."

"Interesting management approach, sir," Ozera said. "But which one is really in charge?"

The Colonel looked up at Ozera and with a wry grin said: "I am."

* _ * _ *

V: The Team

"The Doctor," said the Colonel, handing a color 8-by-10 photo to Ozera. He studied it: A candid, unstaged picture that caught her at some social event. High cheekbones, light complexion, dark blue eyes, shoulder-length chestnut hair. It was his neighbor, down the hall at Mrs. Griffiths' B&B, Room 2.

"I caught a glimpse of the Doctor this morning," he said. "She's quite a looker."

"And brains, too," the Colonel responded. "Daciana Lupescu. Late 30s, we think. Doctor of Medicine, Medical University of Vienna, **and** psychologist. Before that, a degree in physics from Bucharest Polytechnic. You don't see that often – a physicist who then becomes a medical doctor. English wasn't even in her top-three languages, but she picked it up quickly. She speaks fluent Romanian and pretty good German and Russian. Smart gal. And that's one of the reasons you're here."

"You want me to get her into bed and find out what she knows?" Ozera said with a smirk and a smile.

"If you get her into bed, young Captain, it's because she wants you there. Remember that," the Colonel retorted, throwing cold water on Ozera's fantasy. "No, you're here – in part – for Romanian-to-English translation."

"But if she can translate Romanian to English, why do you need …"

"Because she's one of **them**," the Colonel retorted. "She's worked for the Russians for five-plus years, and we know she made several trips to the USSR Academy of Sciences in Novosibirsk. Hell, her boss worked for their Special Department 8, their equivalent to our Stanford Research Institute out in California. I need somebody who understands their lingo and who works for **me**."

Ozera nodded, "I see, sir."

"She's here, and she's our co-director because she was assured she could continue working on the Monastery Project, as we have come to call it. She swears that her role at the Romanian site was administrative, providing medical oversight of the tests and test subjects. And she was liaison with the Romanian locals, mollifying them, assuring their cooperation and participation. She's passed all our lie detector tests," the Colonel added," indicating she bears no allegiance to the Soviets, and that she is in fact Romanian and hates the Russians' guts. Actually, information she's provided has been instrumental to our research. Advanced us years, our boys say."

"But you still doubt her ... motives?" Ozera subtly queried him.

"There are some ... anomalies," the Colonel replied, "Like, we haven't been able to verify where she was born or raised. From my experience, the strongest allegiance a person has is to their country of birth, no matter what happens later in life. In fact, we haven't been able to verify anything about the good doctor before 1968. It grates on me; it's a burr in my saddle."

He continued: "She knows everything we know about the Monastery. That was unavoidable in getting her to come over and take the job with us here. To my knowledge she knows nothing else about classified U.S. psi research – what we know, or where we're headed. And I'd like to keep it that way. Here," he said, closing and handing the file over to Ozera, "It's all there." Ozera took one more look at her picture, then slipped it into the file folder and put it aside.

"Our other co-director is James Bennington," the Colonel continued, handing another photo to Ozera. Like the Doctor, he was 40-ish too. A good-looking guy with a dimpled chin and personable smile, wearing stylish dark-rimmed glasses.

He looked academic, yet managerial, and very sure of himself.

"Bennington has a doctorate," the Colonel elaborated: "Ph.D. from Stanford, in theoretical physics. But don't call him 'doctor.' He's got undergraduate degrees from MIT. No question but he's a smart cookie, too. I've known him, and known of him, for nearly ten years now. He's got a mind as open as the great outdoors, no doubt from the psi work he's been doing since the 1970s. He's got a real talent for theorizing – he listens to all sides, asks probing questions, assimilates all facts and arguments, and then comes up with a solution, or at least a viable working theory – a feasible explanation. He's not always right, but he's not afraid to push the envelope of what we know. He is among the world's most knowledgeable people on ESP and psychokinesis."

"You trust him, sir?" Ozera asked.

"There are very few people I trust, Captain," he replied, "and there aren't many left since my dear mother passed away many years ago." He was serious, and Ozera could readily see that he was a jaundiced skeptic, with little faith in his fellow man. It was an expected attribute, and an occupational hazard in his line of work.

"A lot of people think Bennington can help us find the answer to our enigma," the Colonel added.

"Will he be working here?" Ozera asked.

"No," the Colonel replied. "He works from his own place out on the West Coast. He's been on board for a few months now and he's been here twice. He's married with a couple teenage kids and a hell of a mortgage on a ranch just outside Palo Alto. He's got his finger in more than a few pies out there, besides us. So he's working part-time on our project. He'll be in for his third visit soon, by the way. I'll make sure you have some private time with him."

"Great. Thanks, sir."

"Bennington's been told most of what we know – also necessary for him to take on the job. He knows about the Doctor, but doesn't know about the rest of the team, at least not yet. He's well connected from his years in this business, so don't be surprised if he seems to know everything, including about you. He didn't get it from me. And don't let him hoodwink you. He's deceptive and conniving. Oh, and for what it's worth, his passion is fine wine. Maybe that'll be useful. It's all in here."

The Colonel gave him the file and picked up the next one. "Professor Jeremy 'Jerry' Wainright, from Princeton U," he said, handing him the photo. A rotund man in his 50's, with snow white hair and moustache, red nose. With a white beard and a red suit he'd make a helluva Santa Claus, Ozera thought.

"Full professor in the Electrical Engineering Department at Princeton, right over in Jersey just two hours from here. The Professor's been in and out of here quite a bit the last six months, putting some experiments together in his lab, next door in the Conference Center. Wainright is after a Nobel Prize; he wants to be the first to prove to the world – scientifically and beyond any doubt – the physical effects of psychokinesis. He's been outside the envelope at measuring psi effects since the late 60s; it's made him and his department famous. And it's what attracted him to us, too.

"Can he keep our work here secret?" Ozera asked.

"I think so," the Colonel answered. "In an earlier life he was an officer with Army intelligence. Did a tour in Vietnam. Our paths didn't cross though until a few years ago, but he has a solid record with DOD. So yeah, he can keep his mouth shut. He's hoping our work will lead him to the breakthrough he seeks. And who knows? Maybe it will. He's been in academia quite a while, but he was key in our analysis of the statistical data from the Russian psi screening. He's a damned good empirical scientist, with super math and statistical-analysis skills."

"Next is Henry Hallemeier," the Colonel continued, handing him another photo, "a geneticist with GTI, Gene Technology Inc., of Boston, Mass." He was 40-something and looked like a nerdy mad scientist – thick glasses, disheveled hair, white lab coat with pocket protector no less.

"Looks like Einstein's lab assistant," Ozera offered. The Colonel ignored him and went on.

"Hallemeier is at the forefront of deciphering the human genome," he said. "In other words, he is one of the few people in the world who can understand what our DNA means and, more importantly, how differences in our DNA affect our talents, skills and capabilities."

"Like psi?" Ozera asked. "I know genes affect eye color, height, maybe even our intelligence to some extent. But genetics determining whether we can read minds, or bend spoons …"

"We were told to pursue that line of investigation, too, for this project," the Colonel interjected. "Hallemeier has been advising DOD on this area for some time. They're comfortable with him."

It didn't sound like the Colonel personally held out much hope for useful results from the geneticist. 'We were told to pursue it,' he said. It was an inescapable truth that everybody – even someone as influential as the Colonel – worked for somebody. We all have a boss … though Ozera didn't have a clue yet in the Colonel's case who that might be.

"Hallemeier believes that, within the next few years, we'll be able to break down and analyze the full DNA of peoples from all over Europe and identify genetic differences that may account for the psi capabilities the Russians found. But he says that's still years down the road." The Colonel added:

"His work for us doesn't require that he be here, except for checkpoint meetings and briefings. So you'll likely need to meet him at his place in Boston." The Colonel handed over Hallemeier's file.

"Next is Evelyn "Eva" Gerhard," the Colonel said, handing him her photo. "Born before WWII in eastern Germany. She is a research professor and heads Eastern European Studies at Oxford in England. Impressive credentials." She looked like a librarian – 60-something, bluish-gray hair, and the kind of glasses that only teachers and bookworms wear.

"The old gal is our historian, and a gifted forensic archaeologist. Her whole life has been focused on the early and middle ages in Eastern Europe. She has been researching this particular area for us for years, scouring the archives from Poland to Bulgaria. She's got impeccable credentials, can decipher early Romanian and Cyrillic texts, and can get access to back rooms and sub-cellars anywhere – any cathedral, any museum. She knows we are studying the native peoples of this particular region of northern Romania, and that we are looking for a Monastery that may seem to have disappeared in the ninth century.

"Does she know who we are, or what we specifically are looking for?" Ozera asked.

"Not beyond what I just told you," the Colonel replied definitively. "And we'd like to keep it that way. She'd do anything for us: We get her out of her stuffy Oxford office, and enable her to pursue her true love – roaming the sub-basements and archives of ancient buildings in Eastern Europe. We pay her and her travel bills, and we get her expertise and ongoing dedicated effort in return." He handed Ozera her file.

"Our final member of the team is Father Angelo Del Bello, a card-carrying Roman Catholic priest, who currently hangs his hat in Rome. He was born in Naples, Italy but was brought up here in the U.S. – Jersey City." His photo was apparently taken during a religious ceremony, showing the gaunt, 50-ish Del Bello in full priestly garb.

"Now this character is a little different from the others," the Colonel told him. "Father Del Bello has a weakness, an addiction that I feed. I arrange for him to visit New York a few times a year, and he brings us something that only a handful of people in the world can."

"And that is?"

"Access to the Vatican's archives," the Colonel said. "It's how we got as far as we have with this project. He is a legitimate researcher and continues to scour the incredibly massive Vatican archives for anything that may be of interest … to us. Keep in mind that the Roman Catholic Church has been the only continuous repository of historical documentation from the fall of the Roman Empire through the Dark Ages and Renaissance. Our Father Del Bello has copied or smuggled out documents about our Monastery that have been priceless to our project."

"How can we trust him if he betrays his own church?" Ozera asked.

"Please, Captain. It's basic intelligence gathering," the Colonel implored him. "We exploit people's desires and weaknesses, whether it's pursuit of a Nobel Prize, crawling through Romanian church cellars, intellectual obsession, or something like Father Del Bello. I do not trust him, and don't you trust him. He knows what we are looking for, from a historical documentation perspective, but that's it. We need to indulge him. He'll be coming to New York with his latest findings in a few weeks. And we'll need to repay him. But don't trust him."

"Indulge him? Repay him with what?" Ozera asked.

"He's a pedophile," the Colonel responded tersely. Ozera nodded. He was repulsed, but knew not to show it. The

Colonel was right. It was the way the intelligence business worked. Find a weakness and exploit it. And you could create a resource that could reap dividends for years.

"And that's the lot of them," the Colonel concluded, handing over the last file and pushing back into his armchair. "I hand-picked some of them; a couple were assigned to me. I am the only one here who knows all about every member of the team. And soon you will, too."

"The Doctor and Bennington have been learning about the other team members as they need to know. I have found that it's best to keep some secrets in your back pocket. Knowledge truly is power. Don't worry; both Bennington and Lupescu are used to operating on a need-to-know basis. And for now, I'm the one who determines what they need to know."

"Yes, sir," Ozera snapped back, "I understand." He paused, and then added: "You said you located and picked some members of the team, and some were assigned to you. Can you tell me which is which?"

The Colonel mulled it over for a moment. "I think that's something you don't need to know right know," he said with a smile. "I picked you," he said sincerely. "I just don't want to prejudice your investigation and assessment based on who I think is reliable and who may be suspect."

Ozera nodded.

"Now," the Colonel said, looking at his watch, "Let's get a coffee. It's a nice afternoon. Let me give you the 25-cent tour. Bring the files with you."

* - * - *

Chapter VI: The 25-cent tour
VI: Security Central

They walked out and down the hall towards the back of the building, Ozera toting the armful of green Army file folders. They passed a small kitchenette and stopped at the first door on the right. The Colonel produced a ring of keys, unlocked the door and walked in.

It was a typical office, with all the usual amenities, plus a few more. On the large desk were a multi-button phone, a walkie-talkie, and a radio handset, which was connected to a larger radio set somewhere. Behind the desk was a high-back leather executive chair – the same as the Colonel's – two armchairs for guests, a locking file cabinet, and a small round meeting table with three chairs. It was roughly half the size of the Colonel's office, with two windows looking out to the back. The office seemed unused.

"Whose office is this, sir?" he asked, although he suspected he knew.

"Yours," the Colonel said with a smirk, handing him the key ring. "Big one's for the door, the small ones are for the desk and file cabinet."

"Everything a desk jockey needs," Ozera muttered as he sat down at the desk and tried the lock.

"Go ahead and lock up those files," the Colonel told him. "You'll have plenty of time to go through them later." Ozera slid the files into the center drawer and locked the desk.

Then the Colonel walked around behind the desk, standing next to Ozera. He reached down and picked up the walkie-talkie, switched it on and turned the volume up – then placed it back down on the desk. The white-noise hiss and static crackling were annoyingly loud.

Ozera was perplexed, but tried not to show it. The Colonel leaned down and spoke softly to him, almost whispering in his ear: "In the closet in my office is a safe," he said, "You'll need to look around but you'll find it if you have to." Then he reached over to the phone and put his thumb over the last part of the phone number, leaving just the first six digits exposed – 215-381, the area code and exchange. "This is how you get into it," he said.

The Colonel looked squarely at him with raised eyebrows – his expression asking if he understood. Ozera finally caught on and slowly nodded: Six digits – three numbers – 21, 53 and 81 – for a combination lock. With that the Colonel nodded, leaned over and turned off the noisy radio.

Ozera wondered what it was all about, but didn't say anything. Clearly the Colonel was being cautious, and concerned that someone might be listening. And it was just as clear to Ozera there were things he didn't want someone to know.

* _ * _ *

"C'mon," the Colonel told him, "There's more I need to show you." They locked up and headed down the hall towards the back of the building.

"That's Captain Imhof's office," he said, as they passed a closed door across the hall. "He's our AG paper-pusher – comes in a few times a month, pays bills, handles contracts, that sort of thing. He's Adjutant General branch, but he's not a bad sort." Ozera smiled. It was a testimonial, like saying: 'Yeah, he's an accountant, but he's not a total nerd.'

A stairwell at the end of the hallway led up to the second floor. Up the steps they came to a locked, solid door. Ozera spotted the small camera in the corner just as a buzzer sounded and the Colonel pulled the door open.

It looked like a mini NASA Mission Control: Two men in camouflage fatigues were seated at consoles, facing about 20 small closed-circuit TV screens. A large television set was mounted up in the corner; a report on Operation Desert Storm was airing on CNN. There were PCs, printers, a fax machine and a wall full of VCR video and sound-recording tape machines. A large digital clock on the wall flashed the time: 3:15 PM.

The two men at the consoles briefly looked up, acknowledged the Colonel, and then turned their attention back to the screens. A burly sergeant emerged from the back and walked up to them.

"Sergeant Caldwell," the Colonel addressed him, "This is Captain Ozera, my second-in-command." Ozera was taken aback by the 'second-in-command' job title, but went along with it. They heartily shook hands. Ozera saw the sergeant was Signal Corps, the Army's communications specialists, but he didn't recognize the patch on his left shoulder – an upright sword with lightning bolts – presumably the unit emblem for the command they worked for.

The Colonel explained that the sergeant and his men were 'attached' to the mountaintop facility from their base in Maryland. This detail had just arrived that morning, he added. 'Attached' was a peculiar military status: It meant the troops were on temporary loan, but in reality they worked for and reported to someone else. More importantly, they did **not** work for Ozera, who had been told he was to be in charge of security there. Maybe that's why the Colonel elevated his job to second in command – executive officer – a more prestigious job that gave him authority to act for the Colonel and take charge in his absence.

The sergeant introduced Ozera to the others, who walked him through the consoles and closed-circuit TV screens. There were camera views from all over the mountaintop, and live video and audio feeds from the public areas of each building, as well as motion sensor alarms – from the helipad down to the log gate at the entranceway. There wasn't much that happened in or around or near the compound that they didn't hear or see.

Then the sergeant led him and the Colonel over to one of the tape recorders. "If you don't mind, sir," he said to Ozera, "Would you mind telling us what this is all about?" He turned it on.

It was a recording of a phone conversation, in Romanian, between a local woman and a man on the other end. Ozera thought the woman might have been Maria the cook. He listened intently for a minute and then told the sergeant to pause it. He did.

"Not a whole lot going on here, Sarge," Ozera told him, "The woman, who sounds like it might be Maria the cook, is talking to someone about the rent her parents pay for their apartment back in the old country. She's asking why it's going up so much and she's kind of pissed off, telling him she thinks she is wasting her time even talking to him."

The sergeant looked over at the Colonel and the two exchanged broad smiles.

"Right on the money, Captain," the Colonel said, "and a lot more insightful than the translators." Ozera was taken aback. It was a test. And he apparently passed with honors.

"How about this one, sir?" the sergeant said, fast forwarding the tape. "It'll save us from having to get it translated." It was another Romanian phone conversation, between the same woman but a different man. Ozera listened for a couple minutes.

"Nothing real spooky here either," Ozera said. "The same woman wants to send money to this guy, and he is giving her his mailing address. She's writing it down, line by line."

The Colonel smiled. "We thought maybe he was giving her information in some kind of code." He chuckled. "Just the mailing address, huh?" The Colonel seemed relieved, and maybe just a little embarrassed.

The testing was over, it seemed, and Ozera concluded that he had now been accepted as the local translator.

The door buzzed and opened, and another member of the security detail came in. Apparently he had been on a walking patrol of the compound. The young soldier lifted his robe, exposing a Mark 4 automatic rifle. He unloaded the magazine and placed it and the weapon on a countertop, then turned off his walkie-talkie radio and set that down. It was all routine, it seemed. Then he pulled his robe off – revealing camouflage pants and boots, olive drab T-shirt, dog tags, and a .45 automatic holstered on his hip.

In a deep southern drawl he remarked matter-of-factly about all the deer he'd seen in the thick woods around the compound. But, he pointed out, you couldn't tell the bucks from the does, since they all lose their antlers this time of year. His comrades seemed bored and disinterested, and likely would have heaved some disrespectful responses were it not for their distinguished visitors.

The sergeant turned to Ozera and summarized his detail's standing orders: Secure the facility. Safeguard the "foreigners" and do not intimidate them. No firing of weapons … unless absolutely necessary. Wear robes whenever outside or patrolling the compound, and avoid any unnecessary outward military appearances. Most importantly, bring to the Colonel's attention immediately anything peculiar or potentially threatening. Ozera figured this recitation was more for the Colonel's gratification than his. It was good politics by the sergeant.

They discussed how things work there "on the mountain." The chopper flight is just over an hour from their Maryland base. Once they arrive, one of the men takes an SUV down to town to get groceries and supplies. The NCOIC – non-com in charge – is the liaison with the local State Police, about a half-hour away in Dublin. But the State Police and local government agencies all know the mountaintop campus is under federal jurisdiction and, except for an occasional phone call, they are content to leave things there well enough alone.

Sergeant Caldwell explained that he and Sergeant Ernie Rivera have been tag-teaming this detail for months. It is good duty, he explains, with two weeks on site here, and then a week off when they get back to base. The soldiers, all of them, commiserated for a while, as soldiers do – ribbing each other, telling jokes, swapping stories and recollections.

The Colonel then led Ozera out the back and through the detail's living quarters. All the comforts of home, Ozera observed – private rooms, kitchen, dining area, lounge, and laundry. The fifth and last member of the detail, assigned the graveyard shift, had just awakened and was eating cereal. He started to stand up when he saw them enter but the Colonel put him at ease.

It was all well-organized, manned by professionals, and seemed to run pretty much on its own. There really wasn't much need for oversight or involvement on his part, Ozera concluded. He wondered, though, who the security detail really worked for, and if it was the same commander, or even the same command, that the Colonel reported to. He'd find out … in time. For now, though, he was the new kid in town, and would be best served by just watching and listening – keeping a low profile.

* - * - *

VI: Mind over matter

The Colonel led him back through the control center, downstairs and out the back door. The two officers stood quietly for a moment, relishing the solitude of the mountaintop. It was a pleasant afternoon – warming, maybe 50 degrees – just warm enough for them in their robes.

"I see we have a visitor next door," the Colonel said, nodding at the Conference Center next door. Ozera looked over and saw lights on up on the second floor. "Come on," he said, "It's our next port of call."

They walked around towards the entrance to the Conference Center, and spied a black pick-up truck in the parking lot right in front of the building.

"Oh," the Colonel said, "I know who it is. We'll go up and see him later. Let me show you around downstairs first."

Ozera held the front door open and followed the Colonel in. Just then his eye caught someone walking on the far side of the parking lot. Whoever it was had a slight build and wore their robe with the hood up. He watched curiously as the figure neared the utility building. A hand went up and the hood came down. It was Lisa, who was looking around nervously. Ozera was standing inside and she didn't see him. She pulled open the door to the utility building, stepped in and quickly pulled it shut behind her. Strange. Ozera didn't know what to make of it. But this had been a perplexing afternoon all around.

He turned and caught up with the Colonel – through a doorway and into a large meeting room. There were chairs with writing arms attached, like in a classroom, and a large oval conference table, encircled by a dozen nice armchairs. White boards covered the long inside wall.

"This is the main conference room, where I hold planning and checkpoint meetings," the Colonel told him. "You're welcome to use it, too, if you like. But keep in mind that everything said and done here is videotaped and recorded by hidden cameras and microphones. Actually, most everything that happens in this building is recorded."

Ozera contemplated the implications and asked: "Is my office wired, too, sir?"

"Not for video, I'm sure," the Colonel replied, "But I do know that all phone calls to and from this mountaintop are recorded … including into and out of my office."

"Your office?" Ozera asked, surprised. "I thought you ran this …"

"We all work for somebody, Captain," he interrupted him. "This project has potentially enormous implications on national security. And I am sure there are more eyes watching this mountaintop than even I know about." That said, Ozera knew to let it go, but a certain uneasiness started to churn in his gut.

Walking through the first floor they passed bathrooms, a few smaller rooms, a couple of seemingly unused offices, a kitchenette and lounge. A staircase took them upstairs and onto the second floor. Several rooms were empty there; others were offices in use. A large lounge area had a dozen armchairs arranged in a semicircle, as if for presentations or group sessions.

The light in the next office was on, shining out into the dim hallway. The Colonel walked up and knocked on the open door.

They looked in and saw a large, white-haired older man seated at a desk, on the phone. Ozera recognized him from his picture earlier that afternoon. When Wainright looked up and saw them at the door he spoke a few words and hung up the phone.

The Colonel walked in casually. "Whatcha up to, Jerry?" he asked, familiarly. The two apparently knew each other well.

"Hi, John," he replied, just as informally, although clearly he was caught a little off-guard by the unscheduled late-afternoon visit. "Wanted to put in a couple hours on the test bed before the weekend," he said, nodding to the wall on the other side of the big room. "But I had to sit through a freakin' staff meeting that ran through lunchtime." The Colonel smiled and nodded sympathetically.

Ozera looked over. A wall area about 10 feet wide was covered with hundreds of pegs, uniformly sticking out several inches. The pegs were placed in a pattern, a few inches apart, forming neat diagonal rows. The whole peg arrangement was covered with a large clear sheet of Plexiglas. At the top was a large bin, tapered down in the middle. Along the bottom was a series of bins. It looked like a giant pinball game, standing upright, except without flippers.

"Jerry – or rather, Doctor Jeremy Wainright," the Colonel said, correcting himself, "This is Captain Bradley Ozera, our new security officer."

"Hi, Captain," Wainright said, standing up and extending his hand. Ozera reciprocated.

"Glad to meet you, sir," Ozera said, noting the man's girth. He was larger in life than his photo revealed – truly a big man, a couple of inches taller than Ozera's six-foot frame.

"Infantry, I'll bet," Wainright added, looking back over to the Colonel.

"Better yet, Special Forces," the Colonel added. "Captain Ozera is just back from the Gulf. Had some challenging times behind the lines in Iraq." Ozera smiled warily, and he thought it a bit odd that the Colonel would again relegate him to security officer. But he trusted that the Colonel knew what he was doing. And security officer was probably the appropriate title and entrée to meet with the team members and conduct probing interviews and investigations.

"Doctor Wainright is with the electrical engineering department at Princeton," the Colonel again interceded, "and a well-recognized pioneer in measuring the physical effects of psychic phenomena and energy. We're lucky to have him on the team. So what've you got here, Jerry?"

"Well, you should know that I've got a lot of balls," he said with a smile, making his bushy white moustache curl up. "Seriously, folks, I've got about 4,000 little plastic balls over there." He nodded towards two large, over-stuffed hefty bags against the wall. Wainright was flamboyant and apparently had a sense of humor. Ozera and the Colonel looked at each other, perplexed and intrigued.

"Come on over. I'll explain," he said, leading them to the apparatus on the wall. "We made one of these back in the lab at Princeton last year and got some pretty impressive results. When it's done you'll have a state-of-the-art psychotronic detector here." He looked over and saw a blank look on both their faces.

"Bear with me," he reassured them. "The balls are loaded up here on top. I hit a relay button via the computer and the gate opens – and balls drop into the maze. They fall out at a rate of about four per second in a continual stream." He paused to see if his audience was still following him. They were.

"The balls hit the pegs and bounce back and forth. Eventually they find their way to the bottom and into one of these collecting bins, where they are automatically counted. Takes about fifteen minutes per run. To reload, I pop the catch, the bins release the balls, and a plain old vacuum cleaner sucks 'em all back up into the top bin through this tube." He looked over; both of them were nodding. "You soldiers are a tough crowd," he said with a smile.

So he continued: "Now, **statistically**, the balls end up in a very predictable distribution in the collecting bins. When you plot it – as we have, many times – it's nearly a perfect bell curve. The deviation you see in subsequent runs – the standard from the baseline – is inconsequential."

"And how does this measure, uh …," Ozera began to ask, groping a moment for the right technical term.

"Ah," Wainright pre-empted him, "How does this measure psychokinetic capability?" Ozera nodded. He reached over and picked up a chair – a comfortable armchair – and placed it down squarely in front of the wall apparatus, about six feet back from the center.

"The subject sits here," he continued, "And is given just one instruction: 'As the balls fall, see if you can mentally steer them to the left'. Then we repeat it and ask them to try to make them go to the right. We test for both directions with each subject – one at a time of course. This eliminates any bias in the test bed or apparatus. The test bed and process is thus unaffected by any external influences – wind, vibrations, electrostatic energy, humidity, continental drift, etcetera."

"And what have you found?" Ozera and the Colonel both asked in near unison.

"Remember I said that the normal, expected deviation from a pure bell-curve distribution is virtually zero?" Ozera and the Colonel nodded. "Well, we have confirmed deviations by some subjects of up to a tenth of a percentage point. That may not sound like much, but this change can be attributed **only** to the focused thoughts and mental energy of the subject."

"No shit," Ozera uttered, somewhat stunned at the implications. The Colonel showed no reaction. He'd heard it all before.

Wainright was now obviously getting energized. "And it's pretty much been repeatable, too. A subject tends to affect the falling balls to roughly the same degree in subsequent tests, give or take a tenth of a percent. We've had subjects who could cause full-percentage-point deviations on a regular basis. Not all the time, of course, but much of the time – 30, 40 percent of the time."

"So why build this here?" Ozera asked. "I mean what and who are we going to test here?"

Wainright glanced over at the Colonel. "You haven't told him?"

Ozera looked at the Colonel, who responded directly to him: "As I mentioned, we think some of our foreign guests may have psi talent, maybe even **exceptional** psi talents. And so we've brought Dr. Wainright here to check them out, at least for psychokinesis. I was going to brief you on it next week … I didn't expect we'd run into Jerry tonight," he said apologetically. "You'll be working with them – and the good doctor here – to arrange for the testing." The Colonel looked back at Wainright.

"So how long, Jerry, before you can go live with … this?" he asked, nodding at the contraption on the wall.

"Well, I've got photo-electric counters to wire up, and then shake-down and adjustment for a day or so," Wainright replied, then added: "We might be ready for real testing by the end of next week."

"Super," the Colonel said, "We'll get out of your hair and let you get back to work." With that the Colonel looked at Ozera and nodded.

"Doctor Wainright, a pleasure meeting you." Ozera said in closing. "Can I check back with you next week?"

"Please, call me Jerry," Wainright replied. Ozera smiled and nodded, but did not reciprocate with his first name. Wainright noticed, but went on: "I'll be back up on Tuesday, staying through Friday, Captain. How about stopping in, say, Wednesday or Thursday?"

"Will do. See you then," Ozera responded, turning to the Colonel.

They headed out, the Colonel leading the way. Walking through the doorway he nearly tripped and fell. It was old Alexandru, pushing a wide dust mop just outside Wainright's office. Ozera recalled that Alexandru was the janitor for the Conference Center building.

"*Îmi pare rău. Scuzați-mă,*" Alexandru said in Romanian to the Colonel. Ozera heard and understood his 'I'm sorry. Excuse me' apology, and replied without thinking.

"It's okay. No apology needed," he said to him, his hand on the old man's shoulder. The Colonel noticed and shot Ozera a questioning look.

The Colonel stopped off in the bathroom on the way out. Ozera went back down to the entrance and waited for him. Standing in the doorway, with the lights off, he looked out over the parking lot. The tall trees were casting long shadows as the afternoon sun began sinking in the southwest.

A movement across the parking lot again caught his eye. The door of the utility building opened and a figure emerged. Ozera strained to see and finally made the figure out – it was the same soldier he had met earlier in Control Central. He was apparently out walking a patrol of the compound. Oddly, though, he was pulling his robe down over his rifle as he walked back across the gravel parking lot towards Control Central. Ozera didn't move, and the guardsman walked past the Conference Center without noticing him.

Then he saw the utility building door open again, slowly, and a head popped out, looking around. He stared carefully and could make out Lisa. She stepped out, pulling down and straightening her robe, and then quickly shut the door behind her. She walked off towards the dorm building, looking straight ahead – like a youngster who had done something wrong, trying to exit the area before anyone noticed.

"Well, our prissy little Miss Elisabeta, enjoying her afternoon off," Ozera chuckled to himself. She must have been involved with the young soldier for a while, he reasoned, since the new security detail just arrived that morning. And it must have been two weeks since they saw each other. It just goes to show, Ozera mused, that despite the unusual nature of this installation and their mission, people are still people everywhere.

The Colonel showed up; Ozera opened the door and they stepped out onto the front porch. Dusk was settling over the mountaintop.

"Come on," the Colonel said as he descended the steps and headed out to the parking lot. "One more stop before dark." Ozera dutifully followed as they crunched across the gravel parking lot and past the utility building. On the far side the Colonel led them onto a path into the woods.

* - * - *

VI: New construction

The path through the woods was wide and Ozera noticed deep furrows and tracks. There had recently been a lot of heavy traffic through there, almost certainly made by tracked vehicles, he concluded. The woods on either side were carefully preserved, which tended to obscure the pathway from anyone who didn't know it was there – including Ozera. He'd been in and out of the parking lot several times and hadn't noticed it before.

"Ah, a walk in the woods at sunset," the Colonel uttered, to no one in particular.

"Where are we headed, sir?" Ozera asked.

"You'll see." A terse answer, quashing further questions for the moment. The two robed men stepped purposefully. For a man of 50 or so, the Colonel moved along smartly over the rough terrain, and had to be in fairly good shape, Ozera observed. He wondered whether he would be in as good shape as the Colonel when he reached that age.

The pathway curved left, and what had been a gradual rise grew steeper. They rounded the wide turn and Ozera saw the woods giving way and a broad clearing up ahead.

They crested the hill and both suddenly stopped.

"Holy … shit," Ozera muttered reflexively.

On the flat open field before them was … the Monastery – or at least a structure that looked just like the one Ozera had seen in the ancient images. The sun had set behind the structure; an eerie glow highlighted it. A ring of massive upright stone boulders made up the structure's base. Greek-style columns and cut stones filled in neatly between the megaliths. Above, a colonnade of Roman-looking arches capped and surrounded the lower level. And above that rose walls and a slate-like roof, in the style of an early Christian basilica.

But it was **not** the Monastery – Ozera could see it was a copy. The cut stone was new, not weathered. The pillars and arches – and the cross above the front wooden gates – were all gleaming white, likely made from concrete poured into molds around reinforcement bars. It was all new construction, but it certainly did look, structurally at least, just like the original.

"Where'd you get the money … for all this?" he asked the Colonel.

"My boy," the Colonel replied, with a tenor of boastful confidence, "They've thrown more money at this project than we could ever spend."

"How much **did** this cost?"

"Don't ask." Okay, enough of that line of questioning.

Ozera had a thousand questions. But he consolidated them into a single, one-word query.

"Why?"

"Some of the people involved in this project believe it may have been the Monastery itself – the actual structure – that was the key, and somehow instrumental to what's been happening on that plateau up in northern Romania. There's no agreement, though, on how the structure itself may be involved. One line of thought is that it may serve as a battery, an amplifier of sorts, accumulating the type of energy we are trying to identify and isolate. Remember, we are talking about phenomena that don't follow any of the known laws of science or physics."

"And the other line of thought?"

The Colonel sighed deeply, weighing his words, then responded: "That the structure – its composition, its shape, maybe even divine influence, who knows – enhances human thought, meditation and concentration. That it somehow served, and serves, as a vessel enabling the human mind to somehow expand, reach out and achieve amazing, seemingly impossible things."

He looked at Ozera, who showed an emotionless expression. The Colonel expected nothing else. "It's the spiritual component," he added, "The unity of man with nature, the communal spirit … that sort of thing."

"Do you believe that, sir?" Ozera interrupted him, with a tone of impatient incredulity. He wondered who gave the Colonel this advice.

"It doesn't matter what I believe," he retorted, a tone of defensiveness in his voice. "I'm responsible for producing results, and I'm not about to overlook – or reject out of hand – any line of investigation." Ozera sensed a little irritation on the Colonel's part and he tactfully changed the subject.

"How'd you get measurements to build it?" Ozera asked, "I mean, what did you use for a scale?"

"The wooden front gateway, actually," the Colonel replied. "Our best estimate, based on the drawings and other structures from the same time period, put the gate height at four meters at the center peak, just under 13 feet. All the other dimensions were derived from and based on that." Ozera nodded, impressed.

The Colonel continued, recounting his achievement and the steps leading up to this point: "Ironically, what took the longest was producing a set of prints from the painting and drawing. Then I set up five teams, mainly Army engineers and local concrete and stone contractors, and they worked in parallel. A little careful management, timing, luck, and things progressed pretty quickly … et voila!" he said, gesturing at the imposing structure.

"Where'd all the stone and building materials come from?"

"Actually, most of it came from right around here, this mountain," the Colonel explained. "The stone monoliths were hewn from a rock face on the other side of the hill. The area here was cleared down to the bedrock, and then stone cutters went to work with their saws and hydraulic trimmers. We brought the boulders over and positioned them by helicopter – had to bring in a Chinook for that. And we pushed it to the max. Some of the biggest stones are nearly 15 tons. I have no idea how those poor fuckers in Romania built theirs so many centuries ago."

He continued: "The foundation layer took a couple months, early last spring. Then they placed columns and cut and laid the smaller stones; that took a couple more months. Local limestone and gravel were used to make concrete, which was poured around reinforcement bars to make the Roman columns and arches on the second level. Those were put in place in late summer. And through the fall they erected the basilica level on top. It was getting pretty cold by the time they finished the slate roof."

"What's inside, sir?" he asked.

"Not much … yet. It's pretty empty," he replied. "We think we know what it looked like from the outside, but we have no idea what was inside. To support the exterior structure we had to build a framework of concrete pillars and timber girders inside. We milled the big pines and oaks we cut down for rafters and beams."

"Actually," the Colonel continued, "I was hoping you'd help me out with the inside. After all, you **are** an architect, and they told me you were a good one, with insight into early Christian church design, right?"

Ozera snapped back: "Me?! How the hell am I supposed to know what to put inside? I mean, shit … sir … a structure that **may** have existed a thousand years ago?!" The Colonel accepted his outburst. He'd dumped a lot on him the last couple of days. And he expected, and deserved, pushback.

"Just … give it some thought, okay?" the Colonel said calmly. "And see what you can come up with."

Ozera sighed, and replied with a tone of helplessness. "I'll get to work on it, sir, but I think it's going to take some heavy duty research. How long do I have?"

"Soon as you can," was the terse response. They stood quietly for a moment, side by side, before the massive eclectic structure. Evening was fast approaching. The detail of the Monastery before them was getting harder to see, fading to dark … like a dream forgotten.

"We pushed pretty hard, and fast, but what we have here, we believe, is damned close to the original," the Colonel reflected, "I can only imagine what the builders over there had to go through. I mean, we had diamond saws, steel cables, hydraulics, bulldozers, and a mambo transport helicopter. What did they have?"

"That's what I guess we're trying to figure out," Ozera offered, encouragingly, having regained his composure.

The Colonel nodded. "Well, that concludes today's guided tour," he declared. They turned and headed back down the path, Ozera looking back a few times, as if to make sure it was still there. It was nearly dark. The moon hadn't yet risen, and the clear night on the mountaintop was slowly revealing an awesome display of stars.

* _ * _ *

VI: Weekend off

A long, long day, and Ozera was starving. He pulled into the B&B parking lot, next to the Jeep, and trotted up the stone pathway. He swung the large front door open and entered the dimly lit sitting room.

"Honey, I'm home," he said matter-of-factly to an empty house. He looked around. Comfortable chairs, carpeting, curtains. Inviting.

"Nobody's called me Honey in years," the voice behind him said in a Mae West impersonation. Mrs. Griffiths had quietly slipped in behind him, standing with hands on her hips. Her feather duster was nowhere to be seen.

"Ah, my dear Mrs. Griffiths," he said, in a light-hearted, convivial tone. "Do you ever get out of here for a while?"

"Frankly, Brad, not very often," she lamented, "It's a curse of the business."

"But you've got just two guests," he said, "me and the mysterious lady at the other end of the hall. And I was thinking: I'm starving and would love to try that Fern Valley Inn I saw down over the mountain. But Friday night dinner would go much better with some company, and someone who's been there before." He paused, then offered: "Interested? My treat."

She thought about it for two seconds. "I'd have to change, and so do you," she countered.

She reached under the counter and pulled out a deck of placards. Shuffling through them she pulled out a 'Back in an hour' sign and positioned it prominently on the countertop. She stopped and thought for a moment, then muttered "Oh, fuck it," picking up the sign and replacing it with a 'Closed for the night' card. "Who knows?" she said, "I might get lucky." Ozera laughed out loud.

"Meet me back here in, say, 15 minutes?" he proposed. She nodded approval and dashed out.

He ran up and dug out a casual outfit from the large closet – slacks, clean white shirt, sweater and sports jacket. He jumped in the shower, dried, changed and was on his way back down in 15 minutes flat.

A transformed Mrs. Griffiths was already there waiting – in a low-cut little black dress, which she filled seductively, and a fur-fringed wrap. Stockings, high heels, a tasteful touch of make-up and a satin clutch purse. Her hair was still in a bun, but was fixed up with some curls dangling attractively – seductively – over her ears.

She adopted her hands-on-hips stance, accentuating her delightful figure, and Mae West accent: "Hey, soldier. Looking for a good time?"

"Wow," was all he said, to which she responded appreciatively.

He smiled, walked up to her and held out his arm, which she eagerly accepted.

It was after 8 pm by the time they arrived, and the Fern Valley Inn was abuzz with Friday night dinner activity. Without reservations they were ushered to the comfortable, low-ceiling bar. Early to mid-1800's, Ozera guessed, gazing about. He ordered a Manhattan. She had a new drink – a Cosmopolitan.

"It looks good," Ozera noted with approval, "What's in it?"

She took a long slurp and stared at her half-empty martini glass. "Vodka … and some inert ingredients." He chuckled, and ordered them both another round. He tasted hers, and she had a generous sip of his.

"In some parts of the world we'd be married now," Ozera pronounced with a deadpan expression.

In a little while they were escorted to their table. Appetizers. Prime rib and all the trimmings for him. A gorgeous Chilean sea bass for her. Pinot Noir for him, and a very palatable Pinot Grigio for her. And another round ...

They laughed and talked. If there was an age difference, no one around them noticed, and neither did they. They were enjoying each other immensely. **Mr.** Griffiths, it turns out, had passed away some years ago, leaving her to run everything herself. She spoke of her late husband lovingly, and from time to time with a tear in her eye. He changed the subject at those moments, preferring to keep her engaged – and smiling and laughing – with wisecracking and suggestive repartee.

She was not particularly probing about him or his background. It wasn't that she didn't care. She was too busy enjoying the night out – her first real night out in what had to be a long time, Ozera figured. He told her he worked for the government, to which she cracked "**Our** government, I hope."

He couldn't tell whether or not the Colonel had told her about him. If not, she was one trusting woman, having just met him that morning. He worked into the conversation that he was recently divorced, and she made note of it, but it didn't seem to matter. He saw that she enjoyed the drinks and wine, maybe indulging a little too much, but she apparently needed a night out ... as much as he did. He was her escort and she was his guest tonight. He wanted her to enjoy herself, and he'd make sure she got home safe and sound. And she knew he would.

They finished dinner and decided on a nightcap in the bar– which neither of them really needed. They stopped in the restrooms on the way. He finished first and went into the bar. There were just a couple regulars left in the old inn's cozy bar. Ozera checked his watch; it was getting late.

She walked in, and went right up and embraced him with friendly kiss. He was a little surprised, but reciprocated nonetheless. She looked up at him and said "Thank you," with a sincere look in her lovely eyes that made him melt. He said nothing but smiled a charming smile that said 'You're welcome.'

"Mrs. Griffiths," he said in a romantic tone, as he raised his glass, "To the most gorgeous woman I've met in a long, long time." He was sincere. She thanked him with her eyes.

"And here's to the best-looking guy I've met all day," she wisecracked, lightening the mood, as they laughed and clinked his brandy snifter against her dry sherry glass.

In their own time they left. He sensed her footing was a little unsure as they proceeded down the front steps – a combination, he reasoned, of the heels, the hour and the drinks. So he held her firmly around the shoulders, for her benefit – as well as his.

They rounded the corner toward the parking lot. His was the only vehicle left. The waning moon illuminated the cool evening as he opened her door to the black Ford Explorer. She struggled to climb up onto the front passenger seat of the SUV. She finally did, and then plopped down with a heavy sigh.

They pulled out and he headed towards the road that snaked back up the mountain.

"Thanks for a wonderful time," she said in a gracious tone.

"My pleasure," he replied, and he meant it. The rest of the short ride home was quiet. They were both tired and getting drowsy.

"Home again, home again," he said softly as they pulled into the long driveway of the B&B. It was a line from an old rhyme he remembered from his childhood.

"Jiggity jig," she responded reflexively, citing from the same old rhyme. They laughed. Despite differences in their ages and upbringing, they shared a lot in common, it seemed. The chemistry was reactive between them, and in just a single night out they had become close friends.

He hopped out and opened her door. It took her a second to get a solid footing in her high heels. Ozera held out his arm, as he did when they left. She accepted – appreciating the companionship as well as the physical support.

She almost slipped at the front doorway, then straightened up and walked, carefully, to the reception counter.

"Aw, shit," she said, standing unevenly before the counter.

"What is it?" he asked.

"They're closed," she said disappointedly. "And I was looking forward to a nightcap."

"We should have called ahead for a reservation," he played along.

She turned to him and caressed his arm. "How'd you like to get to know the lady of the house?" she said enticingly, leaving no doubt what she had in mind.

He had to either rise to the occasion or tactfully decline. And given all he had to drink, too, it was a tough call. His spirit, and flesh, were more than willing. But was there a relationship between Mrs. Griffiths and the Colonel? It gave him pause. Putting Mrs. Griffiths to bed would have been the end to a perfect evening, for both of them, to be sure. Ozera considered that they'd just met that morning, and there would certainly be other opportunities. Settled, then: Not tonight.

"What time is breakfast?" he asked, distracting her and redirecting her attention.

She paused, then pouted. "Seven o'clock," she muttered dejectedly.

"I'll be there," he said, smiling and with a very unromantic lilt in his voice.

"Well," she replied, clearly disappointed but accepting of the situation, "Don't be surprised if you have to wait a little bit and get your own coffee. I hear the cook sometimes shows up late Saturday morning."

She leaned up and gave him an amorous – but not quite passionate – kiss on the lips. It surprised him but he enjoyed the intimate attention.

"It'll be nice to have a man around the house again," she confided, adding: "Thanks again." With that she turned and headed towards her apartment in the back, walking carefully.

"Can we do it again soon?" he called to her.

"We better," she replied over her shoulder, adding: "And remember, I know where you sleep."

Ozera chuckled and plodded up to his room. 'What a gal,' he thought to himself. He stripped down and, after evicting a number of excess frilly pillows, crawled into bed under a fluffy feather comforter. Soft, cozy and comfortable. Before nodding off he recounted the evening – a truly enjoyable and fun get-acquainted time together. He chuckled, realizing that he still didn't know Mrs. Griffiths' first name. Despite all the repartee and conviviality, she never offered it and he never asked. They were too busy enjoying each other.

* - * - *

VI: Morning after

The sunrise activated the birds, and the cacophony of twitters and tweets gently woke him. He lay quietly for a moment, looking around. A bordello perhaps? No. Then he recalled it was his new home in the B&B.

His first thoughts were of the Colonel and the new Monastery. It was all real. He threw back the covers and sat up, and a throbbing head made him recall the night before. That was real, too.

Just 7 am. Ozera decided a run around the farm in the cool morning air was just what he needed. He donned a gray sweat suit, sneakers and pulled a brush through his short brown hair. Going downstairs he heard the rattle of dishes coming from a room off to the side of the house.

He walked over and poked his head into a beautiful room with a wall of windows facing the east. A long table covered with white lace tablecloth had two table settings, opposite each other at one end. A sideboard featured a coffee carafe, pitchers of orange juice and milk, and all manner of breakfast cereals.

A door at the far end swung open and Mrs. Griffiths walked in, carrying a tray with coffee cups and glasses, clad in her traditional short dress and apron. She looked over and saw him in the doorway.

"Didn't you have a 7 am reservation, sir?" she asked in a serious maître d' tone.

"I got delayed in traffic," he countered, just as deadpan. She smiled. It was great. She was a heck of a gal. No mention of the night before, just her regular, sharp-witted, convivial self.

"How many eggs would you like?"

"How many you got?" he retorted. She laughed.

"Oh, hungry, huh?" she said, "How about four scrambled, bacon and French toast? Maybe a fruit cup, fresh rolls …"

"Now you're talking. Sounds wonderful," he replied, "How about in 20 minutes? I'm going to go for a run around your place first." He nodded at the two place settings. "Just you and I for breakfast?" he asked.

"Oh, no. These are for you and the Doctor, but she won't be down for another hour or so. I ate a while ago, **after** I baked the rolls, and fed and cleaned the horses."

"Mrs. Griffiths, you are an amazing woman."

"You don't know the half of it," she replied with a wink. "Go, do your run. I'll be all ready for you by the time you get back." They looked at each other and smiled at her double entendre.

It was cloudy and cold – above freezing but not by much – and Ozera could see his breath in the morning air. He picked up a gravel path in front of the big house and took it around back. It felt good to get out and get some exercise – stretch muscles, breathe deeply, get the heart pumping.

The path wound through the fields, past a small waterfall and after a while circled back towards the farmhouse. He estimated he'd gone about half a mile and decided to break off and go cross-country for a while. He finally headed back to the farmhouse, sneakers sopping wet, arriving near the kitchen and breakfast sunroom. He stopped near the house, hands on knees, panting heavily and wondering how to get in from the back. He glanced up and saw her.

Behind a large window in the suite over the kitchen stood the Doctor, clad in a white bathrobe, parted enticingly. She was holding and casually petting a black cat. She looked down at him and their eyes met. He stood up, still panting, his heavy breathing heaving misty trails into the cold morning air. She smiled cordially, then turned and walked away from the window. It was the second time their paths crossed, and the second time she caught Ozera off guard – this time sweating and panting, out in the cold, in a beat-up old gray sweat suit. He grimaced at the situation and the dubious impression he no doubt left on her.

He walked across the patio, past the hot tub, and back around to the front door, then right into the breakfast sunroom.

"Right on time," Mrs. Griffiths said to him, "Sit down and have some coffee and juice. Breakfast will be right out. How'd it go?"

"Dee-lightful," he told her. "You've got a gorgeous property. Made two laps around the whole farm to cover about a mile and a half, I guess."

"Any wildlife to speak of?" she asked.

"Naw, most of the critters probably heard or smelled me coming," he said with a grin. "Only thing to cross my path was a black cat."

"A black cat, huh? Way out back somewhere, I hope. I've never allowed cats inside here. I'm allergic to the little hairballs ... plus I could really do without the bad luck."

Ozera smiled and decided to drop it. No sense getting his attractive neighbor in hot water with the landlady.

Mrs. Griffiths ducked back into the kitchen and re-emerged in seconds with a big tray and several dishes, placing in front of him a substantial plate of eggs and bacon, another with French toast, a fruit cup and a basket of rolls.

"I see what they told me about your breakfast is true," Ozera said, picking up a fork and digging in. She smiled and walked out. When she returned a little while later he was already nearly finished.

"Wow," she said. "Good appetite. How about we try my Eggs Benedict tomorrow?"

"How about Monday morning?" he posed, putting his fork down for a moment. "I was thinking of going to see my parents later today and probably won't get back til sometime tomorrow."

"Okay. My other guest pretty much keeps to herself. She eats like a bird, and I love to cook."

"I'll keep you in practice, don't worry," Ozera promised.

"Well, I like to eat, too, but I've got to watch my girlish figure," the ebullient landlady teased, not missing the opportunity to show off her attributes. Ozera thought it prudent to smile and leave the wisecracks alone. He went back to work finishing the fruit cup. She came over and began to pick up his dishes.

He looked up at her. "Can I leave a tip?" He was only half serious and she knew it.

"You can take me out to dinner again," she said. She was serious and he knew it.

"Next Friday night?" he asked, standing up.

"You've got a date, big guy," she told him, heading back to the kitchen with dishes in hand. "Have a good time, Brad," she added. "See you tomorrow night then."

* - * - *

VI: Home again, home again

It was the start of spring break and a full house at the Ozera household. Youngest son, Pat, had come up for the day from Lehigh, some thirty miles south. And daughter, Liz, had dropped in for a couple days, down from Boston College – in transit to some Florida party town on the beach.

It was a rare treat to have oldest son, Brad, home from the Army. His mom had told Liz and Pat that he'd recently returned from the Gulf and they wanted to hear all his war stories. Brad glossed over his many combat exploits – and his siblings knew not to push it. He focused instead on his new assignment and, as usual, gave few real details. He told them the small secluded government post was a research facility, looking into "the impact of mental processes on military operations." It had a smattering of truth, and sounded like something that a government research center might really be investigating. Liz and Pat glanced at each other, sharing the same blank expression.

They knew big brother Brad was a Special Forces officer and often involved in classified operations – and this sounded to them like just another one of them. But they saw by Brad's tenor and expression that this new job weighed heavily on him. There was something burdensome about the new job deeply affecting their brother – which he couldn't, or wouldn't share.

Even so, it was nice to have him home. The three siblings commiserated for hours, tastefully mixing their old experiences together with current events, bringing each other up to date. Pat was having mid-term difficulties, after moving into a fraternity that Brad knew was the university's party house. Liz was having boyfriend problems and planned to connect with girlfriends to share the long drive to Florida. Her latest fellow turned out to be gay, she confided, while barely holding back tears. Brad and Pat struggled to keep a straight face while they consoled their sister.

Their mom outdid herself with a sumptuous dinner, topped off by ice cream over hot cherry pie. After coffee Pat excused himself and headed back to school, promising to work harder and party less. Liz was on the phone for what seemed like a marathon session with her girlfriend.

"You seem worried, Bradley," his mom commented. "The war in the Gulf is over. The U.S. Army has won. And you are back home with us, safe and sound."

"Yes, Mom," Ozera replied, "That is good news and we should all be proud. But the country faces other challenges, too."

His mom looked at him, confused. "And you are involved in those other challenges, too?" she asked.

He thought a moment before answering. "Yes," he said, with a bothered look on his face.

His mother wisely changed the subject. "Have you heard from Kathy?" she asked.

"Not a word, Mom. I think you and Pop should try to forget her. It didn't work. It's over, and she's out of my life now – and yours." His father, sitting nearby on the couch, just listened and nodded.

"Mom and Pop, let me ask you both something," Ozera began. "There's a town in northern Romania, called … Vatra Dornei. Have either of you ever heard of it?"

"Vatra Dornei? Yes," she responded. His father perked up, squirming on the old soft sofa as if trying to get up. "Your father comes from a small village just north of Vatra Dornei. She called over to him: "What was the name of your village?"

"Iacobeni," the normally silent man replied.

"Yes, that's it. I came from Bistrita, a bigger town further south. Actually, your father and I met near Vatra Dornei, and we got married there, in the old cathedral. Where did you hear of it?"

"I remember you and Pop mentioning it before, and I met some Romanians recently who come from there," he told them.

"Are any of them young ladies?" she asked, re-directing the conversation. "You know, Bradley," she said, "In our church there are several young Romanian girls, some born here and some from the old country. Pretty women, who would love to meet a strong, good-looking young American man like you. I know you and Kathy are divorced now, and I mentioned my oldest son was a U.S. Army officer who also spoke Romanian. Maybe you would …"

"Mom," he interrupted, "I do meet girls, and some are even Romanian." She smiled lovingly at him – in a way only a loving mother can smile at a son – and let the subject drop … for now.

"Munte Manastirea," his father blurted out. Ozera and his mother both looked over at him, puzzled and surprised.

"What'd you say, Pop?" Brad asked.

"You were thinking about it, and you were going to ask me about *Munte Manastirea,* right?" Ozera slowly nodded, puzzled and stunned.

"You're reading my mind again, Pop," he said with a grin. "Actually I **was** thinking about it." He recalled how, growing up, his father would often tell him what he was thinking, and usually he was right. It was as if he really could read his mind. Ozera never could figure it out.

"You've heard of it then, Pop?"

"Not since I was a little boy. There were stories in my village about a monastery high up on a mountain. It was a place where they say angels stay, looking over us. And sometimes they would come down to guide us."

"Have you ever been there, Pop? Is there a monastery up there, on *Munte Manastirea*?"

"I have been all over those mountains," he said, "but I've never seen anything but goats and rocks."

"Then the stories are not true?" Ozera asked.

"There is an old saying in the village where I was born," the elder Ozera responded, in his native tongue: "*God gave us belief and prayer, and the power to know the truth.*"

Ozera sat emotionless, not knowing how to respond. "What does that mean, Pop?" he asked.

"It has always meant to me, where there is belief and prayer, there is truth."

"But how can you say something is there, when it's not?" Ozera asked him. "It doesn't matter how much you believe or how much you pray, right"

"We don't see air. We don't see God," the Ozera patriarch said. "Some things we aren't supposed to see, but that doesn't mean they aren't there."

There was conviction, and a certain logic, to his argument. The younger Ozera could only nod. He knew that his father did indeed believe, and often prayed. He did neither. But maybe one day he'd have to reconsider ...

He decided to change the subject, instead discussing current events on the farm. He volunteered to take care of things in the morning, so his parents could relax and clean up for church. It was also a way to avoid having to go to church.

－－*

It rained off and on the next morning. Mom announced at 8 am that breakfast was on the table – and everyone in the family knew not to keep her waiting. Ozera came in from the barn and cleaned up. During breakfast he told them he would finish the farm chores, then shower and leave before they came home from church. So they didn't need to hurry back on his account.

Liz joined him as they sent their parents off to church. Then brother and sister sat and, over coffee, talked privately a while. It had been a long time, and both had come a long ways in the interim. By noon Ozera was done, washed and packed up. After a long and enduring embrace he bid farewell to his sister and left. He couldn't get over how ironic it was that his own father would know of Monastery Mountain. Angels, his father had said. And what was that old saying about belief and prayer? Must have lost something in the translation, he thought with a smile.

The car followed the familiar roads through the Pennsylvania hills to the river, and then back down the Delaware to his new home at the B&B. Ozera thought about his new job and the week ahead. He had his work cut out for him. He'd meet and hold preliminary discussions with some of the key players on the team – including the mysterious, sultry, Doctor Lupescu. Maybe he'd even find out what that Nutty Professor Wainright's contraption was all about. And in his spare time, of course, he'd try to figure out what might, or should, go inside the Monastery II.

－－*

Chapter VII: Teamwork

VII: The Doctor is in

A quiet night at the B&B – the lady of the house was out. Ozera sat out back, enjoyed a beautiful sunset with a bourbon and branch water, and then retired to his suite. He stopped on the way up the staircase, wondering if his sultry neighbor was in. Not a sound from her end of the hallway. 'The Doctor is out, it seems,' he muttered to himself with a chuckle.

For his morning jog it had turned cold and rainy. A few spots out in the 'North Forty' – what Ozera termed the big field behind the B&B – were muddy and slippery and he nearly took a tumble a few times. He didn't mind the weather, though. He actually reveled in tackling the adversity that nature often threw his way, as if it were a personal challenge, something to overcome or at least contend with. His last few years in the field, from the jungle to the desert, gave him ample opportunity. Training and experience had taught him to ignore 'a little heat, a little rain, a little cold, a little pain.'

Two full laps around Mrs. Griffiths' property – almost two miles, he reckoned – left him soaking wet by the time he got to the back patio. But rather than duck in out of the rain he turned about facing the back yard, raised both arms in a victorious stance, and issued an invigorating – and totally unintelligible – yell. He wiped the dripping rain from his face and turned around. And as luck would have it, there, looking down on him through her large picture window, was the Doctor –dressed in a very businesslike, exquisitely form-fitting dark blue suit and daintily sipping from an ornate cup and saucer. Realizing how he probably looked to her, and not knowing what else to do, he issued a broad smile. She returned a polite, though slightly condescending look, which he interpreted as: 'What kind of idiot are you, standing there in the rain and yelling like a banshee?'

He went inside and checked his watch. Just 7 am. Early for the Doctor. He dashed up to clean and shower, bemoaning the fact that she seemed to always catch him off-guard in embarrassing or compromising situations. Maybe he could be better prepared for their next meeting. In fact, he was to start conducting in-depth personal interviews with the team members this week. And the only one now available at the facility was the Doctor. Maybe he could book her today – as his first official appointment and interview in his new office.

Ozera dressed a bit more respectably than usual – a clean white shirt, pullover sweater and blazer – and headed down to breakfast. He expected to see the mysterious Doctor at the dining room table, but there was just one fresh place setting – awaiting him.

"Good morning, Monsieur," Mrs. Griffiths said, emerging from the kitchen, clad in her typical short, low-cut dress and apron.

"Oh, nous parlons français aujourd'hui?" he responded, asking her if French was the language of the day.

He saw on her face that it was more French than she could absorb, and he made a note to stick to English with the flamboyant Mrs. Griffiths from now on.

"You look very dashing this morning, Brad," she remarked affectionately, changing the subject.

"Thanks," he replied with a smile, "Will I be dining alone this morning?"

"Well, I already ate," she responded, pouring his coffee and orange juice, "And the Doctor just asked for tea in her room; said she would eat at work." Then she added: "Y'know I don't mind delivering room service for certain guests." He looked up at her, a dreamy look was in her beautiful eyes. The meaning he heard was exactly what she intended.

"I will keep that in mind," he replied sincerely, wanting to sound open to the suggestion, yet non-committal.

Yet another wonderful breakfast – fruit cup, French toast, bacon. He'd have to ask Mrs. Griffiths to cut down the menu and portions, or else he'd have to increase his exercise regimen. But how to do that diplomatically, with her loving to cook … and him loving to eat? He decided it best for all concerned to just leave it alone for now.

The rain lightened but still dampened his robe as he walked from the parking lot to Control Central. He saw the Doctor's Jeep parked over by the Conference building, along with another car he hadn't seen before. He walked in promptly at 8:30. Lisa was on the phone; she was making an appointment for something or other. That done, she hung up.

"Good morning, Captain," cute Lisa said with a smile. "How was the weekend?"

"Very nice, thank you, Lisa," he said, adopting a somewhat more professional tone than when they met the previous week.

"Lisa, I'm going to be in my office getting organized today. So if anybody needs me …"

"Yes, sir," she injected, "I met with the Colonel early this morning. He briefed me on things."

'He briefed me on things,' she had said. What things, he wondered: About me, my role in this organization, whatever my job and title are, my access to his office? And 'sir?!' I got a 'sir'! Well, that was encouraging.

"Oh, and Lisa, a request," he posed, "Could you please see if the Doctor can come to my office this afternoon? I'll need her for an hour or so. Early this afternoon would be great."

She wrote it on a pad, at the end of a list of items. Must be her To-do list, he supposed.

"I'll take care of it, Captain," she said. "The Doctor was in with the Colonel earlier this morning." Satisfied, he left and walked back to his office, pulling his keys out from under his habit.

Ozera walked in and sat down in the comfortable chair at his desk. He slowly looked around. The Colonel was worried about bugs, he recalled, but did he know where they were? He unlocked the drawer and pulled out two personnel files: Doctor Lupescu's and James Bennington's. Yeah, Bennington was a PhD and some PhD's liked putting Dr. in front of their name. Personally, though, Ozera thought the title ought to be reserved for medical doctors – of which 'the Doctor' actually was one. What's more, the Colonel had advised against using 'Dr.' with Bennington. Presumably it was Bennington's choice to forego it.

He was reading Bennington's file, thumbing through some of his many published articles, when a knock, knock diverted his attention to the open doorway. Lisa stood with a cardboard box under one arm, a cup of coffee in the other hand. When he looked up she walked right in, placing the hot, black coffee right in front of him on his desk.

"I figured you'd need some supplies," she said, putting the box down. She reached in and, like a magician with a hat, produced all manner of standard office supplies. Paper, tablets, notepads, clips, pens, pencils, markers, stapler, staples – you name it. Ozera looked up at her approvingly.

"So what did the boss have for breakfast today?" he asked her, making small talk.

She didn't miss a beat: "Monday: two eggs over medium, crisp bacon and well-done rye toast," as if she were reading from a menu. "But Maria screwed up and gave him white toast." Ozera shook his head, pretending with her that it was an unforgivable disaster.

"I handle copying," she told him, very professionally, "and I'm pretty good on the computer, so I type in and print letters." She turned to leave, then turned back. "Oh, and the Doctor will be in to see you at 2 o'clock."

"Thanks, Lisa," he said, truly appreciative. She smiled coyly, turned and walked out. She was good, very good, and it's easy to see how the Colonel came to rely on her. He wondered if the boss knew of her extracurricular activities. Probably not, or it would not still be going on.

'Okay, so the Doctor will be in,' he muttered to himself. He put Bennington's file away, then busied himself stowing the office supplies. That settled, and with a hot black coffee in hand, he pulled out and reopened Dr. Daciana Lupescu's file.

Compared to Bennington's, the Doctor's file was anemic, maybe 12 pages total plus a handful of photos. He looked again at her 8x10 glossy. It was taken within the last few years, he guessed, but it was not posed or staged. It looked like she was being introduced to someone, perhaps at a conference, when the photo was snapped. Even so she exhibited a raw natural beauty – high cheekbones, sultry eyes, dazzling smile. And the picture, just head and shoulders, did not take into account the rest of the package.

'Maybe Lisa can get me a wallet-size,' he muttered to himself. He thumbed through the other pictures, including a full-length shot of her in an English horse-riding outfit. Wow, he thought. In another picture she was younger, maybe 25 or 26, and accepting a certificate. Likely graduation from medical school, Ozera surmised.

Her vital stats were sketchy and, as the Colonel noted, there was very little detail about her before about 1969. That's when she first applied to Bucharest Polytechnic. She listed her hometown as Botus, a small village in Suceava County in the Bukovina region of northern Romania. Father deceased, mother deceased. Two step-sisters, one deceased. No grade or high school listed and no transcript – just college entrance exams, which the analysis said placed her in in the top 1 percent. **Believed** born in 1952, which made her some years older than him. But the file noted that, oddly, they could verify nothing before 1968 – her birthplace, age, parents, school – nothing.

She attended the technical school in Bucharest on a full scholarship, earning her degree in physics with highest honors. But interestingly, rather than pursue graduate study in advanced physics, she applied for and was accepted at the Medical University of Vienna, one of the most prestigious medical schools in Europe, also on full scholarship. On her 1973 application she listed a different hometown, and a son, status: unknown. Curious, Ozera thought, but maybe declaring a missing son in Communist Romania was helpful in landing the scholarship.

Doctor of Medicine awarded 1979. There were few details on the record for the years following that. It was believed she returned to Romania, but no medical license for her could be found. References show she co-authored two papers on parapsychology in the early 1980s, but copies of the papers were not available – the publications were impounded by the Communists. An expired Romanian passport revealed she traveled through Russia, Hungary and Czechoslovakia – throughout the Soviet Bloc. Fluent in Romanian, reads and writes German, conversant in Russian and English. No record of marriage or any reference to children or relatives.

Another knock, knock on the doorjamb. Lisa again.

"Would you like some lunch? I'm headed for the cafeteria," she asked. He looked at his watch: after noon already, and he was starting to get hungry.

"I can't get away just now, Lisa. Any way you could get Maria to wrap up a burger for me?"

She nodded and left, and he returned to the Lupescu file.

There was another lapse in her record, five or six years from 1979 to 1986 – when her name showed up in Russian documents as being hired for the research site in northern Romania. So, Ozera mulled, the Russians brought her on board there in 1986, but then had to pull the plug in 1989 with the Romanians in revolt against their Communist occupiers. Barely three years.

Another knock on the door. The Colonel this time.

"All moved in? I heard you have a visitor coming shortly."

"Yes, sir," Ozera smiled, "I'm still going through her file." The Colonel looked around to see if anyone was in the area and then stepped in. He walked up and put an envelope on the desk in front of Ozera.

"For legitimate expenses," he said, "We avoid paperwork here and don't get into expense reports and all that. You're going to need this for expenses, including dinner tomorrow night."

"What's tomorrow night?" he asked, picking up the overstuffed envelope and peeking inside. It was a still-wrapped pack of $100 bills. Looked like a pack of 100, making it $10,000. Ozera tried not to look surprised, and slid the envelope into his center desk drawer.

"Bennington, James R., PhD," the Colonel said. "He's flying into Philly tonight. I'm meeting with him and the Doctor in the morning. You get him tomorrow night, and you get to take him out – not in the Special Forces sense, although I've considered that too," he smiled. Ozera chuckled. "Wine and dine him. See what you can get out of him."

"Will do," he assured the boss. "Is he staying around here?"

"Oh, heavens no," the Colonel said, in a feigned effeminate manner. "I offered him Mrs. Griffiths' place before, but he wouldn't hear of staying in some 'hunters' lodge.' He's partial to the Ritz-Carlton in downtown Philly. Says it's the only place in a hundred miles with a decent wine list." Ozera snickered. The Colonel smiled, then turned and walked out.

He'd just finished the Doctor's file when knock, knock, Lisa was back. He subtly slid the file in his desk as she meticulously placed his sandwich and a bottle of water in front of him. He thanked her profusely.

Ozera opened the foil wrapping to see a mega-cheeseburger, with all the trimmings, and a small note on top. "Bon appetit – Maria" with a smiley face. You don't get a come-on from the chef every day, he chortled to himself.

The burger was as good as it looked. He gobbled most of it in short order, gathered up the wrapping and leaned over looking for a trash can. Just then came another knock, knock at the door. With a mouthful of the last bite of the burger and leaning over behind his desk, he looked up.

The Doctor had arrived.

_ * _ * _

VII: Getting acquainted

It was uncanny, he thought to himself in an instant, how she could appear at the most inopportune moments. She was as he'd seen her at the B&B that morning – same blue, form-fitting outfit. Mid-thigh length. Gorgeous legs. Heels.

"Late lunch?" she asked, her voice conveying a hint of sarcasm. He checked his watch: 2 pm sharp.

"Mrs. Griffiths has me on a starvation diet," he said. It was the best he could come up with.

"That's not what I heard," she said, disarmingly. "May I come in?"

"By all means." Not finding a trash can he put the ball of burger wrapping on the corner of his desk and gestured to one of the armchairs in front of his desk.

She was cool, confident, and laid-back. He was a bundle of uncoordinated nerves and reactions. She noticed, although he tried clumsily to hide it. She looked him in the eyes and for a moment neither said a word. It was weird, like she was looking inside him somehow. He felt the urge to wipe his chin with his hand, and he did, some residual burger juice and ketchup, which he wiped on his robe. She smiled – a faint, wry, subtle smile.

He began: "I was hoping we could privately discuss a few things…" He was going to ask if it was okay to shut the door, but before he could finish the sentence she had already closed the door behind her. She was one step ahead of him – again. He tried to look elsewhere than at her feminine form as she strode in and sat down.

"I hope you're not going to ask me a lot of personal questions about my age and love life," she said with a smile.

"I wouldn't dream of it," he retorted. In fact, he would like nothing more, and probably would dream of it.

"Do you know who I am and what I am here for?" he asked bluntly.

"The Colonel briefed me this morning." That was it. No elaboration. It would have been very nice to know what the Colonel told her. She wasn't taking the bait. She was going to make him work for whatever he got out of her.

He thought a moment how best to proceed. "I am here for the course of this project, just like you, to help in any way I can. One of my tasks is to get to know our key people and help assess our progress." It was a pretty nebulous statement. She sat totally reactionless, which actually was a reaction – one of polite indifference.

"You are military … American military?" she asked. She had an accent, a slight guttural elocution, like someone who was raised in Romania, who then learned German, then Russian and, finally, English.

"Yes, I am an Army officer." She sat back in her chair, apparently satisfied that he was being candid. It seems the Colonel did not elaborate on his background.

"And you are here for security?" Again, did the Colonel tell her that, or was it just an insightful guess?

"Among other things," he replied. But hold on a minute, he thought to himself. Who was asking the questions here? He interjected one of his own, to reverse the flow: "How do you like it here in the States? You're a long way from home."

"It's very nice. Yes, quite different from home. Everyone has been delightful."

"And where exactly is your home?" he asked.

"Isn't it in your file?" she said, with more apparent sarcasm. He didn't want to admit to anything – the file, or the fact that intelligence couldn't verify anything about her youth, including where or when she was born. She leaned over and gave him a hard eyeball-to-eyeball look.

"Sir," she said, as if talking to a cop at a traffic stop, "I was born and raised a Romanian. Please have no misconception about that. Yes, I worked for the Russians on their research project in Romania for a few years – which is what makes me particularly useful to the Colonel on this project. I needed the job and the Russians paid well. And if you lived in that economy, under the Communists, you'd have worked for them, too, or anyone else who would pay you a decent salary. I am Romanian, and like all Romanians, we hate the Russian pigs." She sat back, crossed her arms and huffed, as if to say: 'There, I've said my piece.'

Ozera had hit a nerve, and got a little reaction from the otherwise cool and collected Doctor Lupescu.

"You are Romanian, too, no?" she asked him. "At least your name is. Do you speak any Romanian?" She was taking advantage of the lull and again taking the lead.

He hesitated a moment. "No. I was born and raised here in the U.S.," he tersely replied. And again, he was answering her questions, not asking them. He again countered: "I understand most of your colleagues agreed to work here for two years. You, too?"

"The Colonel could answer that," she shot back snippily. Then, apparently realizing how acerbic it sounded, she composed herself and adopted a more cooperative tone. "It has been a year already, and yes, all of the others agreed to two years. Some want to stay and work or attend school here in America; a few want to return home, if things settle down back there. But for the most part they are all reasonably content. And no, I am not part of the same deal."

"I met most of the people last week," he said, trying to be more conversational and less inquisitorial, "I stayed in the dorm and had breakfast there."

"Yes, I know," she answered matter-of-factly. Ozera felt she knew a lot more about what went on around there than either he, or the Colonel, did.

He, too, decided to adopt a more cooperative tone. "Doctor," he said cordially, "You must have supported the Colonel in building that replica of the Monastery up on the mountain." He already knew she did.

"Yes, I endorsed it," she replied. Good, she was being honest, or so it seemed. "In fact, the Colonel did a magnificent job getting it built in so short a time."

"I agree," he said. "But now he needs to finish – the inside. And he asked me to look into it."

"You?" she countered, almost laughing, "How would you know?" It was a candid question, but with a heavy overtone of indignation.

"I am a student of architecture," he answered. "But I am asking your help in this. Can we discuss this further, maybe work on it together?"

"You think **I** know how the inside of … this structure … should look?"

He merely shrugged and grinned, leaving it to her to interpret. Was he saying 'maybe,' or 'yes,' or 'I don't know,' or 'I just want to see you again'?

"Let me think about it," she said, standing up. "I'll let you know. Are we done for now?"

"I think so, yes, for now," he said, politely, adding: "Thank you for coming in."

She walked to the door and opened it, then turned around at the last minute.

"*Would you like to make love to me?*" she asked in Romanian. He looked up, understanding what she said, but totally flabbergasted by the question. She carefully watched his reaction.

"I, uh … uh ..." was all he could utter, momentarily startled and befuddled.

"Never mind," she replied in English, "I found out what I wanted." As she walked out she again uttered, in Romanian, "*You may still get your chance.*"

He was dumbstruck for a moment, then sat back and let out a long exhale. Well, they did meet and got acquainted. But he'd have to work on his interview techniques: She learned a whole lot more about him than he did about her.

_ * _ * _*

II: Dracula's lab

"An early meeting, that's all she said," Mrs. Griffiths told him at breakfast, when he again asked if the Doctor was in. "Are we becoming interested in our guest at the other end of the hall?" she asked suggestively.

"Just professional curiosity," he tersely replied between mouthfuls of her ham and cheese omelet. "We do work together, you know." On the way out he consoled his charming landlady: "I hear you've got a hot date Friday night." He knew he didn't have to remind her.

"Hot?!" she replied, an expression of wonder on her beautiful face. "That'd be wonderful! I'd settle for lukewarm, even tepid."

It was a bright sunny morning and warming nicely. As he pulled into the parking lot he spotted a sleek new silver BMW M5 in the parking lot, guessing that belonged to the flamboyant James Bennington, PhD. Over by the Conference Center he saw a familiar black pick-up truck. 'So the Mad Professor is in today, too,' Ozera muttered to himself, 'a full house.'

He parked and walked to the Control Center building. Lisa was at her desk. Some loud voices were coming from the Colonel's office. He looked at Lisa inquisitively, nodding to the closed office door.

"They've been at it for a while," she said demurely. "He's got the Doctor and Mr. Bennington in there. They're scheduled to go all morning." He nodded, as if sharing her annoyance at the ruckus.

"Could you stop by my office when you get a chance?" he asked. She nodded, as if happy to be taken away from her post.

She showed up a few minutes later with a hot black coffee and placed it, fastidiously as usual, squarely in front of him. She had a notepad and pencil with her and sat down.

"Three things," he said, imagining her adding them in order to her to-do list for today. "First, can you please make me dinner reservations at that restaurant down over the mountain, the Fern Valley Inn? Two of us at 7 would be perfect. Shouldn't be a problem on a Tuesday night. And second, please call the Ritz-Carlton Hotel in Philly. Tell them you are James Bennington's secretary in California, that you know he's staying there, and you need to find out what wine he's been drinking – because he's been raving about it and told you to get a case."

"And third?" she asked.

"Can you find me a trash can?"

She grinned. The first was a snap, and so was the third. But the second was something different, something sneaky, and something challenging. She welcomed it. "Anything else?" she said with a self-confidence that bordered on swagger.

"Well, yeah," he said. "If you find out the wine, see how we can get a few bottles by dinnertime." She nodded, got up and left. Ozera opened his desk and slipped five of the hundred-dollar bills out of the envelope. Then locked up and walked out.

"This should cover the wine." he said, handing her $200. "Get what you can for this. I'm going to see Professor Wainright in the Conference Center. Be back soon. "

As he walked out another row erupted from the Colonel's office. He recognized the Doctor's accent, but he hadn't heard this intensity of her raised voice before. Lisa winced.

- * - * -

"Professor?" Ozera called, walking into his lab.

"Over here," he heard from the back, "C'mon in, m'boy." He walked back and saw Jerry Wainright at his desk, a computer on his desk linked via a web of cables to the apparatus on the wall, across the room from his desk. There was one comfortable-looking armchair between his desk and the apparatus, facing the wall. Flood lights were hooked up, focusing on different parts of the giant pinball machine on the wall and on the empty chair.

"You by yourself, Captain?"

"Yes. The boss is tied up in a meeting and, uh, heavy discussions with our two project directors."

"Oh, the gorgeous Doctor Lupescu and the equally gorgeous James Bennington," he said with a deadpan expression. Ozera smiled, but was a little taken aback that he knew the two major team members well enough to accurately describe them. Then again, it followed that he would have been interacting with both of them. Ozera decided it wouldn't be wise to ask Wainright which one he reported to; that would have made it clear that he didn't know.

"Looks like something from Dracula's lab," Ozera said, nodding at the apparatus.

"Frankenstein. Actually it was his master, Dr. Frankenstein, who had the lab," Wainright corrected him, straight-faced. "Dracula never had a lab, just a castle and a coffin. And besides, we've got enough Romanians around here already." They both chuckled. Wainright was somewhat blustery, but he was sharp and had a good sense of humor. "Yeah, looks pretty awesome, huh? Ain't she beautiful?"

"What are all the wires for?" Ozera asked.

"They carry the signals from the ball counters on each bucket, right into the spreadsheet here," he said, pointing to his desktop computer. He got visibly enthusiastic that someone was actually taking an interest. "After the test I push a button and get an automatic analysis that tells me the deviation from the norm, left or right. Then I push another button and the computer releases the balls and fires up the vacuum that sucks 'em all back into the hopper on top."

"I'm impressed," Ozera said. He was patronizing him a little, to show a little management appreciation. But it's doubtful he noticed. "How long before we go live?" he asked.

"Well, m'boy," he said, "We are ready. You can be the first victim, er, subject."

"It hasn't been run before?" Ozera asked.

"I've run baseline tests all morning to normalize the software. And of course, another set-up just like this one has been running in my lab at Princeton for over a year. They are both built pretty much the same," he added. "Want to give it a shot?"

"Sure."

Wainright got up and moved his massive frame around the desk and gestured to the empty armchair. Ozera sat down. "Comfortable?" he asked. Ozera nodded. "Now, you must be relaxed, and mentally focused," he said, adding, tongue in cheek: "It doesn't hurt, unless thinking causes you pain."

"When I hit the button, balls will begin to fall, one a time, four per second. They'll hit the metal pins and bounce all over the place and end up in the buckets at the bottom," he said with all the rote of a flight attendant giving a safety briefing. "Your job is to guide the balls, mentally, to the **left**, that way," he said, pointing to the left. "Concentrate now and no talking. Try to stay focused on pushing the balls to the left side. The test takes about 10 minutes. All set?"

Ozera nodded. Wainright pushed the button and the balls started falling, and Ozera tried hard, focusing. But when the last ball fell, it looked like the buckets of balls at the bottom were pretty much distributed in a bell curve, which would seem to be the expected random result.

"Now don't worry about how you did," Wainright said. He pushed some keys and the balls all fell to the bottom compartment. He pushed a toggle switch and a strong vacuum started up, sucking the balls out and up into the top hopper. "It takes a little while to reset," he said.

When it was ready he pushed some more buttons, and then announced: "We are going to start the next run. This time focus all your thoughts on pushing the balls to the **right** as they fall." Ozera again nodded.

Again the test ran. And afterwards, the balls at the bottom again looked like a typical bell-curve distribution. Wainright pushed some buttons and the computer digested the data.

"Hmmm," Wainright murmured, examining the results.

"So how long do I have to live, Doc?" Ozera joked, getting up and walking over alongside Wainright.

"I may have to make some adjustments," he said, "possibly to the pin layout." He paused a moment, silently thinking, then asked: "Have you ever been examined for psychokinetic capability?"

Ozera shrugged and shook his head. "Why? What did you get?" he asked.

Wainright sat back. His chair squeaked under the strain.

"We show a .55 percent deviation to the left, and then a .35 percent shift to the right. The results are apparently legitimate, since they went left when you were mentally pushing them left, and then right. I ran the baseline test six times this morning. That gives us the "norm," against which we measure deviations. And the greater effect to the left is also normal. Those who can affect the balls' movement tend to do better to the left than the right. Might be the way our brains are wired. Who knows?"

"So what's the problem?" Ozera asked.

"Well, if everything is working as it's supposed to, then your results are the highest of the hundreds of subjects I've tested so far. In fact, they're hard to believe. I'll check the wiring, the counters, the software, even the pin placement. Okay if I give you another shot in a few days?"

"We'll see," Ozera said. "Oh, and something to consider," he added: "I bet most subjects try real hard the first time, pushing to the left, and the ol' noodle may just get tired after that. That may explain why the left results are greater than the right. Why not try the reverse order a few times and see if that makes a difference?" The affable Jerry Wainright sat motionless and expressionless for a moment, thinking about it. It made sense.

Ozera smiled and turned to walk out, almost running into old Alexandru, who was quietly sweeping the floor.

"Buna dimineata, căpitan," he said with a nod, standing up respectfully.

"Buna dimineata, Alexandru," Ozera automatically responded. Oops. Then he remembered: Do not let them know you speak Romanian. He bemoaned his own slip-up, and reworded in English: "Good morning, Alexandru."

* ₋ * ₋ *

VII: James Bennington, PhD

"They're still at it?" Ozera leaned over and quietly asked Lisa, nodding at the Colonel's door.

"Yes, but it'll be breaking up soon – almost lunchtime," she said. "Oh, and I found the wine you wanted. That hotel says to get a good Pinot Noir from the French Burgundy region called Cotes de Nuit, 1987 if possible. I checked and there's two choices matching that in the state store." She handed him the note. "Tell me which to get and I'll pick it up at lunchtime."

"Hmmm," he looked at it. Like reading Greek, he thought. Domaine Dujac Gevrey Chambertin, 1987, $55 a bottle, or Domaine Faiveley Les Cazetiers, 1988, $50 a bottle. "Well, my dear, let's get one of each." She smiled and nodded.

The door to the Colonel's office cracked opened a few inches. They heard a man inside with raised voice hollering: "How can we make any progress, Colonel, if the woman won't share what she knows or how she knows it?!"

The door opened and the Doctor walked out, clutching papers and folders in her arms, stopping at Lisa's desk. She looked like she'd been through a verbal harangue, but wore a smug half-smile that looked to Ozera like she emerged the victor. The door quietly closed behind her.

"What a horse's ass!" she huffed under her breath, apparently unconcerned that Lisa and Ozera heard her. She stood still a moment – oblivious to everybody and everything – while she regained her composure. A moment was all it took. Then she looked over at Ozera, as if he had just walked into the room. "Good day, Captain," she said, with a polite, ever-so-slight nod of her pretty head. She walked around him and exited, as if nothing had happened.

Ozera had seen enough high-level conferences and heated exchanges to figure what did happen. The Colonel pitted one against the other and let them slug it out. And based on whose arguments held the most water, he called a winner – in this case the Doctor. But he'd also consoled the loser, assuring him that this was just one round in what would likely be a protracted fight.

The door reopened and out stepped the Colonel, followed by James Bennington, PhD – in all his glory. He looked like the posed picture in his file: handsome, in a rugged, quarterback sort of way; about as tall as Ozera and with a similar athletic build; clean-shaven, dimpled chin; wire-rim glasses. A briar pipe, exuding a noxious tobacco aroma, hung solidly in the corner of his mouth. The pipe-smoke smell was notable; there was a sickening sweetness about it – like someone trying to cover their body odor with a too-sweet deodorant.

Bennington's cardigan sweater seemed out of place among the monk's robes everyone else was wearing. Ozera was sure he was looking at a man who, twenty years ago, was certainly the Big Man on Campus – MIT, Stanford and whatever other expensive private schools he graced with his considerable presence. He looked very confident, in control, invincible.

Judging by his tirade just a few minutes earlier, though, Bennington had to be as worked up as the Doctor. But unlike the Doctor, he didn't show it a bit. Either he recovered quickly or the argument never really bothered him in the first place. Some people are like that, Ozera mulled. They just enjoy the thrill of contention.

"Captain Brad Ozera," the Colonel addressed him, "This is James Bennington, BS, MS, PhD, and a handful of other academic acronyms I don't remember. James, this is Captain Ozera, my second in command." The Colonel added: "I asked James if he would join you at dinner and perhaps share his perspective of where we're at." As they shook hands Ozera glanced over Bennington's shoulder at the Colonel and caught a very quick, very subtle, private wink.

The Colonel was taking Bennington to lunch, at some Bohemian place down along the Delaware River. And they would be back 'later.' He would love to be a fly on the wall at that.

"Where are you staying, Jim?" Ozera asked. He saw the Colonel painfully wince.

"It's **James**," Bennington corrected him. It wasn't a request. "And I'm staying at the Ritz-Carlton down in Philly."

"Sorry about that," Ozera atoned. He already knew where he was staying, but Ozera suggested he consider staying locally tonight, especially after dinner and drinks. Ozera assured he'd make all the arrangements. Bennington reluctantly acceded. They agreed to meet at the Fern Valley Inn at 7 pm, "just a left turn out of the gate and two miles down the mountain," Ozera told him.

Bennington and the Colonel left. He turned to Lisa, who already knew what was coming.

"Somewhere comfortable for the night near Fern Valley," she said with a smile. She was good, damned good. Ozera went to his office, closed the door and pulled out the Bennington file.

He was 42, lived in a 12-room Spanish-style rancher on 4 ½ acres in the hills of Palo Alto, just west of Route 101, just north of Silicon Valley. Estimated property value $3.6 million. Ozera's eyebrows rose. Where did this yahoo get $3.6 million? He read on.

"Hmmm," Ozera murmured. It turned out he came from money. Parents divorced. Father lives in their former beachfront vacation home in Martha's Vineyard, Mass. Mother returned to her ancestral home in Charleston, South Carolina.

But he owes more than $3 million, on an assortment of mortgages and other loans and debts, including a $300,000 investment he made in a winery in Sonoma that went bust in 1989, according to his financial report. This is somebody who needs a regular infusion of big bucks, Ozera concluded.

Married. Wife, Yvonne, age 41. BA, MA from Boston College, Phi Beta Kappa. Two daughters, 17 and 19 – both with multiple-arrest records: drugs, DUI, indecent exposure, disturbing the peace. No convictions. Family picture showed a real nice-looking family. But apparently with a lot of skeletons in the closet, Ozera smirked.

His professional record was dazzling – that is, the record that was public. He was a pioneer in his field, having authored a dozen papers in leading physics and reputable parapsychology journals. Impressively, all were authored by just James Bennington, PhD, nobody else. No co-authors. All were based on his original research – research he thought up himself, conducted and produced solid, apparently reproducible results.

One in particular caught Ozera's eye: a paper he did while at USC in 1979, a first-of-its-kind study into whether someone knows if someone else is looking at them. Conclusion: Definitely. Of two dozen students tested, every one of them could guess more correctly than not whether someone out of sight was looking at them. Why didn't this make the news, Ozera wondered? It was incredibly lucid and legible, and seemed to prove beyond a doubt that some form of ESP exists – that most people did in fact know when someone was surreptitiously looking at them.

His other papers were equally impressive – including one looking at whether psychokinetic effects could be aggregated by multiple individuals focusing in concert. The results in that case, however: Inconclusive, although there were very interesting results. Bennington truly was at the leading edge of ESP and psychokinesis. But his last published paper was in 1983, eight years ago. Then they stopped.

His résumé, compiled by some government background-checking agency, showed nine different job assignments since then. They showed that he worked under contracts for the CIA, DIA, DoD, and a couple other agencies he didn't even recognize. The dates overlapped; Bennington was handling two or three projects at a time – and double-or triple-dipping. There were no details on any of the projects, just a 'Classification: Secret: Contact agency' note on most of them.

But two were different: A job he worked on in 1988/89 was noted just 'NTK basis,' which Ozera recognized as 'Need to Know.' There was no indication of the classified status, the nature of the work or even the agency that contracted it. The real kicker was the last listing: Starting three months ago he began work on another project also listed as 'NTK basis.' It was their project, there in the Pennsylvania mountains. So not even Bennington's résumé would help him find out who he and the Colonel worked for.

Maybe he could weasel it out of him at dinner.

Lisa stopped in, a bag with wine bottles in hand and change. She told him she found a couple nearby spots where Bennington could spend the night.

"What's the closest to the Fern Valley Inn?"

"The Fern Valley Inn," she said with a smile, "It turns out they rent some rooms on the second floor. They don't advertise it, but it's a requirement for their 'hotel' liquor license. $65 a night."

"Perfect," he told her, "Please book a room for Bennington for tonight. She nodded and left. Ozera closed up and left to change at the B&B, then head out to the Fern Valley Inn.

* _ * _ *

He decided on jacket and tie – looked more professional. Then he headed downstairs with time to kill. Mrs. Griffiths was behind the counter, a drink in hand already.

"My, my. Dressing for cocktail hour, are we?" she teased.

"I'll join you for a quick one, my delectable Mrs. Griffiths," he teased, "but then I'll have to leave you."

She feigned pouting while mixing his Manhattan. He explained he had a date at the Fern Valley Inn.

"Tuesday night? That's unholy," she chastised him. "So who is she?"

"**He** is a pompous Californian who looks like Popeye – big dimpled chin, pipe and all, and who, in the medical parlance of the Doctor, is a horse's ass. Someone you should be glad is not staying here. He's not nearly as congenial as you." She smiled seductively. "It's a business dinner meeting."

She chuckled and they enjoyed their drink. He got up, kissed her cheek, and turned to leave.

"I've got a surprise for you Friday night, Bucko," she told him.

"Oh, really?" he looked back. "I shall be at your disposal, M'Lady," he said with a knavish, Errol Flynn bow.

The sun was setting as he drove out the long driveway and down the mountain. Arriving at the Inn down in the valley, the parking lot was almost empty. No sign of Bennington's BMW yet. It was just 6:30. He grabbed the bag of wine and went in.

They were still setting up for dinner. Ozera asked if he could see the owner, and in a few minutes he showed up, introducing himself as Charlie Howe, an affable, balding, 50-something man – who had owned and run the Inn for 15 years, and his parents for 50 years before that. Ozera explained that he was a happy customer, that he worked nearby, and tonight had a very important private business meeting. He asked if they could serve a couple bottles of special wine he brought for the occasion, that he needed a quiet dining accommodation, and that his 'client' would be spending the night in one of their rooms.

"Oh, so you're the one," the innkeeper noted. He told him Tuesday was usually a very quiet night, but that he did have a private upstairs dining room available if they really wanted privacy. And since Mr. Bennington was spending the night anyhow, it might even be more convenient. Ozera asked to see it.

He took him through the bar and up a narrow flight of stairs. Right at the top was a room with two window panels on either side of a paneled glass door. Café curtains on the inside could be pulled shut and block the view into the room.

They went in and flicked on the light switch. It looked like something out of a bordello – a comfortable, softly colored room with a table set impeccably for six, including silver candlesticks. An ornate, cushioned bench along the wall provided two of the seats; four comfortable armchairs provided the rest. The wallpaper was vertical lines of alternating dark velvet and red silk bands. There was a 1930's-style settee at the end of the room. The wall sconces had electric light bulbs that flickered like candles. It was cozy and kind of romantic – but too romantic for dinner with Bennington.

"How about tonight we dine downstairs. I think we can find a quiet alcove somewhere," Ozera suggested. "This little hideaway is charming and I will keep it in mind for future special occasions," he added. "In fact, is it available Friday night?"

"I think so. How many would it be?"

"Just two," Ozera replied. "Special night," he added, with a wink.

He liked Charlie Howe, a customer-oriented innkeeper, anxious to please and with a memory for details. They readily came to terms on Bennington's room and a modest corkage fee for the wine he brought. No charge for using the private dining room, provided it was available, but an extra $20 would go to the waitress for serving everything up and down the narrow stairs.

Back downstairs Ozera took a table in a far corner with a view of the entrance, and awaited the resplendent James Bennington, PhD.

* _ * _ *

VII: Another glass of wine

He didn't wait long. Bennington entered wearing a Bavarian
Herrenhut, replete with feather. His pipe was clenched
tightly in the corner of his mouth. A suede and woolen jacket
matched his hat. He just needed a walking stick and he'd look
like he just hiked down from the Tyrolean Alps. 'What a
peacock,' Ozera thought to himself. He didn't look silly, just
out of place. But more than likely he just likes to stand out in
a crowd.

Ozera greeted him cordially and they sat down. The waitress,
named Jo, one of two working the dining room, promptly
took drink orders: Johnny Walker Black, neat, for
Bennington, and a Manhattan, up, for him. Ozera could see
in Bennington's eyes and manner that he'd had a few drinks
already that afternoon with the Colonel.

"So where am I spending the night, Captain?" he asked.

"Right here. They've got some rooms upstairs. Did you bring
an overnight bag?"

"Never leave home without it," he said with a grin. He raised
his glass and put down the scotch in two gulps, then stood up.
"I'll go get it," he said and walked out, a little unevenly.
Ozera ordered another round for Bennington; he hadn't
touched his Manhattan. Not while he was still on the job, he
thought to himself.

Bennington returned, leaving his satchel by the steps, and sat
down.

They made small talk and looked at the menu. The waitress
recommended the Veal Française and they both ordered it.

"I'm afraid to ask for the wine list," Bennington said
disparagingly.

"Oh, you might be surprised. I keep a private stash here."

Bennington perked up. "Really?" he asked, incredulously.

"Sure. I'm partial to Pinot Noir myself." Bennington's eyebrows went up.   Ozera called the waitress and nonchalantly asked her to get one of his "special" bottles from Charlie and two glasses. Bennington waited anxiously, like a kid on Christmas morning. She returned with one of the bottles and adeptly uncorked it. Ozera deferred to Bennington for tasting and she poured him a sip. He fastidiously lifted it, sniffed, swirled and finally took a sip, which he then swished another minute or two before swallowing. The waitress and Ozera exchanged looks, tacitly conveying the same message: Geez, what an annoying showoff.

"Mmmm. I am impressed, Captain," he said. It was almost a … compliment. Must have been the more expensive of the two wine bottles, Ozera figured. The waitress poured them both a glass. Ozera took a sip and then slid his over by his untouched Manhattan.

For a while they talked about Bennington's favorite subject – Bennington. It was all pretty much consistent with what Ozera had read, with some not-unexpected embellishment. After a while Ozera decided to nudge him towards topics of more mutual interest. He should have been moderately high on the blood-alcohol scale by now, but he hardly showed it. He must have a high tolerance for booze, Ozera reasoned – no doubt the result of many years of intense training.

"I had my first formal meeting with the lovely Doctor Lupescu recently," Ozera said, changing the subject. "Have you known her long?" he asked.

"Actually, we have admired each other for years – from afar. I think she stole from my work for one of her papers – on aggregating individuals to achieve a cumulative psychokinetic effect." It was a mouthful, and not a syllable slipped. "She's a bitch," he snarled. Ah, that was more like it. Maybe the booze was finally doing its job.

"I saw your paper on that." Ozera injected. "Weren't the results 'inconclusive,' though?"

"Yeah," he replied. "But her paper – a year **after** mine by the way – concluded it could be done, though her paper didn't really elaborate. I'm surprised they published it," he added disparagingly.

"How'd you see her paper?" Ozera asked. "I thought the Commies impounded all copies of those journals."

"My last client got me a copy. They 'liberated' the galleys from the print shop in Novosibirsk," he snickered. It seemed Bennington was starting to feel no pain. The first bottle of wine was nearly gone, and they'd only finished appetizers and salad. Ozera hoped the other bottle – regrettably the last of his special stash – would make it through the rest of dinner. Ozera signaled the waitress. The place had almost emptied out and she was standing idly by. He picked up and pointed to the wine bottle and she understood.

"Yeah, I've been amazed how the Company can come up with this stuff," Ozera chimed in.

"The Company?!" Bennington retorted, "They couldn't find their collective ass with both hands. I'm talking about the ... you got any more of this wine?"

"Got an even better bottle coming. Another gorgeous Pinot Noir," Ozera assured him. "So anyhow, if it wasn't our Langley friends ..."

"The Brigade, of course," he replied without a moment's hesitation. "Those fuckers can get anything."

They both stopped talking for a moment when the waitress came with the other bottle of wine and more glasses. As before, she poured a taste for Bennington, who sampled it quickly this time and gave his approval. She filled Bennington's glass and left, returning in a few minutes with dinner.

Ozera leaned over and queried him quietly, "The Brigade?" He didn't want to sound uninformed or out of the loop, but he couldn't bullshit much further on this. He had to ask directly.

"Yeah, the team Nixon put together back in the 1970s," Bennington said matter-of-factly.

"Oh, they're still around?" Ozera said, as if he knew what he was talking about, trying to cajole him on.

"Shit, yeah. And bigger and badder than ever. They're, like, everywhere now."

"Wow," Ozera exclaimed, figuring it would get Bennington going. And it did.

"Smart, if you think about it," Bennington began. "They tag the best, brightest senior agents – in the FBI, CIA, DIA, DOD and a dozen other agencies – pull them aside and secretly sign them up in the Brigade. Super-compartmentalized: They don't even know which of their co-workers may be members. They only know their handler in the Brigade – it's usually the one who recruited him – who also directs and manages him."

"And they report to … "

Bennington shrugged. "Who knows? I guess the White House, like they were originally set up. What's smart is that they can tap the assets and resources of any of our intelligence agencies, just like that," he said, snapping his fingers, "without anyone ever knowing about them – no questions, no paperwork, no approvals from anybody. And they can get to the bottom of anything, immediately. I've seen it. They pull info from all the agencies, who don't talk to each other."

"No shit," Ozera uttered, listening intently. He was pretty sure Bennington was telling the truth as he believed it, and it scared him. An organization like this – with deep-cover agents inside every other intelligence agency –would have access to every file, every project, and every secret in the country. They could literally do whatever they wanted, go anywhere.

"So you worked for them before?" Ozera asked nonchalantly.

"Well, not directly. Nobody ever does. My last job with them – the contract, the money, the day-to-day supervision – came 'officially' from the CIA, I believe."

"And so your work, your research, your reports went back to the Company then, right?"

"Eventually, yeah, but not directly," Bennington replied. "The Brigade boys would review my reports when I finished, and sometimes they'd give me 'sanitized' versions to send back to Langley."

"But how do you know who they really are?" Ozera asked. "That they're on the up and up? That they're working for our side and not some foreign power?"

Bennington showed no concern for what Ozera was intimating. But he really didn't know the answer. "Remember, Nixon set this all up," he rationalized. "The president. Tricky Dick. Because he didn't trust anybody in or out of the government. Then when Nixon left office I guess it just … took on a life of its own."

"Who do we work for, on this project?" Ozera bluntly asked him. Bennington heard the question but sat emotionless for a moment, considering how to answer.

"You don't know?" he queried him. "Didn't you ask the Colonel?" Now it was Ozera's turn to carefully consider his answer.

"I don't know who we **really** are working for," he reiterated.

"Neither do I," Bennington tersely replied – a serious, but not totally trustworthy look on his face. Ozera wasn't so sure.

* - * - *

VII: An after-dinner conversation

The waitress picked up the dinner plates and asked about coffee and dessert. "Nothing now, maybe later," Ozera brushed her off. She walked back out of an otherwise empty dining room.

"James," Ozera said, "The papers **you** published, are **they** real? I mean are they the truth about what your research found?"

"The stuff **I** published? Oh, yeah, absolutely," came his quick reply. "You can take all my published papers to the bank. They were all done before I went to the dark side, nearly a decade ago, with my first classified, government-funded project. That's when my findings would occasionally be 'massaged.' But that was all classified and none of it was ever published."

Bennington reflected out loud, more than a little tipsy: "Back when I submitted my papers to journals, I had to go through endless peer reviews and editing cycles. It was exciting, to design your own research, find out things that no one ever knew before and be the first to publish the results." He paused, then added: "It was clean. It was pure research. Christ, I miss it."

Ozera didn't know what to say, or what else to ask him about the Brigade, or their manipulation of his government research work. If Bennington were military, he would be in very serious trouble for everything he just disclosed. Ozera couldn't be sure about the Brigade story. But he was pretty sure Bennington believed it.

Maybe he could still re-focus Bennington on their project at hand. Ozera held up his glass of wine and toasted with Bennington, who reiterated his approval of the second bottle, the vintage and the contents. Ozera tasted the wine himself, although his glass was from the first bottle. It was good –

medium body, very smooth, light berry flavors. He'd have to try it again, on a more leisurely occasion next time.

He leaned over and queried the well-regarded parapsychologist: "James, is our project heading anywhere?"

Bennington looked at him, apparently stunned and surprised at the question. He collected his composure to issue a response:

"Yours is among the first examinations of the ability of the human mind to alter the dimension of time," he said, with remarkable and unexpected clarity. "That's my assessment of where you are heading."

He elaborated: "You are free of the traditional shackles of academic research. You don't have to publish results. Hell, you don't even have to come up with results. You have unlimited money. You have but one objective: To determine if there is a tangible force we do not now understand, which could account for the movement in time of an entire structure, presumably with the people responsible inside."

Ozera saw that he could be eloquent in any environment, even after having a lot to drink. He was a free thinker, educated and articulate. And he had a rare talent: He could understand and then summarize a complex situation in a few words –like he just did.

"We are the first, really?" Ozera asked.

"Well, I spent the morning in your Colonel's office with Doctor Daciana Lupescu, who believes an earlier research project she worked on in Romania was on the cusp of unlocking the secret."

"Is that what all the hubbub this morning was about?" Ozera asked.

"No," Bennington replied. "The Doctor is pushing a holistic approach to the project. She thinks that the solution is multi-faceted and that, to achieve the effect, we need to address the Monastery physical structure, including a specific internal layout, the right people, the power of prayer – hell, everything, probably including alignment of the stars."

"And **you** believe?"

"It is the people, pure and simple," he asserted definitively. "We need to find a couple dozen people who test positive for the right attributes and we will be able to reproduce the effect."

"What attributes?" Ozera asked.

Bennington thought a moment, then replied: "I'm still working on that." His voice was toned down considerably – almost apologetic. It seems he hadn't yet hypothesized a credible answer to that particular question.

"We'll see what Wainright comes up with, after he fires up his gear and tests that gang of Romanians you have up there now."

"And which approach are we pursuing?" Ozera asked him, adding: "I'm sorry, but I haven't met with the Colonel today."

"Well, there's another Monastery here on top of your fucking mountain. So even you can see that the Doctor gets what she wants," he lamented, his voice rising. He sounded dejected. "And yes, we will be pursuing her holistic approach … for now … until I can come up with the answer." No denying it; Bennington was a cocky SOB. Not 'if I come up with the answer,' and not even a hint that he may end up being wrong.

The waitress came over, correctly sensing a lull in the conversation, and asked if they wanted anything else. Both ordered an after-dinner drink, even though Ozera still had a full cocktail and glass of wine. Bennington poured himself another glass of wine in the interim, finishing off the second bottle.

"James," Ozera asked, "Is this stuff for real – psychokinesis, ESP."

"Oh, fuck yeah. Definitely," he replied. "I've proven it. A dozen other researchers have proven it, and with reproducible results."

"Why hasn't it hit the news?" Ozera asked. "They've reported next to nothing about it."

"I think it's because the press expects some splashy breakthrough – someone bending a bar of steel with their mind, or predicting tomorrow's lottery, or levitating a truck in Times Square by just focusing on it." He continued: "Take Wainright. His research found, with absolute reproducibility, that some people can mentally push his balls to the left 0.06 percent more than chance. But the fucking press, they don't see the significance in it."

"What is it that gives some people this capability?" Ozera asked, "And why is it just certain people?"

"It is something within our brains," he said, pointing to his head of long wavy hair. "We think we know what part of the brain does it. But appreciate this: We're not even sure how the brain works yet. What we're all looking for is a force we have yet to nail down. We know this: It's not electromagnetic, and it's not chemical. And until we figure it out we can't say why some people have it and some don't. It could be we **all** have it, but just some are able to tap it, to express it, to demonstrate it."

Ozera nodded, listening intently. It was a long day, a good meal and – looking at his watch – nearly midnight. He flagged the waitress, who was anxiously waiting to drop off the check.

"James, one last question for now," he said. "How can something huge … a whole Monastery … be moved through time?"

"**That** is the million dollar question," he replied. "Look, Einstein hypothesized, and it's since been proven in spades, that time is another dimension, right alongside the physical dimensions – y'know, width, length, height. It's all tied together, in a fabric called space-time."

"Are you saying we can time travel?" Ozera asked with a skeptical tone.

"I don't believe we will ever go **back** in time," he replied. "Think about it: To change the height or width of anything you add an inch, or cut off a foot or whatever. These are positive values. Similarly, to move in time you can only deal with positive values. You can't put a negative value on time. You can slow time down, almost stop it – we know this from outer-space experiments – but there's no such thing as negative time, and that's what you'd need to go back in time." He paused. "And besides, did you ever ask yourself why we're not up to our ears in time travelers from the future?" Ozera laughed. Again, a clever, articulate explanation for the … unexplainable.

Bennington went on, and still with surprising eloquence: "It may be possible for this force of the mind – perhaps minds, with enough of the right people – to cause a temporal acceleration of the entire locale surrounding them, including a structure, to move it all forward in time. Now, try to understand this: It doesn't really go anywhere, though. It occupies the same location, with the same physical attributes." He saw Ozera straining, trying to understand.

"It's like this table," he told him. "You can make it shorter, longer, or wider. But what if you could change its time dimension, too? What would happen if we added an hour to its position in space-time? I think our drinks would probably fall to the floor," he said with a smile. "But then, in an hour,

our table would reappear." It made sense, and he put it in terms that Ozera could not only understand, but directly apply to the Monastery paradox.

It had been a long day for both of them, and they agreed it was time to pull the plug on their first meeting. Ozera gave Bennington the key to the upstairs room and bid him a good night and a safe trip home. He took care of the bill, including a generous $40 tip, and left. Only Bennington's BMW and Ozera's Ford Explorer were left in the customer parking lot.

Driving back up the mountain Ozera mentally collected his thoughts on Bennington. His motivation, his value to the team – on those points he scored high. But did he care, though, who he worked for? Did he care who paid his bills? Did truth matter to him? Those did not seem Bennington's strong suits.

In Ozera's assessment, Bennington would give them hard work and solid analysis, contributing his considerable technical prowess and innovative thinking. He might even come up with the answers they seek. But with all that, you could not expect loyalty, too.

* _ * _ *

VII: Back at the office

"The Doctor speaks with authority. I think she knows what she's talking about," the Colonel said. "Bennington, on the other hand, has theories, good theories, but doesn't offer much of a real plan for how to get there from here. I'm hoping Bennington can live with following her lead for now," the Colonel said, then added: "How'd it go last night?"

"He doesn't like it, or her, but I think he's accepted her lead, for now," Ozera summarized. "There's a lot of contention between them, but it seems that's what you expected." The Colonel gave a sly smile and a slight nod.

"As far as dedication to the project, I think they're both on board," he told the Colonel. "As far as which is more trustworthy, well, I wouldn't want to count on either one watching my butt out in the field."

The Colonel chuckled. "Captain, in a project like this you need to recruit experts in their field. And I haven't met one yet who didn't have his, or her, own agenda. All I can do is try to keep them headed in the same direction – which, for now anyhow, is the Doctor's direction."

Ozera nodded, then leaned over, "Sir, Bennington had more than a few drinks last night, and told me a bizarre story about some ultra-secret government group, whose members are senior mole agents in all the other, different intelligence agencies. He says they've been secretly calling the shots on a couple of his projects over the last few years." He stopped there. To borrow from the old artillery term he had fired for effect: Shot out a few rounds, to see how close they come to the target.

The Colonel sat back and heaved a sigh. "Our intelligence services are like overlapping fiefdoms. None wants to let the other within their castle walls, let alone into their keep. Yet they all support and work for the same king … supposedly. I've heard this story before. Whether it's true or not doesn't affect our mission or our work here. I'll run interference with headquarters. That's my job; you've got your own job to do." He let that sink in a moment.

Ozera did not get a straight answer, and he'd have to accept that, for now.

"Speaking of which, where are we at on figuring how to layout the inside of our Monastery?" the Colonel asked, changing the subject.

"I've got calls out to a couple reputable early-church archaeology authorities. And I'm poring through some books I ordered on the subject," Ozera reported. "I'm going to go through architecture libraries at Lehigh, U of Penn, and the Firestone Library down at Wainright's place at Princeton."

He added: "I'm working on trying to enlist the Doctor's help. She knows more about it than she's been saying."

"No shit," the Colonel interrupted. "Well, keep your eye on the ball. Thanks for your assessment of Bennington, and the Doctor. Solid stuff; confirms my own opinions. And keep me posted, Captain."

That was it. Dismissed. Five minutes to report his findings, observations and plans. But that didn't bother him – it was Army business as usual. What did bother him was the non-response about Bennington's disturbing story. It wasn't a denial, and it wasn't a confirmation. It was something in-between. But like the boss told him, he'd take care of dealing with higher headquarters … whoever that might be.

- * - * -

Spring had finally sprung and his morning runs have been brighter and, it seemed, the days were getting warmer. He brushed shoulders with the Doctor at breakfast: He was leaving; she was just coming in. They pleasantly exchanged smiles and greetings.

It was a quiet Friday morning of research in his office, then lunch with Lisa at the dining hall. Anton, the cook's assistant, walked by, with his arm in a sling.

Ozera leaned over. "What happened?" he asked Lisa.

"Oh. He was cleaning late last night and slipped on the wet floor," she replied.

"Sprained I guess?"

"No, broken, in two places," she said, matter-of-factly.

"Ouch. Who took him to the hospital?"

"No one. The Doctor took care of him. She was here til 2 in the morning."

"How did she know it was broken, and in two places, without an x-ray?" he asked.

Lisa shrugged. "I don't know. She figured it out. That's what doctors do, no?"

"I guess," Ozera replied, curious.

Maria's daily special: Stuffed Cabbage. Lisa took just half of one, incurring Maria's scorn, as usual. Ozera had two, they were delicious, and then went back for a third.

* _ * _ *

He wasn't back in the office 10 minutes when the phone rang. It was Wainright, quite upset.

"I just got in a little while ago, Captain, and found that somebody's been messing with my stuff over here," he growled.

"Calm down, Professor," he told him, "What happened?"

"Somebody launched a test and got the balls all screwed up. It'd be easier if you came and saw it yourself."

Ozera left and showed up in a few minutes, walking right into Wainright's lab.

"Okay, Professor. So what's the big …" Ozera stopped short.

Wainright stood behind his desk, arms folded, staring at the apparatus on the wall. Ozera looked over. Very odd: All the balls were on the left side of the grid, as if dropped in from the far left side instead of the middle. There were fewer and fewer balls towards the middle. The whole right side was empty, devoid of balls altogether.

"Somebody fucked with it," Wainright charged.

"I see that. How did all the balls get on the left side like that?" Ozera asked.

"I don't know. The apparatus can't be moved. It's all nailed and screwed to the wall," Wainright told him, as if thinking out loud. "I leave it all set to launch another test, with all the balls in the hopper at the top – ready to drop into the middle, as usual. Anybody could have set it off by hitting any key on the computer. But how all the balls got pushed way over to the left like that, I haven't a clue. Beats the shit out of me."

"Could someone have opened the top and dropped the balls into the left side?" Ozera asked.

"No, I checked, it can't be opened and it hasn't been touched."

"Could they have been blown over by the vacuum, maybe by reversing the air flow? Could someone have messed with the computer controls?"

"I don't see how," Wainright replied, plopping his considerable mass into his squeaky chair. "It would have been easy to set it off, which somebody obviously did. But they'd have to know the computer program to do anything else. And the control program wasn't running."

"Who else has been in here?" Ozera asked. "Have you done any tests on any of the subjects yet?"

"No. Besides you a few days ago it's just been me ... and the old cleaning guy," Wainright replied. "I wanted to run some final tests today. Then I was going to come over and see you about scheduling tests for next week."

"So what caused ... this?" he asked, pointing to the wall apparatus.

Wainright shrugged. "Fuck if I know. It's like someone dropped the balls, turned the whole wall sideways and then set it back up straight. I'll check everything over and let you know if anything turns up."

"Do you lock up the lab when you're not here?" Ozera asked.

"No," Wainright replied. "Mainly so the old guy can get in and clean up."

"Well, start locking up now. Old Alexandru can come in and clean while you're here."

Ozera walked out, baffled, and returned to Control Central. He stopped in to brief the Colonel and tried explaining what happened – to the extent he could. The Colonel asked him all the same questions that he asked Wainright. "Spooky," Ozera succinctly concluded.

The Colonel mulled it all over and glanced back with a blank, puzzled look, not saying a word.

"Wainright said he'd check everything over and let us know what he finds," Ozera said, then added: "And Wainright says he's ready to start testing our people next week."

"Good," the Colonel said, nodding. "Please coordinate it between Wainright and the Doctor. She'll get her people to do whatever you need. She's like the shop steward, in case you haven't noticed." Ozera nodded and got up to leave.

"Oh, and have a nice weekend, Brad," he added.

"Thanks, sir. You, too," he replied, walking out.

That reminded him. He went back to his office and called the Fern Valley Inn, confirming his reservation – and requesting the upstairs dining room. Mentioning his previous meeting with Charlie Howe helped. He asked, too, if drinks could be pre-delivered for 7 sharp. The girl on the phone told him to hold on while she checked … probably with Charlie. She came back and asked for his drink order, assuring him everything would be ready.

Ozera looked forward to a fun night out with Mrs. Griffith. Down at the entrance, as usual, he pulled off his monk's robe while waiting for the log gate to swing open. He started to pull out and then braked sharply as a big panel truck unexpectedly zoomed by, heading downhill – "Pocono Spas and Pools" written on the side. Oh yeah, that's right, he reminded himself, I did tell Mrs. Griffiths I'd help get her hot tub up and running.

* _ * _ *

VII: Firewater

"Honey, I'm home," Ozera playfully announced, closing the front door behind him.

"Just in time for Happy Hour," came the response, as Mrs. Griffiths emerged from the back with two martini glasses in hand – one a neat Manhattan, the other a Cosmo.

"You are the best thing I've seen all day," he said.

"You talking to me, or the Manhattan?" she asked.

"Both of you," he quipped. She was already dressed for the night out – little black dress that barely and snugly covered her curvaceous frame. Hair pulled up, with cute curls just framing her pretty face. Shiny red lipstick. Nylons, black heels. She struck a Marilyn Monroe pose, then came over and gave Ozera his drink and a short kiss on the lips. She was being exciting, and she was exciting him.

"Not bad, huh? You'd never guess I was shoveling horseshit two hours ago," she boldly announced.

"Dressed like that?" he asked rhetorically. They laughed. "I've got to go get dressed," he told her.

"Not on my account," she saucily replied.

"Is the Doctor in?" he asked.

"No, she left a while ago with a packed bag," Mrs. Griffiths cheerfully replied, "Said she'd be back Sunday. Looks like we'll have the night alone."

"I guess you answered the phone when they called for her last night."

"What do you mean," she asked, looking perplexed. "Nobody called here for her last night. In fact, nobody called last night, period."

"Then I wonder how she knew to go over when … " Now he looked perplexed. "Aw, never mind. It doesn't matter. So we got the whole place to ourselves. You better watch out, lady," he said, playfully wagging his finger at her. He looked at his watch, then took a slurp and put the drink down. "I'll be bock," Ozera said in his best Schwarzenegger accent, and headed upstairs.

He donned a clean white shirt, paisley tie, and his best suit – the dark blue one, which he recently had dry cleaned. His other suit, the gray pinstriped one, was too business-like and needed to be cleaned. He knocked the closet dust off his black dress loafers with a clean pair of underwear. In minutes he was bounding back downstairs.

They finished their drinks and he held out his arm, which she graciously accepted, and off they went.

"I've got a surprise for you later," she cooed as they meandered their way down the mountain.

"As long it's not that you're a female impersonator," he flashed a smile. They laughed.

They arrived right on time. It was a pleasant night and the place was packed. He dropped her at the door to go find a parking place, and rejoined her a few minutes later. He told the hostess he was Ozera and she looked him up and down, approvingly, and then her. "Please follow me, Mr. Ozera." She took them up the stairs. The door was open.

It was very cozy – all cleaned up, fresh tablecloth, table set for two, with two long white candles flickering. With the wall sconces there was just enough light. A vase held two red roses and some Baby's breath. And on either side, a fresh Cosmo and Manhattan, two menus and a wine list.

Mrs. Griffiths was beside herself. "Ooooh," she cooed, "How did you manage all this?"

"Nothing's too good for my landlady," he said confidently, with a wink. She leaned up, threw her hands up around his neck and gave him another – though deeper and more arousing – kiss on the mouth.

They savored their drinks while listening to the hubbub downstairs at the bar. The waitress showed up – the same woman who handled him and Bennington the other night. "Mr. Howe asked me to take care of you tonight," she said. "My name is Jo." They ordered appetizers, wine and entrees. Service was superb. So was dinner, the ambiance and each other's company. This could get to be a Friday night habit, Ozera thought to himself.

They finished the wine, then moved on to after-dinner drinks.

When they were getting too comfortable, she stood up. "C'mon," she said, pulling him up by the hand. "You've still got a surprise coming." They checked out – over-tipping the waitress for the countless trips she made up and down the stairs. They walked warily arm-in-arm to the parking lot, and drove slowly back up the mountain.

It was a fairly quiet trip back, both were talked and laughed out. They parked as close as possible to the front door, and he helped her down from the Explorer's high seat. He held her tightly as they walked up the walkway. It was not just for mutual support; he enjoyed holding her close.

"All right," she announced as they got inside. "Get a bottle of champagne out of the fridge and a couple glasses, and I'll meet you out back."

"Out **back**?" he asked. She said nothing, turned and walked away sexily towards the back door. He dutifully complied, though he thought they needed champagne like a beanbag needs more beans.

It was a delightfully comfortable night and the sky was crystal clear – no moon, but bright stars. The hot tub had been moved 20 feet from the house and was now out under the stars. He heard the pump humming. The water surface bubbled invitingly and steam wafted up into the cool evening air.

Four patio oil lanterns were flickering off the corners of the hot tub, shedding a comfortable yellow light. A picnic table had been conveniently moved next to the tub. And standing next to it, one hand on the hot tub and the other on her hip, was Mrs. Griffiths.

"What do you think?" she asked, with an adorable smile. Then he remembered the Pocono Spa truck he almost ran into on the way home. They must have been here getting things up and running.

"I'm impressed," was all he said.

"You ain't seen nothing yet. Come here, big boy," she said. It was a directive, not open to discussion. He walked up to her and put the champagne and glasses on the table.

She leaned up on her toes and gave him a light but sensual kiss, then turned around. "Undo me."

"Yes, ma'am," he replied. He was starting to enjoy her dominating demeanor.

He unzipped her black dress, right down to the small of her back. She shook and the dress fell off, down around her high heels. She wore a black lace bra, black panties, and stockings that clung by themselves to her perfectly shaped legs.

"Don't stop there," she ordered. He gulped, reached up and undid her bra. She pulled it off and let it fall. Then she turned around. Her large breasts heaved sensually, nipples hard, as her breathing became heavy. He was speechless, but he was pretty sure he knew where this was going. He felt himself responding.

"I need help with my stockings," she said, lifting one leg easily and putting her high-heeled leg on the table. He complied, starting just below her panties, and taking his time peeling her stocking down her leg. He undid her high heel, and dropped the shoe and stocking on the table. Then the other leg. Same thing.

She stood up. "Turn around," she directed. He did. She peeled off his jacket and threw it unceremoniously on the table. She reached around and undid his tie, then slowly unbuttoned and stripped off his shirt, her breasts rubbing enticingly against his back. "Shoes," she commanded,. He flipped off his loafers and pulled off his black dress socks.

"Turn around." And he did, bare from the waist up, exposing his broad shoulders, tidy patch of brown chest hair and narrow waist. She lifted his hands and applied them to her ample breasts. He massaged them, to their mutual delight. At the same time she reached forward and undid his pants, letting them fall.

"Oh," she said, "boxer shorts." He smiled in anticipation. "I like boxer shorts ... off." She knelt and gruffly tugged them down over the protruding obstruction.

"Uh, Mrs. Griffiths," he said, relishing her attentions. But there was no response; she was occupied.

After a while she stood up and shed her panties. Giving her a hand, she then stepped up and into the hot tub, settling down slowly into the hot water. "C'mon in," she said enticingly, "The water's fine." He did.

They both had a lot to drink over the course of the evening. But he seemed to be regaining his composure – and salacious interests. He still didn't know if she had been involved with the Colonel, but at this particular moment it did not matter. There was no stopping her ... or him.

They coupled – to the extent possible in the hot tub, and before long decided as a practical matter to relocate to a bed inside. They made it to Mrs. Griffiths' bedroom – the closest, inside the back door. She gained the upper hand initially, and then he reversed positions. And on it went. For both of them it had been a long time. And neither wanted the pleasure to end.

When Ozera awoke he was in his own bed, but he looked around and saw that it, too, had been the scene of their liscivious festivities. It smelled like sex, but it smelled good. It was mid-morning. He smelled bacon. Then he remembered the night before, and smiled.

He showered, dressed in jeans and sweatshirt, and then followed his nose to the dining room.

She saw him enter and went into the kitchen. He sat at his usual seat, all prepared for him, and sipped coffee. She came out with a big dish containing pancakes and scrambled eggs. She put it in front of him, emotionless, and he looked up at her.

"I am old enough to be your mother," she said.

"Well," he said, with an almost repentant face, "I guess you know what that makes me." He looked up with a broad smile. She broke into laughter, then leaned over and kissed his forehead.

"I didn't quite have all that in mind last night," she said apologetically, "Not **all** of it anyway."

"I think we both got what we ... needed," he said. His face adopted a more serious expression. "But you do have another boarder here, and we'll have to try to behave ourselves going forward." She looked down, accepting his polite admonition. He looked at her and wanted to share responsibility, and make her feel better.

"Of course, I have to ask my landlady if she's free for dinner next Friday night," he looked up with a smile. She smiled back at him, lovingly.

"And all I ask in return," he looked at her tenderly, "is some clean sheets."

* _ * _ *

Chapter VIII: Filling in the blanks
VIII: Before Christ, and after

Ozera got down to work. His job: figure how to complete the inside of their Pennsylvania Monastery. What would an ancient pagan religious shrine in northern Romania look like? And then how would it change after conversion to Christianity? It soon became clear it was going to be no simple task, if he could come up with anything at all.

He made some calls and arranged phone conferences with two different, prominent experts on early church architecture on separate afternoons. Neither offered much help, as it turned out. There were well-documented migrations of non-Christian to Christian church architectures in a few cases – like Jewish synagogues that were converted to churches, especially in the Mideast. But otherwise it depended, the experts both agreed, on the pagan religion, and adaptability of its holy sites to early Christian church design. Both noted, however, that there was very little historical, anthropological or archaeological record on pre-Christian religious sites in northern Romania or the former Dacia.

Ozera ordered in-depth books on the subject and, as they began arriving, read through them diligently. One of them shed light on the ancient spiritual beliefs of the Dacians, but offered little substantive detail about the layout of their religious structures. He read that the Dacians established hidden religious 'sanctuaries' in the mountains, but nowhere did anyone even speculate what the inside of these may have looked like.

Plan B: To visit and pore through architectural volumes at some of the leading nearby university libraries. He had Lisa call and make advance arrangements, billing him as a Department of Defense researcher who needed to investigate early religious structures, especially in Eastern Europe, for a U.S. Government project. All true, actually. He was welcome at Princeton University's renowned Firestone

Library and the equivalent Furness Library at the University of Pennsylvania in Philadelphia.

He arranged overnight trips to each. The Colonel's only request: check voicemail and check in from time to time for messages with Lisa.

The trip to Princeton was pleasant as spring was blossoming, but uneventful, and regrettably not very revealing from an ancient religious architectural perspective. He did locate a fascinating old volume that documented and speculated on the settlement of the Eastern European area later to be known as Dacia.

That part of the Carpathians and northern Romania, it is known, was already peopled before the last ice age – 10,000 years ago. Indeed, it was believed that the earliest people settled there as long as 35,000 years ago – and may have been the first Homo sapiens to encounter Neanderthals, mankind's predecessors. Some archeological digs in Romania indicate these people and the Neanderthals not only met but may have co-resided, and perhaps even interbred – if such inter-species mating were possible.

The archaeological record concluded that the area of Dacia had been settled by Indo-European-speaking peoples by 2500 B.C. – barely out of the Stone Age. Where these people came from was in dispute: A 'Kurgan hypothesis' maintained these people came from the steppe of what is now southern Russia. A competing theory disagrees, suggesting they migrated over the Balkan Mountains from Asia Minor.

Wherever they came from, the first written mention of Dacia was about 500 B.C. The ancient Greek historian, Herodotus, called the Dacians "the noblest, as well as the most just, of all the Thracian tribes." Decades later, Athenian general and historian Thucydides lauded the Dacians' exceptional horsemanship and archery capabilities.

But what about the Dacian people themselves, their religious beliefs and, especially, their temples? Ozera's next research stop, the University of Penn's Furness Library, filled in a few of the gaps. The next written records were by the Romans, who fought the Dacians for decades before finally claiming victory over them in the 1st century A.D. The Romans referred to some Dacian religious sites as "solar sanctuaries," and noted that the Dacians practiced special religious observances on remote mountaintops. The Romans presumed the Dacians worshipped a sun god, akin to the Roman's Apollo.

But the Romans were wrong. The Dacians were among the earliest monotheists, historians generally agree. Their religious belief, for countless centuries, was based on a single all-powerful God.

Solar sanctuaries? Ozera mulled it over to himself, poring through an old volume in the Philadelphia library. Maybe the Romans were referring to astronomical observatories, he pondered, like Stonehenge and others throughout the ancient world.

The more he learned about the ancient Dacians, the more intrigued Ozera became with them. They were known as fierce warriors, especially as horsemen and bowmen. But they did not believe in or practice slavery. This was thousands of years before contemporary civilizations ever considered outlawing it, Ozera mulled.

The Dacian belief in a single God paved the way for the arrival of Christianity. But it wasn't clear, from what Ozera turned up, how much the Dacians adopted Christianity, and how much Christianity borrowed from the Dacians. History records that the Roman emperor Galerius was born of a Dacian mother. And it was Galerius who, in 305 A.D., issued the decree ending the Roman persecution of Christians. This was shortly after the previous Emperor Aurelian withdrew all Roman forces from Dacia, ending 200 years of occupation.

A century later the first Christian monastic order was founded. Today, historians believe it was Dacian dogma and practices that served as the basis for The Rule of Saint Benedict, which established the structure and procedures for running Christian monasteries.

And the immortality of the soul, another fundamental belief of the Dacians, also seems to have been later conveniently adopted by the early Christian Church.

But Dacia and Christianity seem to have diverged in one key area: Dacian cultural belief embraced the equality of women in all practical and spiritual matters. The Christian Church, by contrast, banned women from leadership positions, advancement and, eventually, from the priesthood.

Ozera turned up another peculiar aspect of Dacian belief: they believed that we did not die, but rather, simply changed location. That had him scratching his head. Not heaven, not hell, nor purgatory. A different location?

The bottom line: Ozera could not find what a Dacian temple or religious shrine might have looked like, before or after conversion to Christianity. He returned with more questions than answers. And he knew the Colonel was waiting – so far patiently – for his report. When he last checked in, Lisa told him the Colonel wanted to schedule an update meeting.

"How about Friday afternoon?" he asked her. That would buy him a few more days.

"I'll ask," was all she said. "Keep in touch, Captain."

He still had one more resource to try – his alma mater, Lehigh University, an hour south in Bethlehem. He hoped that a couple of the architecture professors he studied under would take the time to meet with him … and maybe offer some insightful recommendations.

* _ * _ *

VIII: Doctor's prescription

A glorious, sunny spring morning: The birds were chirping and tweeting noisily, a sign that mating season had arrived in the Poconos. With his bedroom windows wide open Ozera slept soundly. In fact, having returned late the previous night, he overslept.

Glancing at his watch he awoke with a start, throwing back the blanket. In barely 10 minutes he had dashed into the shower, took care of business and emerged, his short brown hair still damp. After dressing he grabbed a book from his bed and headed down to breakfast. The book had just come in at the office and he began reading it late last night in bed, getting through just a few pages before nodding off.

He sat in his usual seat, back to the picture window, and Mrs. Griffiths brought him coffee and orange juice.

"Welcome back," she told him. "Missed you the last couple of days. Nice trip?"

"Actually no," he replied, with an uncharacteristic serious tone. No quipping, no wisecracks and no elaboration. He returned to the book, reading on ancient and pre-Christian religious practices around the world. Mrs. Griffiths noted his preoccupation.

"Okay, grumpus," she lightly teased him. "Your pancakes will be out shortly." He looked up at her and smiled.

"Thank you, my dear. Sorry. I need to get through some of this stuff," he said, nodding at the book. He returned to his reading, a chapter on ancient religious practices of central Europe, 1500 to 500 B.C. The Germanic tribes of 500 B.C. were barely out of their Stone Age hovels. They were belligerent, fighting mainly among themselves. But since they spoke more-or-less the same language they would unite on rare occasions to fight a threatening invader. They worshipped a common set of gods, although names varied from tribe to tribe. Not very advanced, Ozera thought, compared to the Dacians to the east. Religious observances were mainly tribal or family. Some religious sites from the period had been excavated …

"Any progress?" a feminine voice from behind him said. He looked up over his shoulder; it was the Doctor. Wearing a light floral spring dress, accentuating her lithe, curvaceous build, she walked around the table and sat down directly across from him. "A little late for you, isn't it?" she asked with a hint of sarcasm, spreading her napkin on her lap.

"I've been out of town. Got back late and slept in a little this morning," he honestly confessed. He and the Doctor had brushed shoulders a few times at the B&B and exchanged pleasantries. They even had an after-work cocktail together in the parlor last week, an ad hoc happy hour with Mrs. Griffiths. This morning, though, the Doctor seemed to be showing a bit more interest in him than usual. Ozera dog-eared the page he was reading and put the book aside.

The Doctor leaned over, as if talking to an old friend, and displaying enticing cleavage in the process. "I've been thinking about your dilemma," she said to him. "You've got a perfectly fine Monastery up on that mountain, but no idea what should go inside it."

"Do you?" Ozera asked her tersely and bluntly.

"I may," she replied, just as tersely and bluntly. "I was privy to certain information about the Monastery. Remember, the Russians were looking for all possible details on it, too, and they had a two year head start over you and your Colonel."

Her accent was … charming. She occasionally rolled her r's and used the wrong English word or plural or verb tense. She reminded him of a cartoon character from his youth – a Mata Hari-ish spy named Natasha, in an avant-garde cartoon series called Rocky and Bullwinkle. He was becoming enchanted with her, and he was aware of it. She probably was aware of it, too; she seemed very adept at discerning what was on his mind. But he had no idea whether or how to proceed, given their proximity at work. 'You don't crap where you eat,' was the wise, although crass, advice he'd gotten from his first commander in the Army.

"What are you proposing?" he asked, taking her bait.

"A … partnership," she replied, making sure she used the right word. "The Colonel is leery of me. I know it, though he doesn't think I know it. I want to help you complete your Monastery, because it is a key piece in solving the mystery about the one in Romania. If you succeed, I succeed." She paused, weighing her next words. "And you are the Colonel's right hand. He accepts what you say without question." He wondered how true that was, or whether she was just stroking him. He'd let it go for now.

But one thing he especially liked about her suggestion: If he could get the Colonel to buy into it – and he probably could – he'd be able to spend a lot more time with this woman.

"How do you know what should go inside the Monastery?" he asked.

"I'll tell you," she replied craftily, "if we can come to terms."

Mrs. Griffiths came out of the kitchen with his platter – fruit cup, and an impressive stack of pancakes with all the trimmings. She saw the proximity of her two guests at the breakfast table. But she was getting paid pretty well by their employer for housing and feeding them. So she said nothing, except to ask the Doctor what she'd like for breakfast. A fruit cup, some toast and a cup of tea was all. Mrs. Griffiths turned around, emotionless, and walked away.

"What terms?" he asked the sultry Doctor between gulps of pancakes. A bit of maple syrup dripped down his chin. The Doctor smiled.

"You can eat like that and think and talk at the same time? I'm impressed," she laughed and produced a captivating smile. She pointed to her chin, then to his.

He understood and wiped his chin, feigning embarrassment, and then smiled his most charming smile in return. It was a moment of friendship, of nearness – their first.

She leaned forward again – his eyes again unavoidably drawn to her cleavage. She adopted a more serious tone: "Alright. Here's my proposal: I will help define the interior of your Monastery. And you will agree to build it as I specify, without asking a lot of embarrassing questions about how I know. Then I want to be able to hold private meditation sessions, up there in the Monastery, with our people." She reiterated for emphasis: "Private."

"Anything else?" he asked, nonchalantly.

Mrs. Griffiths returned and dropped off her fruit cup, toast and tea. She saw that they were in the midst of discussion and, knowing when to butt out, again turned and returned to the kitchen.

"And know this," she told him, "If we work together, I will not mislead you, and I ask you to be straight with me. Just do not ask me how I know what I know." Funny she should bring that up, Ozera mulled. Whether she could be trusted was the main thought on his mind … as if she could read it.

"I'll need to check out a few things," he told her, "I'm sure you can understand." She nodded. "But let me propose this," he added, "If we come to terms, can you and I meet and can I get some answers from you this week, before Friday?"

"Let me know if we have a deal, and I'll let you know tomorrow," she told him.

"I'll get back to you as soon as I can," he said, and in one motion he gulped the rest of his coffee and stood up. He looked into her pretty eyes, and she looked into his. Neither said another word as he turned and left. I hope she's not reading my mind right now, Ozera thought, smiling to himself as he walked out.

* - * - *

Ozera was energized by the Doctor's proposal, but remained apprehensive about accepting her offer. To do so would effectively mean handing the Monastery's interior design and layout over to her – since he really could not, per her proposal, question whatever she came up with. Still, he didn't have a lot of choice, or any practical alternative to offer the Colonel.

He walked in and Lisa told him the Colonel scheduled their "update" meeting for Friday. He spent the morning on the phone setting up his visit to Lehigh – now his Plan B. There was certainly no harm in seeking advice and recommendations from his old professors.

He learned that a new faculty member had joined the department in the years since he left, a Professor Thibodeaux, who reportedly specialized, among other things, in ancient religious structures. Exploiting his status as an alumnus of the Architecture Department, Ozera called around and finally secured agreement from two of them – Thibodeaux and his old senior advisor, Professor Joe McFadden – to meet with him the following morning.

Ozera also called over to the Lehigh ROTC detachment – the military officer-training program that commissioned him in the Army. Don Kunkle took his call and was thrilled to hear from him. Kunkle was a captain and instructor when Ozera was a cadet in the program some six years earlier. He had left the university for a tour in Hawaii and then, following his promotion to major, was re-assigned back to the Lehigh detachment. He told him how the ROTC cadre heard that Ozera had returned to the states from the Gulf, but then lost track of him. All the usual methods of tracking him down and getting in touch with him failed.

Kunkle insisted that, as he was visiting on campus, he join him and some of the other cadre for lunch. And would he also consider, at some point after lunch, talking to the senior cadet class, who would be graduating and getting commissioned themselves in a few weeks? It'd be great if he, as a distinguished Lehigh military graduate, could share his unique perspective on the Gulf War. Ozera reluctantly agreed. He was planning to wear shirt and tie; now he'd have to spend an hour tonight preparing his uniform.

Knock, knock. He looked up. The Colonel. Uh-oh.

"Heard you were in," he said, "How's the research going? You've got me on pins and needles," he added with a wry smile.

"Glad you stopped over, sir. I'm still pulling everything together for our Friday powwow." Then he gestured for the Colonel to come in. The Colonel raised an eyebrow, sensing he had something sensitive to discuss privately. He pulled the door shut, walked in and sat down in the armchair in front of his desk.

"First," he said, "I'm going to speak with architecture professors at Lehigh tomorrow. Can I take a copy of the ink Monastery drawing with me?"

"Sure, just please don't leave it. I have a couple copies."

"Great. Second item: I am working on getting the support of the Doctor in moving ahead with our interior layout. I'd like to get her on board," he said, looking for a reaction.

The Colonel seemed almost surprised. "In my conversations with her, she's been pretty mum about it," he said. "But if she can help us get this properly finished on the inside, then by all means." That's what he wanted to hear. She would be taking part. Now he had the Colonel's blessing.

"She asked me for one thing, though, in our discussions," he said. The Colonel raised his eyebrows. "After we've finished it, she'd like to hold meetings there with the other Romanians, privately." Before the Colonel could comment he added: "Some kind of religious get-together, meditation of some sort. I don't see a down side to that, or see why she couldn't hold her group sessions up there privately."

The Colonel shrugged, "Fine. Doesn't matter to me. As long as we move ahead on this."

A half hour later Ozera was knocking on the Doctor's office door in the Conference Center building. She was standing at her window, looking out over the back field, her back to him.

"Come in, Captain," she said. She continued staring out the window. He wondered how she knew it was him.

"Okay, you've got it," he said, standing in the doorway. "Help us complete the inside, and you can have all the private meetings you want up there."

"And questions about how I know what I know?" she asked.

"I'll take care of that," he told her confidently, "If anybody asks you anything you don't want to talk about, tell them to see me."

"Even the Colonel?"

He paused a moment. "Even the Colonel," he replied confidently. "So, is that acceptable? Do we have a deal?" He sounded impatient, and she detected it.

"I will let you know," she replied enigmatically. "You are going on a trip," she said. Ozera chuckled. It was the way a fortune teller would broach it – an ambiguous statement, posed with confidence and just a ring of insightful knowing.

"Yes, tomorrow. But I'll be back tomorrow night. Can we get together on this soon?" he asked

"Patience," she said, "I'll get word to you tomorrow." That was it. Conversation ended. The ball was in her court, and she was holding it tightly. She continued gazing out the window and didn't turn around once to speak face-to-face.

"I'll wait to hear from you," he said, an undertone of frustration in his voice. With that he turned and left. The Doctor turned around, a look of smug gratification on her face.

* _ * _ *

VIII: Revisiting the past

Ozera tried to tell Mrs. Griffiths he had to leave early and wouldn't have time for breakfast, but she wouldn't hear of it. Breakfast at 7? No problem, she assured him. It'll be ready.

He abbreviated his morning jog to finish getting ready and get on the road. Promptly at 7 o'clock he went down to the dining room, clad in his black-striped Army Class A pants, poplin shirt and black tie. True to her word, Mrs. Griffiths dutifully had breakfast ready and laid out for him. She must have just made it: Scrambled eggs, sausage and toast – all still warm. But there was no Mrs. Griffiths in sight. Probably went to finish getting dressed and dolled up, Ozera figured. He sat down, ate and had coffee. Still no Mrs. Griffiths. He got up and left, going back up to his room to don his jacket and beret and get going.

Ozera came down the staircase, adjusting his Green Beret, and headed for the front door. Mrs. Griffiths appeared in the dining room doorway, wiping her hands on a towel. She saw him in uniform, coming down the steps, and stopped short, a stunned look on her face – slowly morphing into veneration. He stopped, too, hands at his sides, letting her take it all in. It occurred to him that she didn't even seem to believe that he was in the military.

"I'm a soldier," he said to her softly. She remained motionless, her expression unchanged. He looked awesome – and she was in awe, with his impressive physique, Green Beret and uniform bedecked with ribbons and appurtenances. "I am a captain in the Army, in Special Forces," he said straight-faced. He walked to the front door and then turned to her. He smiled and walked out – melting her heart.

* - * - *

"You're looking good, Brad, and fit," Joe McFadden, his old professor and senior advisor, told him. They poured a coffee and sat down in the department's conference lounge.

McFadden was a short, heavy man, whose hair was quite a bit grayer than Ozera remembered. "So what could I possibly tell a Green Beret Captain that could help out our country?" he asked with a touch of sarcasm. McFadden himself was a World War II Army veteran, and was all too aware that the military sometimes worked in mysterious ways.

"We need to know what the inside of an old, very old, religious structure in Eastern Europe probably looks like," Ozera told him. He had rehearsed exactly what he would say. "It's a structure in a place we can't get access to or into." McFadden raised his peppered eyebrows.

The door to the lounge opened and in walked a short, wiry man in his late 40's, maybe 50, with dark hair, carrying a huge mug of coffee. McFadden stood and made introductions: "Professor Ted Thibodaux, this is Captain Bradley Ozera, one of our department's distinguished alumni, class of '85." Thibodaux made clear he had about an hour before he had to leave and McFadden summarized the situation for him.

Ozera led them to a table, where he unrolled the drawing of the Monastery he brought. He walked through in general terms the key architectural features on the outside – a circular foundation of massive, roughly hewn stones, filled in with smaller stones and mortar. Then over the centuries, Greek and then Roman columns and arches were added, and finally, over top of the whole structure, a Christian basilica roof.

The two professors studied the drawing intently, and admiringly.

Anticipating their questions he explained where it was – high in the Carpathians of Northern Romania, near what is now the Ukraine border, presumably built by the Dacians. He detailed what little he could of its history: likely a religious shrine circa 2000 B.C., the same site continually embellished, and then finally made into a Monastery, likely in the 400 to 500 A.D. time frame.

"And there's no way you can get a man into this place? I mean, it **is** a Christian Monastery now, right?" Thibodaux asked.

"It is not … accessible to us," Ozera tersely replied, avoiding any elaboration.

"Hmmm," Thibodaux deliberated. "Would this structure happen to be on the south side of the mountain?" the old collegian asked, "With a clear view of the east and west skies?"

Ozera thought about it. He didn't recall any shadows in the drawings and pictures, so the sun probably was shining from the south. "I think so, yes," he replied.

"Then this might well have been where the locals constructed an ancient solar or astronomical observatory," he said. McFadden and Ozera both nodded. It jived with his research. The two academicians conferred. Such a monument – uncommon but not unheard of in the area – was consistent with their understanding of Dacian culture and religious practices. The ability to know and predict the solstices and seasons was not only key to farming – planting and harvests. Such structures also tended to become the spiritual center of the people, McFadden added.

"So what would you expect to find inside this … structure today?" Ozera asked them.

They looked at each other. McFadden deferred to Thibodaux.

"There's no way to know for sure without going inside, you understand," he said. Ozera nodded. "But there **may** be the remains – the core – of the ancient observatory inside there. Probably large immovable stones, in a circle or horseshoe shape, oriented towards the southeast – the rising sun. The focal center would have been embellished over the centuries, like with the addition of an altar – likely a large stone slab."

"The priest or shaman or spiritual leader would traditionally conduct rites on one side, facing the congregation." He added that the massive circular foundation stones on the outside might well have been the outer ring of the observatory. When was it first constructed? Thibodaux looked at McFadden, who just shrugged. "Second, maybe third millennium B.C. – could have been five thousand years ago," he conjectured.

"Why or when it was walled in and then covered over to become an enclosed structure is anybody's guess," Thibodaux continued, "That may have been around 700 B.C, with the arrival of the Macedonians, I'd guess."

"I don't think I can add much more with any degree of confidence, except maybe this: The outside circular stone arrangement means it long pre-dated Christianity, and those original stones were probably just too large to later move when subsequent civilizations, and finally Christianity, arrived. It also means that the monoliths were quarried locally – they were just too huge to move over any distance, or uphill. Clearly this site had great significance to the people. And given its long history, and what I know of the people of the region, it's likely the old ways, the pre-Christian spiritual rites and practices, are also still practiced there."

"There is a large stone cross over the entrance," Ozera noted.

"Wearing an Easter bonnet doesn't necessarily make it Easter, Captain," the professor added.

Thibodaux got up to leave. Ozera thanked him heartily. He and McFadden had another round of coffee, reminiscing about the old campus days and their respective times in the Army.

An interesting set of suppositions, Ozera thought, walking down the familiar front steps of the old ivy-covered Cooper Hall that housed the Architecture Department. He still had a half-hour before his lunch date with his ROTC associates – enough time to find a pay phone and check in at the office.

* - * - *

"The Colonel will be out tomorrow morning," Lisa told him, "But he's really looking forward to your meeting Friday. He'd like to shoot for 10 am." Ozera acknowledged, thinking about how little solid information he had so far to report.

"And the Doctor stopped in," she added.

"Oh? Any message?"

"Yes. Her message is: 'I would like to proceed, per our discussion. When can we meet?'"

"Super!" he exclaimed. Salvation! He contemplated when and where to meet. "Lisa, would you please see if the Doctor would join me for dinner tonight? And if she agrees, please book us for 6 pm at the Fern Valley Inn. And book us the upstairs private dining room, if it's available. Ask for Charlie Howe and tell him you're calling for me. I'll call you back later and see if we've got a date."

* - * - *

The lunch, it turned out, was a catered event for the whole Army ROTC cadre – a dozen or so officers, enlisted men, the administrative staff, and even a few senior cadets. Major Kunkle introduced Ozera to everybody, including the new detachment commander, Colonel Jeffrey Hammer.

Ozera figured that after lunch he'd be tapped for a brief talk about his experiences in the recent Gulf War. He had mentally prepared what he was going to say. But he was wrong. After eating, Major Kunkle, who was the adjutant, called "Attention to orders!" and all the military stood up.

"For conspicuous gallantry against the Republican Guard in Iraq on February 26 and 27, 1991," Kunkle read from a citation, "Then First Lieutenant Bradley Ozera led a motorized patrol that was instrumental in targeting and destroying an enemy armored Brigade, saving countless American lives, by calling and directing airstrikes, and then, despite fierce enemy fire that killed half his patrol members, led the rest to safety, and by direction of the President, is hereby awarded the Silver Star with Oak Leaf Cluster." Colonel Hammer pinned on the medal.

Hammer and Kunkle had arranged the whole thing. They had just one day, after he called yesterday, to put it all together. The ROTC detachment knew he was assigned to Special Forces after going on active duty, and that he was sent over to the Gulf last year. But they couldn't track him down after he returned. They learned he was administratively assigned to FORSCOM in Fort McPherson, Georgia, but everything else about his current assignment was classified.

They learned that his second Silver Star had been approved. So they offered, and received permission, to conduct an award presentation. Ozera thanked them both for all the hard work, logistics and follow up.

Ozera didn't know himself that he was officially assigned to the Forces Command. It was just an administrative designation, though, and had nothing to do with his actual classified job. He was nearly certain the ROTC cadre didn't know about the mountaintop facility – ironically just an hour north of the Lehigh campus.

No one asked about his combat experiences in Iraq. It would have been inappropriate. Several did, however, gently quiz him to find out where he was actually working. Ozera avoided any specifics, saying just that he traveled a lot. He found a quiet moment to ask that they excuse him for a few minutes so he could check 'back at the office' for messages. His compatriots insisted that they all go out for a drink after he returned.

"The Doctor is looking forward to dinner with you tonight at the Fern Valley Inn," she told him. He heard excitement in her voice. "She will meet you there at six."

"That's great!" he responded briskly. "Reservations? Did we get the private dining room?"

"Yes to both," she answered, "And I ordered flowers."

"Flowers?! This is a business meeting, Lisa," he admonished her, trying to make sure she didn't get the wrong idea and start spreading rumors. "Who said anything about flowers?"

"She did," Lisa told him. "She told me to order flowers and have them delivered to the restaurant," she said, adding: "She is an aggressive woman, Captain."

He smiled at her assessment of the Doctor's character – candid, and probably also accurate. "What does the card say?" he asked.

"To the future," she replied. Well, that's fairly innocuous, and pretty upbeat, he thought.

"Okay, Lisa. Thanks for taking care of everything, as usual. I'll see you in the morning."

For the next couple of hours, in a small off-campus pub called Rosie's, five US Army officers enjoyed each other's company, reminiscing and storytelling, each outdoing the other. It reminded Ozera of who he was, prior to his current bizarre assignment. The camaraderie was a welcome change from the civilian, surreal, monk-robed atmosphere of the mountaintop facility.

Ozera nursed two drinks. He had to drive. He had a dinner date with the mysterious, luscious – aggressive – Doctor.

* - * - *

VIII: Sealing the deal

Not too busy tonight, Ozera thought to himself, pulling into a parking spot right near the entrance. He got out, making sure beret and uniform were as they should be, and walked along the pathway to the front door, his shiny black shoes crunching on the gravel. The sun was setting and the twilight air was already getting cooler. He checked his watch and smiled – right on time.

He walked in, to the admiring look of the tall skinny hostess. Before she could say anything he pointed in the direction of the bar; she just nodded and stepped back out of his way.

Ozera scanned the bar looking for the Doctor, but no sign of her. Some middle-aged couples were enjoying drinks at tables; a few other customers sat at the bar. The handsome young Green Beret officer, in full regalia, had attracted a lot of attention – especially buoyant attention, given the recent Gulf War.

He walked up to the bar. One man leaned over and offered to buy him a drink. Ozera politely declined, spotting owner Charlie Howe behind the bar. Howe came over.

"What can I get you, Soldier …," then spotted his nametag, "Oh, Mr. Ozera. I didn't recognize you."

"It's **Captain**," interjected the man next to him at the bar, who offered him a drink.

Charlie tried to apologize: "Ooops. I didn't know what business you were in … Captain."

"No problem," Ozera said. "I have your room upstairs tonight?"

"Yes, you do," he replied, "In fact, flowers came for you. They're up there. And so is your … dinner companion. Joanne will be taking care of you again tonight."

Ozera thanked him and headed upstairs.

He stood outside a moment, mentally composing himself, then opened the door and walked in.

She was sitting at the end of the table, facing the door, casually sipping a glass of champagne. A fresh Manhattan marked his place next to her, facing the wall. A tasteful vase of bright spring flowers cheered the room. She looked to him as Ingrid Bergman must have looked to Bogie in Casablanca.

She put down her glass and eyed him slowly, top to bottom and back up again.

"Oh, my," she uttered reflexively. "You look very … military … tonight. Very impressive. And I mean that in a very complimentary way. I have not seen many American Army officers look quite so good in their formal attire."

"It's not formal," he countered, pulling off his beret and walking towards her. "I'm just getting back from a trip out of town." He sat down. "This is a work uniform, for travel and office work. We call it Class A."

"You wear it well, Captain," she said approvingly, lifting her champagne glass in a toast. He hoisted his Manhattan and they clinked glasses. "I like the crossed-arrows Special Forces branch insignia. Hmmm," she said, looking over his four rows of ribbons. Silver Star, Combat Infantryman Badge, Airborne wings, Ranger tab. I'm afraid I might have misjudged you. You're quite an … accomplished soldier."

He was stunned and bewildered. "How do you know so much about the U.S. Army uniform?"

She looked at him with a pleasant, appeasing smile. "I am a student of military uniforms, so to speak. Your American uniforms are attractive, especially your Marines."

"I can't disagree with that. Who has the best looking uniforms?" he asked.

She thought about it a moment. "The smartest and sexiest uniform I ever saw," she said, "was worn by an SS-Sturmbannführer."

He sputtered his drink. "A what? That's a Nazi officer, an SS major, like, 50 years ago, right? They were killers, murderers!"

She casually shrugged. "Aren't all soldiers?" That stopped him cold. She was right. He couldn't dispute that his own profession was, first and foremost, to kill – or cause the death of – whomever his country pointed at and told him was the enemy.

This was a truly unique woman, with unique perspectives. He admired her worldliness, her frankness, the fundamental honesty in her observations and her confidence. He'd never met anyone like her.

And he admired more than that. While her beautiful blue eyes captivated him, his eyes unconsciously dropped to her dress – a form-fitting little black dress, which drew attention to her impressive figure and cleavage. She noted his gaze and responded by sitting up pertly, accentuating her attributes. And she was achieving the desired effect.

"You know, Captain," she said, leaning forward, enticingly displaying her wares, "I look forward to an intimate and satisfying relationship with you."

Intimate? Satisfying? He was about to respond when a knock came on the door, followed by the waitress, Jo, with menus and wine list under her arm. She deftly recited the evening's specials. The Doctor ordered another champagne, he another Manhattan.

As the waitress turned and left, the Doctor stood up. Standing just a few feet in front of him she smoothed her little black dress – or so it seemed. What she did for Ozera was accentuate her figure, slowly, especially the breasts and hips. He gulped.

"I'll be right back," she said, grabbing her small black purse and sexily sauntering out.

Ozera heaved a heavy sigh. It was like intermission at an incredibly arousing stage show. It seemed to have gotten warmer in the small private room since he arrived; he unbuttoned his jacket. In a little while Jo returned with their drinks. He expected her to ask about appetizers or dinner order but she didn't. She just deposited the drinks, picked up the empties, gave him an unexpectedly randy smile, and left. Something was up, he sensed.

A few minutes later the Doctor walked back in. She dropped her purse on the table, gave him a sexy smile and a wink. Then she grabbed a chair and, in a casual almost practiced move, snugly slid it under the doorknob. She checked the café curtains, tugging them a bit to ensure no one could peek in. Watching this, Ozera sat up in curious anticipation. The Doctor turned and sauntered right up in front of him.

She shook her beautiful head of long chestnut hair, and again caressed her body. This time, though, she grasped her breasts and massaged them vigorously, moaning as she did. Her nipples grew hard and stabbed through the thin fabric of her dress. He thought he saw the outline of a bra before, when he first arrived. But not anymore.

She motioned him to stand up and he did. She pushed him hard against the wall, which surprised and yet excited him – and he was already visibly excited. Her hands roamed his chest and reached down between his legs.

"Is Captain Ozera happy to see me?" she asked rhetorically in her sexiest voice. She stepped back and pulled her dress neckline under her breasts, exposing the pendulous orbs. His hands found them. He leaned down and tenderly nibbled one nipple, then the other, as she threw her head back and moaned.

She knelt and slowly unzipped him. She reached in and unceremoniously grabbed his erect manhood, working to free it between his boxer shorts and pants.

"Beautiful," she murmured, kissing and then engulfing him. He moaned, glad he was leaning against the wall for support, and watching the action.

"Careful," he said softly, "That thing is loaded." She looked up at him and winked.

She got up and stepped backwards to the table, pulling her dress up in the process. Nylon stockings on her lovely legs, still wearing her sexy black high heels. No panties either, he noted approvingly, though he was pretty sure she had them on before, too. Must have stashed it all in that little black purse, he mused.

He dropped to his knees as she sidled up on the dinner table, mindful to slide their drinks out of the way. He voraciously returned her oral favors, her legs hanging precariously on his shoulders. She moaned incessantly, and after a while began to shudder. He stood up, keeping one of her legs on his shoulder; the other dangling freely over the end of the table. He penetrated her deeply in one thrust; they groaned concurrently in carnal desire.

She again began to shudder and pushed him back. He withdrew, wondering what she had in mind. She hopped off the table, turned around and pulled her dress up again, and leaned over the table, displaying her shapely posterior.

"Geez," he uttered, "It just gets better and better." He approached. The alignment was perfect and he entered her deeply. He withdrew and re-entered her, again and again. In a few minutes their excitement peaked and, both restraining their loud groans, he nearly collapsed on top of her.

"How long do we have?" he asked, still catching his breath.

"I had a … woman-to-woman talk … with our waitress," she replied, also still breathing heavily. "I asked her to give us … 15 minutes. Just a calculated guess."

"Boy, you're pretty sure of yourself," he said. They both laughed as he stood and zipped up. She stood up, re-covered her bosom and let her dress drop. They plopped down in their respective armchairs, lifted their respective drinks and tacitly toasted their quasi-public debauchery.

"They're going to charge me more for the room next time," he said, and they both erupted in laughter as a knock came at the door. He got up and moved the chair back, and the waitress slowly peeked in.

"Not a minute too soon," the Doctor said with a chuckle, waving her in.

* - * - *

They got down to dinner – he enjoyed prime rib and another Manhattan; she enjoyed a shrimp and scallop medley with Pinot Grigio.

Before long they had entered into a business-like conversation, seemingly oblivious to their earlier activities. Ozera explained that he needed her input desperately on the internal layout of the monastery. She agreed, but asked that they discuss it away from the mountaintop facility.

"Aw, you just want a good-looking Army Captain to take you out again," he said straight-faced.

She chuckled. "That, too. But the walls up there have ears … everywhere. You know it and I know it." He nodded.

They decided she would meet him for lunch tomorrow and they would go for a walk. She would get him what he needed – in time for his Friday meeting with the Colonel.

"So how **do** you know what goes inside the Monastery?" he asked.

She told him a story, about how she was frequently tapped by the Russian director of their research site to translate between local Romanians and the Russian staff. One day they called her in and sat her down with a man, about 50, who claimed he had spent his youth in a now missing Monastery not far from there. They wanted to know all about it: where the Monastery had gone, what it looked like inside, how he managed to get out, and so on.

She would ask him their questions, she said, but would give the Russians bogus answers that she made up. They never got the straight story, she explained, but she did. And among other incredible things, he described in detail the internal layout of the Monastery.

"That's amazing," he said, "You never told anyone this before?"

"No," she replied, adding: "It never happened. It's totally made up. But it's a believable story that you can tell your Colonel when he asks. And he will." He nodded, impressed that she had it all so well thought out in advance. He didn't relish the prospect of lying to his boss, or her assuming that he would so readily consider it. It was a lie, but it was a very credible cover story. And it would satisfy all concerned.

"So how do you **really** know …"

"You are not supposed to ask," she interrupted him, her beautiful face adopting a serious, scornful expression, "Remember?" He nodded. That was the deal. And they had sealed the deal.

She ordered dessert and he had a nightcap. He settled up; he left $200 on the $100 tab. Not a bad deal for Jo, the waitress, he thought to himself.

"You know my name is Daciana," she said to him. "If you like you may call me Dacey, privately. Mostly they refer to me as the Doctor."

"Yes, they do. And please call me Brad. But I think we should keep up appearances not just at the office, but at Mrs. Griffiths' too." She agreed.

They walked arm in arm through the almost empty parking lot. Her Jeep was at the far end. She gave him a sensuous kiss on the mouth. He reciprocated.

"I just can't resist a man in uniform," she said with a smile, climbing into her Jeep.

"And I didn't even have to take it off," he quipped. "See you back at the ranch."

* - * - *

VIII: Doctor's orders

Now they were lovers. Both, it seemed, were secretly hot for
the other – hot enough to satisfy their lust atop a public
restaurant table. It remained to be seen, though, if they could
work together. And who knows, at some point, maybe they'd
even learn to trust each other.

"Would you like to join me for a coffee, Captain?" Ozera
looked up from his desk. It was the Doctor. They'd had
breakfast together at the B&B just a little while ago, but were
notably silent in front of Mrs. Griffiths about their work – or
their sexual exploit the previous evening.

Ozera readily agreed, got up and followed her out,
announcing to Lisa that he'd be back in a little while. Their
robes were just enough protection against the cold. It had
become crisp and cool, just slightly above freezing. Low-
lying clouds engulfed the mountaintop in a foggy mist. The
Doctor led them out across the parking lot, and they walked
the road that went up through the woods to the top, and the
Monastery.

"There aren't many places where we can talk privately on this
mountaintop," she said as they walked side by side through
the eerie, swirling mist. "I know there are video cameras in
each of the buildings," she told him authoritatively, "and
many microphones."

"I really don't know where they all are," he responded, "The
security detail doesn't work for me. I'm just …"

"No matter," she cut him off sternly. "You and I need to
know where we can meet – to talk or whatever – and not be
seen or heard. We know there are no cameras or
microphones in the utility building, but going and coming
there can attract attention. We don't know about the
unoccupied office building."

"Neither do I," Ozera said, "How'd you know about the utility building?"

"I had one of our girls entertain one of the security soldiers in there a while ago," she said, "He wouldn't have joined in such an … extracurricular activity … if there were cameras or microphones."

Ozera just nodded. Was that the time he saw Lisa and the soldier meet there surreptitiously, shortly after he first arrived? Maybe. So the Doctor had set that all up? It was beginning to sound like she was describing a prison camp, in which she was the leader of the Romanian inmate contingent. Clearly there was more to what was going on around this place than he had thought.

"We need a place where we can meet and not be seen or heard," she said. "I do not believe the B&B is bugged. Do you know?"

"I'm pretty sure it's not," he told her, "It's private property, not government, and Mrs. Griffiths wouldn't stand for it."

"Have you had … relations with Mrs. Griffiths?" she asked bluntly. He stopped in his tracks, a bit startled.

"And if the Colonel asked about you and me," he replied sternly, "I wouldn't answer that either."

"Okay. That answers my question," she said, casting him a disappointing frown. Both tacitly knew it was best to change the subject. They continued walking up. They neared the top and just came into view of the Monastery. It looked eerie, appearing and then disappearing in the foggy mist, as if it really wasn't there.

"Where are we going with this?" Ozera rhetorically asked, nodding at the ominous structure before them.

"This isn't going anywhere," she replied. "But we can still help get the Colonel the answers he seeks." He wasn't sure what she meant. She produced a sheet of paper from under her robe and handed it to him.

He unfolded it. It was a simple diagram, showing a floor plan of stones. A circular shape at the middle was marked 'Communion Stone.' Around it, in a horseshoe curve, were five rectangular shapes labeled 'Guardians.' An outline of the Monastery showed the relative position of these within the structure.

"It is enough to get you started," she said. "Beneath these there needs to be a stone foundation that is laid directly atop the bedrock of the mountain. And all these stones must come from here, from this mountain."

He studied the diagram. "What is this, the axis line that runs right down the middle, right through the access tunnel and out the entrance gates?"

"That points to the rising sun on Midsummer day," she explained. So, he thought to himself, the access tunnel was a sighting mechanism: it aimed at the point where the sun would rise on the longest day of the year, and on that day the sun would beam directly into the heart of the stone circle.

"That means the whole building has to be oriented towards this point on, what, June 20th, 21st? What if it wasn't built …"

"It was," she replied with a tone of smug confidence, "I made sure of that when I reviewed the Colonel's plans. He built it that way, the way we agreed. And he didn't ask a lot of questions." Ozera did not catch her mild admonition.

"How big is this round one in the middle?" he asked, studying the diagram.

"The communion stone. It is, oh, four or five in diameter across," she said.

"Four or five feet?"

"No," she said, "Meters."

"Holy shit. These are some big stones. How are we going to get them in …"

"That is your problem, Captain," she said, turning and heading back down the path. He followed her. She looked over her shoulder and asked him: "Do you know how to ride a horse?"

"Yes," he replied, wondering what the connection was to the topic of discussion. "I was raised on a farm, not far from here actually …"

"Good, then I know where we can meet from now on. Do you have access to the Monastery?" she asked him.

"Well, I'm sure I can arrange …"

"Good," she interrupted him. "Then do it, and come to Mrs. Griffiths' stable Saturday morning at 8 o'clock." They had arrived back at the parking lot. She stopped, turned and gave him a beautiful smile. "See ya," she said, and then headed off to her office in the Conference Center.

* - * - *

VIII: Command briefing

He returned to his office and got to work. He had a report to
prepare and a day to do it. He pulled his pile of notes
together, the centerpiece being the Doctor's hand-drawn
diagram.

Ozera fed paper into the typewriter and started tapping away.
"Preliminary Recommendations for Interior Layout of
Monastery," he titled it. He was a passable two-finger typist,
but he was rusty. It was not his preferred method of
communicating – he preferred oral briefings. But this was a
classified communique from him to the Colonel; he could not
pass a pack of scrawled notes to Lisa for typing into the
computer, although that would certainly have produced a
more professional looking document.

There is little documented evidence of what the inside of such
an ancient structure should look like, Ozera noted in the
introduction. However, architects familiar with the people
and religious culture of the area at the time – circa 2000 to
1000 B.C. – conjecture that a solar or astronomical
observatory was originally built on the mountain site where
the Monastery in northern Romania later evolved.

Such an observatory would have consisted of immense stone
monoliths, painstakingly cut and transported into position
from nearby cliffs. The large rough-hewn stones that make
up the exterior wall – in the drawings we have – support this
conclusion. And if these huge stones remained integral to the
structure since the beginning, then, by extension, we can
reasonably conclude that the stones at the center of the
original megalithic arrangement would have remained as
well. That assumption underlies the internal layout proposed
here. Dr. Lupescu independently confirms from her own
sources that is what lies at the heart of the interior.

A key recommendation from Dr. Lupescu actually describes
the relative size, position and spacing of the stones inside the
Monastery structure. Again, this is wholly consistent with the

independent conjecture of experts. The stones were simply too large to later move, even though the religious beliefs of the culture continued to evolve. What's more, retaining the original stonework served to spiritually connect succeeding generations with their distant past.

The massive stone megaliths that make up the circular exterior foundation were not moved as time passed, but rather were filled in with Macedonian/Greek columns and stone walls, circa 500 to 400 B.C. A second tier of arches was subsequently erected atop the original wall, and at some point, circa 100 A.D., as Christianity permeated the area, the whole configuration was enclosed and subsequently rebranded as a Christian church and Monastery.

Recommendations: 1) To promptly further research and define the internal stone structure and layout described in the diagram, in terms of source of the stone, foundation and dimensions. 2) To expeditiously finalize the floor plan, specifying what needs to be done and in what order. 3) To develop a work plan and time frame for contractor work – masons, transport of the stones and modification of the existing structure, as required to implement the internal layout. 4) To execute the finalized, approved plan without delay.

He made clear throughout the report that he expected Dr. Lupescu, with her support, to play a key role. The interior design is based in large part on her input, reportedly based on intelligence she obtained during her time at the Russian research center. Her details, though, are consistent with the independent judgment of architectural professionals whose input and speculation were solicited.

Ozera then spent time redrawing and clarifying the Doctor's diagram. He ended up with a six-page report – tight, to the point and clear. He checked his watch: 8:30 pm. He was exhausted, but pleased, and locked the draft in his desk drawer.

When he got back to the B&B Mrs. Griffiths had a nightcap waiting for him. What a gal! They joked and talked up their regular Friday dinner the next night, but he still had work – and his conversation with Dacey – on his mind.

He casually asked Mrs. Griffiths about her horses, and she lovingly described them – George and Gracie, her aging gelding and mare – both just longing to be taken out for a ride. Trails snaked all through the mountain, she told him, and Gracie had just been re-shod. Both Western and English saddlery were in the tack room, she explained.

Ozera assured her, and she accepted, that he knew how to saddle, mount, ride and care for a horse. She suggested he give it a whirl that weekend, with an outstanding weather forecast. She added that, coincidentally, the Doctor had just recently talked with her about the same thing. He finished his drink and, tactfully fending off other suggestions by Mrs. Griffiths, went upstairs and turned in.

* - * - *

Ozera got in early and checked over his report, fixing and tweaking here and there. He put the final in an envelope, sealed it, marked it "Confidential: Eyes Only," and left it square on the Colonel's desk by 8 am. The Colonel hadn't shown up yet.

At 10 am sharp he knocked on the Colonel's open door. He was reading Ozera's report, looked up, pulled off his glasses and waved him in. Ozera closed the door and sat down, in the uncomfortable wooden chair opposite the Colonel.

"I like it," he said. "I like the way you think. And you got the Doctor to play ball. I'm not going to ask how you managed that," he said with a chuckle. Ozera smiled. "And you independently got corroboration, more or less, to verify she isn't just yanking our chain."

"You realize, sir, it's the best I could come up with," Ozera inserted. "There's no guarantee …"

"I know that, Captain," he assuaged him. "But you took an impossible assignment and turned it into a solid plan. My grand plan, you probably already figured, is to finish off our Monastery – that's what this is all about," he said, holding up the report. "And then we find the right people with the right … capability. That's what Bennington, Wainright and the Doctor are all working on." Ozera nodded.

"So you think it was originally some kind of Stonehenge, huh?" he asked, "Up there on that Carpathian mountain plateau."

"That's what everything and everybody are pointing to," Ozera replied.

"And the Doctor?" he asked. "I would not have expected her unqualified commitment to this. Her support with me so far has been … somewhat soft – steady but soft. What's your take?"

Ozera mulled it over. "I think she does sincerely share our goal: To learn and understand whatever force or power could be behind this … and, if possible, to recreate it."

"What does she get out of it?" the Colonel asked. They were all the right questions. Ozera would be asking all the same questions if he were sitting in the Colonel's chair. They were of a like mind, he and the Colonel.

"I'm not completely sure," he answered. "I've told her, with your approval, that she'll be able to use the place for meditation sessions with her people whenever she wants. That's important to her. I do not sense any deception. What are her long-term motives? It could be she wants this – us – to succeed, for her own fame and fortune down the road. That, and the ability to rub Bennington's nose in it."

The Colonel chuckled. "Yup, **that** would definitely drive our Doctor. How much did she learn about the Monastery from her time with the Russians over there?"

"More than she has told us so far," Ozera replied.

"Amen to that," the Colonel echoed in agreement. "Alright, Captain. Let's go ahead. How long before you can get me solid details of this layout, so I can muster the logistics?"

"Give me a week, two tops." Ozera confidently assured him. "A lot of fine-tuning from this point is going to be worked out with the Doctor. Oh, and I'll need to get into the Monastery."

"Help yourself," he told him, "It's a simple combination lock." The Colonel scratched a note and handed it to him. A simple combination: 11-22-33.

*　-　*　-　*

VIII: Gathering stones

He pulled on jeans, an old Lehigh U. sweatshirt and well-worn sneakers. It was a beautiful May morning, despite the residual grogginess of a mild hangover. Already warming outside, he opened his windows and relished the rich, morning spring air.

"Enjoyed our dinner last night, Brad," Mrs. Griffiths told him as he sat down at breakfast. He smiled.

"I did, too, as much as I remember. How'd we get home?" he asked, embarrassingly.

"I drove, you bum," she chided him. "And I wasn't in much better shape than you. When you had that last Manhattan I had a coffee; I figured I'd end up driving. You were out cold in the car by the time we left the parking lot."

"Yeah, it's all coming back to me now," he joked. "Where's your other shameless tenant?"

"She ate earlier. I believe she was going horseback riding." That reminded him. 8 am. He looked at his watch: Oh, shit: it was 8 o'clock.

"Got to run. I am sorry, Mrs. Griffiths," he said as he jumped up and dashed out. He grabbed a windbreaker he kept at the front door and ran out to the barn.

The Doctor was tightening an English saddle on her horse, the larger one. She was wearing a tight English-riding outfit, replete with the cap, vest, jacket and gloves.

"Good morning, Dacey," he said playfully, a lilt in his voice. "You're taking George?"

"I prefer to wrap my legs around a male," she said in a deadpan serious tone, then turned around and looked at him. "My, you didn't have to get so dressed up on my account.

You could have dressed more casually ... I think." He looked down. He did look like a slob.

"C'mon, c'mon, farm boy," she prodded him, "Gracie's afraid she's going to be left behind, aren't you, girl?" The smaller horse whinnied in her stall and nodded her head in agreement, as if on cue. Both were quarter horses – stocky and muscular, though typically docile beasts. George was bay colored, a reddish-brown coat with black mane and tail. Gracie was a sorrel, a copper-red coat, with a conspicuous white patch on her nose. Both were past their prime but healthy and strong, well cared for by Mrs. Griffith.

Ozera led Gracie out and fitted her with blanket and Western saddle in no time. He turned to see Dacey mount up – one swift smooth move and she was up and in the saddle. This was a woman with experience, Ozera thought to himself, in more ways than one.

"Don't forget the knapsack," she said to him, nodding to a black satchel by the barn door. He grabbed it, mounted his horse and followed her out the barn. They headed past the house and proceeded in single file along the winding driveway to the front. They didn't see Mrs. Griffiths watching through the dining room window as they passed by, a look of longing in her eyes.

They walked out to the main road and turned left, then right into the entranceway of the mountaintop facility.

"Good morning, boys," Ozera said to the post-mounted camera and microphone. "The Doctor and I will be scouting the mountainside." In a few seconds the log gateway whirred and swung open. It wasn't necessary, of course. The horses could easily have gone around or stepped over it. It just showed they were watching and listening, and that Ozera and the Doctor had been identified and granted access.

They arrived up at the parking lot and tied up the horses by the dorm building. They agreed to meet back at the cafeteria.

Ozera went to his office; he wanted a pad and pen, and his Geologic Survey map of the mountaintop.

In the cafeteria he went and poured himself a coffee. The smell of breakfast had him nearly salivating, but he would follow the Doctor's lead, and Mrs. Griffiths said she had already eaten breakfast. The dining area was bustling with breakfast activity. The Doctor was seated at a table, looking out of place in her English riding outfit. Lisa and Maria the cook stood before her, all conversing in Romanian. It looked like the Doctor was in control, not surprisingly. He couldn't quite make it out, and the conversation abruptly stopped when he neared them and sat down.

"We can talk more later," she said in English to Lisa and Maria. "I must tend to some other things now." She stood up and Lisa and Maria left. "I've got us some goodies for lunch," she said to Ozera with a smile, handing him the black knapsack. It was notably heavier. He gulped down the rest of his coffee and they left.

They mounted and headed out the back, around the helicopter landing pad and along the mountain ridge.

The weather was delightful, in the mid-50's now and still warming, sunny and dry. The trees were quickly greening and the otherwise impressive views from the mountaintop were now being obscured by budding leaves and blossoms. Ozera was studying his folded map as they rode, noting their location and progress.

"I hear water," she said. "The horses could use a drink. Come on." She veered to the right and cautiously walked the horse down into a draw. It was rocky but she found a deer trail and walked the horse along that. Ozera followed close behind.

She was right, a spring was gurgling out of the ground just down the slope. It flowed over and splashed across several rock faces, and collected in a little pool. She rode up to it and dismounted. He did likewise and walked Gracie up next to George. The horses politely took turns slaking their thirst.

"Hungry?" she asked him.

"Hell, yeah. I missed breakfast," he groaned, "This crazy gal I know wanted to go horseback riding at 8 am … on a Saturday. I'm pretty sure that's against the law in Pennsylvania."

"Oh, quit whining. You're worse than an old woman," she chided him playfully. "There's a sunny spot over there. Give me the backpack and tie the horses." He did, as he watched her, in tight pants and riding boots, step furtively through the brush and rocks to a small clearing.

She pulled a small blanket out of the knapsack and spread it out. Then she took off her hunt cap, undid her ponytail and shook her head, letting her chestnut hair swirl and fall. God, Ozera thought, what a doll!

He went over and sat down Indian style on the blanket. She sat down opposite him, reached in pulled out a bottle of French Beaujolais and handed it to him with a corkscrew. She produced two small water tumblers, then reached back in the knapsack and pulled out a small loaf of French bread and a dark sausage of some sort. She emptied the rest of the contents on the blanket: two knives, napkins and a small brick of cheese.

"I'm impressed," was all he said, popping open the wine bottle. She was slicing the bread and the sausage, and looked up, giving him an 'Oh, it was nothing' look. He poured some wine, then took a knife and sliced off some of the cheese.

He controlled himself from wolfing it down, as he was prone to do when hungry. She ate small bites, daintily, as if she was rationing their modest food stash to last for a few days. They exchanged some pleasant conversation and, when finished, he laid back on the blanket.

"It's still just a little cool," he noted. "But I'll bet this would be a great spot to come and relax in the middle of the summer." She got up, going to explore, she said, and walked downhill. He laid back down, still nursing a dull hangover from the night before, and closed his eyes. He would have nodded off, when she called to him.

"Do you know where we are on that map?"

He got up on his elbows and look at the map. "More or less," he called back.

"Well you'd better make sure," she said. "I just found our centerpiece, the Communion Stone."

He jumped up, excited, and quickly traipsed over to where she was, watching out for rocks as he stepped. She was standing further down by the running water. At this point the water flow had become a regular stream.

"Look," she said, pointing to a pool just downstream. The water, just an inch or two deep, was flowing over and covering a large flat rock. It was smooth, likely eroded by running water over the ages.

He stepped out onto it and knelt down, feeling around the edges, and moved around to determine its dimensions. It looked like the massive rock – 9 or 10 feet across and nearly round – might be able to be loosened and removed. He only had his Geology 101 experience to call on, but he guessed it was a sedimentary stone – sandstone, or perhaps shale. It had a reddish tint, which normally indicated the presence of iron.

Ozera got pretty wet, but after he finished his examination he nodded approvingly. Then he looked up overhead, assessing the tree cover.

"Yeah, we can get probably get this out," he muttered to himself. "Depends how thick and heavy it is."

They returned and packed up. The Doctor was pleased. Ozera carefully marked the location on his map and made notes about the stone's estimated size. They mounted up and headed back.

* _ * _ *

They'd found what would probably end up being the Communion Stone. Ozera wanted to ask why she picked that particular stone, but decided against it: She wouldn't want him asking, and he probably wouldn't understand the answer.

It turned out she was not so persnickety about the other stones, what she referred to as 'the Guardians.' Sauntering back she told Ozera that most of the stone for the initial construction was cut from an outcropping just down the mountain ridge from the Monastery, and Guardian stones of the right size could likely be cut from there too.

She would take him there, but he said he first wanted to stop and see inside the Monastery. They rode the horses back through the compound and across the parking lot, and headed up the road to the structure.

As they crested the top Ozera got his first good look around. It was the peak of the mountain ridge. The noon sun was high and it was comfortable, nearly 60. There was a thick old oak tree about 100 feet from the entrance and he headed there. There were not many trees on the mountain ridge and the still-leave-less oak stood alone, looking like it had single-handedly fought against wind and weather for the last century or so.

They tied the horses under the tree and walked to the entrance. Ozera readily undid the combination lock and struggled to pull the door open. He figured she would have liked to have seen the combination, and he would have given it to her if she asked. But she didn't.

"You've been in here before?" he asked, as he slowly swung one of the two massive wooden doors open.

"Yes, frequently, during construction, but the Colonel locked it up after it was finished, just before the winter."

"Well, welcome back," he said.

It was eerie, and dark. They walked into a passageway that was stone walls on the sides, up to about five feet, and then curved concrete arches over the stonework, creating a tunnel eight or nine feet high in the center. There was some light at the other end, about 25 feet ahead.

"I see there's light at the end of the tunnel," Ozera quipped, adding: "We should have brought a flashlight." They proceeded slowly. The floor was stone, flat stones set into a poured concrete base, like a wall-to-wall flagstone patio.

"Yes," the Doctor responded, "The central roof was made with about two dozen portals – holes in the roof, covered from rain or snow but allowing direct sunlight. At any given time through the day three of four sunbeams illuminate the central hall."

"That's pretty clever," he said, "I don't recall seeing portals in any of the drawings. Whose idea was that?"

"Mine," she replied. "I made several modifications to the initial blueprints."

They exited the tunnel and entered the main hall. It was a cavernous, circular chamber. About ten feet inside the outside wall was a circular colonnade of simplistic, round cement columns, about 12 feet high and 12 feet apart. Above them were crosspieces and above that, the roof infrastructure. Inside the circle of 35 or 40 columns shone several sunbeams, like spotlights on a center stage that, for now, was vacant.

"Who decided to put in this circle of columns?" Ozera asked.

"The engineers," she said. "Apparently the columns had to be there, internally, to support the structure as seen from the outside." Ozera nodded.

The roof at the peak was about 40 feet high. Ozera strained through the dim light to view the roof structure. He saw a large triangular portion that might possibly be removable. It was the only way that large round Communion Stone could be brought inside the center of the structure. Breaching a section of outside wall would threaten the stability of the whole structure. And it would not fit through the access tunnel. But removing a portion of the roof and dropping it in from a helicopter ….

The inside floor of the central hall was irregular, weathered stone – the native bedrock of the mountain. Laying a flat stone floor on top of it would be fairly straightforward, by comparison.

"Okay, I've seen enough," Ozera said. "I'll need to come back with some better light and take some measurements." The Doctor stayed close, but remained quiet. He looked at her pretty face, and she looked back at him. She seemed like she was a thousand miles away. He turned back to the tunnel and she followed.

They saddled up and sauntered down the ridge, arriving in a half mile at a large rock cropping on the south face of the mountain. It was clear that stone quarrying had been done here recently. The rock looked like granite, and excellent stone to cut and work, but also fairly heavy.

"What dimensions are the other five stones," he asked.

"I don't know your feet and inches all that well," she admitted, which was her first admission to him of any shortcoming. "The first two stones are the height of a tall warrior."

"Taller than me?" he asked, adopting a he-man pose.

"No, about your height." She explained that the next two stones were half-again as high, and the last stone was the tallest – double the height of the first two. So he asked her how deep and how wide. Only their height was different; all would be about 1 meter wide and maybe a half-meter deep.

He wondered again how she knew these details, how she seemed so sure. But the subject was verboten. He packed up the map and his notes in the knapsack and they headed back.

They moseyed back down to the B&B, arriving mid-afternoon. She quickly unsaddled and watered George, and then began brushing him down. Ozera took longer; it had been quite a while since he had ridden. The Doctor led George back into his stall. He finally finished and put Gracie away, and looked around – but no sign of the Doctor.

"Hey, soldier." He heard a voice and looked up. A ladder went up the side of the barn to the hay loft. And the Doctor had her pretty head sticking out, her chestnut locks released and hanging down. "Any of that wine left?" she asked.

"About half a bottle," he answered matter-of-factly.

"If you bring it up here I've got something to show you," she said in a pleasant, almost playful tone.

He grabbed the knapsack and scampered up, stepping off into the hayloft. She was standing akimbo, silhouetted against the large window behind her – wearing only her black leather riding boots. Ozera stood for a moment, in awe. He had never seen anything, anybody, so sexy.

"I hope you don't mind," she said, "I didn't shower."

He didn't.

*_*_*

VIII: Debriefing

Ozera finished his report and, early the next morning, positioned it prominently on the boss' desk. It wasn't long before he was called in.

"So, in a week you got the interior stonework all figured out," the Colonel said approvingly, "How many stones, sizes, even how to air-drop the stuff in through the roof. I'm impressed," he said with a broad smile.

"All of the pieces can be cut from the granite outcropping where you mined the stone for the initial construction – except one," Ozera summarized.

"Yeah, I see," the Colonel said, nodding at the report, "But you did find something for this centerpiece altar stone – the Communion Stone – right?"

"Yes, sir. It's in a stream bed just a half-mile out back from here. On the south side of the mountain."

"Why that one?" the Colonel asked.

"It's the Doctor's pick. It's round and almost perfectly flat, about 10 feet across," he replied. "It's sedimentary, with a reddish hue throughout."

"I see your weight estimations are based on it being no more than two feet thick. Do we know that?"

"No, sir. Not yet. But it's a reasonable estimation. This stone was deposited on this mountain by a glacier, probably the last glacier, 10,000 or so years ago. It's not from around here. But it looks impressive. It meets the Doctor's requirements and will be a good centerpiece of the interior. And if it's too thick in spots we can cut off any excess," Ozera told him confidently. "And like I detailed in my report, if we assume two feet thick we are looking at 157 cubic feet, or about 28,000 pounds, at 180 pounds per cubic foot."

"Do you know what the maximum payload of a Chinook helicopter is?" the Colonel asked.

"Well, the spec is 13 tons, 26,000 pounds," he said, "and we're asking for a ton more. But that's worst case, and we know the specs are a tad on the conservative side." The Colonel chuckled and nodded.

"And the other five upright stones?" he asked.

"They have to be cut and moved, but they're not as big or heavy. All are two feet deep by four feet wide. Two of them are six feet high; two are nine feet high. And the last one is 12 feet high. The biggest one should come in under nine tons – well within the Chinook's lift load capacity."

"I see your roof specification," the Colonel said, reading from the report. "We remove this section, roughly 10 by 20 feet. Pretty clear. All great work. I think we can figure it out."

"Well, I'll be here to direct …"

"Oh, no you won't," the Colonel interrupted him. "You are going on the road." Ozera perked up, confused. "I'm flying down to Maryland tomorrow to get the ball rolling on this. I'll need the Corps of Engineers, carpenters and some top-notch stone masons. And then some big choppers when we're ready. I'll lay that on the jarheads at Willow Grove."

"And where will I be, sir?" Ozera asked.

"Over the next two weeks, New York and Boston," he said. "And I heard from Gerhard yesterday – our gal in the U.K., remember? She's got some goodies for us, which you have to go retrieve. But first take care of the Big Apple and Boston. When you get back we'll look at your trip to London."

* - * - *

Chapter IX: On the road
IX: Father Del Bello

By the time he arrived at the office the next morning the Colonel had already come and gone. Lisa told him that he came in very early and a helicopter picked him up just after sunrise. Ozera settled in his office and pulled out the file of Father Angelo Del Bello.

Born in Naples, Italy in December 1943, the illegitimate son of a German soldier and an Italian girl of 15. Raised by mother and friends in a brothel and on the streets. Migrated to the U.S. at age 9 to stay with a distant relative in Jersey City, N.J. Altar boy. Some minor flaps with the law growing up, but typical for young guys in that area. Average grades in public school. So he was 48, Ozera looked again at his picture. He looked older, and gaunt. He did not look well.

Attended Montclair College in northern New Jersey, then transferred to Princeton Theological Seminary. Graduated with Master of Divinity in 1966. Average grades. Ordained in 1969. Served 10 years in various positions in the Archdiocese of Newark, N.J., then was approved for reassignment to the Vatican. Has worked in Vatican Archives and Records since 1982.

He never applied to become a naturalized American citizen. Never married. Never owned property. No known political affiliations besides the Catholic Church. Travels several times a year between U.S. and Italy on his Italian passport. Speaks fluent Italian and English. Medical status unknown. Photo enclosed from September 1987, when Del Bello accompanied Pope John-Paul II on his trip to the U.S.

Hmmm. Nothing in the file about his pedophilic orientation. Ozera wondered how the Colonel managed to keep it below the radar and out of the file. Either he was being shrewd and careful about concealing that aspect of Del Bello's life, or else he kept the arrangement to himself for years. That sounded much more plausible.

Ozera recalled his initial briefing about Del Bello. 'I don't trust him, and you shouldn't either,' the Colonel had said. He has an addiction that we are feeding.

It was a beautiful May morning; the sun shone brightly and it was already in the 50's. It would be time soon to switch to the lighter robe, Ozera thought. He'd just settled down with a coffee when he heard the chopper. He walked out front and around the side, sipping his coffee. By now it was a familiar routine: Lisa would go out to meet and greet him, the Colonel would jump off. The chopper would hover a moment and then zip off and out of sight.

The Colonel saw him standing out front and waved for him to come and join him. Ozera acknowledged and gave the boss a few minutes to get in and get settled.

He walked in as the Colonel was hanging up his jacket. "C'mon in, Brad. Grab a seat," he said, slipping on his robe and sitting down at the conference table. He held up a finger to his lips. In a moment Ozera found out why: Lisa walked right in and deposited a coffee in front of the boss. She turned and walked out, closing the door behind her. Efficient, quick … and seemingly able to read their minds.

"They love your reports, m'boy," the Colonel said enthusiastically, "Tight, unbiased, solid. And in this business – psi research – there hasn't been much solid and unbiased anything. I think some of them are jealous I've got you here." Ozera smiled, politely accepting his kudos. "Now, thanks to you, we have unqualified approval to proceed. I've got masons and a construction crew coming in next week. It's my top priority now. And from what you've said the Doctor can help oversee the work and position the stones inside." Ozera nodded.

"That's the good news," the Colonel took a deep breath and continued. "Now, there are things I expect these people to know; there are things I expect them to find out – and then there are things I don't want them to know." Ozera wasn't sure what he meant and returned a confused look. "I heard something that none of them should have known: One senior guy joked to me, in passing, about Wainright's balls hanging to the left. He thought it was pretty funny. I did not."

He spelled it out to Ozera: "It means somebody here is leaking – and we better find out who it is, Brad. Now I can exclude me and you. There's the Doctor, and her minions, and of course our favorite preppy, the self-absorbed James Bennington."

"I can grill the Doctor, sir," Ozera offered, "But I don't talk to Bennington much."

"Go ahead then and check her out – and you know what I mean. I'll make some not-so-subtle inquiries about who Bennington might be talking to. I have my own sources in low places; we're not the only ones with a snitch in their midst." Ozera nodded. "And when you've gotten back from Del Bello, we'll send you to check out our geneticist in Boston. Doctor what's-his-name knows a lot about us. He does have connections in our business, and he does know Wainright."

"Del Bello first though, right?" Ozera asked, casually producing a notepad and pen from under his robe.

"Go meet him," the Colonel said, "Get him his fix and retrieve whatever he's got for us. We can exclude him as the source of the leak, though. He knows we're government-affiliated but that's about it. He doesn't know anything about us, or this mountaintop, and he's never even heard of Professor Wainright. He's purely on a quid pro quo basis." The Colonel looked down at some papers on the table, avoiding Ozera's eyes. "Just make sure he has a good time, Brad," he added.

"When and where do I meet him?" Ozera asked.

"Get up to New York early next week. You may want to train up from Philadelphia, or Trenton; you won't need your car. Anyhow, check in at the Hotel Penta New York, right across from Penn Station, under the name Adam West. Lisa's taken care of reservations – for you and Del Bello. He'll call you there when he arrives. He wrote me a couple weeks back and gave me his arrival flight and date. He's getting into JFK next Wednesday, noon-ish, from Rome. He'll be expecting me, so you'll have to handle that." Ozera nodded confidently.

The Colonel reached out and spun his Rolodex, wrote down a note and handed it to Ozera. "Call this creep when you get in town. He'll help arrange … entertainment … for Del Bello. He's a …"

"Pimp?" Ozera finished his sentence. The Colonel searched for the right words but couldn't find them.

"Take ten grand with you," he said. "Spend what you have to. And Brad, be careful. We have a rat among us. Don't share anything outside this room. Not even with Doctor Drop-Dead Gorgeous." Ozera nodded, then got up and turned to go.

"Keep your back to the wall," the Colonel said.

"…and you'll see them coming at you," Ozera finished it – one of the truisms from the Special Forces Rules of Combat.

* _ * _ *

"Lisa, I'm going to need …"

"The hotel in New York City is all taken care of … Mr. West," she smiled, handing him an envelope with all the details. "The Colonel told me to book you at the Hotel Penta

New York and another room on another floor for your visitor. His room is in your name too."

"When am I arriving?" he asked her.

"Monday night?" she asked, leaving open the possibility that she would change it if he wanted. Ozera peeked into the envelope.

"What? No train tickets?" he asked, with just a touch of irritation at her infallible insightfulness.

"I wasn't sure where …," she offered apologetically.

"That's okay. I'll take care of it," he told her, "Thanks, Lisa. Great job, as usual."

* _ * _ *

IX: Arrangements

"Skip's not here anymore," said the male voice who answered the phone. "Who's calling? Maybe I can help you."

'Damn,' Ozera thought to himself. "This is Adam West," he said. "Skip has helped arrange entertainment for a client of mine who comes to town from time to time."

"Hang on a second." The phone went silent. After what seemed like five minutes he picked up again. "Yeah, we have you in our records. A little-boy set-up, for a couple sessions – that'd be this week, right?"

"That sounds about right." Ozera wondered what kind of record-keeping system they had. Probably a wall covered with stick-'em notes. Another Special Forces adage came to mind: If it's stupid but works, it's not stupid.

"Yeah, we can handle that. But prices have gone up. $1,500 a session now," he said, and then waited silently for the response he wanted.

After an appropriate, uncomfortable silence Ozera replied, trying to sound grudgingly accepting. "Yeah, okay. We can do that. But I want to meet you and the boy first."

"Sure. How about at the Fox and Hound, down in Penn Station, say, tonight at 9 o'clock?" Ozera agreed.

Penn Station was eerily quiet on weeknights by 9 pm. In about eight hours it would be an ant hill of commuters, scurrying in every direction. Ozera went early and located the bar – in the first sub-basement of the labyrinthine train-station complex. He ordered a drink at the bar and looked around. He, the bartender and a young couple at a table in the corner, seemingly engrossed with each other, were the sole occupants.

At 9 o'clock a couple of characters walked in – a black man, about Ozera's age, and a young boy, certainly underage. He looked like 15, at most 16. He was slim and clean-shaven, though he probably didn't shave much yet. He had a cute boyish face and a rich head of jet black hair.

Walking in, the black man looked around and quickly focused on Ozera, giving him a slight nod. Ozera returned the acknowledgement. They sat down at a well-lit table by the back wall.

The bartender suspiciously eyed the two, and Ozera decided to intercede and placate him. "I've been waiting for them," he told the burly bartender. "They won't be here long. I'll take care of them," he said, and got up, leaving his drink and a $20 bill on the bar. The bartender nodded.

"You Mr. West?" the black man asked as he sat down. "I heard you was older. Ozera assured him he was Mr. West. The boy said nothing and sat quiet and emotionless, eyeing Ozera with only slight interest. "My name's Jones, and this is my boy, Ralphie. So what's the gig?"

"I've got an important business client coming to town in a couple days," he replied, "He's staying in the Penta Hotel across the street. He's looking for a good time and needs some, uh, entertainment in his room Wednesday and Thursday nights."

"Is he an older Italian guy?" the boy asked, quite unexpectedly. Ozera looked at him and nodded, trying not to show his curious surprise.

"I know him. He makes me wear an altar-boy outfit. Real kinky," the boy said. His words didn't seem to match the youthful face, though it was clear to Ozera that any shred of innocence this boy ever had was long gone.

"Same gig," Ozera said to both of them. The black man looked over at the boy and gave him an 'okay, get out of here' nod. The boy understood, got up and nonchalantly walked out of the bar.

"So my little man's taken care of your guy before," he said to Ozera. "It's going to cost you three grand, up front."

Ozera already decided to offer him just half up front – fifteen hundred. He told Jones, and then pulled out a wad of folded bills and put it on the table. Jones quickly glanced around and then readily accepted and pocketed the cash, not bothering to count it. Ozera would call him Wednesday afternoon and give him the time and room number for Wednesday night. Then they would meet again at the bar and he'd get the other half for the Thursday night session.

"That business client of yours must be pretty important," Jones said, standing up.

"Just make sure he has a good time," Ozera replied. He didn't want a discussion. Their business was concluded. A handshake would have been customary but neither offered their hand to the other. Jones learned that, in his business, few wanted to shake his hand.

"Don't worry. My little man'll take care of him," Jones said, adding: "Call me Wednesday when and tell me where you want him. And I'll see you here then Thursday." He turned and walked out. Ozera went back to the bar and downed the rest of his drink. He nodded a tacit 'thanks' to the bartender and walked out. He heard the bartender say "Thanks" as he scooped up the $20 tip.

Ozera called room service for a late meal in his hotel room. Afterwards he took a shower, his second of the day. He felt … dirty.

*_*_*

IX: Report to the Pope

With Del Bello arriving Wednesday, Ozera didn't have a lot to do Tuesday. So he slept in, and around mid-morning enjoyed bacon and eggs in the little café off the lobby of the hotel, nearly choking on the $35 bill for the modest breakfast.

He went to the desk and coordinated Del Bello's arrival and room, paying for two nights on the second room that Lisa had booked. He put it in the name Del Bello and told them to expect his arrival Wednesday afternoon. He would be getting room 666, they told him.

Ozera called back to the office and spoke with Lisa. She was inordinately cheerful, apparently because of all the activity. The mountaintop was alive with engineers, contractors and stone masons.

"They all started yesterday up on top at dawn, including the Colonel and the Doctor, and I took them up some lunch," she explained. "They didn't come back down until after dark. This morning a helicopter dropped off a half-dozen engineers from God knows where. They'll be staying in the dorm for a week." She went on about the stone-cutting equipment that was hauled up and how busy she was making hotel and restaurant reservations and handling all manner of things.

"Anybody need me for anything?" he asked.

"I haven't been told or left any messages for you," she said. "When are you coming back?"

"Probably Friday, late morning. I expect to leave here early Friday," he told her.

"Okay, I'll tell everybody you called. Talk to you tomorrow. Take care, Captain."

A pleasant afternoon – a gorgeous spring day and, Ozera observed, notably warmer here than the Pennsylvania mountaintop. He spent it walking around Manhattan, a sort of self-guided tour. And the people! So many people! It was still cool, in the low 60's, and Ozera took an outside table at a café on Avenue of the Americas for a late lunch and to watch the people go by. Businessmen, punks, Hassidic Jews, and an endless procession of gorgeous women – all shapes, sizes, ages and colors.

The next day it was back to business. Ozera stayed in his room, awaiting the phone call that came in the early afternoon.

"Adam West?"

"Speaking."

A pause, and then: "You don't sound like Adam West."

"I'm filling in for the other, older Adam West," Ozera replied, trying to put his mind at ease. "You must be Father Del Bello."

A pause, then: "Okay. I'm at JFK. Where do we meet?"

"Like last time," Ozera said, "There's a room for you, in your name, at the Hotel Penta New York, in midtown."

"I'll be there about 3 or 4," he replied, "When should we meet?"

Ozera had prepared what he'd say. "Why not check in, relax and go get some dinner. We can meet in the morning. I thought you'd like some … company later tonight. I have made arrangements. How's 8 o'clock sound?"

"That sounds wonderful!" Del Bello replied enthusiastically. "Thank you. Where can we meet tomorrow?"

"How about 10 am, at the café off the lobby of your hotel?" Ozera asked. He had observed that the restaurant emptied out after about 9 am, until nearly lunchtime. It had several nooks where they could meet and converse privately.

"I will see you then. I'll be carrying a black leather valise, with papers for you."

One last detail: Jones answered the phone. Ozera recognized his voice.

"Yes, Mr. West. I was expecting your call."

"Have your boy at room 666, Penta Hotel, tonight at 8 o'clock. Okay? And how about we meet at the bar at 3 pm tomorrow to settle up?"

"See you tomorrow, Mr. West. A pleasure doing business with you."

* _ * _ *

Ozera went down early and found a quiet table in the back of the café. He asked the hostess to be on the lookout for a slim, 50-something man with a black valise, and please bring him back to his table.

It wasn't long and the hostess escorted him back. Del Bello looked considerably older and skinnier than he remembered in his photo. He was gaunt and walked hunched over slightly. He looked ill, as if in the late stage of a debilitating disease.

Ozera stood and, remembering the unique value this man added to the project, extended his hand.

"Father Del Bello, I presume," he cordially greeted him. "Please, sit. How about some breakfast?"

With a deep raspy voice, Del Bello ordered just coffee. Ozera was hungry and ordered a hefty omelet with all the trimmings.

They both sipped coffee and Del Bello asked if he could smoke. Ozera nodded and passed an ashtray. It was likely, he thought, that smoking accounted for the deep raspy voice, and maybe whatever else caused this 48-year-old man to look like and act like he was much older.

"I have two presents for you and ... the other Mr. West," he began, unzipping the valise. "This all is for you," he said to Ozera, indicating the valise and the file folder he pulled out. He handed it to Ozera.

The folder contained a copy of a document, apparently reduced in size to fit on one page. It was barely legible but appeared to be Latin. The next eight pages were full-sized copies of parts of the original document, so the document could be pieced together.

"So what is this?" Ozera asked, studying the sheets with a puzzled look. Del Bello reached into the satchel and pulled out a typed report.

"Here's the English translation from the Old Latin," he said, handing it to him. "It was a report to Pope Benedict IV in 903 A.D. We don't know if it was ever read, and if it was, whether it was ever acted on. It was one of the last documents on papyrus in the archives. It was also one of the last things ever seen by Pope Benedict IV. He died a month later and Leo V became Pope. They were tumultuous times in Rome and Popes came and went every few months. Some Popes are believed to have actually murdered their predecessors to assume the office."

"So what is it about?" Ozera asked.

"Sometime in the late ninth century, Rome learned that a remote monastery in the Carpathian Mountains, at the furthest edge of the Roman Catholic world, went missing. So the Pope at the time, John VIII, sent an investigator to find out what happened, and this is the resulting report. Now I'll be honest, it doesn't make a lot of sense. Most of it details the conduct of the investigation and the people interviewed."

"So what did they find?" Ozera asked.

"It's right there at the end," he said, pointing to the bottom of the second translation page. He quoted: 'It is our conclusion that the Monastery and its occupants were delivered by God from pagan attackers'." Ozera looked over at Del Bello, who shrugged his shoulders.

"Now here's a weird one," the priest said, reaching into the valise and withdrawing another folder. "I came across this just two weeks ago – another report that mentions the same Monastery – but 130 years later, in the year 1021. It was by a papal delegation touring the remotest area north of Walachia, the former Dacia. The author says they found the 'missing' Monastery, presumably rebuilt on the same mountaintop. He says he not only saw it, but actually visited inside the Monastery." Ozera looked up at Del Bello, intensely interested.

"The author describes it as 'almost pagan.' There was an ancient, circular altar, where all participants joined in rites he called 'heretical.' He notes there is no further cause for concern, however. When the delegation returned on their way back a few weeks later, it was gone: the Monastery, all of it, every stone. He summarizes: 'The Almighty had taken the Monastery – the structure, the occupants – for their heresy'." Del Bello let it sink in for a moment, then handed him the now empty valise.

Ozera crammed it all back in and zipped it closed. "You've done well," he told the aging priest. "Please continue. How are the accommodations? And the entertainment?"

"Excellent. Everything is excellent," he said, adding: "Thank you very much."

"Would you like … company tonight?" Ozera asked.

"That would be wonderful."

"I'll take care of it. 8 o'clock?" Del Bello nodded appreciatively. "And the room is paid through tomorrow."

Del Bello sensed they were about to part. "I've got to share something with you," he injected. "I've been working with you and your predecessor for over a year now. You've told me what you're after. And I've found and leaked you guys over a dozen Vatican documents – about that Monastery in Romania that seems to come and go."

Ozera sat silently and expressionless, not wanting to confirm or refute Del Bello's allegations.

"I've met people in the Vatican the last few years, including people who investigate alleged miracles," Del Bello continued. "And they have told me stories, about people who somehow connect with the Holy Spirit and make things happen that defy any natural explanation. Now it doesn't matter what you think of me, or the Catholic Church, but people – some people – have these God-given gifts. It is the power of prayer. And that could be what you're looking for."

Ozera stood up and extended his hand. "Father Del Bello, thank you for your … research. Enjoy yourself and the Big Apple." And with that he walked out.

* - * - *

He went to his room … and washed up. Then he called back to the office.

"The boss wants to talk to you, Captain," Lisa told him. "He's having lunch in his office. Hang on." Pause, click, then a ring.

"Brad, how's it going there? We've been slicing up the mountain here."

"So I've heard, sir," Ozera replied. "I have a couple gifts from our associate. Good meeting. Interesting. He had a good time last night, and is looking forward to more of the same tonight. I'm checking out in a little while. Will be back in the morning."

"Good, good," the Colonel replied. "The Doctor has been terrific, by the way. She's become a real take-charger. You've had a real positive influence on her. Okay, back to work. Have a nice trip. See you tomorrow."

Ozera packed, checked out, and headed out, bag in hand. A short trip, across the street to Penn Station for his 3 pm meeting. It was busy in the bar. Ozera ordered a drink and, in mid sip, was surprised by Jones coming up behind him.

"How'd it go? Everybody happy?" Jones asked him. Ozera nodded, and held his hand out with the wad of 15 hundred-dollar bills. Jones accepted it under the guise of a quick handshake.

"Same place, same time, tonight," Ozera told him. Jones nodded and the two men parted company, leaving the bar by separate doors.

On the Amtrak train Ozera settled in, then pulled out and read through the translations of both documents. It was curious, the account of the Papal investigator of the late ninth century disappearance: "The Monastery and its occupants were delivered by God from attackers." But delivered where?

The account of the Papal delegation of 1021 was even more puzzling. An ancient circular altar. How did Dacey know? They were conducting rites that the Pope's people considered pagan, heretical. And in retribution for that the Almighty had taken the Monastery – the structure, the occupants. He put the reports away.

Ozera thought about Jones and that poor kid, Ralphie. A hell of a life. Was it of his choosing? No, he was too young. He could well have been on some kind of drug habit. Still, he seemed lucid and aware, though somewhat withdrawn. The rocking of the train had a soothing effect and, as it pulled out from the Newark station, leaving New York behind him, Ozera peacefully nodded off.

* _ * _ *

IX: Stone work

Ozera pulled into the parking lot and saw the fervent activity that had besieged the otherwise tranquil mountaintop. A contractor's trailer was at the end of the lot. Men were walking to and from Control Central and the Dorm building. He sat in his car a moment and watched as two men climbed in a construction pick-up truck and spun out of the lot and up the pathway to the Monastery. He left his robe in the car, given all the company. He grabbed the valise, got out and walked to Control Central.

It was a good call. Lisa was behind her desk, absent robe.

"Welcome back, Captain," she said, energy in her voice.

"Just another quiet day, huh?" he asked rhetorically.

"We haven't had this much going on since last year," she said. "Please go right in; the boss is waiting for you."

He knocked and the Colonel looked up, putting down whatever he was reading. "Come in, Captain," he said, waving him in. He looked ebullient, alive, in charge. Lisa brought them both fresh coffee and left, and Ozera briefed him on the Del Bello episode, passing him the two document folders. He briefly reviewed the translations and looked up.

"I see two items of immediate useful information here," he said to Ozera, thinking out loud. "First, the interval between disappearances and reappearances of the Monastery is no longer than 150 years – based on the timing of these two events, one in 888 and another in 1021." Ozera thought about it.

"There may have been more … reappearances … in between those dates though, right? Anyhow, what's the second?" Ozera prompted him.

"The ancient, round altar stone," he mulled. "Looks like we're right on the mark with the one the Doctor found. We wrapped chains around it and pulled it loose with a bulldozer, just to have a look at it and take measurements. But because of its location we're going to wait on the Chinook to haul it up to the Monastery. It's about 18 inches thick. The engineers estimate it at 16 to 18 tons, so we'll have to see if the pilot can handle it. Come on, I'll show you." He got up and donned a light jacket and baseball cap.

They walked up the pathway – along the two tracks that had been worn in by tractor wheels – and stopped before the Monastery. The large front gates were wide open. They went in. Ozera heard generators running and saw bright lights illuminating the floor area, where a half-dozen workmen were finishing the floor at the center. Granite slabs and smaller filler pieces, professionally laid – all apparently brought in via the tunnel entrance.

Only a small area of the flooring remained to be laid, and the masons were busily finishing that up. The finished surface looked like it had been there for years. That was the nature of stone: timelessness. A stone wall laid yesterday looks like it's been there forever.

A workman walked up to the Colonel. "It'll be done by close of business, sir," he proudly announced, "Right on schedule." The Colonel nodded approvingly. "You need to give the mortar a good 48 hours to set before placing heavy objects on it," he added.

Ozera looked up and saw a larger portion of the roof opened than he initially recommended. The sunlight poured in, deluging the center of the Monastery like an atrium.

The Colonel looked up, too. "We had to take out another section, mainly to get that round altar stone in." They walked backed out, turned right and walked downhill. A bulldozer was dragging a large cut granite stone.

And there was the Doctor, standing atop a rock pile, waving directions to the bulldozer operator. Clad in tight jeans, sweatshirt and work boots, she had her hair pulled back into a ponytail. She looked like the centerfold from a lumberjack girlie magazine, Ozera mulled with a smile.

They looked over at where the bulldozer was headed. There were four large granite stones, lying across several tree trunks. Behind them was a crane, with a long boom hovering over the stones.

"This is the last of those 'guardian' stones," the Colonel told Ozera, "It's the biggest one, nearly 16,000 pounds. We're laying them there on the logs so we can get cables and chains around them. Next week the Chinook will lift and lower them into place. Wish you could be here to help direct that."

"Where am I going to be?" Ozera asked, bewildered. The bulldozer had pushed the big stone onto chains near the logs and powered down. The driver jumped off and started hooking the chains to the crane boom.

"You have a date Tuesday with Herr Doctor Henry Hallemeier, in Boston," he said. "I need you to find out where he's at ... and who he's been talking to." Ozera nodded, and then turned his attention to the Doctor, who was looking back at them. He waved and she returned a lovely smile.

They proceeded back down the mountain. Back on the parking lot they noticed a familiar black pick-up outside the Conference Center.

"How's Wainright coming along?" he asked.

"He started testing the staff a couple days ago," the Colonel said. "The Doctor's been great in setting up the test schedule. Don't know what if anything he's come up with yet; I've been too busy with all the rest of this. Why don't you check in with him? I've got to get back."

Professor Jerry Wainright was seated at his desk, clad in a white lab coat, looking over at the apparatus on the far wall. He looked deep in thought. Ozera walked in and Wainright looked over.

"Hey. Welcome back, Captain."

"What's the matter?" Ozera asked, "You look like your wife ran away with your dog."

"Yeah, wouldn't be at all surprised," he shot back. "He's got a bigger dick than me."

"I like the lab coat. Makes you look … medicinal."

"Yeah, sometimes the subjects react better when they think you're a professional." The corpulent professor looked over at Ozera and grinned.

"Speaking of subjects," he said, "I hear you've been testing some of our distinguished Romanian visitors."

"You're information is correct, Mon Capitan."

"And what are we finding?"

"**We** are confused," he replied. Ozera looked at him askance. "Yeah. Look at the big board," he said, gesturing the apparatus on the wall. "It's from a test I ran yesterday. The cook, Anton. Y'know, young stud with his arm in a cast?" Ozera nodded.

"See how all the balls are in the middle?"

"I thought that's what you'd expect to see," Ozera said. "So what's wrong with that?"

Wainright was shaking his head. "They are in the middle. That's the problem. They are **too** much in the middle – much more so than the baseline. It's an eight percent deviation from the baseline." He turned and looked hard at Ozera. "It's like he tried hard to make sure that the balls were in the middle – not left or right, but in the middle. They're packed tight in the middle," he said, gesturing with his hands.

"How many others did you test?" Ozera asked.

"Two others before Anton," he said. "And that's why I am confused; both of them had almost identical results – all the balls packed in the middle. One was 7 percent more packed that the baseline; the other was 12 percent."

"So what are you saying?" Ozera asked, though he suspected where he was going. He wanted to hear Wainright say it in his own words.

"It's like they can control the balls ... but have been told to make sure the balls stayed in the middle," he said, "Not left or right, but in the middle." Ozera stood silent and emotionless, not knowing what to say.

"I'll go brief the boss," Ozera told him. "Keep him posted, okay? I'm going to be out on the road again next week. Going to see a friend of yours, by the way – Henry Hallemeier, up in Boston."

"Oh, haven't seen or heard from Henry in years. Tell our favorite geneticist that Jerry Wainright says Hi."

"I will. Oh, by the way, you share your test results with whom?" Ozera asked – a point-blank question that smacked of an accusation.

And Wainright caught it. "Uh-oh. Something leak out? I share my results equally and concurrently with the Dapper James Bennington and our Delectable Doctor – and the Colonel, of course, usually through you."

"Why not keep these tests to yourself for now, okay?" Ozera requested. "And run tests on a couple more of them before you report anything officially. I'll let the Colonel know." Wainright nodded.

Ozera thought about Wainright on his way back to Control Central. Despite his larger-than-life, somewhat sloppy appearance, he was an exceedingly bright man, and very perceptive. Yes, he was engrossed in his work, but he was also well aware of the world and events around him. He was a former Army officer. Ozera believed him, and he believed that he had not seen or heard from Hallemeier for years. He also surmised that Wainright reported his results to both Bennington and the Doctor. Any leaks almost certainly originated from one of them.

Ozera stopped in and briefed the Colonel on Wainright's latest findings. Like last time, his face contorted in puzzlement, not knowing what to make of it.

"As if the test subjects – all three of them so far – intentionally kept all the balls in the middle?" the Colonel asked, feeding back his understanding, to make sure he had it right. "Why would they do that, even if they could?"

"What if," Ozera postulated, "one of our Romanians was playing around in there before and mentally drove the balls way to the left – the way we found them, remember?" The Colonel raised an eyebrow. Such a psychic capability was almost beyond belief. "And what if," Ozera continued, "After word got out, they were told – remember they were all research subjects in Romania – that when tested by Wainright, to make sure the balls all stayed in the middle?"

"But the deviation from the baseline?" the Colonel asked.

"So far 7, 8 and 12 percent – incredible," Ozera injected. "Maybe they didn't know there was a baseline they'd be compared to. Maybe they thought keeping the balls in the middle would avoid any suspicion, because that would show no psychic ability."

"But instead, it aroused Wainright's suspicions," the Colonel completed the thought. He contemplated the scenario. "So you're saying they may think they're being inscrutable and not showing their hand, when in fact they're showing us what they can really do. And it's pretty spooky."

"I asked Wainright to keep these latest results... and his observations ... to himself for now," Ozera said. The Colonel nodded approval.

"I'll work up a course of action with Wainright next week," the Colonel volunteered. "You'll be in Boston, checking out Henry the geneticist," he said, adding with a smile: "And I'll bet by the time you get back we'll be damned near done with the Monastery up there." He muttered under his breath: "I should have been a construction foreman."

Ozera smiled, got up and went to the door. "See you sometime next week, sir," he said, and left.

He stopped in front of Lisa: "So, my dear, where am I going, and when?"

She smiled pertly and handed him the envelope.

"Boston," she said. "Flying out Monday 9 am, from ABE to Logan. Open return. Got you booked two days in The Westin Copley Place. The boss says that's pretty close to where you are going."

Ozera spent the rest of the day quietly in his office, reviewing Hallemeier's file.

Chief Scientist at GTI, Gene Technology Inc., his dealings with the Colonel were all refreshingly above board. He found a document authored by the Colonel 18 months ago – a Statement of Work to the CEO of GTI. For $2.4 million, plus reimbursement of documented expenses, the private firm would provide two years of confidential written monthly reports to Colonel John Smith, Chief of the NEPA Facility, summarizing the latest industry progress toward deciphering the human genome – "focusing on the potential of human genes and genetic structures and arrangements to enable psychic ability, on an individual or collective basis." Wow! He'd have to check out the past reports when he got back.

Henry Hallemeier was designated the principal researcher, report author and contact. The background intelligence had only glowing assessments of his academic and research credentials with regards to genetic science. He knew everybody, went everywhere and heard everything.

Earned his PhD from MIT at age 24. Impressive. Well paid, with juicy stock and investment options. Single at 48, never married. No evidence of hetero- or homosexual relationships found. No evidence of drinking, gambling or drug problems.

Mr. Clean, Ozera concluded. Let's see what he knows about genetics and psi.

* _ * _ *

IX: Welcome back

The weekend was rainy and cold. It had become a Friday
night tradition – the Fern Valley Inn with Mrs. Griffiths. She
was buxom, funny and enticingly dressed. They ate and
drank too much, and a good time was had by all, as usual.
When they returned to the car after dinner, in the rain, both
were hanging onto each other for warmth and support. They
climbed in and, unexpectedly, she called him 'my love' and
gave him a long kiss on the lips. Ozera wasn't sure how to
respond, but accepted her affection.

It was just too wet outside for his morning jog, so Ozera did
push-ups and sit-ups in his room. He went down to breakfast
disheveled, unshaven, in sweatshirt, sweatpants and sneakers.
The dining room was empty, but the coffee urn was hot. He
poured himself a cup and stood by the window, looking out
over the yard, the barn and the parking lot. It was a steady
rain, thoroughly drenching everything.

"Welcome back, Captain. How was the Big Apple?" He
spun around, surprised, splashing coffee on himself. The
Doctor was seated, sipping a cup of tea. She must have
quietly sat down and been watching him for a while. "Oh,
my," she said, looking him over, "I didn't know we were
dressing for breakfast." He looked back at her snidely,
walked over and sat down across from her. She wore a light
blue blouse with lots of buttons. She looked good. Ozera
thought to himself: Hell, she'd look good wearing a burlap
bag.

"Alright, wise guy," he said. "If April showers bring May
flowers, what do Mayflowers bring?"

She thought a minute and shrugged.

"Pilgrims," he said with a smile, "Get it?" She did not. He
groaned in frustration. "We'll see if we can get an American
to explain it to you." She jokingly sneered at him. As if on

cue, Mrs. Griffiths walked out, a bit groggy it seemed from the night before. They ordered breakfast.

Mrs. Griffiths returned to the kitchen and the Doctor leaned over: "We need to talk, Brad. How about ten o'clock in the loft?" He nodded.

Showered, shaved and cleaned up, he snuck out. Gracie whinnied, as if heralding his arrival. He climbed up the ladder to the hay loft, stuck his head up and saw the Doctor already there. Her back was to him; she was looking out the window at the rain. She likely watched him walk over from the house.

"It's cold and raw this morning," she said. She had on a jacket and tight jeans. He went up to her and put his arms around her lovingly. She responded, enjoying it and turned around.

"I'll try to keep you warm," he said, "But we could use a blanket up here.

"Like that?" she said, nodding to a large comforter, rolled up in the corner beside a bale of hay. Ozera smiled, impressed at her talent to forecast such things.

He spread out the comforter as she took off her jacket and pulled off her jeans. They kissed and climbed in together, snuggling up to each other as he pulled the blanket over top of them.

Mrs. Griffiths stood looking out the dining room window, through the rain, at the barn. A tear formed in her eye.

* - * - *

"Welcome back, mein Soldat und mein Liebhaber," she said to him afterwards, with a sultry Marlene Dietrich accent, and kissing him on the cheek.

"So you wanted to talk, huh?" he lovingly chastised her. He leaned down and kissed her nipple, grateful and obviously satisfied with their roll in the hayloft.

She cooed, enjoying the post-play. "Actually I wanted to ask a business question: Are the Colonel and Professor Wainright satisfied with his test results so far? I mean, nothing spooky or alarming so far, right?"

It surprised him. He asked Wainright to keep the results quiet for now. So she likely did not know what they suspected – that the Romanians tested so far exhibited potentially powerful psychic power, but were apparently all trying to make it appear like they had none. Ozera didn't want to dwell on it – she seemed able to pick up on whatever he was thinking. He preferred to concentrate instead on their lovemaking.

"So no concerns?" she reiterated.

"Just one," he responded, trying to keep his mind on the fun and frivolity at hand. "How long can we stay here and play before Mrs. Griffiths comes looking for us?"

* _ * _ *

IX: In the genes

The Back Bay had become the glass and steel antithesis of quaint old-town Boston. The cab from Logan pulled up in front of the Westin Copley Place and dropped him off. It was to be a quiet night, with a room-service dinner in his corner room on the 26th floor, offering an impressive, panoramic view of Boston.

GTI had its offices and labs in a skyscraper a few blocks away, and Ozera decided to walk over – after an incredibly overpriced breakfast. He entered the lobby promptly at 10:30 and saw Henry Hallemeier waiting for him. Thick glasses, disheveled hair, but wearing an old suit, instead of the nerdy lab coat he remembered from his file photo.

"Doctor Hallemeier, I presume," Ozera said with his trademark smile.

"Mr. Ozera?" he stood and greeted him, "Colonel Smith told me you were coming." They agreed to call each other Brad and Henry. Hallemeier seemed a little nervous, Ozera suspected, as if he had control over the millions in business his company had with the NEPA facility.

They went up to an ostentatious conference room apparently set aside for VIPs – luxurious wood and high-back leather seats – pastries and coffee and a hostess to serve them. Ozera explained he wanted to converse with Hallemeier privately about the project and the state of their research, and appreciated the VIP reception. Hallemeier seemed more than willing to accommodate in any way he could.

"I'll confess I haven't read all your reports," Ozera started, "But I was hoping we could chat and I could get a better appreciation for the state of your genetics research."

They talked … mostly about the state of the decoding of the human genome. It had been underway for a couple of years, financed mainly by the U.S. Government's Department of

Energy. But it would be years yet, maybe a decade, Hallemeier said, before the 3.3 billion 'base pairs' of mankind's DNA, aggregated in some 23,000 genes, would be fully mapped.

"Do you know what we do?" Ozera asked him bluntly.

"Not specifically," the scientist replied, "But it seems your research focuses on understanding where psychic energy in people comes from. And if that source could be something written in the genes is where we get involved." Ozera thought a moment and nodded in agreement.

"So can our genes account for who has psychic ability, and who doesn't?" Ozera asked outright.

Hallemeier heaved a heavy sigh, as if he had been asked an unanswerable question. "You must first believe whether 'psi' exists," he answered, "and I do. I've seen incontrovertible evidence from multiple independent researchers that capabilities including telekinesis and ESP exist. I know respected scientists, who have documented the ability of some people to move falling balls with their mind, and to know whether somebody unseen is looking at them."

"Speaking of falling balls, I met Professor Jerry Wainright recently and he mentioned you two know each other."

"Oh, how are Jerry's balls these days?" Hallemeier replied with a touch of levity, not the least bit shaken. "I haven't seen him in some time. Is he involved in your … work … too?" Ozera didn't want to elaborate. Besides, based on his discourse with Wainright and now Hallemeier, it seemed unlikely that either was the source of the leak that worried the Colonel. So he changed subjects.

"Let's say psi does indeed exist," Ozera posed, "So could the reason someone has it, and someone else does not, be some combination of those 3.3 billion genetic base pairs?"

Hallemeier considered the question. "We are finding that a very small percentage of our DNA is actively involved in encoding protein sequences – that is, only about two to three percent of our gene sequences serve the purpose of creating proteins and other biochemical building blocks that we need to live, procreate, fight disease, and so on."

"So what does the rest of our DNA do?" Ozera asked.

"You tell me," Hallemeier rhetorically countered. "The press has coined the term 'junk DNA' to refer to all the DNA that doesn't directly manage biochemical functions, what's called non-coding DNA. But that's a pretty derogatory assessment. I, on the other hand, am one of the geneticists who believe that 80 percent, perhaps more, of our genes do have direct functions. We just don't know what they all are … yet."

"So if it's not biological or chemistry stuff, what do they control?" he asked.

"Well, some are relics of our evolution. We have some of the same residual gene sequences as jellyfish and amoeba. Some of us have more than others," he said with a grin. Another shot at levity that missed its mark.

He continued: "But I believe there's a host of other non-coding jobs that our genes handle. I believe a lot is genetic memory – and a lot of other leading geneticists agree with me. People know things, things that we are born knowing, that we never learn and are never taught. We are remarkably well-endowed with inborn survival instincts, for example. We smile when we see a new baby. We all do. We can't help it. We hurt and cry at the loss of a close loved one. We get hard-ons when we see a sweet young thing bend over, or hang her boobs in our face."

"Those are caveman responses," Ozera inserted. "Still, you think they're genetic memory?"

"Yes, I do. And it's not just caveman reactions. I believe we are likely to someday find advanced conceptual thought enabled by certain genetic combinations, too. Maybe even …"

"Psi capabilities?" Ozera queried.

"I think so, yes," Hallemeier admitted. "But analyzing the genes of people who test high for psi, and confirming what unique gene sequences they have that other people do not … that's a few years away yet, I'm afraid."

"But how can you attribute so much to genes, when we don't know that much for sure yet?"

"Oh, we've known a lot about genes for a long time, Brad," Hallemeier said. "Chinese farmers became genetic engineers 10,000 years ago. They experimented with grain seed and found that plants with shorter stalks produced higher yields, because plants with taller stalks were prone to fall over. We learned **long** ago that we could manipulate the genetic composition and characteristics of future generations. It was the mid-1800's when an Austrian monk discovered the genetic rules of dominant traits. And our genetic knowledge has grown exponentially since then."

"You're talking about plants," Ozera interrupted. "I'm talking about people."

"People, too. Since the dawn of man, how did tribal wars usually end?" Hallemeier asked him.

Ozera thought for a moment and shrugged: "The last man standing?"

"In many cases, yes, that was unfortunately the resolution," he replied. "But then a new trend emerged: Often a marriage was arranged, usually between the children of the warring tribes' leaders."

"Yeah, but wasn't that to bring the two sides together, politically?" Ozera responded, "Not really to improve the human species."

"Oh, really?" Hallemeier countered. "It turns out a whole new subspecies of human emerged – royalty, nobility. People figured that genetically they could preserve the character – the leadership, bravery, even wisdom – of past great leaders. Of course this unintentionally also spawned inbreeding issues – recessive disorders like hemophilia, seizures, infertility and a gamut of other physical deformities and emotional issues."

"So now we know better?" Ozera asked.

"Human genetic engineering has been going on for thousands of years, Mr. Ozera. Today we know **why** inbreeding causes problems – it's the way deleterious recessive traits promulgate when the genes are too similar. We've known inbreeding's problems for a long time. That's why the inter-marriage of young, healthy children from warring clans became so … practical."

"Can a people improve their genetic … capabilities … by selective inter-breeding?" Ozera asked.

Hallemeier raised an eyebrow. "I'm sure it's been tried, but any such project involving humans would take generations – hundreds of years – to produce results. And how do you decide which people to bring into a population, which people to mate? We're only starting to understand which genes control which attributes. And science today is forbidden from screwing with human genes and then breeding people just to see what happens."

Ozera had to ask a key straightforward question. "Could it have been possible, hundreds of years ago, for a people to have conducted selective breeding that produced, like, psychic abilities?"

Hallemeier thought about it. "Yes, I believe it's scientifically possible, even though we still couldn't knowingly do that today. I doubt any ancient people would have known what they were looking for. If it happened, and psychic ability was the result, it would have been an unintentional byproduct."

They chatted for another hour, but Ozera learned what he had come to find out. He met a few of GTI's senior officers – an unavoidable diplomatic chore – who thanked him for the work and revenue. They had a catered lunch in the lavish, richly paneled conference room, and then Hallemeier conducted Ozera on a guided tour through GTI's many labs.

It finally dawned on Ozera that mapping the human genome was not the same as knowing what each gene, each base pair in each DNA strand, actually did. As Hallemeier pointed out, the vast majority of our gene combinations were labeled 'junk' – simply because we didn't know what they did.

It was a pleasant walk through Back Bay Boston back to his hotel. The late afternoon sun was warming; it was in the 60's. He sat on a park bench on Boylston overlooking a fountain, contemplating the day's events. Soon the sidewalks were full of commuters as the evening rush hour got underway.

He judged Hallemeier to be a straight shooter – a lab scientist just trying to survive in the corporate world. It seemed out of character that this lab geek in a worn pin-striped suit would have the inclination or aptitude to peddle secrets with spooky government agencies. He seemed to respect secrets. So did Wainright for that matter. They were both basically scientists who did what they were told. And he believed that they hadn't been in touch with each other for a long time.

Boston was the place to enjoy a dinner out. And his work there was done. Ozera had a hankering for lobster and dry white wine. He'd be back on his Pennsylvania mountaintop late tomorrow. But tonight he'd enjoy Boston.

* _ * _ *

IX: Gifts

"So, personally, Henry Hallemeier conceptually accepts that genetics could be behind psi," the Colonel asked.

"He says it **could** be, but he's pretty fluffy on any specific details or scientific findings," Ozera replied. "And I am reasonably confident that he and Wainright have not been in cahoots – or even in touch – for some time. I saw no evidence that Wainright's data got leaked through Hallemeier." He let his assessment sink in. "I didn't know, sir, that you've had them sending you monthly reports. It might've been helpful to know that before I went up there."

"Their reports didn't really say anything," the Colonel retorted. "Not really. Their corporate lawyers sanitized them, and you don't want intelligence reports sanitized. You want all the suspicions and gut feelings from the author, whether a scientist or a field operative. Anyway, those reports hinted at stuff that you and I already knew about – like the Russian psi demographic study – and some possible new indications of psi genetic inheritance. But there was not much new or solid. Pretty fluffy," he said with a grin.

Ozera accepted his boss' explanation. He had not lied or misled him so far. "So how're things going here, sir?" he asked, refocusing the discussion.

"Let me show you," the Colonel said, standing up. Ozera saw him grab an envelope from his desk drawer and stick in in his pocket. They walked out and across the parking lot as a big truck with a long flatbed came rumbling down the road from the Monastery. An extensible crane was folded up and loaded on the flatbed.

"That might be the last of them," the Colonel said. "So next week it's back to robes again."

"You're all done?" Ozera asked, incredulously. "How'd it go with the Chinook?"

"We nearly lost the chopper Monday getting that big round flat stone out," he said. "Must have been 18, almost 19 tons. But I worked with these jarheads from Willow Grove before. They're a little nuts and don't let little things like load limits slow them down. Anyhow, they yanked it out Monday and lifted it up to the Monastery. Then Tuesday was the big show. Everybody was up there watching. The Chinook first dropped in the big round one, the Communion stone. The masons had built stone pedestals to lay it on. Worked perfectly. The rest of the day they dropped in the Guardians, one at a time, while the Doctor guided them into the exact positions."

"How's it looking?" Ozera enthusiastically asked.

"Awesome. C'mon." They trudged up the pathway, with two pronounced ruts worn by the heavy equipment. They rounded the crest at the top and there, before them, stood the Monastery.

The front gates were open. The stone walkway through the tunnel was completed – a beautiful patchwork of square and rectangular pieces, a mix of stone types and colors.

They entered the main hall and Ozera had to stop and admire the work that had been done. The sun streamed through the large opening in the roof. It was done tastefully, a roughly 30-foot round opening, right above the center. The architect within him looked it over in admiration.

"Awesome," he muttered under his breath. "They didn't close up the roof?" Ozera asked.

"No. And they may not. Keeping it open for now was the Doctor's idea. We had to open it up even more so the Chinook could lower the stones straight down into place."

They walked through the colonnade and onto the newly finished stone floor of the main hall. The round Communion stone was right in the center. Around it, tastefully spaced, were the five Guardian stones.

"Can you imagine them building this a thousand years ago … with no Chinook, no bulldozers, no crane, no stone saws?" the Colonel asked, not expecting an answer.

On the other side of the altar there were a half-dozen wooden benches, like large park benches.

"The Doctor asked for those," the Colonel explained, "So she could hold her meetings up here. And the carpenters put them together before they left. We had a lot of rain here this weekend and everything got soaked with the open roof. But as you see, most everything inside here is stone and mortar, and the water drains down into the mountain very quickly. It's actually nice having the open roof. You don't need torches or flashlights, except at night, of course. And the air is always fresh and cool."

The two sat down on the closest bench. "We have some problems coming up, Brad," he told him. "Our operation here is attracting a lot of interest, from organizations that would normally care less. We have to be very careful about what gets out. It's like we're getting close to something – I sense that and maybe you do too. And the wrong people are taking interest."

"Has Wainright been keeping quiet?" Ozera asked.

"I'd sure like to think so. He's tested more of our gang –with the same results." Ozera looked at him, surprised. "All the balls were squeezed in towards the middle. He runs a baseline with no one around and comes up with the same consistent metric – always within a .02 percent standard deviation. Then he tests another subject and all the balls get squeezed again. We are talking 7 to 15 percent deviation from the baseline. That's like a thousand times more than chance. It is a … power, a measurable power. I'd give anything to find out how the Ruskies measured telekinesis when they did their study."

"So where to from here?" Ozera asked.

"I have Wainright working on the next phase: the group effect," he replied. "Can two or three or ten of them aggregate the effect? But I have my concerns."

"About what, sir?"

"Two things," he replied. "First, we found out largely by accident about their individual capabilities. We know, but they don't know we know. Their attempts to conceal it actually revealed it to us. So how do we get them to knowingly cooperate on TK tests with several of them?"

Ozera nodded. "And the second thing?" he asked.

"Well, follow me here. If someone off the street – someone with a strong psi capability – can move a plastic ball a half-inch, what can somebody with a thousand times that ability do? And then – and here's where we're at – what if a bunch of them could aggregate this … power?"

Ozera sat quietly, emotionless, cogitating what the Colonel said. The Wainright experiments were designed to measure telekinesis – mind over matter, the psi effect most likely related to a disappearing Monastery. But what about telepathy, ESP, clairvoyance, remote viewing?

"Be super-careful about what gets out of here, Brad. There are people in our government who know about these capabilities and what they can do. They've got the black money and influence to do whatever they want. And that could mean taking us over, shutting us down, or moving all of this, and us, into the dark. That's why I brought you up here. No one can see or hear us here. It's just you and me."

They got up to leave. "Oh. I almost forgot. I've got something for you," he said, reaching into his pocket and pulling out the envelope Ozera saw before. "You'll be going to Europe soon, and it's not good to travel abroad using your own name. Here," he said, handing him the envelope.

Ozera opened it and pulled out two passports. One was a new U.S. passport. He opened it. It was his passport – his picture, all proper and sealed – but with another name, Victor Livingston.

"Is it real?" he asked.

"You bet your ass. It's better than real," he replied. "I still have friends in low places and I got these for you. Using that passport you are Victor Livingston, a real American with a real past, real military credentials, and government databases that tag you – Mr. Livingston, that is – as an asset of the U.S. Government. Nobody will fuck with you."

Ozera was impressed. The other one looked like a Romanian passport, also new. He opened it and, again, it was his passport – his face. He read the name. "Stefan Ionescu?" he asked.

"It's a special gift, in case something happens. And it's as real as the other one," he told him. "You speak Romanian – as well as a Romanian. If you need it, use it. You'll know if and when you need to. And if and when you need to, I may not be around."

They walked out and, locking the front gate, proceeded back down to Control Central.

* - * - *

The Monastery

IX: Seven sisters

In the weeks that followed the Colonel became increasingly wary that unidentified outside interests were watching them closely … and waiting. If it were anyone else Ozera would have considered it wild paranoia. But after surviving so many years as a Special Forces officer in the murky intelligence community, the Colonel's paranoia was probably justified. The boss knew what was going on, though he often did not share all he knew with Ozera.

And in the weeks that followed Ozera and the Doctor grew closer, and closer. Neither would admit it, to themselves or to each other, but romance was blossoming. At work it became a sort of playacting – pretending everything was strictly business in front of the Colonel and others, including Mrs. Griffiths.

George and Gracie saw things as they were. Every few days the Doctor would come in, pet and talk to them for a few minutes, then climb up into the loft. And not long afterwards Ozera would show up, usually bearing some gift – wine, champagne, lunch, chocolate, once even flowers – and scamper up to the loft with her. After-dinner trysts became increasingly common. Saturdays were special, though, especially if the weather was nice. The Doctor and Ozera would saddle them up and go for a ride.

One Saturday morning she presented Ozera with a pair of custom-made, black leather riding boots – and she forbid him from wearing sneakers again on their horse rides. They fit incredibly well, and he wondered how she managed it without a fitting. He reciprocated the next Saturday, giving her a suede, wide-brimmed Australian bush hat. She loved it, and looked great in it.

There was sex, yes, and great sex – at least twice a week. And they would talk – playfully, intimately, sometimes even seriously. They reached an accord, though, that she wouldn't query him about his work, and he wouldn't ask about her sundry activities. Their relationship deepened as the days lengthened.

May warmed the way to June, and summer waited patiently in the wings. Dacey, as he came to call her, told him after their lovemaking one Thursday night that she had to turn in early. Without thinking he asked why.

"That's my business, mon cher," she said, holding her finger to his lips, shushing him.

It got Ozera wondering. Why tonight? She never pushed him away after lovemaking before – and under the guise of having to get up early? He had to know. He tossed and turned in bed until 2 am. Then it hit him. Tomorrow was June 21st – midsummer night. He set his alarm for 4 am, got up and quietly dressed. He opened his door and looked down the hall. Not a sound. 4:15, then 4:30, still nothing. 4:45. It would be dawn in another half-hour.

He decided to go check the parking lot. Her Jeep was gone. Damn! He got in his SUV and tore off, heading to the mountaintop. He waited impatiently at the log crossing and flashed his lights a few times. It swung open at last and he gunned it up the winding access, almost going over a sharp drop-off on one curve.

He remembered: the access tunnel to the Monastery, and the rising sun on Midsummer's morn. He tore into the parking lot and jumped out. Lights were on in the Dorm building, and on the second floor of Control Central.

He headed to the access road up the mountain and took off, almost running into the walking sentry, wearing his robe, who had braced for a collision.

"Oh, it's you, sir," the guard said, recognizing him in the dim twilight. "Don't know what's going on. They're all up there."

"I'll check it out," he said dismissively. Ozera looked up; sunlight was just peering up over the mountain. He took off in a run up the road. He rounded the top and stopped, gasping for breath. The main gates of the Monastery were wide open; the sun was streaming into the access tunnel.

He ran to the entrance, the bright sun at his back. His body cast a long shadow into the tunnel, darkening the stone floor before him as he walked down its length. He emerged into the great hall and then stepped aside, to let the sunlight fill the spacious chamber.

There they stood – all of them, in their robes, standing silently, side by side, behind the Communion stone. In the middle stood the Doctor. A vision of Michelangelo's Last Supper flashed through Ozera's mind. Something had just happened. They had all just experienced something. Ozera felt it. It was … gratification of some sort. But whatever it was, now it was over.

"*Go, now*," the Doctor said in Romanian to her entourage. They walked around both sides of the large altar stone and into the tunnel, passing single file by Ozera. He cast a puzzled look at her. She looked back and flashed him an innocent "Who, me?" smile.

"Did the sun deliver, as planned?" he asked.

"It was glorious," she said, walking around the altar and up to him, planting a friendly kiss on his cheek. He wanted very much to ask her what happened, but he did not. He followed her out. At the entrance they closed the large wooden gates and she secured the combination lock.

"The Colonel gave you the combination?" he asked.

"No. He didn't have to," she said with a smile. "You did, a month ago."

"But I never told you …"

"You didn't have to," she interrupted him. They turned and sauntered back down. It was a glorious morning on the first day of summer.

Dacey never did volunteer any additional explanation for the events of that midsummer morn. Nor did any of the other Romanians, not even the usually talkative Lisa.

The Doctor had come to accept Ozera's Friday nights out with the landlady and never asked about it, in the interest of keeping her relationship with Ozera private. And that evening he had his usual night out with Mrs. Griffiths – typically festive, saucy and over-indulgent.

And as usual, Ozera was too tipsy at the end of the night to engage in coherent conversation – or engage in anything else. He would trudge upstairs and in a few minutes, would crawl in bed and fall soundly asleep, oblivious to the fact that, as usual, the Doctor noted his return, and that he had gone to bed – alone.

* - * - *

It was an afternoon meeting in the Colonel's office – a benchmark meeting with Professor Wainright. He handed Ozera and the Colonel a three-page report, "Results of Phase 1 of TK Testing of Romanian Subjects." It was dated June 25, 1991 and marked: "Highest Confidentiality." Ozera and the Colonel scanned through the document, as Wainright sat back with a coffee, nonchalantly noshing on a cream doughnut.

"An **average** of 840 times the telekinetic capability of the most adept subjects you previously tested?" the Colonel asked, shooting right to the bottom line. "And every one of them has it?

"That's right, Colonel, although to varying degrees," Wainright explained, wiping powdered sugar from his chin.

"It is virtually certain that our initial presumption was correct: Each of them was apparently trying to keep the balls in the center – as it seems someone told them to do, to make it look like they had no special telekinetic capability. These fuckers probably sit around at night drinking beer and bending spoons for fun."

"Who else has seen this?" the Colonel asked, holding up the report.

"Nobody but me, you and the Captain. I typed it myself, on a computer and printer only I use."

"Not the Doctor?" Ozera asked.

"No one else," Wainright repeated with added emphasis, irritated at being questioned.

"We've got to be very careful, Jerry," the Colonel told him. "I know that some spooky outfits want to get in our shorts. All they'd need is to find out we have some psychic super mensch here – and they'd be all over us like flies on shit!" Wainright nodded understandingly. "I know you'd like to be able to test this bunch more and use the results in your own research, and you will, as we agreed. But you've got to make sure that nothing gets out about this for now." He looked Wainright in the eye and got the tacit acknowledgement he wanted.

"So how do we proceed?" the Colonel asked him, "What's your thinking about how to test for aggregate TK capability with multiple subjects?"

He did have a plan. He had been testing a motorized pendulum apparatus in his lab at Princeton that could carefully record movement in any direction, and any TK effect that speeds it up, slows it down or changes its swing direction. He showed a floor plan that would enable up to three subjects to sit in booths, unaware of the others, and be tested individually or concurrently, based on instructions given them via a headset.

Wainright added: "I'd like to plant sensitive clocks in each booth and around my lab here." The Colonel looked askance at him. "I want to see if any temporal anomalies are recorded," he explained.

The Colonel nodded approvingly. "That's why I keep cream donuts around for you, Jerry," he said with a smile.

They worked out a timetable and budget: The pendulum and lab set-up would be done within a month, and Wainright was authorized $500,000 for the next phase. The Colonel thanked him; Wainright assembled his belongings and left. Ozera got up to go, but the Colonel asked him to stay for a moment.

"It's time you got over to England, Brad. Our gal, Frau Doktor Eva Gerhard, says she has some interesting stuff for us. I have you going out Sunday, if that's okay. You'll connect with her on Tuesday. She'll get in touch with you at your hotel. She hangs her hat at Oxford, a couple hours northwest of Heathrow. Use a hired car; you'd be nuts to drive yourself. Take your time; come back when you're done with business. Assure her we value her help. Keep her stoked."

Ozera nodded and stood up. He thought about telling the Colonel about the dawn activity up at the Monastery, but he didn't know what to say, and really didn't know himself what happened.

"I haven't said lately how great it is to have you here, Brad. You've become a super second-in command. I'd trust you with my command ... and my life. I'll just say once more: A lot of eyes are watching us ... and this project ... now. Please be very careful who you talk to and what you say."

"I will, sir," he said, and snapped a loose salute. The Colonel returned it – a conditioned response.

Ozera wrapped up some paperwork and headed out. Lisa said she was waiting for hotel confirmation and would have his travel documents for him in the morning. He walked out to a simply splendid late afternoon. It was warm, dry, and would be light for a few more hours.

He walked out towards his SUV and came to a sudden stop. Two horses were saddled and waiting by his car, with a gorgeous gal seated on one.

"There may not be enough room on this mountain for both of us, pardner," she said as he approached. Her attempted cowboy twang was tainted by her subtle eastern European accent. She wore her riding boots, tight jeans, a loose denim shirt and her favorite hat. Her sunglasses obscured her gorgeous eyes, but he saw she wore just the right touch of lipstick and makeup. She looked scrumptious.

"Your boots are in your car. And don't take all day. C'mon, I've got to show you something." Her horse, George, whinnied and nodded in agreement, as if on cue. She had a blanket rolled behind her saddle. A backpack stuffed with goodies was hanging on Gracie's saddle horn for him. "I've brought dinner, too," she said, for added enticement.

He was touched. She had obviously spent quite a bit of time and energy planning this. He threw his robe in the car and pulled out his boots. In a moment he had saddled up and the two were sauntering out back of Control Central. A tired Colonel was looking out his window and saw them ambling in the warm afternoon sun along the wood line. He smiled. Security told him long ago that Ozera and the Doctor frequently rode horseback around the facility.

They strolled past where the large flat altar stone was excavated. "I found this when I went exploring further back along the mountain ridge." Ozera's curiosity was aroused. They descended slightly onto a small, flat, heavily wooded enclave. It was isolated, surrounded by the mountain. In this natural shelter the trees – a mix of deciduous and evergreen –

grew tall and created a high canopy, competing for sunlight. It was dark and notably cooler in the shade.

The horses' hooves crunched the leaves and twigs on the ground. She stopped and dismounted. "Here," she said, "Let's tie off the horses and walk." She took her blanket and they walked towards a lighted open spot they saw up ahead in the woods. They walked to the middle of the small circular area with knee-high grass.

"Isn't it wonderful!" she exclaimed turning around in a circle. "It's seven sisters. See them?" He looked around and didn't understand. "The trees. The big oak trees? Seven of them. They all came from the same parent." He looked and nodded; she was right. Seven nearly identical, thick, old, 30-foot-tall oaks.

"This is a holy place," she said. "Their father was here, right here where we're standing. He lived a long time ago. He left these seven daughters, and now they stand here, respecting their father's grave. It did seem odd to Ozera that the circle was devoid of any other trees, or any growth besides the grass. Dacey spread out the blanket. They sat and he started to unpack.

"No, no. First make love to me," she pleaded, leaning over and undoing his shirt.

"With all seven sisters watching?" he teased.

"Shut up and love me, you fool," she playfully growled in his ear.

* - * - *

IX: Double date

They dined afterwards on Brie, French bread, pate and, to wash it down, a bottle of Beaujolais-Village. She was wearing her panties and shirt; him just his boxer shorts. She looked at him lovingly. He looked at her, as enthralled with her beauty as the first time he saw her – and he knew he had fallen in love.

Then her loving expression turned serious, as if she just thought of something. "You are going on a trip," she said. It was not a question.

"How'd you know?" he asked, bewildered. "I just found out myself a few hours ago."

"I just found out ... from you," she answered.

"So how long have you been reading minds," he asked, only half-jokingly.

"All my adult life," she replied, not joking at all. "It's easy with you."

"And why is that?"

"Because you are like me," she said. "And I have a special gift."

"A gift?" he asked.

"**The** gift. Those with it have special ... abilities," she said. "We can do things – sense things, people's thoughts, and do amazing other things – that others cannot. You are leaving Sunday, right?" she asked.

"Yes," he said, somewhat surprised. "I'm going to ..."

"England," she interjected. He was amazed, which was apparently what she wanted. "I assume you are going out

Friday night with Mrs. Griffiths, as usual," she said with a frown. "But please promise me we can be together Saturday. It's very important, Brad."

He was puzzled but agreed. She began to dress and so did he. What she said troubled him. It wasn't about her 'gift' – he suspected for some time that she could somehow read his thoughts, though he attributed it to keen insight and intuition. He didn't quite believe her, but he didn't disbelieve her either. No, what troubled him was her insistence on seeing him again before he left. Why would that be so important?

* _ * _ *

Mrs. Griffiths hefted her first Cosmopolitan of the evening and toasted Friday nights. They drank, they ate, and they laughed. After dinner, though, he adopted a serious note for a moment.

"I am leaving on a trip overseas to the U.K. on Sunday," he told her. She smiled and they joked about the Queen, and she toasted the upcoming 10-year anniversary of Charles and Diana.

In the parking lot he opened the door to his Ford Explorer and was about to help her in. She unexpectedly turned and embraced him amorously. "Just promise you'll come back to me, Brad," she said softly to him, then leaned up and sensually kissed his ear.

"I promise," he told her.

* _ * _ *

Dacey looked stunning as she walked down the hall – a mid-thigh length, black, spaghetti-strap fringe cocktail dress, her legs in stockings and high heels, and her long chestnut hair swirling playfully. Ozera looked on longingly. No one watching would ever have guessed that just hours earlier, after an afternoon horse ride, they were making passionate love in his room.

It was summer – vacation time for many – but it was still a busy Saturday night at the Inn. Even with a reservation they still had to wait for a table. They enjoyed a drink in the interim and were eventually escorted to a cozy corner booth table.

After a wonderful dinner they awaited coffee and dessert. "Dacey," he asked her, "What **did** you uncover after your years in that research center? You must have come up with something, right?"

She hesitated before responding. "I can tell you now," she said. Something about what she said bothered him. Why now? What was different? What was going to happen?

"It seems some people in the area of northern Romania have a trait, and are able to pass it on to their progeny. It is a form of natural clairvoyance. Those with it, we discovered, can actually change the magnetic field around them, and that of the earth in their immediate vicinity." He sat silent, astonished. "The Russians suspected, and had developed a hypothesis, which they were in the process of proving. But then the world around us changed and they hastily left, leaving it all behind – their research, and their research subjects."

"What happens," he asked, "When a group of people with this … trait … get together?"

"What happens when enough fissionable material is brought together?" she asked him rhetorically. "At some point you reach critical mass."

"How many of your people here have this?" he asked.

"All of them," she said, "Though to differing degrees."

"You, too?" he asked. She looked in his eyes and slowly nodded.

"The gift you talked about?" Again, she nodded.

He was astonished and wanted to ask a lot more questions, but this was not the night. She was worried about something, something affecting them, and he needed to concentrate on the two of them, not work.

They walked out to the nearly empty parking lot after dinner and saw a beautiful, nearly full moon in the clear starry sky. They stopped to admire it.

"Grandma Moon is watching over us tonight," she said. Then she turned to him: "Brad, let's go up to the Monastery."

"Dacey, Honey, it's almost midnight," he said discouragingly, "And it's getting cool." She returned a 'I don't care, let's just do it please' glare. And so up to the mountaintop they went. It took a few minutes longer than usual for the log gateway to finally swing open – understandable, given the hour. Ozera drove up and onto the parking lot, then looked around and told her to hang on. The SUV took off onto the rough trail that ascended to the Monastery. The ride was bumpy and slippery, given the ruts, the overgrowth and the evening dew. The light from the high-beam headlights bounced erratically, along with them and the SUV, until finally they reached the crest at the top and stopped. His headlights shone on the locked front gates.

They sat a moment, recovering from the bumpy ride. Then he watched as she reached down, took off her high heels and rolled the stockings down her long, sexy legs, one at a time. Leaving the lights on, they got out. It was noticeably cooler on the mountaintop, so he took off his jacket and threw it over her spaghetti-strapped shoulders. He opened the lock and swung open the left front gate.

They entered and the yellow light from his headlights faded quickly as they walked through the tunnel. Ahead, they approached the main hall, bathed in a white light by the overhead moon. It was like crossing between two worlds. As they entered the great hall the view stunned them both. The moon was shining down brightly over the round altar stone and the attending Guardian stones. It looked beautiful – eerie and surreal, but beautiful.

They walked to the large round altar stone. Ozera sat down on the front bench while Dacey walked around behind and caressed the smooth stone surface. She looked up at the bright moon and raised her head and arms, as if basking in it, being nourished by it. Then she lowered her head and looked at him.

"My history begins in the year 1429, Brad," she said to him, matter-of-factly. "I have seen kings, and kingdoms, come and go. I have memories of different times, of people long dead, of conquerors and the conquered." He sat spellbound, listening intently.

"My birthday is March 15th," she went on, "But in the year 1582, I had no birthday. They changed the calendar and eliminated my birthday. Poof. There was March 11th and then it was March 21st." Ozera still didn't understand. She made it sound like it happened yesterday.

"So much time, and yet not enough," she lamented. She walked back around the altar to Ozera, who stood up. "You are leaving tomorrow, my love," she said, tears welling in her eyes. "And I fear we may not see each other again." He looked at her startled. "But who knows?" she said, embracing him. "Maybe someday. Hold me. Love me tonight."

* _ * _ *

Chapter X: Crisis
X: Night in jail

Ozera was puzzled when he reviewed the envelope Lisa had given him for his trip to the U.K. His flight and reservations were all in his name – his real name, despite the Colonel's warning about not traveling abroad using one's own name, and the passports he gave him for that purpose.

The car taking him to Newark airport was due in an hour. Sunday afternoon: Lisa would not be accessible in the office until tomorrow. And he couldn't call the Colonel and talk about phony names and passports, given that it was all recorded – and possibly reported to who knows where?

Simple command decision: He would be gone for maybe four or five days, and everything was already in his real name. He would take his real passport, and stash away the passports the Colonel gave him in a nook somewhere in his room. He'd be careful and keep a low profile.

The Continental flight out was comfortable and uneventful, despite the drudgery of an overnight flight. He ordered a drink and settled down to read Gerhard's file.

Evelyn "Eva" Gerhard. Born 1928 in Leipzig. Ozera chuckled. Leipzig was a key German city before World War II, and then a key East German city under Communist control since 1945. And it was only last year, after the fall of the Soviet empire, that the divided Germany again reunited. He wondered if Frau Doktor Gerhard had revisited Leipzig since then.

She escaped Germany in 1944 at age 16 and went to Switzerland, where she attended undergraduate school. Thank God she wasn't a 16-year-old in East Germany under the Russian occupation at the end of the war.

She did graduate school at and obtained her doctorate from Christ Church College at Oxford in the 1950's. While there she married a Brit, who spent 30 years with MI-6 British Intelligence before retiring. Gerhard rose to head Eastern European Studies. Fluent in German, English and Russian. Deciphers Latin, Romanian, and a half-dozen other ancient Eastern European languages. Can translate early Romanian and Cyrillic texts. Impressive credentials.

Recruited by the Colonel 18 months ago for historical research and forensic archaeology. She knows we are studying the native peoples of this particular region of northern Romania, but she knows nothing else about the Pennsylvania installation. She has focused her whole academic life on the early and Middle Ages in Eastern Europe. An ardent anti-Communist. She gets paid – £48,500 so far – by direct check from Lloyds Bank, a special account arranged by the Colonel. Spends her summer in northern Romania, digging through the archives of monasteries and churches. The last entry: A memo notes that she notified Col John Smith, says she has hit pay dirt and please arrange for retrieval. Capt. Ozera dispatched.

He looked at her fairly recent photo, taken at age 63. Bluish-gray hair, glasses. Tenacious-looking. She knows how to get what she wants, Ozera surmised.

It was the end of June and tourist season, so the plane and everything else was crowded. Like most Americans on the flight, Ozera walked in a half-dazed state after just a couple hours' sleep, through the long airport corridors, through passport control and customs and finally, out to local transportation.

It was a bittersweet trip. Ozera had taken Kathy to England on their honeymoon a few years back. It was a minimal one-week trip, on a cut-rate plane fare, in cut-rate hotels and eating fish and chips every night. But when you're young and in love …

"It's about an hour, right up the M-40," the car driver told him. They agreed on $100 U.S. cash and they were off. A delightful summer drive, early morning and little traffic and hub-bub. It was noon when the car pulled into the Malmaison.

"An unusual looking hotel," Ozera commented.

"That it is, sir. It was a prison until the 1950's. Originally it was a battlement built by William the Conqueror in the 11th century. You'll enjoy spending the night in this jail," the driver told him with a smile. "They've replaced the bars, but you'll be sleeping in what was a dungeon 900 years ago."

An hour later Ozera was sitting on the patio of the restaurant, sipping a gin and tonic; they apologized for not having bourbon. He looked at the ancient stonework around him and thought about what Bennington had told him. What if a structure like this could be moved – not physically, but in the time dimension? Was there some set of rare conditions that could reveal this structure today, as it was back in 1061?

After lunch and a drink he couldn't stay awake any longer, and returned to his room for a nap. It seemed he'd just nodded off when the phone rang. It was Gerhard, asking for "Mr. Ozera?" She wanted to arrange their meeting and proposed the following morning.

"If you don't mind, I'd rather we meet at Salisbury," she said. "Too many people know me around town here in Oxford. I know it's about an hour's ride, but it's supposed to be a very pleasant day. "

"Sure," Ozera said. "Where in Salisbury?"

"I was thinking Stonehenge. Have you been there before?" she asked.

"No."

"Then you'll get to see England's most striking Neolithic ceremonial structure." She sounded like a professor, with a faint but unmistaken German influence underlying the British accent.

"It's quite a tourist trap, isn't it? Won't it be crowded?" he asked.

"Not in the middle of the week," she countered. "How's, say, 11 am sound?"

"That'll be fine," he agreed.

"I'm in my late 50's, and I'll be wearing a red hat," she said. He kept to himself the fact that he knew what she looked like, and that he knew she was really 63. He told her he was 30, with short brown hair and would be wearing a white scarf.

Ozera called the concierge and arranged for a car the next day to Stonehenge. Pick-up at 10, return by 2 pm. And could they find him a white scarf? With that taken care of, he turned in again, sleeping through dinnertime.

*_*_*

It was a long, interrupted night – acclimatizing to the five-hour time change. At 11 pm he got up and got dressed, deciding to head out for a late-night, self-guided walking tour around town. Oxford was a lively, cosmopolitan college town, and there was no shortage of pubs and restaurants for snacks and meals.

With the hotel's map in hand he plotted a course around the city, up and down hills, stopping for drinks and then a late dinner. On the return he strolled through an old, eerily lighted cemetery, and was in awe of the still-legible gravestones dating from the 15th, 14th, even 13th centuries. He looked down at a big one and smiled: John Smith, born 1323, died 1401.

Ozera returned and slept, off and on. Just before 5 am came the sunrise and he decided finally to get up. He showered and dressed and at 6 am went down and was the first hotel guest for breakfast. He'd eaten at midnight but was very hungry and enjoyed a full English breakfast. Afterwards he stopped at the desk and the bleary-eyed receptionist handed him a small shopping bag. Inside was a new, £35, white silk scarf. "Perfect," he said, stuffing it in his pocket. He checked on his car and was told the charge for car and driver for the four-hour round-trip would be £190 – and that a tip to the driver was **not** expected.

He watched some exceedingly boring morning British TV fare, then donned his tan blazer and headed back to the lobby. He exchanged five hundred dollars for British Pounds and found that his driver was already waiting. Ozera introduced himself and they shook hands – the driver, Robert, had an exceptionally powerful grip. He was a large, good-looking man, built like Ozera, and well-groomed in immaculate chauffeur garb.

They got in the uncommonly large black sedan and took off. Although cloudy, damp and cool, Ozera enjoyed the ride through the rolling hills of southwest England. They arrived and pulled into the large parking lot across the highway from the ancient monument. He tried to hide his excitement: he'd seen pictures but never visited the legendary structure in person. An ancient observatory, that much was known. But despite hundreds of archaeological studies they still didn't know who built it, or when, or how.

* _ * _ *

The Monastery

X: Summit at Stonehenge

There were some summertime tourists, though Gerhard was right: it was not very crowded. Ozera got out, leaving his car and driver, and draped the white scarf around his neck. He walked along the path towards the imposing structure.

Several cars were parked right next to the pathway, and a short woman – wearing a long gray overcoat and a striking red hat – stood next to one. She had already seen him and was walking to intercept him. Her blue-gray hair clashed with the vivid red headgear. She had two manila envelopes in hand.

"Mr. Ozera?" she asked with some trepidation. She bore the face of a prim and proper, aging librarian.

"Dr. Eva Gerhard, I presume," he said with an endearing smile, hoping to put her at ease. It worked and she returned a modest smile. They shook hands warmly, then she gestured towards the pathway and they walked along side-by-side. Ozera saw her slip on her thick glasses. They must be for close-up, Ozera reasoned; she had no problem spotting him across the parking lot.

"I hope you stay and enjoy the monument," she said. "It really is a magnificent structure."

"I'm afraid I'll have to be on my way," he replied. "My boss says you've dug up some treasure for us."

"Yes, I have," she replied excitedly. "I have found two cryptic, though definitive, references to Manastirea Munte in northern Romania. There is no doubt: There **was** a monastery there somewhere, even though we still don't know where that location actually is, or was. I spent a month in the area late last summer. It's pretty remote. I met several older people who indicate they've heard of the place, where a monastery once was but is now gone. But nobody was willing to discuss it outright. They just … look away. Very peculiar."

"So what have you turned up?" he asked, indicating the envelopes she was carrying. She handed him one. He opened it and pulled out a copy of a portion of a very old document with very faded and very small handwriting on it. He couldn't make out much of the writing or the language. He looked at the other papers in the envelope, which apparently were translation details, written on modern notepaper.

"The original is on a piece of paper that isn't doing too well," she told him. "I copied this for you soon as I could after I found it. I estimate the original came from the 12th or 13th century. You can barely make it out today anymore. I spent two months on the translation, and really just finished it last month."

"What is it? What's it say?" he asked impatiently.

"I finally determined that the language is a flavor of Istro-Romanian. It's pretty much extinct today, though it is spoken in a few scattered villages in Croatia, a small part of what's left over from Yugoslavia." Ozera nodded. He'd heard of the break-up and growing in-fighting between factions of the former Yugoslavia. It was all going on about the same time as the revolution in Romania after the Russians' departure.

"And so what is it?"

"A prayer," she told him. "It's religious prattling, reminiscent of the Catholic mass. But what is particularly notable is the first line, which says this prayer comes from Monastery Mountain in the north of Romania."

"And so what does the prayer say?" he reiterated, with growing impatience.

She sighed. "There are a few words that I had to give my best guess to, but I believe this is a pretty close translation. It's some sort of rite … or prayer, or incantation. It reads like a prayer begging God for deliverance from impending doom. My best guess at the title is "Rite of Transition," or "Rite of Crossing. The church where I found it had no idea where it was from originally, or what the rite was for. I could only make out and translate part of it. There is at least one more page, but the rest of it was nowhere to be found. So you have the translation of just the first part of it."

Ozera nodded. "Okay, good job. And the other?" he asked, putting the papers back in the first manila envelope.

"Well, this is more peculiar," she said handing him the other envelope. He opened it and pulled out a piece of heavy paper, sealed in a clear plastic binder. "It is some sort of birth register. To be honest I don't know exactly what it is. It is Latin, circa 1650."

"A birth register?" he asked.

"It's nice handwriting, and it's all legible. And it's unquestionably pre-1700, from the ink, paper and Latin style. It was in a frame on the wall of an old home in Izvoarele Sucevei, or Izvoarele Springs, where I spent a few nights. It was the home of an old woman, who told me it came from her great, great-Uncle, who was a Monk in a monastery nearby. The thing is, there isn't a monastery within a hundred miles of her town today. And she hadn't a clue of which monastery or where it was."

He looked it over. It was listing of some sort. Maybe 30 or so entries. "So what's it all about?"

"Well, here, the top line, 'Monasterium in monte,' means the Monastery on the Mountain, or perhaps Monastery Mountain. Can't be sure. The second line, 'filii monasterium,' means the children of the Monastery. And it's a table with four columns. These mean: birth year, child's name, sex and mother. The first date was 946; the last 1651. That's how I figured it was a 17th century document. There are about 30 or 40 years between entries."

He looked and saw the first was a girl, born in 946 A.D., named Maria de Magyar. The mother: Ilinca de Lup.

"What does this mean?" he asked, pointing at the first line.

"Well, in Latin, it would mean Maria of the Magyars, and Ilinca of the Wolf," she answered.

"Of the wolf?" he muttered.

"The ancient peoples of the area were the Dacians," she told him. "Their emblem was the wolf."

The last entry was a girl born in 1651, named Carol de Prussia; mother: Celestina de Lup. He scanned the list and his eyes were drawn to an entry halfway down the list – a girl born in 1429, named Daciana de Lup; mother: Ilinca de Lup. The same mother, Ilinca de Lup, had given birth three times – in 946, in 1039 and then again 1429.

"Ilinca?" he uttered out loud, "Couldn't be the same mother. Three children – over a period of, what, 500 years?!"

"You've heard the stories and legends, I'm sure," she said to him. "Maybe there's some truth to it?"

Daciana de Lup. It couldn't be his Dacey. "De Lup," he said to Gerhard. "There's a lot of them. "What would that be in today's language?"

She thought about it. "Well, in today's Romanian, I'd guess … Lupescu," she said, then chuckled. "The same word would mean 'she-wolf,' too."

Ozera thought about it and smiled. "Okay. Anything else, Frau Doktor?" he asked.

"Just the latest bill, which I'll send in the usual way."

"And that is ... ?"

"I post it to a mailbox address in the states that the Colonel gave me," she said, adding, with a smile: "It takes a while but the check does show up eventually."

Ozera thanked her and folded the envelopes and slipped them inside his jacket. They turned and headed back down the path to the parking lot.

The video camera was equipped with a high-powered zoom lens. The chauffeur in the large black sedan turned it off and slipped it under the front seat.

* _ * _ *

X: Skullduggery

In his gilded cell of the former prison, Ozera sat back in the comfortable armchair. He replayed in his mind the session with Gerhard and the curious documents she gave him. Daciana de Lup. The Rite of Crossing? Two more pieces of the jigsaw puzzle.

He had an urge to call the Colonel and brief him about the Gerhard meeting. He checked his watch; it was early afternoon back there. But he thought about it and decided against it: He couldn't call – it was all intercepted and recorded – and with the boss' growing paranoia …

Ozera was getting hungry and would need to go get some dinner. But something wasn't sitting well. It was a feeling. He couldn't nail it down, but making a copy of the Gerhard documents seemed like a good precaution.

He grabbed the two envelopes headed out to the front desk, hearing his room door click closed behind him. Ozera didn't see the door ajar down the hall, or the familiar face that was watching him as he left his room. The door opened and he stepped out into the hallway, dressed neatly in the black uniform of the hotel staff. Hotel staff, chauffeur, bobby, repairman, FedEx courier. He chuckled to himself: clothes did indeed make the man.

Ozera went to the front desk and pulled the documents out of both envelopes.

"I need a copy of each of these," he said, handing the documents to the attractive woman in the black uniform behind the counter. "And this Latin document in the plastic pouch, do the best you can." She nodded and took it all into the back room.

Guests were coming and going in the busy lobby as he stood idly by. The doorman was escorting couples out for the evening and politely loading them into taxis. Then a glass door opened nearby and a waiter clad in black came out with a tray of drinks and scurried up a nearby staircase. As the glass door swung closed, though, Ozera caught a whiff of something familiar. What was it?

He walked to the door and looked in. It was a smoking lounge and bar, now empty. He opened the door and stepped in. His nose caught a pungent tobacco smoke. He'd smelled the same thing before, and recently. It was a sickening sweetness, like … Could it be? Bennington? Here in England? Why would he be here?

Ozera went back to the reception desk. The lady reappeared in a moment with the originals and the pile of copies, which he folded and stuffed into his jacket breast pocket. He returned to his room, but didn't notice that everything had been meticulously and professionally searched.

He decided to check out and leave the next day. There was no sense staying on, and he was anxious to get back and share the documents, and his thoughts, with the Colonel. He stashed the original documents in his suitcase, kept the copies in his jacket pocket, and left for dinner.

He found a cozy pub a few blocks away, sat at the bar and enjoyed the traditional ambiance. Given the dearth of bourbon he decided to try a decent scotch, and then toasted the picture of the Queen on the wall. He grimaced after the first sip – tastes like rusty water, he thought – and ordered a more potable substitute – gin and tonic. A delicious dinner of bangers and mashed potatoes ensued, and afterwards some delicate international diplomacy – with a pair of local lovelies who dropped in and sat next to him.

The streets of Oxford were fairly deserted on his walk back. It was 11 pm and a weeknight. Going back through the hotel lobby he stopped to look again into the smoking lounge. Two young men with their dates were puffing cigars and enjoying brandy. But no pipe smokers.

At the desk he advised the night clerk he'd be checking out the following day, and returned to his room. Everything looked in order, and he went to check the documents in his suitcase. They were there, right where he left them. Maybe his gut feeling was unfounded, he thought.

It was his last thought for the time being. A single, professionally delivered blow to his neck struck from a silent assailant. A sharp pain screeched through his head and down his spine, and he collapsed unconscious.

* - * - *

Ozera awoke with a blinding headache, which began to subside slightly as he sat up and looked around, disoriented. Hotel room. That's right, Oxford. He struggled to get up, his knees still a little unsteady. Looking at his watch: 2:30 am. The papers! He reached over into his suitcase. Not there. He groped around the whole suitcase. Nope, gone. Then he remembered the copies in his jacket and reached into his pocket. Empty, too. Gone. He checked his wallet and passport. Whew! They were still there. So he could still get back home – but empty-handed.

"Oh, shit," he muttered, sitting down at the desk, dejectedly.

Now what to do? He'd been out cold, on the floor, for hours. He looked over at the door. Closed. Whoever it was had a key, or they may have been in the room when he got back, or they may have quietly followed him in. But they knew what they were doing; they could easily have killed him, but didn't. So they just wanted the documents, it seemed.

No sense calling the cops; that'd just delay him from leaving in the morning. But who was it, and why? Maybe the Colonel was right. Maybe someone was looking to take over the project.

To catch his scheduled return flight he'd be checking out and leaving in about six hours. He wouldn't have a chance to call the Colonel; it was late at night back home. But … he could call the B&B, check in with Mrs. Griffiths, and maybe get Dacey on the phone.

It took 20 minutes to place the call. The Griffiths' Bed and Breakfast, Narrows Hill Road, Upper Black Eddy, Pennsylvania, in the U.S. Finally it rang through and Mrs. Griffiths' familiar voice answered.

"Brad! Geez, it's nice to hear your voice. It's a beautiful summer night here. Just got out of the hot tub. All alone. Could sure use a lifeguard."

"Is the Doctor around?" he asked her.

"No. That's the weird thing. We had a drink together earlier … well, I did. She didn't want anything. She looked sad and, well, sort of desolate, despondent. She was preoccupied with something. She said she'd be leaving and she wouldn't be back."

"She said she wouldn't be back? Ever? Where'd she go?" He asked.

"Beats me. I don't think she meant forever, though. She didn't take her stuff. I checked her room and it looks like almost everything is still there. She took her Jeep, and poof, gone. Something's very wrong, Brad."

"Look, I'll be back late tomorrow. Hang loose, okay? Things have been a little weird here, too, in England. I should be back in Newark airport around dinnertime."

He lay down and tried to get some sleep but still had a throbbing headache and couldn't clear his mind. And going home empty-handed; he felt ashamed. Calling the front desk or the police wouldn't help. Whoever got his stuff was long gone.

Getting replacements for the documents from Gerhard shouldn't be that hard – as long as she was still alright. They could certainly trace the documents back to her. She would still have good copies, even if just the translations. Hopefully she would remain under the radar and out of their sight. But her only exposure of late was out at Stonehenge, and who could have seen them meet there?

He showered and got dressed as the sun came up. At 6 am he went for a hardy English breakfast. It would be a long day. It was still just 1 am back home.

*_*_*

X: Fallout

The flight back to Newark seemed to last forever – the way it always is when you are going home. In this case though delays accumulated and they arrived two hours late. Despite the long tedious flight he couldn't nap on the plane. He'd always had a hard time sleeping while traveling, whether in a car, train, helicopter, tank, you name it. He managed to pass right through immigration and customs, though he still had a ways to go.

He stopped at the first available pay phone, desperate to get a call through to the Colonel and bring him up to date. It was probably too late in the day, but maybe Lisa would still be around and answer. He dialed, then waited, but it didn't ring.

"The number you are dialing has been disconnected," the recording mechanically said. He must have misdialed, so he hung up and tried again. Same message.

"What the hell?" he muttered to himself, hanging up the receiver. Well, that was damned peculiar. Why would a U.S. Government research facility have their phones disconnected?

As he descended the escalator to the exit he saw his driver waiting, holding a sign for him. 'Well at least someone is still on the job,' Ozera mulled to himself. It was late and dark, but at least traffic along the interstate was light. In due course the sedan turned off River Road and headed up Narrows Hill Road. He wanted to find out if Mrs. Griffiths knew what was going on, so he told the driver to pass by the facility entrance and drive on ahead and turn into the B&B.

The car dropped him and left, and Ozera rushed up to the door. Mrs. Griffiths was sitting in the front parlor with a drink – quietly and apparently alone – with a worried look. Relieved to see him, she stood up and they embraced.

"When you called last night everything was kind of normal," she explained. "Like I told you, though, the Doctor left earlier, saying she wouldn't be back." He nodded. "And then, just before morning, things up there went nuts. I don't know what happened, but helicopters arrived – several of them, woke me up. They were buzzing the mountain for hours. Things finally calmed down this afternoon and it's been quiet since then. I tried calling John but the call won't go through. The phones are out – disconnected, the recording says."

"Yeah, I know," he said, "I tried calling too a few hours ago and got the same thing. Did anybody come here – like, looking for the Doctor or me?"

"No."

"Let's get to bed. I'm dead tired. I'll go up and check things out on the mountain at first light. There's nothing else I can do now." They went to her room, undressed and climbed in bed. He kept his shirt, pants and shoes nearby – handy. She held him and fell right asleep. In a few minutes he nodded off, too, but slept lightly, starting at every sound.

* - * - *

Still on European time, Ozera awoke and slipped out of bed about 4 am. He washed and got dressed. Then after checking that Mrs. Griffiths was still sound asleep, he quietly left. The night sky was just starting to lighten as he drove out and up the road to the mountaintop entrance.

Everything looked normal. The same 'Government Property' and 'No Trespassing' signs were still in place. He waited for the log gate to click, whirr and swing open. But it didn't. He waited a while longer. Still nothing. He glanced over at the camera on the nearby post. Something was different; a small, inconspicuous green light that used to glow on the top of the unit was off. The camera didn't move. Curious.

He decided to get out, lock his Ford Explorer and hoof it the half-mile up to the top. It was eerily quiet. On a pleasant summer morning like this the birds singing would normally be cacophonous.

The parking lot looked normal too, but there was no sign of any activity. Two of the facility's SUVs were parked in their normal spots, and outside the Conference Center was the Doctor's Jeep. He stood a moment and looked around. No sign of life. But he felt something – a gut feeling he sometimes got out in the field. And usually he was proven right. Somebody was watching him. He didn't know from where, but he'd bet a month's pay that somebody was watching him.

He cautiously went into the Command Center. Nobody there, and the office was trashed. All drawers had been pulled out and emptied. All doors were wide open. Lisa's computer was gone. He went into the Colonel's office. It had been turned upside down. Somebody was looking for something. Almost everything that could be carried away was taken. The Colonel's closet door was wide open and had been thoroughly ransacked, too.

The Security Center? He dashed up the steps. The access doorway was open and the camera was missing. All the electronics had been removed from the inside, leaving dozens of dangling cables and power cords. In the rear quarters things were less disturbed. The light on a coffee pot was on and the coffee in the glass carafe had dried up and burnt. So power was still on, Ozera reasoned. He turned the coffee pot off. There was food in the fridge. But there was no trace of the security detail, or their clothes or weapons. It's like it had been evacuated in a hurry.

Downstairs and out the back door, Ozera ran over to the Conference Center. The conference rooms and lounge furniture were all in place. In the Doctor's office the filing cabinets had been ransacked and papers were everywhere. In Wainright's lab the filing cabinet was similarly trashed. His wall apparatus and plastic bins were cracked; plastic balls were all over the floor.

Over to the Dorm building next door. It looked like everybody had just gotten up and walked out. The kitchen and most everything else was neat and orderly. No meals or cooking were in progress. Upstairs the bedrooms had been searched – mattresses overturned and personal items thrown about. Ozera checked the utility building. Generator and pumps still on. Still a few weeks' worth of fuel in the oil tanks.

Ozera walked back over the parking lot, slowly, shaking his head. What the hell happened here? It looks like someone gave the order to shut down and terminate the project. But it had to be someone way up the food chain, given all the people and equipment involved.

The searching and seizure, Ozera concluded, was frantic and careless. The evacuation of the people, though, was controlled and orderly. There was no sign of blood, violence or any forced abduction. Nobody put up a fight, he concluded. It had to be a U.S. government operation, he guessed. Clearly the security team was involved, so whoever was behind this must have had their cooperation.

But who controlled the security detail? Was it the same people the Colonel worked for? He never bothered to confront the Colonel to find out. That just didn't seem necessary, and might have been seen by him as distrust, questioning. The Colonel seemed to be quietly, and securely, in charge, and he trusted Ozera with everything else. They had grown close, and Ozera did trust him, explicitly. 'But we all work for somebody,' he remembered the Colonel told him.

Then the Monastery flashed through his mind. Could anyone be up there? Might the Romanians be hiding in it? He turned and headed up the pathway through the tall grass, quickening his pace as he neared the crest.

He rounded the top and stopped cold. A chill went up his spine. "What the shit?!" he muttered. It was … gone. There was only the original bedrock foundation – as if all the construction above the natural, solid rock base was just … never there.

Ozera walked over the area, looking for evidence – any indication – of what had happened. Nothing. There was no sign of any demolition or tearing down – no bulldozer or crane tracks. Nothing. It was just gone. There is no way, he reasoned, in just a day – or even two or three – that every trace of the Monastery could have been removed so thoroughly. And why would anybody – any organization or agency of the U.S. Government – want all trace of the Monastery removed so quickly and completely?

He paused for a moment. Another feeling had come over him – an unusual feeling he hadn't felt before. He felt that Dacey, the woman he loved, was somehow there, nearby … and yet not there.

*_*_*

What to do now? Who could he call? Hell, he didn't even know for sure who he and the Colonel worked for. And what happened to the Colonel? He didn't know where he might be, or even where he lived.

Then he remembered what the Colonel told him, about a safe in his closet, and he didn't want anybody else to know about it. He said it was somewhere in his closet, hidden – but he said he could find it if he looked for it. His office was a shambles, and it's doubtful anything was left unturned. Still, who knows? He'd go take a look.

He retraced his path back to the parking lot. He got that gut feeling again: Despite the appearance of abandonment, someone was still around … watching. It was a good military tactic. When you pull out of an area, leave a rear guard to see who turns up.

There was nothing left related to the Monastery project remaining in the Colonel's office. He entered the closet and flipped on the light. One bare light bulb came on. Another at the back of the closet was out. It was the same chaos in there, stuff strewn everywhere.

He shuffled through the rubish on the closet floor with his foot, and for the first time noticed the black and white linoleum tile pattern. He looked out into the office: The tiles were laid in a perfect checkerboard pattern. Then he looked at the back of the closet and saw a change in the pattern. He went over and tapped the back light bulb and it flickered. He twisted it and it came on. The Colonel had it slightly unscrewed, to keep the back of the closet dark.

Ozera bent down and pushed away the trash, revealing a section of floor with a flaw in the pattern – there was a black tile missing. Since it's the back of a closet they might simply have used whatever tiles they had left. Or maybe not. He felt around the floor. Two of the tiles were slightly loose and he plucked them up, revealing the concrete underlayment. There were two holes in the concrete under each of the removed pieces. He put his fingers in and yanked up hard. A floor section came up, revealing the square metal door of a combination safe. Well, they didn't find this, he thought with a smile.

The combination? Then he remembered what the Colonel told him: It was the phone number, the first six digits. He looked out and saw a phone on the Colonel's desk. He went and lifted the receiver. Dead. He saw a pencil, got a scrap of paper and wrote down the first six digits: 21, 53, 81. Back to the closet he knelt down and tried the combination, spinning the dial clockwise to 21, then left to 53, and back again over the 21 to 81. He took a deep breath and pulled the handle. It turned and he swung the door up.

There were some papers on top. He grabbed them: it was a two-page, handwritten, hastily scrawled letter to him, from the Colonel.

Brad,

I sure hope it's you reading this. I have to write fast, so pardon the brevity. They're coming, I'm sure, and I don't know what they're going to do. What Bennington told you is true: There are agencies in our government that nobody speaks of, like a government within the government. Some of them do have our country's best interests at heart. But this is a deceptive business and you can never be sure. The only one I really trust, believe it or not, is you. And I've tried to keep you out of all the backroom bullshit.

Security called last night to tell me they found the Dorm building empty. The walking patrol said he saw some of the Romanians heading up the path to the mountaintop. We were going to install cameras overlooking the area, including the Monastery, but we hadn't gotten around to it. Anyhow, security called me back and told me: the Monastery was gone.

It looks like whatever it is <u>can</u> be reproduced, Brad. Whatever's been happening there in northern Romania, it happened here last night, to our Monastery, on our mountaintop. In the light of the full moon I dashed out and went up last night. The Doctor's car was here, so she was in on it – probably arranged the whole thing. I went up and looked for myself. The whole thing – disappeared. Just bare bedrock, like it was before we started building.

Whatever it took to make it happen – the right people, prayer, the structure itself, maybe even the full moon, who the hell knows – it was all there last night. What happened to it, and the people in it? I haven't a clue, but I'll bet you dollars to doughnuts that someday we'll find out.

Security reported all this back to HQ, I'm sure, and it won't be long now. If it's the people I think, they'll keep me incommunicado somewhere, debrief me for a few weeks, and then reassign me. But if it's the others, they may take this all and move it into the deep black void, and me with it. You don't know these people, Brad; they are ruthless and they do what they want.

Assuming the worse, I'd advise you to get out of here. I mean, leave the country, at least for a few months, until things settle down. They can't get at you as easily overseas. The more remote the better. What's here in the safe should help you get by. Sorry I couldn't do more. Get going now, and don't look back. If they find you, well, I don't know. Just be sure they don't.

I hear choppers coming. Take care. See ya.

John S
Col, Inf, USA

Ozera smiled. The Colonel was no doubt under a lot of pressure, but he was used to pressure and stayed cool. But despite it all he still had to sign off – as a U.S. Army Infantry Colonel. It was in his blood. He played the spook game in the dark swirling world of intelligence, but who he was, first and foremost, was a U.S. Army soldier.

* - * - *

X: On the run

Ozera tucked the letter in his pocket. He reached down into the safe and felt … a gun. He pulled out an Army .45. He popped the clip; fully loaded, and slipped it in the belt in the small of his back. He reached in and pulled out a black canvas satchel. He unzipped it and looked inside. Bundles of cash, maybe thirty or forty bundles – of hundred-dollar bills.

He shut the empty safe, zipped the bag, stood up and flipped off the lights. If there was somebody nearby watching, he was likely to soon find out.

He needed a plan. His boss had advised him to run, get away, for at least a few months. He would high-tail it down to his car, stop in the B&B, grab his passports, and head off to the airport. No time to stop at his parents' home, he reasoned. Whoever shut down the NEPA Facility would be looking for him. His military training, experience and instincts were coming into play.

He cautiously walked out of Control Central, satchel in hand, and across the parking lot. He looked around nervously; he was very exposed, unavoidably. He crossed the parking lot and as he turned to head down the gravel road towards the entrance, a rifle shot rang out. Immediately a bullet struck the ground just a few feet in front of him. He froze, fighting his instinct to hit the ground or run and seek cover. The edge of the woods was 15 to 20 feet away.

The round hit the gravel road just downhill from where he stood. Ozera knew a sniper could easily have killed him, but did not. He had enough experience with snipers to know what it meant: Stay put. Even a novice sharpshooter could have put the round into his temple if he wanted, and this shooter was probably a seasoned pro.

Someone was trying to keep him there, probably until they could close in on him. They were likely watching him since he first showed up at the compound. They would have seen him come in empty-handed, and now was walking out with a satchel – something they hadn't found. And they wanted it, and probably also him. They probably knew that a U.S. Army Captain Bradley Ozera was assigned to the Colonel and this project. But did these people know it was him – and that he was on the same side as them? And if so, did they care?

Ozera slowly glanced over his shoulder to where he thought the shot came from. Snipers setup in a hidden spot with a clear field of fire. And Ozera figured he, or maybe more than one of them, were probably in the wood line on the other side of the open field. That's where he would have set-up – maybe 200, 250 yards away – offering a commanding overview of most of the compound.

Snipers locate their target through the magnifying scope of a high-powered rifle. They center the crosshairs on where they want the bullet to go and, when everything is right, they exhale and slowly squeeze off their shot. Then there's the recoil, which takes the shooter a second or two to re-orient the scope back on the target. That would be his edge, his moment. Make the sniper shoot again, and then he'd dash to the wood line. In a couple seconds he would be under cover and out of sight.

So now he had a plan. His body tensed and he took a big step forward. As expected, another rifle crack. But just as the gravel kicked up in front of him he took off, satchel in hand, making a break for the woods. He heard another shot, and this time the round hit the gravel behind him. He dove into the woods and, staying low, crawled on elbows and knees behind a tree – his heart racing. The woods were good cover, fully leaved and shady on this warm summer day. He looked down at himself – jeans and a brown, short-sleeved shirt. Not bad. He would not be easily spotted. But he had to keep low, keep moving and get out of the area. They would be coming after him.

He slowly backed off, turned and crawled further into the dark woods. He got up and, hunched down, moved stealthily down the mountain, paralleling the gravel access road. He approached the entrance, looked out and immediately hit the ground. A black SUV had pulled behind his and three men in dark suits were walking around. One was discreetly carrying a Mark 5 rifle with a scope. Another was talking on a scratchy walkie-talkie, probably to his cohorts up on top of the mountain.

So now what? Knowing the Colonel's penchant for secrecy, and distrust even of the people he worked for, the chances were he didn't tell anyone that Ozera lived in the B&B down the road. That made sense, Ozera reasoned, since there was no paperwork, and nobody showed up there to question Mrs. Griffiths or search the place. That's where he'd go, through the woods … and hopefully they weren't already there waiting for him.

He backed up slowly … then heard a branch snap behind him. He froze, expecting a bullet in the back. A few seconds passed, and nothing. He slowly turned his head and looked over his shoulder. Just ten yards away stood a big, beautiful buck with proud antlers. They looked each other in the eye for a moment. Then the buck turned and stealthily bounded away. Ozera, who had been holding his breath, slowly exhaled.

Crouching low and moving quietly he followed Narrows Hill Road through the woods towards the B&B. He stopped, still hidden in the woods across the road from Mrs. Griffiths' driveway, and scanned the grounds carefully. Nobody in sight. He looked back up the road towards the mountaintop entrance. A slight turn kept the three men and their SUV out of his view – and him out of theirs. He knew the grounds around the B&B well from his morning runs. If he could just cross the road unobserved, he could slip behind the hedge and into the wood line that leads down to the main farmhouse.

He looked both ways, took a deep breath and decided to go for it. In two seconds he was on the other side and behind the hedge. Ozera looked up the road and now could see the SUV

behind his, but he did not see any of the men. They probably
went into the woods looking for him. He had to stay low.
His heart raced as he ran to the wood line. Made it. He was
panting – from the physical exertion as well as the adrenalin.
He warily made his way to the house, which now was
between him and the men out on the road.

* _ * _ *

X: Escape

He looked around. Mrs. Griffiths' red pick-up truck was in the driveway. The tailgate was down and bales of hay were in the back. But no one was around; no Mrs. Griffiths, no visitors. He opened the door and stepped inside, quietly closing the door behind him.

"Mrs. Griffiths?" he called out to her with a guarded voice. Nothing. He started to worry and walked quietly and carefully into the front sitting room.

"What is it, Brad?" the voice right behind him said, scaring the hell out of him. He spun around to see her and heaved a sigh of relief. She had an innocent but concerned expression on her pretty face. "What's the matter?" she asked, "You look like you've seen the devil."

"I think I have," he said, "Out on the road."

"Oh, those guys out there?"

"You've seen them?"

"Yeah. They pulled up about an hour ago," she replied. "It looks like they've got your car blocked in."

"That's the least of my problems," he said. "They're after me."

"Why, Brad? What have you done? What happened up there?" she asked.

Ozera mulled his answer, a frustrated look on his face. "We've been conducting research up there. Research that could yield something very powerful."

"A weapon?" she asked.

"I don't think so, but who knows? Maybe someday. Anyhow, while I was in England they had a breakthrough of sorts up there. And different agencies in our government are now tripping over each other to get hold of it."

"What kind of research, Brad?"

"Well, it has to do with certain people, and groups of people, with certain backgrounds and capabilities," he said. "We were looking into capabilities of the mind that nobody even knew for sure were there."

"And you and the people up there did?" she asked.

"Seems so," he replied.

"And they would kill you, or John, over it?"

He shrugged. "I don't … think so. They could have done that already if that's what they wanted. They'll probably take me away for a long time," he said, "Probably to wherever John Smith is."

"Where's John? Is he okay?" she asked.

"I don't know," he answered. "He was nowhere around up there. Gone … somewhere. I think they took him."

"What can I do?" she asked with loving eyes and a sincere smile. Not a second's hesitation. What a gal!

"I need a ride out of here," he said, "To get by those people. When I get off this mountain I'll head for an airport – probably to Newark over in Jersey."

He had to get some things out of his room. She told him to get what he needed and meet at her truck outside. He ran up and packed a small carry-on suitcase with some clothes and underwear. He took about half the money packs out of the satchel and tucked them in a suitcase pocket inside. He grabbed his three passports – his own, plus the Colonel's two alias gifts – and stuck them in his pants.

He took his suitcase, and the satchel with the rest of the money – he guessed maybe $200,000 or so – downstairs. He stopped at the reception counter and wrote Mrs. Griffiths a short note:

> Make the most of this, my dear.
> I'll be back when I can.
> Thanks for everything.
>   Love, Brad

He tucked the note in the satchel and threw it behind the counter, out of sight. Stepping outside he looked around carefully. Mrs. Griffiths was waiting by the back of her truck. She had thrown a tarp over the bales of hay in the truck bed and tied it down. She opened the tailgate, revealing a hiding place between the bales. Ozera looked on approvingly.

"So where to?" she asked.

"Let's see if we can get past them, and then a few miles away. Head south down the river road a while. Then pull over and I'll get out and come around, okay?" He threw his bag in the front and came back around where Mrs. Griffiths was. Unexpectedly, he reached over and undid two buttons of her blouse, exhibiting more of her ample bosom and bra.

"Diversion," he said. "Basic military tactic. If they're looking at those bouncing beauties they won't be concentrating on looking for me." She smiled, pulled her shoulders back and gave a jiggle.

He climbed in between two bales of hay. She pulled the tarp over and tied it down, then stood back and eyed the result.

"Looks good, Brad. I think we can pull it off."

"I know we will. Just act friendly when you drive by them. Try to stay cool."

She got in and saw his suitcase. She moved it onto the floor and threw a denim jacket over it. They pulled out, bouncing along the winding driveway, and turned left onto Narrows Hill Road. She slowly approached the two SUVs at the entrance. Two men were standing. A taller one held an M-16; the shorter one looked unarmed, but she figured he probably had something holstered under his dark suit jacket.

As she approached the short man, apparently in charge, walked across to her side of the road and signaled her to slow down. The other subtly slipped his rifle down to his side – keeping it handy, but less visible and threatening. She decided it was best to stop. She opened her window and slipped her arm under her breasts as she leaned over, enhancing the provocative view.

"You boys lost?" she asked the short man. He walked up and, upon noticing the impressive cleavage, offered a lascivious smile.

"No, ma'am," he replied. Then he shifted his gaze to her face. "Have you seen a guy walking around here, maybe with a black bag?" In her rear-view mirror she saw the other man looking over the tarp and hay bales in the back. Her heart was pounding; it was everything she could do to appear calm. Depending on what happened, she was prepared to hit the gas and tear out down the mountain.

"Ummm, nope," she replied, and after a pause: "I've got to go feed the horses, fellas," she said, her thumb pointing to the back.

He looked over the back of the pick-up to his colleague and nodded, then turned back to her with the same smile. "Okay, thanks, ma'am," he said, stepping back. She nodded and took off slowly. In a few moments they were out of sight. She looked at her hand shaking, and only then realized how frightened she was.

In a few minutes she had turned south onto the river road. She leaned out the window and yelled back: "All clear, Brad. I'll find a spot up ahead and pull over." A mile or so ahead was a gas station with a convenience store. She pulled over and drove behind it, then got out and dropped the rear gate. Ozera shimmied out, stood and they embraced.

He kissed and hugged her. "You were wonderful!" he gushed. She was still calming down, but accepted his glowing praise with a wistful smile. Ozera re-tied the tarp. He brushed himself off, moved his suitcase into the back and climbed into the passenger's seat.

"So where to now?" she asked.

"Newark airport," he said.

"Where are you going?"

"Out of town," he replied. "Way out of town, like out of the country." He didn't want to elaborate. He wasn't sure himself yet where he'd go. But they might still come and interrogate her, trying to find out where he went. And if she didn't know, she couldn't tell.

They drove a few miles and got onto the interstate, headed east across the Delaware River and through New Jersey.

She broke the silence. "How long will you be gone, Brad."

"I'm not sure," he answered. "Could be a while, months." He figured she deserved to know that much.

He wondered himself what was next. Where would he go? Europe? That would make the best use of his language skills. Would he use his U.S. alias, Victor Livingston? Or maybe he'd be Romanian, Stefan Ionescu. He would **not** be Brad Ozera; he'd learned his lesson in the U.K.

It was mid-day on a sunny, summer workday. Traffic was light and she was moving along at 75.

"Who were they, Brad? Cops? Spies? Thugs?" she asked.

He chuckled. "Probably a little of each. I used to work confidential missions all over the world, and I've seen all kinds in that business. These guys were neat and clean, polite, armed, and operating on a short leash. Kind of like cops." She looked at him, puzzled. "And they weren't very good at what they do," he added.

"How do you know that?"

"Because they didn't get me," he replied with a broad Brad Ozera smile.

As they drove along he reflected on the night he and Mrs. Griffiths made mad, passionate love. The dinner, the hot tub, the night of unbridled lovemaking. It was fun. Both were incredibly horny and both needed it desperately.

They got off the interstate and onto the maze of highways circling Newark International.

"Head for International Departures," he told her. She pulled up to the curb and he got out. He reached into the back and pulled out his suitcase.

"There's a black satchel under the reception counter," he said. "It's a present for you."

"I'd rather have you," she replied tenderly, a tear in her eye.

Ozera poked his head through the window. She leaned over and they kissed.

He turned and began to walk away, then remembered. He walked back, looked around, reached back and slid the .45 from his belt, placing it on the front seat of her pick-up.

"I'm not checking the bag, and they sure won't let me on board with this," he said with a smile.

"Take care, my love," she said to him, and pouted at his leaving. She stayed at the curb and watched as he entered the terminal and disappeared.

It was barely five months, but oh, what a wonderful five months it was. He gave her life back to her. Tears running down her cheek, she drove away.

* - * - *

Ozera looked at the U.S. passport the Colonel had given him and ruffled it a bit to make it look used. He packed the other two passports in his suitcase. He would now be Victor Livingston. He grabbed half a bundle of hundred-dollar bills, folded them over in a big wad and stuck it in his pants pocket.

At the counter he pulled out the wad and peeled off 24 bills for a one-way, first-class seat to Vienna, Austria.

"Mr. Livingston, I presume," she said with a smile, handing him his passport and boarding pass. The Lufthansa flight boarded at 7 pm, giving him a few hours to kill in the airport. He stopped at a bar, keeping a close eye on his small suitcase.

He boarded the 747, sticking his bag under the seat in front of him. The flight attendant brought him champagne. *"Ich danke Ihnen sehr, Fraulein,"* he told her. She feigned surprise and they chatted for a while in German. "*I'm pretty rusty,*" he explained in German, *"But it's coming back to me."*

In due course they took off. It was a long overnight flight. Ozera stretched out, and, with thoughts of Dacey in his mind, fell soundly asleep.

* - * - *

Chapter XI: The Shades of Eastern Europe

XI: Vienna

For millennia Vienna had stood at the frontier, of sorts. In ancient times it marked the furthest edge of the Roman Empire – the civilized world; to the east were marauding tribes – savages and pagans, or so the Romans believed. More recently, Vienna marked the boundary separating the Western world from the Communist East – heartless and Godless, or so the West believed.

Ozera always wanted to visit Vienna and Austria. Now ironically he would, but not quite in the way he envisioned. Rather than touring the sites and enjoying the trappings of a well-to-do tourist, he was on the lam – traveling under an alias and hiding from his own government.

The big plane landed smoothly and taxied about the airport. At one turn the bright rising sun blinded Ozera for a moment. Vienna's *Flughafen* was in a desolate area southeast of the city. The Hungarian border lay just a few miles to the east, and beyond that his ancestral homeland, Romania. It was only recently that the shroud of Communism began lifting, as the former Soviet Union disintegrated. All those lands and their millions of oppressed peoples were getting their first taste of freedom in generations.

"Geshäftsreise oder Urlaub?" the Austrian immigration officer said, asking if his travel was business or pleasure.

"A little of both," he replied in English, "I'm a tourist, but I'm also an architect." The inspector seemed impressed, maybe just because he understood the German question.

"Willkommen, Herr Livingston," the short stocky official said with a smile, stamping his passport and waving him on. On the way out he stopped for some local currency, exchanging a thousand dollars for some 12,000 Austrian Schillings.

Ozera wondered whether government agents from the U.S. could still track him, even though he used the U.S. passport the Colonel gave him. If they were really determined, they could find out that someone meeting Brad Ozera's description flew out of Newark airport to Vienna, but could they make the connection and nail down that he was now traveling as Victor Livingston? It would be hard, he concluded, but given the resources of the people likely looking for him, not impossible.

He decided to play it safe and use his Romanian identity for now, and he became Stefan Ionescu. He took a cab into the heart of the city and checked into a small, innocuous hotel inside the Kärntner Ring – the Old Town of Vienna. His plan: keep a low profile, change his appearance and hide out. The next day he went shopping, buying some clothes and a bigger suitcase.

The first week was one of adjustments. He worked on his German, exploiting the opportunity to converse with locals and solicit grammatical and vocabulary corrections. He started growing a short trimmed beard and letting his short brown hair grow out. To blend in he added an Austrian Herren Hut – a gentleman's walking hat. Every day he exercised, including a morning jog.

Wiener Schnitzel became his new nemesis. He loved the butter-sautéed breaded veal dish, and had to fight to keep off added weight – despite an active schedule of exercise and walking tours. He found an acceptable substitute for bourbon, developing a taste for Kirschwasser and the occasional after-dinner pear or peach schnapps.

Food and drink aside, Ozera had developed disciplined habits from his military experience. He kept an eye on everything around him. He didn't spend a lot. He limited his contact with strangers and took the subway and public buses.

After a couple of weeks he became curious about things back home. He fought the urge to contact Mrs. Griffiths. Her phone may be tapped or traced, he reasoned. And any postcards or letters would point to him in Vienna. They probably found out by now that he departed from Newark airport – the one revealing fact that Mrs. Griffiths could disclose – but would they figure out his Lufthansa flight?

And who were "they" anyhow? He jogged past the U.S. Embassy almost every morning and would think of how his own government – the government he served for years in rat holes around the world and on the field of battle – had forced him to run.

The weeks grew into months. After dinner one October evening he returned to his hotel and stopped to speak with Freddie – the night manager of the 12-room hotel, who he had come to know pretty well.

"Guten Abend, Friederich. Wie geht's?"

"A quiet day, Herr Ionescu," he said, thumbing through some papers. *"One guest left today and two arrived."*

"My, my. Busy, busy," Ozera chided him.

"And then one man came in just asking questions."

"Oh? What did he want?" Ozera casually asked.

"He was looking for someone – an American, a soldier I think. He had a picture. Actually, come to think of it, he looked a little like you," Freddie said with a deadpan expression. A rush of adrenalin shot through Ozera. It's possible Freddie was kidding. He tried not to seem worried or overly interested.

"Who was asking? An American?" Ozera casually asked.

"No, Austrian, I'm pretty sure, but not police," Freddie said. *"The man he was looking for was named, uh, something like Ossaria. I told him we had two Americans staying here –*

both old ladies on the fourth floor. And then he left. No big deal."

So, months later and they were still after him. And they were looking around Vienna. But apparently they didn't know about the other passports or aliases. Ozera didn't know how the Colonel got those passports – he said he knew people in low places. And he said they were good as gold.

Freddie almost certainly didn't make the connection. Even if he did suspect that the man in the picture was him, he likely didn't volunteer any information. It was the way Freddie was – paranoid and with contempt for authority.

The people looking for him came close. And he wasn't going to hang around to see if they return.

He took the small elevator up to his room on the third floor, peering around carefully when the door opened. In his room he grabbed his suitcase and hastily packed his clothes and toiletries. In the bathroom he cleared off and carefully lifted the toilet tank cover. He reached in, and withdrew a plastic baggie. He opened it and pulled out another baggie, containing the money and his two U.S. passports. The first bag, with a small pile of stones in it for ballast, he let drop back into the toilet tank.

He called down to Freddie, told him there's been an emergency and he'd be checking out shortly. Would he please prepare the bill?

Ozera was an efficient planner and worked best under pressure. He had been considering an escape route – a way out of town, just in case. Plan A was by boat, avoiding the airport.

After first checking the hallway again, he slipped out of his room and took the elevator back down to the lobby. He paid the hotel tab with Austrian cash, telling Freddie he was grabbing a flight to see his sick mother in Romania, who lives south of Bucharest. None of it was true, of course. But it might throw trackers off his trail for a while, if he did talk.

"Need a ride to the airport?" he asked.

"No thanks, Freddie," he said. *"I'll take care of it."* If Freddie arranged a cab there would be a trail for them to follow. They shook hands and Ozera walked out with his suitcase and bag.

* - * - *

XI: Down the Danube

He walked two blocks and hailed a cab, taking it down to the docks on the Danube riverfront. It was late and, despite the eerie yellow light from the sparse streetlamps along the riverbank, still quite dark.

Ozera stopped and talked to a couple passing deckhands, who pointed him to a small freighter. He walked over to it and called up to a sailor on deck, asking if he could talk to the skipper. A few minutes later the captain appeared and walked down the gangway to Ozera on the dock.

"*I need to get to Bucharest*," he said in German to the skipper, who bore a distinctive odor of booze.

"*As a crewman or passenger?*"

"*Passenger,*" Ozera answered, "*And no questions.*"

"*6,000 shillings,*" the skipper snapped back. It did not sound like he was willing to negotiate. Ozera pulled out a wad and peeled off six "Tausend Schilling" notes, about $500 U.S. dollars. The seaman looked at the wad admiringly, took the money and pocketed it.

"*Welcome aboard,*" he said with a smile. "*We leave at first light. You can stay on board tonight if you like.*" Ozera nodded. "*It's a three day trip,*" he continued. "*We'll spend tomorrow night in Budapest, and then in Belgrade. So if you're not in a hurry, sit back and enjoy the ride. The food on board is pretty good, too.*"

He walked up the ramp and Ozera followed, looking around and behind him as he boarded..

* _ * _ *

It was a lazy three days for Ozera. He slept well in his small but comfortable cabin. And the food in the galley was good.

He was the only passenger and so got to meet and interact with the five-man crew. He became accustomed to them, and they to him. Each crewman had a couple of jobs. The second in command was mechanically inclined, and so was also responsible for the diesel engines and fuel. Two of the crewmen handled loading and unloading cargo, and spent their travel time on ship maintenance – one did carpentry and plumbing, the other painting. The cook had full responsibility for the kitchen. He was a good cook, and put out especially good Hungarian dishes. And the skipper … well, he was the skipper.

Ozera spent most of his time up top. He had a lot of time to think, and he thought a lot about what he left behind … Mrs. Griffiths, his home at the B&B, his parents and siblings, but most of all, Daciana.

A few times the skipper, a Hungarian named Konstantin, in his 40's, would sit down with Ozera and share a bottle of something to drink. The first time he produced a bottle of vodka – "the only thing of value the Russians brought to Hungary" – and then Tokaji, a sweet Hungarian wine, which "we didn't let the Russians take back with them."

The two conversed mainly in German, sharing their backgrounds and insights as the freighter – its engine thumping monotonously – wound its way down the Danube. Konstantin lost his father in the 1956 Hungarian revolution, and still spoke with deep disdain about the Russian Communists. Then there was the second bloody revolution, this time in 1989, when the Communists finally pulled out of Hungary. Konstantin shared his speculation that Ozera was Romanian, that he was raised on a farm and that he had been a soldier. Ozera smiled and nodded in feigned amazement. He said nothing about his American upbringing.

The freighter docked in Budapest. While the crew unloaded and then loaded, Ozera hopped off and wandered the city for a while. The people were bundled up as they walked in the cool October evening. Ozera saw a marked contrast with

The Monastery

Vienna, which was cosmopolitan, vibrant. Budapest was gray and destitute – left by the Russians in much worse shape than when they occupied the country and its capital at the end of World War II. Ozera brought back a bottle of vodka, and a flask of Tokaji to give Konstantin as a present when they reached their destination. He couldn't pass up the $20 US price for the small 7.65-mm semi-automatic Walther, which he tucked in one coat pocket, and the extra clip and nearly full box of ammo in the other.

Very late the next night they chugged into Belgrade, the Yugoslav capital. At the skipper's request Ozera stayed on board. *"This country is disintegrating,"* Konstantin told him, with a tone of sorrow. All through the night Ozera heard the familiar clatter of tanks and tracked vehicles, and occasional machinegun fire. The crew unloaded its cargo in the middle of the night, waking Ozera. He wondered what they'd be delivering to a war zone, and to whom. But it wasn't his business. There was no cargo to load, and the ship pulled out shortly afterwards, still in the middle of the night, continuing down the Danube.

Already awake, Ozera stayed up and went up top with a coffee to watch the sunrise. After a while the skipper came by and put his hand on Ozera's shoulder. He pointed to the left bank.

"Welcome back to Romania, Domnule," he said in flawless Romanian. Apparently Konstantin spoke some Romanian, in addition, it seems, to German, his native Hungarian, and who knows how many others. Given his business – a boatman shuttling between these eastern European countries – it was not surprising.

At a hearty breakfast with the skipper and several of the crew, he learned they'd be arriving late afternoon at Bucharest. The waterfront and dock were in a town south of Bucharest, called Giurgiu, they explained. Bucharest was some 30 miles north. At Giurgiu the Danube was the border between Romania to the north, and Bulgaria to the south.

Ozera packed up, threw his carry bag over his shoulder and grabbed his suitcase. The freighter docked with characteristic jerks and bumps. He handed the flask of wine to Konstantin and the two embraced. It was raining lightly as he headed to the ramp, waving goodbye to the skipper.

"*Mult noroc,*" Konstantin yelled to him in Romanian, wishing him good luck.

He walked to the end of the docks and saw a solitary cab at the end of the street. He was quite wet by the time he walked the hundred yards to it. The cab looked like it had been driven around the world without a wash. Ozera wasn't even sure what color it was under the grime.

He looked inside. The driver was sleeping. He put his suitcase down and rapped on the window, jolting the driver awake. He jumped out, grabbed his suitcase and flipped it in the back seat. He reminded Ozera of an old friend.

"*Where to?*" he asked. Ozera thought for a moment. It really didn't matter. He just needed to settle in somewhere for a while.

"*Well, let's head up north,*" he replied.

"*Bucaresti?*"

"*Yeah, okay.*"

The driver hit the gas and they made a sharp U-turn. In 15 minutes they had zigzagged through Giurgiu and were motoring through the countryside. The driver appeared a bit slovenly and unkempt, but he was nevertheless a sharp judge of people. And it seemed odd to him that this passenger wasn't very interested in going anywhere in particular.

* - * - *

XI: Ras

"You come from up north, Transylvania, no?" the driver asked.

Ozera thought for a moment, placing his family's origins. *"I do. How'd you know?"*

"Your accent. I recognize it. Same like mine. "Where are you from?"

"Near Vatra Dornei," he replied, remembering the town his parents told him about.

"Oh, I know it well. Small town in the foothills of the Carpathians," he said proudly. *"I come from the big city, Bistrita,"* he added with a laugh. Bistrita was hardly a big city, although it was one of the larger towns in that remote, north-central part of Romania.

"So what are you doing way down here by Bulgaria then?" Ozera asked him.

"Had to go where the fares were," the driver quipped. *"There hasn't been much business or travel activity up in our area since the revolution, but now it's getting better. I left Bistrita a week ago, taking a man to Targu Mures, and from there I took another fare to Brasov – a really big city. A couple of days around Brasov and I ended up taking this rich guy to Bucharest. And then, yesterday, I drove an old couple down here, to catch a boat to Odessa."*

"What's your name?" Ozera asked.

"Ras," he said. *"It's short for Rasvan."*

"So how far are we from home, Ras?"

"Oh, 250, maybe 300 miles." It was beginning to get dark.

"Why don't we head back up that way, then? Is there a good place to spend the night nearby?"

"You got money, no?" Ras asked.

Ozera thought he'd reassure him. He pulled out a 100-dollar bill, reached over and put it down next to him on the front seat.

"You take U.S. dollars, Ras, no?" Ras looked over. His eyes got wide and he smiled.

"This will get you wherever you want to go, Domnule," he said grabbing the bill and tucking it quickly in his shirt pocket. *"I know a nice place to spend the night, just north of Bucharest. Clean, private. We will be there in an hour or so."*

Ozera sat in the back seat and let his mind wander. He had time to kill. Probably another month or two before he should even think of slipping back to the U.S. He had enough money to go where he wanted. Where would he go? Why not where his parents came from – Vatra Dornei? What was his father's hometown? Iacobeni? Yes, that's it. He would go there. Maybe he could travel around the area. It looked like Ras was available. Who knows, maybe he could even find where the original Monastery was, or used to be. It wasn't much of a plan. But it was a plan.

It was very dark and still raining lightly when they pulled up to the old inn. It was at an intersection of two country roads, and about the same size as Mrs. Griffiths' B&B spread. Ras got out and went in.

"Good room for just 20,000 Lei," Ras came back and told him.

"Cripes," Ozera exclaimed, *"How much is that in dollars?"*

"Oh, in that case, $10 ought to do it for the night." Ozera popped out and grabbed his bag. He went in and booked a room. He was about to go upstairs and settle in when he thought of Ras. He walked back out. Ras had settled down in the front seat and was ready to fall asleep.

"Where are you staying?" Ozera asked him.

He looked up and smiled. *"Right here. It is pretty comfortable. It is where I usually sleep."* He nodded, appreciating that Ras was probably pocketing whatever he could to take home. But it was a cold, raw, rainy night. And he wanted Ras to stay with him for a while. After all, they were practically neighbors.

"Come on in, Ras," Ozera gestured. *"Come and get a good night's sleep. And you could use a shower, Vlach. I'll take care of it."*

Ras shrugged, giving him an 'Okay, why not?' look, and got out and followed him in. Ozera paid for another room. The owner recognized Ras and congratulated him for finally being a **paying** guest **inside** the Inn.

They settled in, cleaned up and then met for dinner in the small dining room of the inn. They were the sole guests. Ozera thought of his Friday nights with Mrs. Griffiths at the Fern Valley Inn, and looked around. Not quite as elegant, he thought, but cozy nonetheless. They talked, enjoyed a peppery chicken stew and had a few drinks. Ras was voracious and had two full bowls of stew and half a loaf of bread. He hadn't eaten in a while, it seemed.

"What shall I call you, Domnule?" Ras asked. *"My name is Ionescu, Stefan Ionescu,"* Ozera replied. Ras' innate understanding of people, and the expression on Ozera's face, told him it was not his real name. But he let it go. It didn't matter.

Ras was about 40, stocky, with a slight paunch that betrayed his Spartan lifestyle. His face and build, even his demeanor and speech, reminded Ozera of his old Army friend – Sergeant Jerry Carpenter. That was probably why Ozera was quick to extend him his friendship … and trust.

Well-fed and comfortable, they turned in.

Both men took their time and washed up in the morning, and then had a good breakfast. By mid-morning they were on the road again, driving through the gray countryside. Ozera likened it to the early 1900's in the U.S. – rural, mainly agricultural, few signs of electricity or telephone, many people on horseback or riding horse-drawn wagons.

They learned more about each other with each mile, and were becoming friends. They stopped for gas and, over Ras' half-hearted objections, Ozera paid. The U.S. dollar was welcomed like gold everywhere. Ozera needed change, though and they stopped at a bank. He changed several hundred-dollar bills for all the U.S. 10's, 20's and 50's the small bank had on hand. Then he also bought a pile of Romanian Lei and, for good measure, a few hundred Russian Rubles, which the bank teller was glad to dispose of.

By late afternoon they were pulling into Bistrita, Ras' hometown. It was a sizeable town for this isolated part of northern Romania. The dirt-encrusted cab wound through a few streets and came to a stop by a small standalone house on a back street. It was an old, two-story, gray stucco structure with steep roofs. It was in need of some repair, but looked comfortable.

"We'll stay here tonight," Ras said, *"And tomorrow we go to Vatra Dornei – maybe three hours' drive."*

"Where are we?" Ozera asked.

"My home," he said, grabbing trash from around the cab and getting out. There was no discussion; Ozera was spending

the night there. Inside he met Ras' wife, a handsome woman named Marian, and their two children – a boy of about 10 and a little girl, 5 or 6. He was touched and honored to be invited to spend the night in their home.

Marian was cooking dinner when he saw Ras go over and hand over his take – about $80 in assorted bills and currencies … and the $100 bill he gave him. She put it all down on the counter and hugged and kissed him. She would have been just as pleased, Ozera supposed, if he had come home empty-handed.

After a delicious lamb and rice dinner she cleared the table and served coffee. Ras brought out some wine – probably the best he had – and they talked.

"*On a good day, Ras, how much do you bring home?*" Ozera asked.

He shrugged. "*After gas, $25, maybe $30. On a great day, $40,*" he said.

"*I'd like to hire you – and your cab – for a week or so, at $50 U.S. per day – plus I pay for gas, meals and lodging. And I'll pay you for the first week in advance.*" Ras looked over at his wife, who smiled and nodded. He returned a big smile to Ozera.

"*To Vatra Dornei? Yes!*" he said, raising his glass. They had a deal.

* _ * _ *

XI: Vatra Dornei

It was a Thursday morning. Ras was already outside, with his young son and bucket and soap, cleaning the cab. Later, while the family had breakfast together, Ozera washed up and did some laundry in a sink. He got a cup of coffee and watched as Ras' son took his little sister by the hand and led her off to school.

Marian made them a big plate of eggs and ham, and he devoured his. Afterwards they talked.

"*Is your home in Vatra Dornei?*" Marian asked him.

"*No. My father's family comes from near there.*"

Where is your home now?"

"*In America,*" he confessed. Ras and Marian looked at each other, both somewhat surprised. Marian started to ask him questions, but Ras held his hand up to her and she acceded.

"*I want to see where my parents and family come from, north of Vatra Dornei. I am like a tourist,*" he smiled.

* - * - *

"*Do you know where we are going?*" he asked him, as Ras fueled up at a roadside gas station. Ozera was under the raised hood, adding oil to the engine. "*I'd like to get to the town called Iacobeni, somewhere north of Vatra Dornei, and find a place to stay there for a couple days.*"

"*Okay,*" Ras replied. "*I know of Iacobeni. We will be in Vatra Dornei in another hour or so.*"

They drove along a highway most of the way, past a half-dozen small towns. Traffic was unexpectedly light. Ozera noticed the mountains getting steeper, the woods darker and thicker, and the populated areas sparser as they drove on.

They were both hungry by the time they got to Vatra Dornei. It was an unexpected island of urban presence in the foothills of the Carpathians. It was much smaller than Bistrita, but just as gray and in a similar state of disrepair. There had been little renovation or re-construction for decades and time had taken its toll. Electric cables and phone lines were strung willy-nilly overhead, as if just done in a hurry and temporarily. Many buildings were deserted, their windows either broken or boarded up.

They parked outside a restaurant that looked open. It had gotten colder since they left Bistrita, and a cold north wind would kick up occasionally. It was late afternoon. An attractive young lady waited on them. The waitress was attentive, and clearly taken with Ozera. They enjoyed a substantial meal of pulled pork, noodles and dark bread. Ozera asked if she knew where he could get a detailed map of the area. She said to check a stationary shop two blocks away.

They finished and drove over to find the store. It was still open. A little old man was tending shop.

"We need a map of this area, especially north of here," Ozera said.

"Well, 30 miles north of here is the new independent country of the Ukraine," the old man said with a broad smile. *"They threw out those barbarian Cossacks, too,"* he said, making clear his view of the former Russian occupiers.

"We are interested mainly in the area from here to the Ukraine border."

The old shopkeeper went over and rummaged through a box, pulling out two folded maps. Ozera looked and smiled as the old shopkeeper tried to wipe the dust off the documents on his pants without them noticing. *"This is a map of Romania,"* he said, handing it to him. *"Not a lot of detail of this area, though. 1,000 lei."*

Ozera looked over at Ras, who shrugged. *"A dollar or so, at the official exchange rate,"* he said.

"And then here's a map of Suceava County. Much more detail around here, up to the Ukraine. 1,500 lei."

Ozera reached in his hip pocket and pulled out a mishmash of bills and coins, which he plopped on top of the glass counter. Some 500 and 1,000 lei notes could be seen, as well as a potpourri of coins.

"Any dollars?" the old man asked.

Ozera fumbled through the pile of bills and coins and pulled out a crumpled dollar bill. The shopkeeper reached over and snatched it, and handed Ozera both maps. Business concluded.

On the way out of town Ras explained that inflation was rendering the Romanian lei increasingly worthless, yet for decades people were forbidden by the Communists from owning foreign currency. Now they could, and the U.S. dollar became the gold standard, worth many times the official exchange rate. Ras said he could get a thousand times the official Lei rate per dollar.

It was starting to get dark as they turned off the main road that curved through the woods and hills, and pulled into Iacobeni. It was a sleepy little town, maybe thirty or forty houses and a church, lying along a valley. Ras drove up and down the two streets of the town, looking for a place to stay. They were about to give up and leave when, at the end of town, they saw a small sign and pulled in. The lights of the cab shown on an old inn set back off the road. They parked, went up and knocked.

A middle-aged woman who owned the place said she'd be happy to take on two guests. She reminded Ozera a little of Mrs. Griffiths – same age, height and energy – but a rather stodgy personality. Ras handled the negotiations. Apparently she had no other guests. How much for three nights, both of them, if they paid in dollars? Ten dollars would take care of the rooms for all three nights, she eagerly offered. Boy, this was the place to be with a bag load of dollars.

Ozera gave her twenty dollars – payment in advance … plus. She accepted it graciously and volunteered to also provide breakfast and snacks. He thought of asking her if she ever heard of his family but decided against it: He didn't need to throw around his real last name.

They settled in their rooms and then met downstairs, sitting at a small table in the corner of the front room. The landlady, *Doamna* Silivasi – Mrs. Silivasi – brought Ras and Ozera some bread, sausage and red wine. It was a light dinner, but it was good and would more than suffice.

After they ate Ozera cleared off the table and spread out the map of the area to the north. They looked it over.

"*I am looking for a monastery, Ras, or the place where this particular monastery used to be. It's somewhere up in these hills,*" he said, circling a mountainous area with his finger.

"*There are monasteries on mountaintops throughout Romania,*" Ras countered. "*Why this one? Why here?*"

"*This monastery may not be there anymore,*" Ozera replied, "*But I need to find where it was.*"

"*If it's not there anymore, how will you know?*" Ras asked. A good question, of course. Ozera avoided a direct answer.

"*We will need to ask around throughout the area, until we find somebody who knows. Some people out there know where it is, or where to look,"* Ozera said confidently. Ras gave him a puzzled look, then shrugged.

"*You are paying the bills,*" he said resignedly, ending his questioning.

The two plotted their course. Tomorrow they would take the main road northeast, through the villages and towns of Valea Putni, Pojorata and Sadova . They would ask around at each and, if no leads turned up that way, then they would head north towards the Ukraine border – through Botus, Briaza, Moldova-Sulita.

"*And then what?*" Ras asked.

"*Then you can go home,*" Ozera told him with a smile.

* _ * _ *

XI: The Quest

Mrs. Silivasi was up and greeted them the next morning. She made an adequate breakfast, and they were anxious to take off on the first leg of their investigative journey. They walked out and the cold air enveloped them, like a blanket flung over a fire. It was near freezing, and yet still only early autumn.

They drove an hour to the first town, and stopped at a cozy-looking old inn. There were a half-dozen customers in the dining room.

"Does anyone know of an old monastery up in the hills around here?" Ozera asked the waitress. She said no, and he asked her if she would query the other staff. She returned with coffee and pastry and reported, sincerely it seemed, that nobody else there knew anything about an old monastery around the area.

They stopped at a restaurant on the outskirts of Sadova. Walking up to the entrance Ras put his hand on Ozera's shoulder.

"Why not let me do the talking this time?" Ras asked. *"I understand now what you want, okay?"*

"Sure, give it a shot," he told him. They entered and sat at a little table by the bar. A fire flickered in the fireplace behind them. Its warmth felt good and there was the pleasant smell of burning wood.

"My friend here is visiting from America," Ras told the 30-something waitress who came over to take their order. *"His grandparents came from around here, and it's like he's coming home for the first time."* She eyed Ozera approvingly.

"Welcome home," she said with a pleasant smile. Ozera gave her a wink.

Ras continued: *"All he knows for sure is that his family lived on a small farm in a valley below a mountain there was a monastery on. Do you have any idea where that might be?"* She said she didn't know of any, but she'd ask around and come back. Ozera saw her talking to the others in the pub, and then taking notes.

They finished eating and she returned, pulling out and reading from her pad. *"There are four monasteries in this region, but two are pretty far away – 60 or 80 miles. The two closest ones are near Putna and Arbore, maybe 30 or 40 miles away."*

"Are those two still open?" Ras asked.

"I think so." She tore off the page and handed it to Ozera. The monastery towns were listed, and conspicuous at the bottom was her name, phone number and the note *"I get off at 6,"* with a little smiley face. Ozera tucked it in his shirt pocket.

"I can't thank you enough," he told her, *"But I need to go to Iacobeni tonight."* She pouted. *"But I'll be back,"* he added. Another customer called; she smiled and left.

"You are wasting your time in a taxi, my friend." Ozera said to Ras with a smile as they left. *"You should be a tractor salesman ... maybe even a politician."*

It was much the same routine over the next two days –with the same results. They'd been to a dozen inns and restaurants, in villages and towns along a hundred miles of back roads. Ozera got two more waitress' phone numbers, but they got no leads on whether, or where, in the surrounding mountains a monastery might have been.

The morning of their third day was sunny and warmer, and they were off again, this time headed north. They drove along the Bistrita River, headed upstream. An hour later they were having coffee in Ciocanesti, a quaint little town in a valley surrounded by farmland. The attractive and outgoing waitress canvassed the other diners for them, but came back and shrugged.

They drove on. The road ascended into the mountains and Ozera's ears popped. The mix of broadleaf and evergreen trees gradually gave way to thicker and darker woods of ancient conifers – spruces and firs. By mid-afternoon they had reached the end of the road, in a small mountain village past the town of Sesuri. They stopped and waited as a young man led two horses across the road in front of them. There were a handful of houses, a few barns, a church – and the inn.

They parked outside and walked in. Bright afternoon sunbeams shone in through small wavy glass windows – providing spotlights for the dancing dust particles. A klatch of old men was enjoying the afternoon and each other's familiar company. The barmaid was a stocky, matronly woman in her 50's. She probably owned the business, Ozera figured, as she amiably greeted the two. The other patrons eyed the two younger strangers warily.

"*There was a monastery up on a mountain somewhere near here,*" Ozera said to her, loud enough for the others to hear. "*But it is gone now. Does anyone remember that?*" Silence. Then one of the old timers spoke up.

"*I heard something of that when I was a young man in Benia, where I was born. But that's 20 miles from here, northeast across the mountains.*" He was trying to remember. "*It was up on a mountain ledge, near the Russian border. Hard to find. I went there once, as a boy, hiking with friends. There was nothing there, not even rubble, just bare rock, but they said it used to be a Monastery. I came home and told my parents, and they scolded me and told me never to go there again, and never tell …,*" he paused.

"*Where was that, Domnule?*" Ozera asked politely.

The old man thought a minute. *"I don't remember. Sorry,"* he said.

So, Benia. It was their first solid lead. The next day they left early, driving to Pojorata and then turning off the highway and onto the back road, heading northwest up into the mountains.

They stopped in a small town for breakfast. Ras gave his pitch to the waitress. Then, unexpectedly, she asked Ozera: *"What is your family name?"*

He thought a moment and decided to tell her the truth. *"Ozera,"* he said.

"I have known Ozeras," the 20-year-old said.

Ras raised an eyebrow and looked over at him. *"So have I,"* he said.

He asked her whether anybody has heard of a place in the mountains where a monastery used to be. She said she'd check, and Ozera watched as she politely asked around among the other customers.

She returned to report: *"A few people said they'd heard legends and rumors of an old Monastery somewhere north of here, near the Ukraine border, but nobody knows where. Sorry."*

*"Where to from here, Domnule **Ozera**?"* Ras asked, emphasizing his last name, as they got back in the cab.

"North, towards the Ukraine," Ozera responded resolutely. They drove through a few small towns and villages, stopping in each to ask if anyone knew where an old monastery was, or used to be. None did. They stopped and gassed up at a station outside the village of Colacu.

In the next town they stopped in a corner store and spoke with a few of the local old-timers. They were talkative enough, offering the 'youngsters' advice on everything from dressing for the upcoming winter to keeping a wife happy. But when Ozera asked about an old monastery up in the mountains, they looked at each other, shook their heads and, uncharacteristically, said nothing. It seemed odd to Ozera, as if choreographed. They knew something, he sensed … but they said nothing.

Further on they finally arrived in Benia. They found an inn and parked. As they went in, Ozera asked Ras to let him do the talking this time.

A handful of regulars were eating and drinking. They picked a table near them and sat down. A friendly, middle-aged woman came over to serve them and they ordered.

She left and Ozera began his story, loud enough for those nearby to hear. He and Ras saw that they had perked up and were listening. He had moved to America with his parents when he was young, he said. But his brother, Mihai, remained with relatives in Botus. Then four years ago, Russians came and took him away for some kind of research. They took him to a research site up in the mountains somewhere nearby. Ozera watched their expressions; a couple nodded in understanding.

"*Yeah, in the mountains near Bobeica,*" said one of the men, a burly worker about 50, wearing coveralls.

"*Well a few years ago,*" Ozera continued, "*just before the revolution, the Russians shut it down. And my brother never came back.*"

It was a poignant story, well delivered. Even Ras was impressed, though he had no idea if any of it was true.

"*Yes, I heard they were doing strange experiments and even operating on our people,*" said the waitress, who joined in the conversation. *"It's possible your brother may be gone,"* she added, looking at Ozera with sincere, sad eyes.

"But maybe not," the workman interjected. *"I heard some of them went to America after the Russians abandoned the place."*

"Bobeica?" Ozera asked the man who spoke up. *"Where is that? Far from here?"*

"It's that way, up in the mountains," he replied, pointing with his thumb over his shoulder. *"Maybe 20 miles. Up near the Russian border. But they say there's nothing there of the Russian site anymore but a few empty buildings."*

"How do I get there?" he asked. The workman gave him detailed directions to Bobeica.

"And the Russian research site?"

"Ask them in Bobeica. You'll need to go by foot from there. It's a half-mile or so up in the woods."

"Were you there?" Ozera asked him.

"I'm a repairman," he replied. *"I fix motors, appliances, heaters, pumps, you name it. Yes, I was called to the site several times and yes, I did work there for the Russians."*

He thanked them and they left, driving north and following the repairman's direction. They passed many small farms, which eked a living from the narrow fertile valley that snaked between the mountains.

Another few miles and they stopped for gas. The attendant walked up to him and asked if he wanted to fill, with an unmistakable accent. *"Russian?"* Ozera asked. *"Ukrainian,"* he retorted. *"No more Russians in the Ukraine; we are independent now. And we have thrown the Russian bastards out."* Clearly it was a sore subject; Ozera let it go.

"Excuse me," he apologized to him in Russian. The attendant accepted it with a nod, not even noticing he was speaking to him in Russian.

"You speak Russian, too?" Ras lightheartedly asked him. *"You are a handy person to have around, Tovarich."*

A little further and they spotted the turn-off to the west – a narrow road, barely a single lane and only partially paved. They headed up into the darkening woods. Ras turned his lights on. Most of the remaining daylight was being absorbed by the woods; precious little penetrated down to the roadway.

"Domnule, I must make a request," Ras said, his head and eyes forward and his attention focused on the road ahead. *"It is Thursday night. We have been on the road now for a week. I need to go home, at least for a couple days. My children need to see their father, and my wife needs her husband. Where do we go from here? Are we getting closer to what we are looking for?"*

Ozera considered his plea. *"Let us check out Bobeica, Ras, okay? I promise then we'll get you back home."*

* - * - *

XI: Bobeica

A mile up the road and Ozera's ears popped. And it was getting dark. They could see little anymore except where the headlights flashed along the road and into the woods. Even Ras slowed down as they took hairpin curves, and even Ozera gulped as they barely skirted some steep drop-offs.

"A Russian research site?" Ras asked. *"We are not looking for a Monastery anymore?"*

"They are two different things," Ozera replied, *"But if we find one, we'll be close to the other."*

They passed several religious stations along the road. Then the precarious road leveled off and straightened. The deep, dark woods receded and they entered the small village of Bobeica.

It was eerie in the late twilight – a dozen or so houses and farm buildings, scattered over a few acres, surrounded by steep mountains. It was a peaceful and pastoral setting. Lamp light already flickered in many of the homes. Ozera saw no streetlights, no power lines or telephone poles. The village probably looked today much as it did a hundred years ago – maybe a millennium ago – he supposed.

They drove ahead slowly and at the end of the village an old inn came into view – a large two-story stone structure. Outside an old car and a tractor were parked, alongside hitching posts for horses. Ras pulled up and turned off the engine.

"You did well with that story about the Russian research site," Ras said ingenuously. *"How did you know about it? How much of that was true?"*

"Everything but my brother, Mihai," he said. *"I do have a younger brother, but this one was made up."*

"Hmmm. I would leave him in," Ras replied, as the two climbed out of the car. *"But what is the connection between the Russian site and the old monastery?"*

"Like I said, they are near each other."

"But how do you know ..."

"I know," Ozera interrupted him. *"If I find one, I will find the other."*

"Okay. You do the talking." Ras conceded. They walked in.

Two men in their 50's were seated at a window table, eating, and both were somewhat surprised when Ras and Ozera walked in. It was a very old place, with a large stone fireplace on the front wall. A small fire crackled, radiating comfortable heat and flickering light into the room. They sat on two well-worn wooden stools at the bar.

"Ruski?" asked the attractive, 30-something lady who walked out from the back, wiping her hands on her apron. She wore glasses and had her dirty blond hair pulled back in a ponytail.

"Nu. Noi suntem români," Ozera retorted, adamantly assuring her they were Romanian.

"What can I do for you?" she asked.

She was pleasant and polite, but not overly friendly. She seemed curious about them – not threatened or frightened, just curious. They ordered wine and she returned with two glasses of *Zaibă* – a popular red wine from southern Romania. She talked them into the house special – a chicken and cabbage dish.

"Why are you here?" she asked, bringing them their meals.

"For dinner and drinks," Ozera responded straightforwardly.

"*No, no,*" she responded, "*I mean, it's too early for skiing, and it's too late for hiking. You could be hunters, I guess, but you don't look it. We don't get many visitors here, especially at this time of year.*"

Ras looked over and cast him a 'You do the talking' look.

"*There used to be a lot of Russians around here, I'm sure you know, up to a couple years ago,*" he said. "*And then, just before the revolution, they shut down in a hurry and left.* She nodded slowly, suspiciously. "*Whatever they were doing, they took quite a few Romanians up there to study them. And some of them never came back. One was my older brother, Mihai. They took him from my aunt and uncle in Botus. I don't know what I might find up there, after two years, but I'd like to go up and look around.*"

"*You won't find anything,*" she said. "*It's been scoured for anything of value.*"

"*Can you tell me how to get there?*"

"*Sure,*" she said accommodatingly. "*It is only a mile or so up the mountainside. But don't go now, not at night. You'll break a leg or worse, wolves will get you.*"

"*Do you have rooms here?*" Ozera asked.

"*Yes. All share a shower and bathroom,*" she said, adding: "*No one is staying now.*"

"*How about them?*" Ozera asked, nodding towards the two other customers.

"*Oh, they live here in the village. The ugly one is the brother-in-law of the owner,*" she said, loudly enough for them to hear. They turned and laughed.

"*Who's the owner?*"

"I am," she said with an attractive, confident smile. Ozera responded with his most irresistible smile. She returned to the kitchen.

"Ras, let's go back to Iacobeni tonight," Ozera proposed. *"Let's check out in the morning, and you drop me back here. Then go home to Bistrita. I'll stay the weekend and look around. I know what I'm looking for. Can you come back Monday and give me a couple of more days next week?"* He reached in his satchel, pulled out three hundred-dollar bills and handed them to Ras, who nodded.

"It's a deal. Thanks," Ras replied.

The innkeeper returned. *"How much for a few nights' stay?"* Ozera asked her. *"In dollars?"*

"How's $10 a night ...," she asked. They looked at each other, then she added: *"... with three meals a day?"* He reached in his pocket and withdrew a wad of notes. He thumbed through it, pulled out two twenties and handed them to her. She held one up to the light, as if she could tell a real one from a fake. And she probably could, Ozera thought.

"It'll be just me; I'll be back with my things tomorrow," Ozera told her, *"and I'll be staying through the weekend. My name is Brad Ozera."* He glanced at Ras, who rolled his eyes.

"My name is Sonia," she said, extending her hand. *"I'll have your room ready for you tomorrow."*

They drove back two hours and returned to Iacobeni very late, and after a nightcap turned in. The next morning they washed, packed up, thanked Mrs. Silivasi and checked out.

It was colder but sunny. They headed back up the tenuous mountain road to Bobeica. Most broadleaf trees were already bare of leaves but a few still stubbornly hung on, waving the last remnants of autumn color. As they ascended, monotone evergreens took over.

It was a much nicer drive in the daytime, Ozera mulled, enjoying the fresh mountain scenery. The road truly was perilous, snaking around some precipitous cliffs – worse than they knew the night before.

Arriving back in Bobeica they saw that the village was not quite as ageless and isolated as Ozera had thought. A line of poles bearing electric and phone lines ran along the road, but was mostly obscured in the thick woods. They drove ahead slowly through the quiet mountain village.

"See you in a few days, Ras," Ozera said as they pulled up to the old inn.

"I'll be back for you Monday, Domnule Brad Ozera," Ras said with a smile, extending his hand, which Ozera shook warmly.

Ozera got out, grabbed his suitcase and swung his satchel over his shoulder.

It was late morning and the place was empty. Everything was wiped down, clean and smelled pleasant – not dusty and smelly like a typical corner pub. He heard some commotion in the back and sat down at the bar to wait. Sonia emerged and saw him, giving him a big smile – much more congenial than when they met the night before.

"Welcome back," she greeted him. *"Want some lunch?"*

"What's cooking?" They both had a bowl of her chicken and dumpling soup, sitting together at a table. It was delicious.

They chatted cordially. She was widowed. Her husband was an ardent opponent of the Communist regime, though not a member of the armed resistance. No matter; one day the Securitate came for him, and he never returned. They found him after the December 1989 revolution – in a prison near Bucharest, shot in the head, she said.

"*He is buried in his family's plot down the road,*" she said. She did not seem angry or hateful. She must have gotten it out of her system.

Ozera extended his condolences. With that, Sonia got up and took the dishes in, and returned in a few moments with a key.

"*Room 1, top of the stairs; bathroom is down the hall,*" she told him, pointing to a narrow staircase beside the bar.

He went up and dropped his things in the room on the bed. It was a small room, but it was closest to the pub – probably kept warmest from the downstairs fireplace. It was dim in the room, but it was just as neat and clean as the tavern and smelled just as good. There was a single bed, a dresser with an oil lamp and matches, and a chair. A small window overlooked the valley and mountains to the rear of the inn. On the wall above the dresser was a mirror, and on the back wall hung a painting of a church.

He unpacked and put on his hiking boots and overcoat. He looked around the dark room for a place to stash his valuables, but nothing seemed suitable. So he tucked a few of the remaining packs of cash in the deep pockets of his coat, and the passports in another. He threw the satchel with the rest of the cash under the bed.

He was ready for his trek, and went back downstairs. Sonia was tending to a couple customers. He waited until she came to the back.

"*The Russian research site: Can you tell me where it is?*"

She told him to go a half-mile south, up the valley, then right, up the mountainside. He would know when to turn when he saw a large cleared area off to the right. It was the old helicopter landing zone. And just up the hill from there, in the woods, he would find the research site.

* _ * _ *

XI: *The Forest and the Trees*

Ozera set out in the afternoon sun and hiked up the valley. After a while he saw the clearing, deep in the woods off to the right. It was a flat area, a couple of acres. The trees there had all been cut very close to the ground. Ozera walked across it and saw that whitish rocks and stones had been strewn in an 'X' pattern on the ground. He looked up; it was a subtle marking, but it would make a landing zone a lot easier to spot from an approaching helicopter. He looked up the hill into the woods and faintly saw the buildings of the research site, or what was left of them, right where Sonia said they'd be.

He scanned the site from where he stood. There was no access to the place by road. Other than by foot, the way he came, the only way in or out was by helicopter. He remembered what the Colonel had told him: that his men walked right up to the place. They must have herded the Romanians, with all the research materials they could carry, the half-mile or so down to the nearest road – where he came up from.

Ozera walked carefully around the research site. There were five single-floor buildings, all about the same size, on stone foundations with wood-framed walls and wood-plank siding – probably sawn from the spruce and fir trees cut down to clear the landing zone. Each had several small windows and front and back doors. The roofs of two of the buildings were damaged or collapsed. It was not that different from their NEPA mountaintop facility, with one notable exception, Ozera mulled. This one was clearly designed to remain out of sight and unnoticed – from the ground or air. Ozera doubted whether even U.S. satellites could have seen anything through the heavy canopy of the evergreen woods, except maybe infrared imaging of the chimneys in cold months. But even that would not have raised any concern or interest.

He entered the closest building, stepping over debris and broken furniture. Sonia was right: it had all been picked through pretty well. The first building had numerous small offices and closets, with busted wooden desks and chairs, a few mangled file cabinets – and an area that looked like a medical facility, with gurneys and what could have been an operating room. He walked through the next building, where he saw two open bays with barracks-type bunk bed frames and scattered ripped mattresses. Sleeping quarters for 30 or 40, he guessed.

The next was the mess hall, with plumbing, sinks, a coal-burning cooking stove, and a sizeable dining area. Then there was the dormitory, with individual bed rooms – probably for staff, Ozera surmised. The last was a utility building, with the remains of a water pump and tank, and storage bins for firewood and coal. There must have been an electrical generator at one time, Ozera reasoned, since there was rudimentary electric wiring in the buildings, but that was now missing, too. It was older and somewhat more Spartan than his mountaintop facility in Pennsylvania, but functionally not that dissimilar.

Ozera walked out of the last building and up the hillside to get an overview of the site – hidden in plain sight, like so many trees in the ancient forest. It was already getting darker; the sun had dipped behind the mountain that rose steeply behind him.

He heard a growl and automatically spun around. There was a wolf – a large well-fed one, barely 20 feet away from him, with teeth bared. Ozera stood frozen, nervously scanning the area with his eyes. He had nothing to fight with; there wasn't even a branch or a stone within quick reach.

Then, as unexpectedly as it appeared, the wolf turned and loped away, on a trail winding up the mountainside. Ozera was still coping with the adrenalin rush, but relieved, watching as the wolf climbed nearly out of sight. Then he saw it stop and turn back towards him. It raised its head and let out a piercing howl. It was calling out … to something. And Ozera was not going to hang around to meet the rest of the pack.

He backed away slowly and retraced his path back down the valley to town and the Inn. The sun was setting and, like a mystical spell, casting a darkening pall over Bobeica and the entire valley.

Back safely at the inn, several patrons were drinking in the pub downstairs – a universal Friday after-work pastime, Ozera thought with a chuckle. Sonia was not around, probably out in the kitchen. He exchanged greetings with the two locals he'd seen the day before and went up to his room.

He walked in and turned on the light, and curiosity got the better of him. He checked under the bed and confirmed his bag was still there as he left it. Ozera washed and stood before the mirror on his wall, combing his hair. In the mirror's reflection he saw the bare light bulb and reflective shade illuminating the room – his bed, the small curtained window on the side wall, and the picture on the back wall. It looked like an original painting, of an unusual looking church. He looked again into the mirror, straining to see it better.

Then he spun around, standing for a moment, a look of bewilderment on his face. He walked around the bed and pulled the framed picture off the wall. It was the Monastery. He felt the painted surface – it was original, and it wasn't that old. 'What the hell …,' he muttered.

He finished dressing and took the picture downstairs. Sonia was at the bar, pouring drinks.

"*Can I talk to you about this*" he asked her softly, showing her the picture. "*It's important.*"

"*Give me a couple minutes,*" she said over her shoulder, looking at the painting in his hands. "*I'll meet you in the kitchen,*" she said. A few minutes later she joined him.

"*Who painted this*?" he asked. She seemed puzzled by his excited state and examined it.

"*I believe it was ... my husband's mother. I never met her. She died in 1966, many years before we met and married. I moved here with Anton in 1979. But this is imaginary,*" she added, nodding at the picture in her hands.

"*Why do you say that? How do you know?*" he asked.

"*She frequently went up into the mountains to paint scenery,*" she replied. "*She was pretty good. Her paintings sold well to tourists and visitors. But this one was not a landscape. She told her son – my husband, Anton – that she saw the church on a mountaintop ledge where she often went, and painted it. But there is nothing up there, nothing but bare rock. I've been there.*"

"*The mountain,*" Ozera asked her, "*Was it a mountain called Munte Manastirea?*" She looked at him, surprised.

"*Yes, I believe so. But that name comes from the shape of the mountain – not from any church or monastery up there. At least that's what I've been told.*"

A call came from out front and Sonia excused herself, assuring him she'd be right back as soon as she could. He waited patiently as she reappeared, prepared a few dishes and took them out. She returned, wiping her hands on her apron. She seemed a little harried, but could see Ozera was anxious about the painting.

"*Do you know when your mother-in-law painted this?*" he asked her.

"*They told me it was just before my husband was born, during the war. The Germans had massed around here for months before they invaded Russia in 1941. I'd say she painted this in 1942, because that's when Anton was born. Why do you ask?*"

"I have heard of this ... church," he said, nodding at the painting.

"But how could you?" Sonia asked, a puzzled look on her face. *"Maybe there was something up there once, but not anymore. Anton told me it was her last painting. She married my Anton's father after he was born, and then she worked in this inn for twenty-five years."*

"Can you tell me where this place is at, and how I can get up there?" he asked her. She got called away again, but returned in a few minutes.

"Okay, how to get there," she said, restarting where they left off. *"It is best to start from the old Russian research site, which I guess you found this afternoon"* He nodded. *"It is up the mountain from there, another good hour. It is a tough, steep climb, but there is an old trail that winds up Munte Manastirea. You'll find it uphill from the Russian site. Look for groups of three stones. They mark the trail and point the way."* Ozera turned as if to walk away.

"I assure you," she implored him, *"There is nothing there but stone and wind. Go, put the picture back, and come back down and have some dinner."*

He did as she asked, and took a seat at the bar. He conversed socially with Sonia as she ministered to the other guests, and brought him a delicious venison stew. She ran the whole place by herself, and she ran it well. He complimented her.

"Best food in the area," she bragged to him, adding: *"And if I didn't cook for them, half of these Vlachs would starve."* In a few hours most of the place had cleared out. Just one old man remained, who had fallen asleep at a table in the corner.

"That's Domnule Patrascu," she told Ozera. *"He raises pigs and chickens. He lost his wife six months ago. Now once a week he comes in, eats and has too much to drink. But he'll*

wake and go home in a little while." He was impressed with her. She was an innkeeper with the sense of a good businessman, and the heart and soul of a nurse. She would be successful anywhere.

They chatted for what seemed like hours. She asked if his room was okay. It was nice – clean and comfortable, he told her. At some point the old customer in the corner stirred and looked around, then got up and staggered out. They both chuckled.

"Have you ever heard the word, Arcobadera?" he asked Sonia. She seemed surprised.

"Where in the world did you hear that?"

"You've heard of it then? It's supposed to be the name of a place somewhere around here."

She smiled. *"Well, you found it. It is here. You are remarkably well informed, Domnule. Years ago I heard the term, Arcobadera, from one of the old timers of the village. He was old, but sharp. He could read your thoughts, that one, I swear it. Anyhow, one night he mentioned Arcobadera. I asked what it was and he explained it was the name for this area, this part of the valley ... from a long, long time ago, when an ancient people lived here. They are gone now, but the old-timers still use the name, Arcobadera. In the ancient tongue it means Snowy Passage. And if you're here in the winter, you'll see how it got the name. We have snow here from November to April, sometimes even to May, often two or three or four feet deep."*

Ozera saw that Sonia was getting tired. He asked her, matter of factly, if she had a flashlight he could use. She nodded, casting a curious look at him.

"There's an oil lamp and matches in your room," she said, *"The electric goes out frequently here, especially in ice and*

snow." She thought for a moment and then asked: *"Are you planning to go up there tonight?"*

He smiled and looked away coyly, but didn't answer. *"Please don't. It's getting late and you're tired, too. You'll break a leg or twist an ankle, and no one would find you."* She waited for a response, but got none. *"I'll get the flashlight,"* she said resignedly, adding: *"Just be careful."*

Ozera went and stoked the fire, adding a few hefty logs for heat through the night. He stepped out the front door to see what it was like. Cold. Close to freezing, he guessed. It was a clear night, full of stars. Above the trees to the east a nearly full moon was rising. He took a deep breath and exhaled slowly, his breath exuding as a mist in the cold night air.

He was tired, too, and it would have made a lot of sense to wait until daylight. He knew, though, that he could never get to sleep; he was too close to where it all happened – just a couple miles from here. Yes, probably all he'd find would be a cold mountain plateau. But it looked like he'd have bright moonlight to help him find the way. Besides, if he got lost, he could wait til dawn and find his way back.

Sonia was waiting for him at the bar, a flashlight in hand. He took it and thanked her.

"Don't worry," he said with a gentle smile, *"And don't stay up waiting for me. I may be late."* He started up the stairs.

"And if something happens?" she asked, *"Who do I call?"*

"No one," he said as he went up the narrow staircase. *"There is no one to call."* He turned around, facing her, and in a comforting voice said, *"It may be a while, but I'll be back."*

Up in his room he pulled on his coat. He threw his suitcase on his bed and opened it. He picked up a pair of fur-lined leather gloves and shoved them into a hip pocket. Then he groped around in the suitcase and pulled out his Budapest

souvenir – the small black Walther automatic. He checked
the magazine clip and slipped it and the extra clip inside a
breast pocket of his coat. 'In case of more wolves,' he said to
himself.

He hit the light switch and walked out, leaving the flashlight
on the bed. He'd been on enough patrols and night operations
to learn the hard way that a flashlight could be a two-edged
sword: It let you see what was out there, but it also let
whatever was out there know where you were.

* _ * _ *

Chapter XII: Now and again
XII: Epiphany

As he left the inn and headed up the valley, Ozera's thoughts
were on Dacey, the woman who worked for years in this
enigmatic Russian research site – a woman of intrigue, a
scientist, a mystic, a psychic. A woman who, it seems, may
have somehow been born centuries ago. A woman who could
look into his thoughts, his heart and his soul. A woman he
fell in love with, possibly for the first time in his life.

As Ozera approached the old clearing for helicopter landing
his thoughts changed – to wolves. Sonia at the inn had
warned him and he'd seen one there himself earlier. He was
prepared this time. He told himself he would fight back only
if attack was imminent. The Walther with two 8-round clips
would handle that … if and when the need arose.

Even with the full moon, traveling at night through the woods
is imposing and daunting for anyone. Ozera had the benefit
of his Army field experience and Special Forces training. In
fact, he considered this nocturnal trek quite a bit more
pleasant than a combat operation: He didn't have to worry
about moving silently, keeping to a timetable, trip strings,
booby-traps or ambushes. Plus, once his eyes adjusted to the
night, there was enough ambient moonlight to see where he
was going – not as good as night-vision goggles, true, but
acceptable. He didn't know the terrain and had no map, no
detailed directions, not even a compass, but he knew
generally how far he had to go, and he knew to look for trail
markers.

He bypassed the old research site and headed uphill, as Sonia
told him. He buttoned up his coat; it was getting colder. His
breathing became harder and more labored as he climbed.
His breath pierced the cold night air with short-lived spears of
frosty mist. He passed by the stone outcropping where he
saw the wolf howling earlier in the day, and headed for it. He
stepped out on it and paused, panting, to catch his breath and

look around. It had a commanding view of all approaches up the mountainside.

He turned around and, stepping off the rock ledge, he saw three large stones back in the woods. Even in the moonlight he could see they were lighter colored than the surrounding rocks. Had it not been for Sonia telling him of the trail markings he would have overlooked them. They had been placed there, forming a line pointing up to the right. That's where he headed.

Ozera found he was on a trail. It wasn't a deer or animal trail; it was too wide. And rough stone steps, strategically situated, revealed an unmistakable human influence and orientation. The trail snaked left and right but headed continually upward – a fact his leg muscles increasingly realized. He couldn't see the peak of the mountain; the heavy woods obscured it. So he couldn't guess how far he still had to go or in what direction.

At one point he feared he might have lost the trail. He looked around and, sure enough, three more distinctively colored stones were nearby, pointing the way to go. It was reassuring. It was dark in the woods, but the trail wound through occasional clearings in the forest that were well lit by the moonlight.

He had trekked most of a mile up from the research site. He advanced slowly and came to a sharp left, up a few steps and then into a small clearing. On the other side of the clearing was a stone-cut stairway, bound by massive stone boulders on either side. His military sense told him to proceed carefully. It was a bottleneck – a defensive measure, a trap, designed to funnel a large attacking force into a small area, allowing just one or two soldiers to advance at a time. You could hold back a company of attackers here with just a handful of defenders.

But there was no sign of danger this quiet and peaceful night. Just the occasional hooting of owls and the chatter of night birds. He wondered how long ago this defensive gateway was built, and when it was last used in that role. In any event, it afforded him confidence that he was on the right path.

He crossed the clearing and looked up the rough-hewn stone stairway. It was a sight to behold: Centered in the sky at the top of the stairway hung the nearly full moon. And in front of it, at the top of the stairway – silhouetted before the moon – stood a wolf, motionless. It was not showing any overt sign of aggression. Ozera slowly reached inside his coat and felt for the automatic. He started up, slowly, gun at the ready. As he did the wolf turned and walked back, away, out of sight.

Halfway up the stairway he noticed passageways off to the right and left, between the boulders. Soldiers would hide here, he reasoned, the first line of defense. But defending what?

Ozera approached the top cautiously and bent down, just peering over the last step. No sign of the wolf. Ozera stepped up and out onto a large, flat plateau – a vast clearing of perhaps 15 or 20 acres. It was wide open and stark in the eerie glow of the moon – mostly bare rock, no trees and just some scattered patches of grass. The plateau was surrounded by boulders on the front and sides, and sheer mountain cliffs loomed at the back. It could not be seen except by someone who came up these steps and stood here – or by satellite.

There was something familiar about the mountain skyline in the back. In a moment it came to him. He had seen this place in a picture the Colonel had showed him in his initial briefing. It was the skyline in the painting and drawing of the Monastery. He was standing at the place where it all started, where the mystery began and ended. But just like everyone said, there was nothing here – no Monastery, no structure of any kind.

Ozera scanned the entire plateau, straining his vision in the dim moonlight, looking for the wolf. But there was no sign of it. Must have snuck off somewhere through an opening in the rocks. He tucked the gun away in his coat and started off across the vast open field. A cold wind blew steadily from behind him, across the field to the mountain cliffs.

The flat rocky surface reminded him of the bedrock on the Pennsylvania mountaintop where the Colonel built the other Monastery. He stopped and turned completely around. He was alone – and fully exposed – in the middle of a wide open field, a hundred yards in all directions to the boulders and cliffs. If someone were out there with a sniper rifle and night-vision scope, he'd be finished. Ozera looked back towards the stone stairway, but despite the bright moonlight it was too dark to make out where it was.

Then all at once it became very quiet and still. Not a sound. Even the cold, biting breeze had suddenly stopped.

A feeling came over Ozera, something he hadn't felt before, and a chill went up his spine. He looked down and saw his own moonlit shadow on the ground before him. But then, in an instant, darkness consumed his shadow. Something had blocked off the moonlight.

Expecting to see clouds obscuring the moon he spun around and looked up. But he didn't see clouds, or the moon, or even the sky. His heart stopped a moment, and when it started again it beat very fast. Just inches from his face stood a massive stone wall, which wasn't there before.

"What the …," he uttered, stepping back reflexively and looking around. It was huge. The sheer flat stone wall rose high before him. Above it was a mortared wall of smaller stones and, above that, he saw a colonnade of columns and arches. He looked to the right. The wall extended quite a ways, then curved back out of sight. Same to the left. The structure was round, perhaps circular, he concluded.

His mind settled down, and it came to him – he was standing within arm's reach of the Monastery … the original, mysterious, missing Monastery. He had to assure himself the massive stone structure was really there. Ozera reached his hand out to touch it. It was real. He stood immobilized for a few moments, stunned. Part of him accepted what he was seeing, part of him did not. How could it have just … appeared here? Where did it come from?

Then, voices: He thought he heard voices from around the structure to the right. He looked over and in a few seconds they came around into view, two hooded men, in monk's robes, walking towards him. They were speaking what sounded like Romanian; Ozera couldn't fully make it out.

* - * - *

The Monastery

XII: Retrospective

A solitary, hooded figure trudged through knee-deep snow, down the valley towards Bobeica. Wind gusts swirled a snow squall. It was late afternoon on a cold, cloudy day and the sun was going down. Ozera reached up with a gloved hand and pulled back his snow-covered hood. His face showed wear. He was tired and cold.

As he approached he saw that the village had changed. There were telephone poles and power lines throughout, and a tall tower with some kind of radio equipment at the top. Most of the snow-encrusted houses had oil and gas tanks, with smoke puffing from their chimneys.

The old stone inn had been expanded. A two-story wing had been added alongside the original, more than doubling its size. A new kitchen wing had been added on the back. A neat macadam-paved parking lot was half full, kept clear of snow by the plow parked off to the side. His feet were cold and numb as he came around the front of the building and walked up the shoveled sidewalk to the entrance. It was now the Bobeica Mountain & Ski Resort, a large sign out front said – in Romanian, Russian, English and what looked like Chinese.

Inside was a small lobby and reception area, abuzz with people coming and going. Off to the side was a small restaurant and bar. He walked in and up to the bar. A young, clean-shaven man with jet black hair, in a tie and neat waiter attire, came over.

"Can I help you, sir?" he asked, in English. Ozera was surprised. He hadn't heard English in months and it startled him. He smiled, wondering why the waiter decided to broach him in English.

"I would love a hot coffee," he asked. The waiter nodded and returned in a few minutes with a steaming cup.

"What's the date today?" Ozera asked him

"It's the 21st today."

"The 21st of what?" he asked.

"February," he replied, wondering if Ozera was pulling his leg.

"There was a woman named Sonia who used to own this place … a long time ago," Ozera said, "Is she still around?" The waiter seemed taken aback by the question, not typical for a guest.

"Yes, sir. Mrs. Vasilescu still owns the establishment. She lives nearby, in a big stone house up the hill."

"How can I contact her?" he asked.

The waiter paused a moment, thinking. "The lady at the front desk can probably help you."

He relished the hot coffee, rich and dark, and drank it down. After warming up a bit more he went back out to the front desk.

He spoke Romanian to the slender, sharply dressed young lady at reception, explaining with a smile what he wanted. She agreed to call the owner. *"Please tell her that a guest from long ago has returned,"* he said, *"Tell her the guest forgot the flashlight, and thinks he left something under the bed."* She responded with a puzzled expression but agreed to relay the message. She placed the call and related what he had told her. Silence, as she listened. Then she smiled, spoke a few words he didn't hear and hung up.

"Doamna Vasilescu thinks she remembers you, Domnule," the receptionist told him politely with a smile. *"She asks if you could please wait. She is nearby and will be here shortly."* Ozera agreed and went back to the bar to wait.

*"It **is** you,"* a voice behind him said. He spun around. Sonia stood as he remembered her, but graciously older, 60-ish. *"Please. Come and let us talk,"* she said, gesturing him to follow her.

They went down the hall and into her small, tidy office. He sat in an armchair across from her desk, snuggling in with his heavy coat still on. She opened a decanter and poured them some țuică, handing him a glass, and sat down at the desk.

"I like what you've done with the place," he said, sipping and savoring the plum brandy.

"Well actually," she began, *"you made it possible,"* adding, candidly, *"with what you left in your room."* She sighed, *"How long has it been?"*

"I don't really know," he said. She continued to stare at him with a puzzled expression. He echoed back to her: *"How long **has** it been, Sonia?"*

She thought a moment, reflecting. *"I don't know. A quarter century, more or less,"* she said, shrugging her shoulders. *"You look pretty much as I remember you. You look no older. Why didn't you come back before? "Where have you been?"*

"A lot of questions, Sonia." He leaned over and looked in her eyes. *"I've been up the mountain... in the Monastery."*

She looked neither surprised nor disbelieving. She sat back and heaved a deep sigh, and then spoke softly to him. *"The day after you left two men arrived. They said they were from the Monastery and needed to get supplies. I didn't know them, never saw them before. But they had money – rubles, lei and dollars – and I gave them all they could take with them."*

"Before they left I spoke with them in the bar," she continued, *"I told them one of my guests had gone up earlier looking for*

the Monastery, but didn't return. They told me not to worry, that you would be alright. And then they left. It was Saturday afternoon and a couple of my old timer regulars were there, who heard and saw everything. **They** *seemed to understand it all, but I certainly did not. All they told me later was that you would be back ... someday. Those old timers passed away many years ago, but I remember that day, and what they told me."* She paused, then added: *"They were right, weren't they?"*

Ozera slowly nodded.

"A couple days later I was cleaning your room and found the money in your bag under the bed. I waited and waited, for years, and then," Sonia looked down, avoiding his eyes. *"Then, I spent it,"* she confessed. She looked back up at him: *"Eighty thousand U.S. dollars. I will try to pay you back, of course."*

He saw the sorrow and relief in her dark eyes, respecting her honesty and her wanting to atone, even after so many years. The guilt of many years had now been lifted.

"Did you remarry? Any children?" She looked down again, as if embarrassed, and shook her head. *"Then I have an alternative proposal for you,"* he told her. She looked up, inquisitively, eyebrows raised.

"Then I am asking you to leave a trust, and instructions, to whoever succeeds you in this place, and whoever succeeds them. Write and tell them that others will come – from the Monastery that isn't there. They will be seeking provisions, just like those who came here to you many years ago. And they are to provide them whatever they need, at no charge."

He looked over at her, a serious and pleading look in his eye. *"Promise me you will do this, Sonia, and you will owe me nothing."*

She nodded in agreement. And he knew it would be done.

"*You have been at the monastery all these years?*" she asked, the look of puzzlement returning to her face. He did not respond. "*Are you going back? Back up ... to the Monastery?*"

"*No,*" he said to her, "*It's time for me to go home now.*"

* _ * _ *

XII: Ghost town

A snow squall that morning had left the Pennsylvania mountaintop with a thin white dusting. It was the first snow of the season, late November. Ozera knew that it might well last until spring – and by then insulated under several more layers of ice and snow.

He looked back over his shoulder, noting the tracks he'd left in the fresh snow. Anyone following who saw them would know someone had recently come up this way … and hadn't yet left. But Ozera wasn't too worried. Since the Big Crash the federal government had been pared by more than half, across the board. Even the untouchable U.S. intelligence community had been gutted and was just a shell of its former self. It was doubtful there would still be any active surveillance of the mountaintop, despite what happened there so many years before.

He knew he was exposing himself by traversing the mountaintop in plain sight, especially in the daytime. It was still restricted government property. He didn't have much choice, though. He'd been receiving automated alerts for several days: The battery was dying.

Snow coated the bare rock where the Monastery once stood. Looking over the site today, no one would guess there was ever anything there but a rocky mountaintop, let alone an expansive and elaborate stone and concrete structure. Ozera made his way over to an old oak stump. He stopped and smiled, remembering when it was an oak tree in its prime. It offered a shady refuge from the summer sun when he and Dacey picnicked under its powerful branches. They'd even made love there, just a short distance from the front gate of the monastery.

It had to be lightning that brought down the old oak, Ozera reasoned. It was one of only a couple large trees on the high rocky summit, which made it a target for lightning. Some of the massive branches still lay nearby, slowly decaying.

The camera pack attached to the tree stump was barely noticeable, and its small, powerful battery normally lasted for a year or more. He reached down and pulled the device off. Lightweight, not much bigger than a digital camera, it was the latest in monitoring technology. Not even a visible antenna. The remote-controlled security camera took high-resolution digital pictures through the day – and night-vision pictures after dark. Then it automatically transmitted these, via the nearest cell-phone tower and out over the Internet, to a remote computer that could be anywhere.

Ozera had made the trip up here once already to replace the battery. This time it was running low after just two months. He peeled back the black tape and saw the blinking yellow "low-bat" light. He plucked the battery off the back of the unit, slipped a replacement out of his pocket and snapped it in. He smiled when he turned it over and saw the light change to a steady green.

He re-attached the camera pack to the tree stump, making sure it was pointing in the right direction, to where the Monastery once stood. Then he reached in another pocket and pulled out a roll of metallic foil.

"Okay, let's see how this works," Ozera muttered to himself. He unrolled it, about two feet of green colored foil, with a dangling wire. He wrapped it around the south-facing side of the tree trunk, above the camera pack, and attached it with push pins. The dangling wire he plugged into the camera pack. It was the latest in solar panels – flexible, in whatever color you wanted, and high capacity. Ideal for remote, outside, battery-operated electronic devices – like the camera pack. During sunlight hours it would automatically recharge the device's battery.

Ozera stood up and eyed his work. It looked good, and it was barely noticeable to someone who wasn't looking for it. He pulled out his smartphone and pushed a few buttons. The app launched and automatically established a wireless connection with the camera pack. In a few moments the picture of the mountaintop popped up on the smartphone. He waved his hand in front of the camera and smiled to see it appear on the smartphone display, after a second or so delay. Seemed to be working as expected.

He pushed a few more buttons and launched another app – this one to check for active nearby radio transmitters. He started with a three-mile radius. After a few moments the display flashed the results – 16 active radios detected. He narrowed the search to two miles and ran it again: four radio transmitters found this time. He set for a one-mile check and re-ran it. Just one solid transmitter detected – his camera pack. He smiled, relieved. Slipping the smartphone in his pocket he turned to leave.

Ozera had concluded he was born decades too soon. In his previous life, as he had come to privately refer to it, the Internet was something only college geeks knew about. Mobile phones – still mainly **auto**-mobile phones, were just starting to come on the scene and were too bulky to carry around. Their cost back then limited them to the well-heeled elite. PCs were proliferating and costs were dropping, but they were hardly transportable.

Wireless and mobility had proliferated while he was away. Despite the economic turmoil, smartphones and wireless service were fairly cheap and, so, everybody had a smartphone. Coverage was universal and so everybody had instant Internet access and voice communications with anybody. The latest operating system, "V," based primarily on voice interaction, was now nearly universal. Oh, there were still some iOS and Androids out there, but almost all apps were now written for V. The latest computers were the "flips" – quickly replacing tablets, netbooks and laptops – which folded up to the size of a small paperback and were powered by battery or ambient electro-magnetic energy. Ozera had an affinity for electronics and reveled in the unending deluge of teeny, affordable electronic marvels and gadgets.

A chill permeated him. It was getting dark and the shadows were growing, which Ozera knew could play tricks on the senses. His military experience kicked in: He carefully followed the same path he came up, obscuring his tracks as best he could. He kept a sharp eye on the woods as he went by, but fortunately, didn't see anyone or anything amiss.

He arrived back down at the old gravel parking lot, which had grown over with trees and vegetation. The two-story, cement-block buildings had been abandoned – some showing cracks in the outside walls, a few with missing or broken windows. He paused for a moment to listen – another good military practice. A crow cawed in the distance, but everything else was stone-cold quiet – desolate; it was like a ghost town. The old NEPA Facility he knew hadn't been used, or seen many visitors, for decades.

The gravel road that snaked down the mountain to the entrance was similarly overgrown; some sections had been washed away by storms and water runoff. Ozera descended slowly, quietly, and finally came within view of the entranceway. The swinging-log gateway was long gone. Instead a long, waist-high row of boulders had been placed along the road. This was effective; you couldn't get a vehicle through without a lot of effort.

Ozera ducked off the road and moved stealthily through the woods, the same way he had come up. He avoided the entrance, figuring that if anyplace was still being monitored or under surveillance, it would be there. He stopped at one point near the road as an SUV went by. It sure wasn't like his old Ford Explorer. It hummed, running on its electric motor. Ozera reflected for a moment: With the new solar panel charger he would hopefully not have to come back up here again anytime soon … not unless, or until …

* _ * _ *

XII: Getting around

"Chevy Volt, one of the first models, 2012," the used-car salesman said to Ozera, "She's a beaut, though, Mr. Livingston. Just 40,000 miles, and American made. Yeah, the batteries are first generation, and it's a hybrid. So, if you can manage eighty bucks a gallon, you can make it 500, 600 miles or more on a fill."

"How much?" Ozera asked, point blank.

"Ten grand will get you the title in 20 minutes."

"How about nine … in cash … and that covers sales tax and all the paperwork?"

The salesman hadn't been offered cash to sweeten the deal in some time. "Sold!" he snapped back, and they shook hands.

Ozera went to the bathroom, opened his bag and pulled out a pack of the old money. He pulled 10 bills out of a pack of 100 and went back to pay.

"Pretty old bills," the salesman said, thumbing through the wad, "and yet they look like you printed 'em just last week. Mind if I check 'em out?"

"Suit yourself," Ozera responded smugly. With that the salesman put one bill on a blank piece of white paper and then pushed some buttons on his smartphone. He leaned over, hovering about a foot above the bill, and snapped a flash picture. After a few moments he read the results.

"They're the real deal," he said with an avaricious grin. "Sorry 'bout that, but since the Big Crash you can't be too careful. Here's your key," he said, tossing it unceremoniously on the table before Ozera. "Your title, registration, contract, inspection sticker and temp plates will be out on the printer in a minute. Glad to do business with you, Mr. Livingston."

It was getting late and he wasn't going much further tonight. Ozera spent the night in a cheap motel right off Exit 8 of the New Jersey Turnpike. $200 a night, for a really barebones room. He still had two packs of hundreds left, $20,000. He recalled how valuable the U.S. dollar was in Romania in times past, where he could live luxuriously for a month on $200. But here, now, it sure wasn't worth what it used to be. And at this rate, he lamented to himself, his cash wouldn't last long.

He looked out at the turnpike. Rush hour, but traffic was eerily light – mainly just electric and some hybrid cars. Gas for standard combustion engines was now about $80 a gallon, having slowly crept down from over $100 a gallon right after the Big Crash. The streets everywhere were littered with abandoned gas guzzlers; only the very well-to-do could afford them anymore.

Oddly, electric power was plentiful, driven now mainly by relatively cheap U.S. natural gas. Oil imports, however, had all but ceased, and the Middle East's vast oil reserves would remain radioactive for many years to come. Commuting to work became a thing of the past, but then Internet 'telecommuting' flourished in its place.

It was now three years after the big crash, and he had yet to learn the details of precisely what happened. It occurred a few years ago, triggered by the White House announcement that the government could borrow no more, and had to temporarily stop paying interest on the debt and issuing checks.

Within an hour the stock market had tanked, shedding 60 percent of its value. A run on the banks started Monday morning. Riots ensued. A mushroom cloud of bankruptcies ensued within weeks: blue-chip corporations, banks, investment houses – taking most retirement funds with them – as well as many state and local governments. Inflation kicked in and prices across the board shot up five-fold –

twenty-fold for gas. The government at this point was powerless to do anything to stem it.

Only within the last year or so have things slowly begun to return to normal. America was slowly starting to climb out of the hole, much as it did after the great stock market crash a century ago. It was not unlike what Ozera had seen in Eastern Europe, with the collapse of the Soviet Union. A whole new economy had to emerge and take root. The inevitability of overspending and massive debt. You'd think we would have learned our lesson by now, Ozera thought to himself.

* - * - *

XII: Aunt Jane

Ozera had to know, and curiosity got the best of him: What had become of the mountaintop and, more specifically, Mrs. Griffiths? It was a bright, sunny, late winter morning. The hybrid car purred quietly as Ozera drove along the river and turned onto Narrows Hill Road, like he had done dozens of times before. He'd come in the opposite direction last time, he recalled, hiding among hay bales in the back of Mrs. Griffiths' red pick-up.

As the road ascended the hybrid's gas engine kicked in regularly. Ozera grimaced, but he had little choice. To get where he was going he'd just have to bite the bullet and drive on. He looked over and saw he still had half a tank. It was $800 for his last fill-up.

There were a few new houses and barns. And some of the ones he remembered had either been rebuilt or expanded, or were gone completely. There was a lot more cattle than he remembered, including now sheep, too. He passed a middle-aged couple on bicycles, toting groceries in baskets on the side. Near the mountaintop he passed a man on horseback riding towards him, on the other side of the road. Nothing unusual these days – just signs of the times.

The road crested and he approached the entrance to the mountaintop facility. He slowed and looked around cautiously. After all, the last time he was there he was shot at and almost nabbed by a squad of government spooks – something you don't soon forget.

A row of boulders had been placed along the road, only about a foot apart, effectively closing off the entranceway to vehicles. Small innocuous signs – some very worn and a couple that he remembered – forbid trespassing and pronounced the area as still restricted U.S. Government property. The road was narrow and there was no place to pull over or park on either side. He passed by slowly and looked it over. The access way was overgrown; it looked abandoned and unused for a long time.

He continued on up the road, to the familiar entrance to Mrs. Griffiths' place. He pulled over and paused a moment before turning in, scoping out the landscape. There were a few subtle but notable changes. The open fields he used to jog through had been crisscrossed with white paddock fences. There were several large, chestnut horses in a large corral in the front field. The big old barn, which was quite dilapidated, had been totally rebuilt and expanded.

A hand-lettered "Horse Riding & Boarding" sign was nailed on a post near the entrance. It looked amateurish; whoever did it had little calligraphy aptitude, Ozera noted. Mrs. Griffiths would never tolerate it. With mixed feelings about what he would find, he turned in and drove along the familiar gravel driveway, down over the brook and up towards the parking area near the barn.

There was only one other working vehicle in the parking lot, an aging blue Toyota Prius hybrid. Behind it, grown over with weeds he saw an old, dilapidated and rusting, gas-guzzler. He took another look and recognized it. It was, or used to be, Mrs. Griffiths' shiny red pick-up truck.

He strode up to the front door and knocked. After several minutes the door swung open. A man about Ozera's age stood there, a little shorter, unshaven, longish brown hair, clad in workman's clothes.

"Is the lady of the house at home?" Ozera asked him, flashing a playful smile. He knew it sounded a little corny, like a door-to-door salesman.

"There hasn't been a lady of the house here for some years," the young man replied in a serious tone. Ozera thought he detected a slight undertone of annoyance.

"Are you the ... owner?" Ozera asked.

"That's right. What can I do for you?" A quick, terse reply. If he didn't say something relevant soon he'd have the door slammed in his face.

"I was wondering if ... Mrs. Griffiths." He wasn't sure what or how to ask, so he just dropped her name, awkwardly.

The expression on the man's faced changed. He softened. "Did you know her?"

"I did."

"Then, please come in," he said, holding the door open for him. "I'm sorry I was so ... I was preoccupied. You are ...?"

"Name's Livingston. Victor Livingston." It was as good a name as any. And it was the alias Ozera officially adopted even before his return to the states.

The inside had been completely redone. What used to be a cozy Victorian sitting room was now a hodgepodge mix of living room and home office. The charm, and it seemed the charming innkeeper too, were both long gone.

The young man turned and looked Ozera in the eye. A sad and somber expression came over him.

"Aunt Jane passed away a few years ago," he said. "Just before the Big Crash. Fortunately she didn't have to live through that. You must have been a pretty young guy when you knew her."

Ozera felt a pain in his heart. He suspected the fun-loving Mrs. Griffiths might have passed on. But he didn't know for sure ... until now. "**Aunt** Jane?" he asked.

"Yeah, I was her great nephew. Patrick, Pat Schafer's the name. I was living in California when I got word that she passed away."

"She died here, Pat?" Ozera asked softly.

"Yes. She was 80 and all alone," Pat Shafer replied. "Her couple horses almost starved to death by the time the neighbors checked in and found her. You know she used to run all this as a Bed and Breakfast, right?"

"Yes, she was quite a woman," Ozera replied, thinking aloud. "She left you the place in her will then, I guess?"

"Actually, no. She left no will," he said, "My grandmother was her older sister, and as it turned out her only relative. She passed away a long time ago, and my mom, her daughter, and my dad both died in an auto accident when I was in college. So I ended up her only surviving next of kin and it all passed to me. I'd only met Aunt Jane when I was very young. Used to stay here for a week or so in the summers. She was feisty and fun, ran everything herself."

"She never re-married?"

"No. Maybe you knew that her husband passed away when she was in her 40's, when I was just a small kid. So I never met him. She is buried next to him in a church cemetery in a small town up north of here. She died alone, but they told me she pined for years and years for a young man she met and fell in love with, who left her. It was a May-October romance, and she took it with her to her grave."

Ozera was dumbstruck. He choked up and could say nothing for the moment. He felt terrible for the lonely Mrs. Griffiths, who he … abandoned. He turned and began slowly walking to the front door.

"How did you know her, Mr. Livingston?" Pat interrupted him, apparently wanting to continue the conversation.

"I was a border here for a while, when Mrs. ... your Aunt Jane ... ran this as a B&B. We got to know each other pretty well after a while."

He saw that Ozera was distressed talking about her. "Geez, that was a while ago," Pat said, contemplating the time frame. "Yeah, I thought of reverting to a B&B, back in the BBC days. But you know, since the Big Crash, attracting well-to-do tourists here on the mountaintop has been next to impossible. So I made a go of boarding horses instead," he said with a smile, hoping that would lighten the atmosphere. "With the gas situation, horses have become more practical. Now I board horses for a half-dozen local families. A Livery Stable. That's what they used to call it back in the 1800's."

"Well, thanks for the time, Pat," Ozera said, returning a pretend half-smile, and again turning to go.

"You wouldn't have known that beau of hers, or what happened to him, would you? Nah, probably years before your time. Irish, I think – O'Shea, O'Shera, something like that."

He perked up. "How do you know the name?"

"She left a letter addressed to him – I guess figuring ... hoping ... he'd show up again someday. I settled her affairs and moved in here. And then, after the funeral, her lawyer stopped by and dropped it off. Still got it in a box with her other stuff, stashed away in a closet in the back."

"What's it say?"

"Kind of a love note," Pat replied. "Hang on. Let me go get it." He ran into the back apartment – where Mrs. Griffiths' lived – and re-emerged in a few moments.

"Ozera, Brad Ozera," he said, reading from an envelope.

"Hang on a second," Ozera said, and went out to his car and retrieved his real, original passport. He returned and handed it to Pat.

Pat looked at the passport picture, and up at Ozera.

"I don't understand," he said, "This passport's like, decades old, but it's … you. How …"

"I'm older than I look," Ozera responded, with a smile.

"I thought you said your name was Livingston?"

"It's a phony name I picked up after the Big Crash," Ozera interjected, "I'm sure you understand."

Pat Shafer nodded, then handed Ozera the letter. He folded it and stuffed it in his pocket.

"Thanks, Pat. You take care," and he left again, for the last time.

* _ * _ *

If you're reading this, Brad, I was right! I knew you'd come back. I'm sorry but I can't wait for you any longer. Too many small ailments are adding up. I know you're alive somewhere and I know you will come back someday. And I'm sorry, Honey, but I won't be here to greet you.

I'm leaving this with my old lawyer, named Ellison, in Hellertown. He assures me you'll get it, if you come back. Please be sure to stop by and thank him.

I was lonely when I met you, Brad. You'll never know how lonely. And our months together gave me renewed life. It all came to an end, though, when I took you to the airport that day. But that was the most exciting day of my life. And an old gal thanks you. I only wish I didn't corner you more often and insist on a happy ending to our nights out together. That night we christened the hot tub will go fondly with me to my grave.

As I guess you found out, everything came to an end up on the mountaintop there, too. They closed the whole place off. You, John ... the Doctor, too ... all gone. When the rent checks from the Government stopped I started taking in boarders again, but in the last few years I haven't been up to it. I got word that John was living somewhere near Pittsburgh. But when I finally located him on line I found out he had just died from Alzheimer's.

Remember to thank Ellison in Hellertown for getting you this letter. I shall always remember you ...
With all my love,
J.G

Ozera wiped away a tear. He had meant so much to her ... and he never knew.

Mrs. Griffiths made a point to mention, twice, that he should stop in and thank the lawyer Ellison in Hellertown ... so he did. Using the return address on the envelope he found it, a small lawyer office on Main Street in the little town.

"Mr. Ellison? Yes, this is his office," said the thin elderly woman in the front office. "His partner is gone and he is kind of semi-retired. Y'know, not much court activity since the crash."

Ozera explained he just wanted to thank Ellison for the letter from Mrs. Griffiths. She responded with a puzzled look and he showed her the letter. She took it with her into a back office. He watched as she called someone, spoke a few moments and hung up.

She returned and asked Ozera for identification. He again produced his old passport. She looked it over and handed it back to him with the letter.

"Please hang on a minute, Mr. Ozera. I have something for you in the safe." She disappeared and re-emerged in a little while with another envelope, the same size, but taped closed and signed on front and back. It had been sealed. He signed a receipt and she handed it to him. He thanked her, put it in his pocket and left.

A short note said simply: "*Brad, I didn't take a penny. Just invested it, and paid for the safe deposit box rental. I know you'll be back. And I hope you're proud of me. Love, J.G.*"

A safe deposit box key had a tag on it with a box number, a local bank name and address. Ozera went to the address and found a bank, still open and operating, but with a different name. Most banks had closed after the crash, but now some were re-opening. The attractive bank manager checked and told him the key was still good, that the box rental was in his name and had been prepaid for 50 years. She led him into the vault, brought him the metal safe deposit box and left.

He opened it and recognized the bag he had retrieved from the Colonel's safe, the same one he had left at Mrs. Griffiths' the day he made his escape. He pulled it out and unzipped it. Inside he found the loaded .45 Army automatic he had left with her that day, and a treasure trove – a still-wrapped bundle of $100 bills from the original packs he'd left; a pile of "Bearer Bonds" of various denominations up to $100,000, and several stock certificates – a thousand shares of "Apple," "Cisco," and others he didn't recognize. There was a heavy plastic tube containing gold coins – U.S. double eagles, in mint condition – and another filled with pristine Morgan silver dollars, all from the late 1800's.

"I miss you, Mrs. Griffiths. And yes, I'm proud of you, Honey. Be at rest," he said.

That night Ozera searched the Web and found a biography – and the obituary – of Colonel John Smith, U.S. Army. It was his real name, it turns out. No middle initial. With the bio was a grainy photo of him in his prime, in Green Beret, captain's bars and crossed rifles on the collars of his jungle fatigues. It was reportedly taken somewhere in Vietnam in 1972. He was born 1944 in Pittsburgh, where he moved back after retiring in 1997, after 30 years military service. Died September 30th. Age 71. Wife Suzanne, deceased. Survived by a son, Thomas, in Georgia, and a daughter, Christine, of Scranton, Pennsylvania.

Nothing about his later assignments – where he served, who he worked for, or anything that he did after Vietnam. Ozera wondered if it really was natural Alzheimer's; even back then he had heard of drugs routinely used by Government agencies, undetectable, which could produce symptoms of heart attack, stroke, even senility. He sat back from his computer and raised his glass of bourbon.

"Well, sir, I got your note, and everything you left for me in the safe. They came looking for me, but they didn't find me. That arrogant asshole Bennington was working for them – whoever 'they' are."

He took a sip. "I found it, Colonel – the Monastery, the original. Or it found me, I'm not sure. You were right. Whatever's been happening on that mountain in Romania, you managed to recreate it here, on our mountaintop. Rest in peace, sir," he said, and then took a big gulp.

Ozera felt very alone. He'd felt lonely while out on his Army assignments, too, of course. But back then he knew that there were friends, family back home – who he'd see again if he kept his head down and made it home alright. Now, however, there was no one left in the world anymore that he could confide in, who knew him and could understand what he knew and experienced.

He thought of his family, back on the farm. Surely somebody he knew was still there. But what if nobody there still knew him? It was a frightening thought. He would find out.

* - * - *

XII: Reunion

It was still dark. Cold and dark. And it wouldn't be dawn for a while yet. He had parked on the road below, overlooking the long driveway. He doubted that he could be seen from the house. Ozera sat and looked lovingly up at his home. He saw himself driving for the first time, on the rumbling tractor's big metal seat, his dad standing behind him, back-seat driving. He saw himself running up to the house with his unconscious little brother in his arms. Pat had been thrown by a horse and hit his head on a rock. Ozera had never seen anyone knocked out before; he was afraid his little brother had died.

He took the last sip of his coffee and looked up again, this time seeing himself arriving home on a cold winter day, after two years away in the Army. It was colder than this. He remembered that he couldn't get warm, despite the overcoat, having spent the previous six months in the tropical jungles of Central America. God, it was good to be coming home again. From the house Mom saw him walking up the driveway, duffel bag in hand. She had called to Pop and then came running down to meet him – no coat, just her apron flapping, despite the biting cold. She threw her arms around him, and began planting kisses frantically all over him, knocking his beret off. He looked up and saw his broad-shouldered father standing near the house. Ozera waved. His dad waved back, smiling broadly – hoping that no one would see the tears in his eyes.

That was years ago … to Ozera. To anyone here, now, it was … a long, long time ago, if anyone here still remembered it at all.

Lights flickered on in the barn, drawing him back to the present. He watched attentively and, in a little while, saw two figures – one large enough to be his father, the other not quite a full-grown man – walk from the barn back into the house.

The sun was lightening the sky over the hills behind the farmhouse and barn. Ozera started the Chevy Volt and, with lights off, purred quietly up the driveway. Like driving an electric golf cart, Ozera often thought. He parked off to the side of the barn, out of sight, and got out, quietly closing the car door. He entered the barn and was confronted by the smells and sounds of the cattle, reawakening pleasant memories. No one around. But it wouldn't be long; the cows had to be fed and milked. He sat on a bale of hay under the light, and waited.

Shortly he heard the house door creak open and the screen door slam shut. In the barn-door opening a large-framed man appeared, holding a shiny, stainless steel bucket. It wasn't Pop, though. It was his 'little' brother, Pat, now in his 40's. He'd grown into a burly figure, just like their dad, and now wore a short-trimmed beard.

Pat flinched, not expecting someone to be sitting on a bale of hay in the middle of the barn at 5 am. He walked slowly towards the stranger, prepared to confront him, a confused and defensive look on his face. Then he stopped short. The bucket fell to the floor with a clang.

"Brad?" he said softly, his head tilting slightly in confused disbelief.

"Yup, it's me, Bro," Ozera said, standing up and flashing his trademark smile, as if to reaffirm it really was him.

"It can't be. Are you a ghost?" Pat asked seriously. Ozera extended his arms and the brothers passionately embraced. After a few moments Brad looked Pat in the eyes.

"Mom and Pop?"

Pat shook his head slowly. "Both ... gone," he said, with sorrow in his eyes. Pat was always the sentimental one. Empathic. He felt for others. Now he felt his brother's pain.

Sister Liz, by comparison, was more of a 'Woe is me,' self-absorbed type, often wallowing in self-pity.

"Mom died in '99," Pat explained. "She was just 66. She had gone through years of depression, which started after you went missing. And then she got worse after they declared you dead. Medication, nothing we did, seemed to help. Pop lamented her passing every day, for years. He dropped dead of a heart attack right here. That was, oh, five years ago now."

Pat grabbed his big brother's arms. "Brad, where the fuck have you been?! You look like you did when we last saw you – like, 25, 30 years ago!"

Just then a young man appeared in the barn doorway, interrupting them. Pat glanced over at him. He was lean but already fairly muscular and broad shoulders. He looked eerily like Pat, when he was a teenager.

"Brad, this is your ... nephew – my oldest, 16-year-old David," Pat said, adding with a smile: "Just started driving. David, this is your ... Uncle Brad."

David looked blank-faced at Ozera, not sure what to say, or think. Yes, Pop had an older brother, Brad, but they told him he died years before he was even born. Brad nodded at him and smiled cordially.

"David, go tell your mom we have company for breakfast. Your Uncle Brad and I will finish up out here and be in shortly." David nodded, but continued staring at 'Uncle Brad.' "Go on now!" his father repeated. That broke the young lad's spellbound gaze. He turned and walked out.

Pat let loose with a barrage of questions: "Where have you been? In the U.S.? Overseas? Were you in prison? Suspended animation? Some kind of medical experiment? What?"

Ozera chuckled nervously. He had to explain his predicament for the first time, and he weighed his words carefully. Yes, he was overseas most of the time, he explained. Yes, it was part of a classified project, the research project he mentioned to Pat and Liz all those many years ago. No, it wasn't suspended animation. But he had aged very slowly, and that, too, was related to the project. Ozera knew it sounded ludicrous, but what he told him was, more or less, the truth.

Pat listened, dumbfounded. It was all too incredible. He nodded from time to time, but didn't much buy into his brother's explanation. Still, he had to admit and accept that, standing next to him, was his brother, Brad, in the flesh, and looking like he hardly aged in the decades since he last remembered seeing him. There was no denying that.

It was the kitchen where Ozera grew up, though it had been totally remodeled. He met Angie, Pat's wife of 18 years, a little stocky, wearing a flowered apron he recognized as his mom's. Short dark hair framed her pretty face. She had heard all about Brad, but had long ago put him out of her mind, to rest, believing he had died in the 1990's. Angie, son David, and their daughter, Rachel – 14 and just blossoming into a young lady – looked at and treated 'Uncle Brad' as if he were a ghost. So did Pat, for that matter, although with a modicum of cordiality.

They had breakfast, with little talking. Afterwards, Pat politely ushered the children away. Angie cleared the table and started dishes as Pat poured another round of coffee, sat down and brought his brother up to date.

"I don't know where you've been, Brad," his brother began, candidly, "and I don't know how it's even possible that you're here with us now, after all these years." He looked at Ozera with sincerity in his eyes, "But you **are** here, bro, and I'm happy to see you're okay."

"You went missing when, early 90's, Brad? Well, spooky government types kept a pretty close eye on the place here for quite a while afterwards. They wouldn't talk with us but we were pretty sure they were looking for you. That went on for … months. Then Mom and Pop said one day it just stopped and they never showed up anymore.

"We called all around the Department of Defense and the Department of the Army, but got nowhere. They would check and then come back and tell us you were involved in classified operations and couldn't tell us anything else. We even went to the local State Police and tried to report you missing. We located that government site you were at, but it had been abandoned. The police came back and told us they checked with Washington and got the same runaround we got. And so, that was that.

"Life went on, Brad. '93 came and went. '94. Still nothing. Mom got increasingly frustrated and despondent. You were always her favorite, y'know, Brad."

Pat continued: "Anyhow, I did graduate from Lehigh, finally," he said with a wry smile. "Class of '96, B.A. in accounting. Married Angie a couple years later and set-up a small accounting practice over in Lehighton.

"Liz married that year … for the first time. Some guy in real estate she met in Boston. I didn't like him. Anyway, a big wedding, at the French Manor Inn up in Sterling. Pretty much cleaned Mom and Pop out. It perked Mom up a little, though, I remember. Liz and Ralph moved to Florida, had a little boy, then broke up a year later. She says he abused her. Beats me. Liz married twice more over the last dozen years. Still married to the last one – an electrician in Florida, named Don, I think. He had four or five kids, she had two and she had another one with him. She's still got five or six young ones still living at home. I visited a couple times, but not since the Crash. Cripes, couldn't afford the plane ticket today. And sure couldn't afford to drive.

"Then one summer afternoon an Army sedan pulled up. You had been gone seven years or so. I was here. An officer – a major I think – got out and came in. Mom and Pop figured out why he was here when they saw him get out of the sedan. Told us you were missing on a classified mission since 1992, and were now being carried as 'presumed dead.' It tore Mom apart. And you know Pop; he tried to be strong and not show anything, but he was pretty devastated too. The officer really didn't know anything else. He just got the job of coming and notifying us.

"Like I said in the barn, Mom didn't last long after that. Pop tried like hell to cheer her up – dinners out, a couple vacations, even a cruise they couldn't afford. But Mom kept sinking. Then in the spring, 1999, she went up to her bedroom, laid down and just … died." Pat had tears in his eyes. He never thought he'd be relating this to anyone, especially his older brother, after all these years.

"Angie and I moved in here afterwards. I was still doing accounting and Angie and I helped Pop with the farm. David came along and then a couple years later, Rachel. It's their home here now, too, Brad. Same as you and me.

"Were you around for the Crash?" Pat asked him. Ozera shook his head.

"No, I was out of the country. But I heard about what a mess it was."

"Mess!? The Federal government of the United States went bankrupt. We are just now climbing out of the hole, but unemployment is still 22 percent. We fared better than most here on the farm. It's quite a barter economy today, and we have fresh dairy products to trade. At least with the Government shrunk we don't get hassled as much for taxes and with new regulations.

Pat shook his head. "At least we did finally get a balanced budget amendment to the Constitution. More than half of our population is back living in the country. Government is just skeletal, but that doesn't bother a lot of people. Older folks are moving in with their children. Big changes. What are you driving, Brad?"

"Got an original 2012 Chevy Volt."

"Not bad," Pat said approvingly. "You can still pick up one of those for, what, $10,000 or $11,000? But the new all-electrics are impossible to get, even for $40,000 or $50,000, which nobody has to spend anymore."

"Pat, I am sorry to have imposed on you …," Ozera said, apologetically.

"What impose?! You're my long-lost brother, back from the … God only knows where."

"Please bring Liz up to date," Ozera said in a serious tone, standing up, and preparing to leave. "I'll try to get back from time to time. Angie, it was great to meet you, and your … my nephew and niece. And thanks for the breakfast." Angie smiled, standing quietly by the sink counter, drying her hands.

"Brad, you don't have to go already," Pat implored him. "I've got a thousand more questions for you."

"Next time, Pat." Ozera was visibly tired. His day had started at 4 am, and the time with Pat and his family was especially … draining. They stood facing each other. Ozera saw his brother's eyes well up again with tears. They embraced for what seemed a long time. Then he pulled away, donned his coat and smiled his characteristic, endearing smile. He turned and walked out. Pat and his wife watched as he walked out to his car. The kids watched from upstairs.

He got in and drove away. The Ozera brothers both shared the same thought: That they may never see the other again.

* - * - *

XII: Return

Adaptability. Special Forces training could be summarized in one word: adaptability. Ozera remembered one particularly grueling field training exercise, near Stone Mountain, Georgia. After several days and nights of patrolling with next to no sleep or food, he learned it was his turn in the barrel.

"Okay, Lieutenant. You da man," the senior sergeant snarled. Successful completion of the course – a key one to getting assigned to Special Forces – would depend on what he did over the next few hours. "Two of your team have just been seriously wounded by a land mine, which also knocked out your radio. You're 10 miles behind enemy lines and five miles from the objective. What do you do now, Lieutenant?"

Ozera looked out the front window of the little house he had rented, overlooking the Delaware River and the adjoining canal. He sipped his coffee and imagined that sergeant's dread-instilling voice now:

'Okay, Lieutenant. You've been dropped into a different world, a world you don't know – a world where the country is reeling from a self-inflicted economic collapse. Most of the people you've known are gone. And there is no going back. So what do you do now, Lieutenant?'

"I'll bide my time, Sarge," he muttered to the empty room. "I've got wheels. I've got a roof over my head. I'm adapting." He thought he had settled in pretty well, in fact – thanks in large part to what Mrs. Griffiths had left him. You could live well in the ABC world, he was finding, if you had money. Some things never change. What Ozera needed, and knew he needed, was a plan, something to focus on, a goal or objective to pursue and achieve … until something better came along.

"Computer!" Ozera announced. "Status!"

A few seconds, then: "Good afternoon, Brad. There have been two motion-sensor alerts since you last checked," the synthesized female voice replied.

Ozera sat down in the armchair at his desk, brimming with all manner of electronic gear. "Computer! Show me the mountaintop now!" The voice-response program took a few seconds, but dutifully replied in due time.

"This was taken one minute and 45 seconds ago," the synthesized voice said, while at the same time displaying a picture on the large, high resolution display screen. It showed the mountaintop view from the tree stump-attached video camera. It looked just as he remembered when he last went up to replace the camera pack's battery.

"Show me the last motion-sensor alert!" he said.

"This was taken at 0814 this morning," the voice said, displaying a picture of the same view, except with a large, white-tailed doe in the middle of the screen, right in front of the camera.

"Show me the previous motion-sensor alert!" he commanded.

"This was taken at 0813 this morning," the voice responded, showing the head of a large animal, filling the screen. It was comical and Ozera laughed out loud. The same deer he'd seen in the later picture was sniffing the camera pack.

"Are infrared and night vision working okay?" he asked.

"Yes," came the reply in a few moments.

"And is the alarm for motion detection still enabled and working correctly?" Again a brief delay, then "Yes," with the same dispassionate, synthesized voice.

Ozera sat back and closed his eyes. A mélange of memories flashed through his mind. One in particular took center stage: His return from Romania.

* - * - *

The driver wanted 200 Euros to take him from remote Vatra Dornei to the outskirts of Bucharest – a day-long, 300-mile journey. But he'd alternately take $400 U.S. dollars, in advance. Christ, Ozera thought to himself, times have changed. He could have lived like a king in Romania for six months on $400 U.S. … before.

He checked into a modest, although cosmopolitan-looking hotel. One hundred U.S. dollars, or 50 Euros, per night. The Euro … impressive. The same currency was now used virtually throughout Europe. There were no more Romanian coins or currency. And while the U.S. dollar was still accepted, Ozera could see it had lost much of its relative value, and respect. And like it or not, all the currency he still had with him was U.S. dollars.

His plan: to spend a few days here, rest up and get some new clothes. Then he'd work on two other, more important objectives: First, he'd mingle with locals and foreign visitors and try to find out what was going on in this world and back in the U.S. Secondly, he'd need an updated passport and papers to get home.

He noticed that, surprisingly, many of the foreign visitors in Bucharest were Chinese. And it was clear that local stores, restaurants and businesses were now catering to the Chinese. He stopped in a few bars and cafes and casually mingled. Oddly, he could find no Americans. At one pub he met and wrangled an invitation to settle down with an older Canadian couple, who gave him an earful about American folly.

He learned of the bankruptcy of the U.S. Government, the subsequent stock market crash and the economic collapse. The United States was just now starting to come back.

Canada, with one of the soundest economies, was marginally affected, although exports to the U.S. slowed to a trickle. With U.S. prominence gone, China was uniquely positioned to expand and fill the void.

The Canadian couple was growing suspicious with Ozera's many questions, but acquiesced and continued. Ozera sat spellbound as they recounted U.S. history for the last couple of decades. George Bush, president when Ozera went on active duty, was not re-elected, despite the success of the Gulf War. They made note of the fact that this was the **first** President George Bush, and the **first** Gulf War.

That night Ozera slept uneasily, worried about the America he would find when he finally returned home.

* - * - *

In Romania, Ozera would use the Romanian passport the Colonel had given him, and the name Stefan Ionescu. Since he spoke fluent Romanian and it was his face on the passport picture, there were never any issues or questions. Now of course that passport had long since expired. He often wondered where the Colonel got it, and chalked it up to the bottomless resources and resourcefulness of the American intelligence community back then.

But he'd need a current U.S. passport to get home. Both his own Bradley Ozera passport and the one the Colonel gave him – Victor Livingston's – had also expired decades ago.

Ozera walked around his hotel and found an upscale beauty salon. He waited patiently to meet the lady in charge and explained what he wanted: to look like he was 50. She asked no questions but looked his face over carefully, then concluded: "*No problem, Domnule.*" She booked him two hours for hair treatment and facial make-up. Afterwards, Ozera looked at the final production in a mirror and nodded his approval.

Next stop: a passport photo shop. They told him that color photos were now used in passports. In fact, it would cost considerably more to have picture taken in black and white. It didn't seem to matter much: all photos were digital now, they explained – no more film or development, or waiting. He left with his pictures a half hour after he arrived.

Finally, to the U.S. Embassy – a sprawling complex in the center of Bucharest. An overworked receptionist – who Ozera determined was a Romanian national – was pleasantly surprised when he spoke to her in Romanian. He explained that he was a U.S. citizen with an expired passport, who had lived with family in northern Romania for many years.

She was considerate and understanding, and told him that the embassy staff had been cut to the bone due to economic circumstances in the U.S. Still, she would get him an appointment with the person who handled passport renewal as soon as she could.

"This passport is quite old, Mr. Livingston," the man in the suit – Mr. Harrison, according to the nameplate on the counter – said to him, "Where have you been all this time?"

I have relatives up north, near Vatra Dornei, where my family comes from. I've been working with my uncle, who does telephone and communications services."

Mr. Harrison considered the story, while comparing his photo in the old passport with his now-aged face. "Photos?" he asked.

"Color, I assume," Ozera said. Mr. Harrison nodded and he put the envelope with the photos down on the counter. The man took the photos and his old passport and walked away. Ozera got nervous. This was a real passport the Colonel gave him, he was sure, but as far as he knew it was a fictitious identity. If he came back and asked a lot of questions about Victor Livingston, he'd be in trouble. He started to double-guess his decision to use the passport the Colonel gave him, instead of his own …

In a few minutes the suit returned. "Where were you born, Mr. Livingston?" he asked.

Ozera gulped. He knew the old passport listed his birthplace as Maryland. So he told him Westminster was his hometown. It was the first place in Maryland to come to mind – a small town north of Washington D.C., where he once spent a weekend with an Army buddy.

Apparently that was acceptable. "Okay, it checks out," was all he said. So he did check it out and it still came back clean. Given the age of the passport it's possible Mr. Harrison didn't or couldn't ascertain any more details of Victor Livingston. "You wouldn't happen to have your Social Security card with you, would you?" There's no way he could come up with the social security number, let alone the card.

Ozera leaned over the counter, as if confiding to his bartender. "Mr. Harrison, I haven't used my social security number for over 20 years, and haven't seen the card in all that time."

He mulled it over. "Okay," he said, accepting the story. "Are you returning home soon?"

"I was hoping to. How long before I can get a new passport?"

There was a $200 fee for expedited handling, and the suit told him he could pick it up there at the embassy in three days. Ozera peeled off and handed him two hundreds and told him he'd be back to pick it up Monday. He then matter-of-factly turned and walked out, letting out a deep breath and loosening a knot of tension in his gut. It could have been a lot worse. So it would be just a few more nights in Bucharest and he'd be on his way home – for the first time.

* _ * _ *

The Monastery

Chapter XIII: Reflections

XIII: Welcome

The Fern Valley Inn was open now just three nights a week. Like most remaining local businesses it was a faint echo of its former self. On this Friday night just three couples had come in to dine. Yes, it was late summer, traditionally a slow time for the restaurant business. But even so, few families were vacationing in the Poconos, and even fewer locals could afford to go out for dinner and drinks.

Ozera ate alone in the barroom. The only other customers were a couple of regulars at the bar, nursing their libations. The owner's wife, he found out, doubled as dining-room waitress and bartender. He fondly recalled the rowdy Friday nights he and Mrs. Griffiths wined, dined, wined some more, and usually closed the place. Those were better times, much better times, he recalled fondly.

On his way out he stopped and looked up the dark stairway that led to the private dining room, where the Doctor first introduced him to her passion, her luscious body and wild abandon. The room had long since been closed off. Much better times, he mulled to himself.

The front door of his house swung open, revealing the dark, sparsely furnished living room. Ozera stood teetering slightly. He reached for the light switch, but changed his mind when he saw the moon glow streaking in through the bare windows. He tossed the remote fob for the Chevy Volt on the table and flopped down in the comfortable armchair in front of the computer.

"Computer!" he said. The large screen crackled and lit up. "Good evening, Brad," the synthesized female voice said, "What would you like?"

He thought a moment. "Any motion-detection alerts?"

A brief pause, then a terse "No."

"Show me the mountaintop now, with night vision and infrared."

"This was taken one minute ago," the voice said and the mountaintop displayed, with the faint green tint of night-vision processing. Night-vision pictures are incredibly clear using just ambient light, but the pictures are even better with star light, and downright remarkable with moon light. The picture on the screen looked like daytime. Again, he noted, no difference in the view from the last time he checked.

"Alright, good night," Ozera said, and the computer screen went dark. He sat alone in the moonlight and his thoughts turned to Dacey. Looking up the staircase at their private dining room had reawakened memories. He loved her, yes, but more importantly, she was one of the few people in the world who knew what he had found and experienced on that mountain plateau in the Carpathians. They could not discuss it when they were together because, at the time, he could not understand. Now he did.

He sighed and sat quietly in the dark room, save for the moonlight that infused a pale, soothing glow through the windows. The moonlight. The Monastery. Earlier times. His eyes closed.

* - * - *

"*Do you understand?*" they asked Ozera as they approached. It was Romanian, but with a marked accent he'd never heard. He could tell that the young, bearded men were trim and muscular, even in their monk's robes, and even in the moonlight.

"*Da, am înţeles,*" he answered, telling them he understood.

"*Then come with us, please.*" They turned and gestured for him to follow. The three of them walked back in the

458   The Monastery

direction they had come. Ozera looked at the immensity of the structure and still could not conceive what had just happened. There wasn't a sound. One moment it wasn't there, and then … it was.

He remained incredulous, even astonished, but not scared. Yes, these two were big and strong, but he felt they posed no threat to him. Even so, he would have faced the devil himself to find out what was really going on here.

"Who are you? Where did you come from?" Ozera asked them.

"Father Radu will answer all your questions," one of them replied dismissively.

They rounded the front of the Monastery and Ozera stopped short. It was an ominous view: Here it was, before him, the structure he had seen in centuries-old paintings and drawings. The near-full moon was centered behind the stone cross atop the entrance. Below it, one of the two massive wooden front doors was open. The yellow light from the sconces inside the entrance flickered warm and invitingly.

The doors of the front gate were about the same size as the structure the Colonel built on the Pennsylvania mountaintop. He was right about that. But, as he scrutinized the whole structure, he saw that this Monastery was much, much older and weathered.

The two robed men waited for him by the open front gate. He joined them and they all entered. The massive wooden gate door closed slowly behind them, shutting off the Monastery and its occupants from the rest of the world.

As an architecture student Ozera was mesmerized. He had stepped back in time. They walked through a cavernous tunnel featuring a vaulted stone ceiling. It was semicircular, unlike the pointed-arch vaults of Gothic cathedrals of the

Middle Ages. This was much, much older – Roman, Ozera estimated, circa 100 AD.

The entrance tunnel was not the oldest part of the Monastery. It was added on much later. At the end of the tunnel they entered the great hall. One of the robed escorts stepped in front of Ozera.

"*Please wait here,*" he said, pointing to the last pew in a large circular basilica. "*We just crossed, and Father is still praying. He knew you were outside, looking for us, and sent us to get you.*"

Ozera didn't fully understand, but he did as he was told. His escort stood nearby as he sat down and beheld the view. The inside of the Monastery back home did look similar, structurally, after the Doctor's interior decorating was finished. But the Pennsylvania Monastery was not nearly as elaborate – or as ancient – as the original masterpiece here before him.

Like the one back home, this great hall was circular, some 50 or 60 feet in diameter. Surrounding it was a ring of tall stone columns. The columns were cleanly dressed and fluted, but preceded every classic architectural order that Ozera recognized. These predated even the early, simplistic Doric order of ancient Greece, circa 700 BC.

He looked skyward and saw pitch black, like a night sky but without any moon or stars. The ceiling had darkened over the years – centuries, perhaps millennia – coated by the carbon and soot from burning candles and oil lamps. The flickering wall sconces showed only occasional glimpses of the ceiling support – a latticework of massive wood timbers and stone arches. A span of 50 or 60 feet without a center support – that was impressive for so ancient a structure. Back home they used steel and white concrete beams for the same overhead span.

There were a dozen rows of wooden seats – moveable benches towards the front, more stationary pews making up the back rows, where Ozera was seated. All focused attention on the massive stone slab in the center, which looked like the raised stage for performers he'd seen at concerts. But here it was not a stage. Clearly it was an altar. Surrounding it were huge boulders, five of them of varied heights, roughly hewn. Just a few feet apart they stood, stoically, like an honor guard, encircling the back of the altar stone.

He recalled Dacey's painstaking specification and selection of the stones for inside the Pennsylvania Monastery. The Colonel was very pleased, even excited, that Ozera had managed to gain the Doctor's cooperation – something he had failed to do in over a year of trying. The Colonel made it a top priority and, in just a few weeks, despite an incredible engineering effort, all of the huge stones had been unearthed, quarried and moved in place. Looking now at the original, the stones Dacey specified **were** all similar in size, shape and position. The Doctor had done a good job replicating this critical part of the Monastery.

This was not built as a Christian church, Ozera concluded, at least not in any traditional sense. The layout wasn't consistent with any early church architectural evolution. No apse, no transept. There was no statuary, no crosses, no reliquary. None of the traditional Christian accoutrements.

But it was a holy place. Ozera knew it. He could feel it, and in this great hall he could see it.

Behind the altar stood a praying figure, head bowed, white haired. He was in prayer, or perhaps resting. Several male and female associates milled about him, waiting patiently. More underlings sat across the altar stone from him on the front wooden bench. This was the person in charge, the Abbot, Ozera reckoned.

The Abbot raised his head and Ozera saw his face. It was a familiar face. He had seen it somewhere before, but how could he have? The old man looked drained and tired. But even so, the retinue started to approach him, one at a time. They would discuss something briefly, or the Abbot would listen and just nod, and then turn to the next one.

Another whispered something in his ear and the Abbot looked up, across the great hall, to where Ozera sat. Their eyes met and, for a few moments, they gazed at each other from afar, expressionless. For Ozera it was a strange experience – as if he could feel the Abbot looking at him, into him, and he could not hide from it. He reached up and rubbed his eyes.

The Abbot looked away and uttered a few words to the aide, who turned and walked around the altar, heading towards Ozera. He was sincere and friendly looking with a clean-shaven face, about Ozera's age and height. When he reached Ozera the escort backed away – as a subordinate does when a superior arrives, he noticed.

"We are happy to have you here," he said to Ozera. *"You understand our language, I am told."* Ozera nodded. *"Father Radu asks your indulgence, that he may meet with you later. It has been a very long day and Father is exhausted. And in your time – outside – it is very late too, no?"*

"Yes," Ozera tersely replied. It was the middle of the night and he, too, was exhausted.

"Please stay here with us for now. Father looks forward to meeting with you in the next few days. Dimitrie here will get you settled in," he said, nodding at Ozera's escort.

Ozera nodded. *"Please tell Father that Domnule Ozera is grateful for his hospitality, and I am honored to be here among the ancient communion stone and Guardians."*

His expression changed, startled. How could he know about that? He wanted to ask Ozera but he did not. His self-control re-emerged and his look of bewilderment quickly changed back to an expression of composure. He smiled, nodded to the escort, then turned and left.

Dimitrie led Ozera out a rear doorway, through a narrow, winding hallway maze and up an ancient set of well-worn steps. How many feet, over how many years, did it take to wear down granite steps like this, Ozera wondered.

Somewhere on the outside periphery of the second floor they turned into a small room. Dimitrie nodded and Ozera walked in. It was comfortably warm. No windows but there was a noticeable draft: A single candle was flickering on a small desk. When he turned back a moment later Dimitrie had quietly gone. Then he caught a familiar smell: cattle and manure – horses and cows, he guessed, maybe pigs and goats too. Clearly somewhere nearby were stables. He didn't hear anything; it was just the unmistakable smell, which Ozera found somehow comforting.

He took off his heavy coat, laden with several packs of cash, a gun and other assorted odds and ends. Dimitrie reappeared, quietly placed a clean folded robe on the chair and left. Ozera stretched out on a straw-filled bed and, despite the amazing events of the day – or maybe because of them – fell soundly asleep in minutes.

* - * - *

XIII: Father Radu

Ozera was awakened by a cock rooster and the lowing of cattle. It was dimly lit – his candle had burned out and only the flickering flame of a hallway sconce illuminated the room. There were no windows or openings to the outside, but the animals knew: Here in this ancient Monastery it was morning. The stables apparently were just below his room, the aroma was as pervasive as the night before.

He sat up and looked around at the Spartan surroundings – small wooden table and chair, washbowl and pitcher, crockpot on the floor beside the straw bed. "Pretty luxurious," he muttered to himself. "Should have booked the honeymoon suite."

He cleaned up and looked at the folded robe on the chair. It was a sign of acceptance, he reasoned, but how could they know anything about him? Well, he did speak the language, more or less. And the head Abbot, that Father Radu, had given him a good hard look last night.

Ozera left his coat on the bed and slipped on the robe. He pulled it down over his head and then recoiled: Standing quietly in the doorway a few feet from him was Dimitrie, who was sizing him up in the robe, approvingly it seemed. Ozera wondered whether the large young man might be in religious training but discounted that. No, spirituality was not this young man's forte. He moved quietly, despite being tall and broad. Clearly, he was following orders. He was a defender … a soldier.

"*Please come with me*," he said. It was more than a request, but less than an order. Ozera nodded and, leaving his coat on the bed, followed Dimitrie as he turned and walked out.

They retraced the maze-like path back to the great hall. A couple of robed figures sat on the benches. They walked around and into the entrance tunnel, where it was noisy chaos: Other robed men herded chickens and a small flock of sheep out the front gate. As they neared the end a piglet scurried between them, squealing, with a frazzled young boy in close pursuit. The lad wore an expression Ozera recognized – himself as a young farm hand of 11 or 12.

Both of the large wooden gate doors were wide open as the animals and their keepers headed out to their respective grazing spots. The air was cool with morning moisture. The sky was cloudless and a bright sun was rising. The coating of snow from the night before had melted away and the warm sunlight felt good. Ozera saw a few milk cows munching the tall, sparse grass. Two horses were saddled, awaiting passengers.

A robed figure with bushy white hair was standing alone, his back to them. They walked up and Dimitrie addressed him: "*Father?*"

He did not turn around, but knew they were both there. "*Late October, it seems,*" he said, scanning the countryside.

"*Today is the first of November,*" Ozera replied. He paused a moment and then added: "*1991.*"

"*All Saints Day*," the old man said, turning around and facing Ozera. He was about Ozera's height but leaner. His full white hair and short white beard framed his furrowed, wrinkled face. Ozera remembered the dark deep-set eyes from the previous night. And in the bright morning light he remembered something else: This was the figure he had seen in his dream many months ago, before he arrived at the Pennsylvania facility. His expression was comforting, radiating understanding and a lifetime of experience. There was a certain timelessness about him. He could have been 60, 70, or 90 – Ozera couldn't tell.

"*I am Father Radu*"," he said to Ozera, a hint of a smile on his lips. "*You know a lot about us – the communion stone, the guardians.* Again, it was a subtle question.

Ozera hesitated. How to respond? *"My name is Ozera,"* he started. *"I know of this place, the Monastery, because I studied it. I learned everything I could about it."*

"You are not from around here," Father Radu said. It was a statement, but contained a question.

"No, I was born far away, but my parents and ancestors come from nearby – from Iacobeni." The old man nodded.

"Do you know why this place is ... special?" the old man asked, an uncharacteristically straightforward question. Their eyes locked. That was what he wanted to know, Ozera realized. And it's why he brought me out here, with a guard nearby – in case he didn't like the answer.

"Yes, I know," he replied. There was no expression on either of their faces. *"I was here looking for the Monastery when you ... arrived. And I know someone who was here, who lived here with you for years."*

"Oh?" Again, a subtle question.

"Her name is Daciana ... "

Father Radu interrupted: *"How is Domnisoara Daciana?"*

"She was fine when I last saw her," he replied, *"That was several months ago."* Father Radu obviously knew her, and that was a big plus. They shared a mutual acquaintance.

Two men walking out of the Monastery – wearing peasant garb, not robes – approached Father Radu and interrupted them. One Ozera recognized as the man with Dimitrie who brought him into the Monastery the night before. Both were lean, tall, muscular. They were soldiers, too, Ozera concluded.

"Excuse us, Father," one of them said in a low voice, not intending for Ozera to hear – but not avoiding it either. *"We*

are headed down to the village for provisions. Căpitan said to check with you before we go." The old Abbot thought a moment and glanced at Ozera. It was a cue, and then Ozera realized that this meeting was not a coincidence.

"*Do you know the inn in Bobeica?*" Ozera asked them. They both nodded. "*Then go there and ask for Sonia. Tell her you are from the Monastery, and tell her what you need.*" He went through his pockets and emptied the contents into his cupped hands – a potpourri of coins and paper money – Russian rubles, Romanian Lei and a few U.S. bills. One of the men held out his hands and accepted the clump of cash; the other looked over at Father Radu, who subtly nodded his approval.

"*You know what's needed?*" Father Radu asked the one in charge as they stuffed the money in their pockets. They nodded, then walked over and mounted the two horses.

"*You are welcome here, Domnule Ozera,*" the old man gently told him. "*Stay with us a while. I would like to talk to you.*"

"*I, too, would like that, Father.*"

"*Tell me though, my son, will others be coming now?*"

Ozera knew exactly what he was asking: Whoever is in power out there, do they know of the Monastery, might they find out about our arrival, and will they then be sending someone, perhaps troops?

Ozera considered carefully how to answer. In a moment he thought through the current political situation – the Soviet Union in political and economic collapse, the recent Gulf War, the eviction of the Communists from Romania … and the state of psi research in Russia and the U.S., including their investigation of the Monastery mystery.

"*In time, yes,*" was Ozera's terse answer.

"When?"

Ozera deliberated again, this time about the awesome network of American and Russian spy satellites, which would certainly spot the Monastery on this open plateau in time. But it's doubtful it was on either major power's priority monitoring to-do list. Still, it would be seen and someone would raise questions and follow up. Certainly the U.S. intelligence community was still avidly looking for the missing Pennsylvania Monastery … and him. But to what extent did the Colonel report his latest findings, conclusions and suspicions about the Monastery here in northern Romania?

Factoring it all together in his mind, in seconds, Ozera told him: *"A few weeks – maybe a month."*

Father Radu nodded, a look of sincerity and gratitude on his face. He said nothing but Ozera felt it. The old Abbot leaned over and said a few words to Dimitrie, then abruptly walked past Ozera and back into the Monastery. He had the answers he sought.

*   -   *   -   *

XIII: The Gift

For three days Ozera awaited his meeting with Father Radu and enjoyed the run of the Monastery in the meantime. He didn't mind, spending some time exploring and relishing the unique architectural features of the ancient place. Or he'd go outside, enjoy the clean mountain air and help with the animals. Or he'd sit in a pew in the great hall – the center of activity – watching the ebb and flow of life in the Monastery.

It was a simple but organized life. Men and women dressed alike in their robes and, from what he could tell, were treated equally. The only exception: The guard unit was all male. It turned out that the guardsmen – a sergeant and a half-dozen burly soldiers – were headed by Căpitan Bălan, the friendly-faced, clean-shaven aide to Father Radu who came over and welcomed Ozera the night he arrived. Ozera learned that his men were proficient with bow and arrow, knife, and now also the AK-47. They drilled regularly and one or two were on sentry duty all the time.

Several novitiates were responsible for the animals, including one who was a capable blacksmith. A few others handled cooking and kitchen operations. Someone in regular civilian clothes would leave the Monastery or return on a regular basis. Most went by foot, and occasionally on horseback. Ozera did not know where they were headed or their missions. Many returned in a day or two with various supplies and other wares and packages; one man on a horse returned with several large bags of provisions – likely oats, wheat and beans. He must have walked the heavily laden horse most of the way back up the rocky mountain trail, and then carefully up the stone stairs, Ozera surmised.

All considered, Ozera mused to himself, the staffing and structure here in the Monastery was not that unlike his NEPA mountaintop facility.

He was becoming restless, though, and had a lot of questions – questions for Father Radu. He was relieved when, late on the third day, Dimitrie came to take him to the Abbot.

The room he took him to – on the first floor, not far from the great hall – was an office, featuring a large desk, a round wooden table, several chairs and bookcases. Through an open door at the end Ozera saw adjoining living quarters. These rooms, unlike any other he'd seen in the Monastery, featured ambient daylight. There had to be small windows or portals above somewhere. He looked up and saw several beams of light illuminating the area and the dust floating in the air. The light beams moved very slowly with the sun, like synchronized, slow-motion spotlights.

"*I apologize for the delay in our meeting, Domnule Ozera,*" Father Radu said, walking in from the adjoining quarters and settling in behind the big desk. "*I have many matters to attend to, especially after a crossing. Do you understand crossing?*"

"*I think so,*" Ozera responded. "*You, all of you ... this whole place ... can somehow move across many years of time.*"

"*That is one part of the gift, yes,*" Father Radu replied,

"*The gift?*" he asked. Dacey had told him about it, but he thought it best to not let on, and leave it to the old Abbot to explain.

"*Our gift,*" he replied, "*A gift from God. It protects us. It protects this place. I suppose you learned about it from Daciana.*" Father Radu again asked a question without asking a question.

"*She told me that some people are able to see things, feel things, do things that others cannot,*" Ozera said, adding: "*How do you know who has the gift?*"

"Those with the gift can learn to tell, to spot others with it," he responded. *"Try it. Go ahead. Look me in the eyes and concentrate. See into me. Then make a harmless suggestion, that I fold my arms or scratch my nose."*

"Father Radu, I don't even know if I've got ..."

"You've got it, my son," the old priest interrupted, and again implored him: *"Try it."*

Ozera leaned forward and looked into his eyes. He recalled the night he arrived, when the old priest had stared at him from the altar, and then he had to rub his eyes. So that was it! He stared across the table into old man's eyes and imagined him reaching up with his right hand and stroking his bushy white eyebrows. He imagined he could see him do it. A moment later Father Radu, still looking intently at Ozera, smiled faintly. He lifted his right hand and stroked his eyebrows.

"Damn," Ozera uttered.

"That's just the beginning," Father Radu said, *"I knew the night we crossed, that you were on the mountaintop looking for us, and I knew you had the gift, even before we crossed here to your time. Those with the gift can see and do such remarkable things."*

Ozera sat quietly for a few moments, contemplating the implications, then asked: *"How long have you had this ... gift?"*

Father Radu contemplated his response: *"We are born with it. But when it first appeared among us, no one knows. Some say it was after the Romans left, many centuries ago. Daciana is named for Dacia, the ancient name of our land. It seems all people with the gift are descendants of the Dacians."*

"Yes, I've heard of Dacia," Ozera injected, *"But what happened to the Dacians?"*

*"**We** are they,"* he replied. *"Not just the people here in the Monastery, but many of the people living in the surrounding area. We continue the same culture, even the heritage mission."*

"The heritage mission?" Ozera asked.

"She didn't tell you," he said – again, a question in a statement. He sat back, took a deep breath and heaved a sigh.

"Since ancient times we have been beset by invaders. It is because of our land here – we lie precariously between Europe, the Mediterranean and the Middle-East and Asia. Every generation of us has seen a new invader. They have come from every direction and land – from Macedonia, the Balkans, Greece, Serbia, the steppes of Russia, Rome, Persia, Germany."

"If we fought them," Father Radu continued, *"we would have died out as a people long ago. Our ancestors wisely decided instead that we would patiently step back, retreat to the mountains and woods, and let the invaders come and go. It could take decades, even centuries. In the meantime we would quietly assimilate them, and add their blood and skill to our culture, to our people."*

*"*The heritage mission,*"* Ozera uttered.

"Our ancestors trained and sent out our most attractive, fertile and dedicated women, to mate with the invader's leader or his bloodline. They would return with their seed, and into our people would be born their progeny, who eventually would mix with our people. And in the years and generations to come the invaders' strengths would be added to ours."

It was the answer to a lot of questions. So there **was** a genetic component in this mystery after all. "*And it still goes on?*" Ozera asked him, incredulously.

Father Radu slowly nodded. "*We will not undertake a heritage mission here, in this time.*"

"*Why not?*" he wondered.

"*We don't have the time. **You** said so,*" the old Abbot reminded him. "*We need six to nine months, and we have, what, barely a month here?*"

Ozera nodded affirmatively. "*When was the last heritage mission?*" he asked.

"*Most recently we added the scion of a Russian Communist leader,*" Father Radu recalled. "*That was in the year 1968 – for you. For us, here in the Monastery, it was six months ago. You see, we crossed to here from 1968 three days ago.*"

It was getting hard for Ozera to fully comprehend. To Father Radu, years in time were places. 'Crossing' from one time to another was for him like crossing a bridge across a river, from one side to the other.

Ozera had many more questions – and it seemed this old man had all the answers.

* - * - *

XIII: Time after time

"When you cross, how do you know when you'll arrive?"
Ozera asked.

"We do not, not really," Father Radu told him. *"We can determine when we leave, but not when we will arrive."*

"You cross, and you do not know where, or when, you are going?" Ozera asked.

"Does any traveler really know, when they leave, where their journey will end, or when?" the old Abbot learnedly asked him. *"There is one thing we know that does influence our destination… the number of us that take part in the crossing rite. The more that participate, the further we cross in time."*

Ozera's puzzled look betrayed him. He didn't understand.

Father Radu saw his bewilderment and sought to elaborate: *"In the old days, we had two dozen participants – men and women, all with the gift – and we crossed 40 or 50 years at a time. But as our numbers dwindled over the years, so did the time we crossed. By the 1500's we were crossing 30 years at a time. The latest crossing was just 24 years."*

"With how many people?" Ozera asked.

"The last time, in 1968, was with 13 gifted men and women, including me." Curious, Ozera thought. There were 13 Romanians at the Pennsylvania site, including Dacey – likely all of whom, like Dacey, had the gift. And that night all of them, including Dacey, vanished … along with the Pennsylvania Monastery.

"How long have you been crossing?" he asked the old Abbot.

Father Radu sat back and collected his thoughts to answer. *"I was there, the first time,"* he said, *"It was the year 888. I was just 12 years old – a frightened young oblate. My parents* had given me, the second of their nine children, to the Monastery in return for the blessing of our small farm. The Abbot was the legendary Father Bogdan, a complex man with an uncommon wealth of experience – worldly ... and otherworldly."

"It was late on a cold autumn night," he continued, "The Monastery came under attack – a raiding party of Magyars. They had been pushed out of central Asia and, like many migrating marauders, they came through Dacia looking for new lands to settle. They ended up in what is now Hungary. Four hundred years earlier it was the Huns who were plundering their way through here."

"This place," Father Radu said, gesturing the whole structure, "is now a Monastery, but it has evolved over many thousands of years," Father Radu related. "We sit here on ancient holy ground, ground blessed by God in the creation. And all that time God has protected this land and its people."

"Father Bogdan convened a service, as the enemy was besieging us. He had us hold hands around the communion stone and pray. At the time I did not know of the gift, but Father Bogdan did, and he knew who among us had it – including, I was to find out later, me. I remember clenching the hand of a woman, an incredibly beautiful woman named Ilinca, of our heritage mission."

"The invaders battered on the front gate as he preached. I believed, as most of us did, that it was just a matter of time, that we would be horribly killed by the Magyars. I couldn't stop shaking, but this woman consoled me. She told me not to worry, and I was sustained."

"Father Bogdan unleashed a fiery oration. I remember it, and I have repeated it many times since then. He prayed to God – not just mouthing the words of someone praying to God. He was speaking to the Almighty – asking Him to preserve these people and this place, the Soul of ancient Dacia."

"He had us all look into his eyes, each of us, one by one, telling us we could be saved if we believed. At the end he uttered the words: 'We pray to live on to see our future. Thy will be done.' And it was done. It was all over. There was total silence. No more siege. No more Magyars. When we went out we found a bright warm summertime morning. No one understood, except Father Bogdan. We later discovered that we had crossed that night, some 56 years."

He stopped and looked over at Ozera, who was spellbound – absorbing the narrative with the relish of a young boy engrossed in a campfire tale.

"That was also our furthest crossing. Twenty-three of us with the gift participated," Father Radu said. *"The crossings since have been shorter and shorter."*

"How many times have you crossed?" Ozera asked him.

"I have crossed 26 more times after the first," he replied somberly.

"You have led your people in this since Father Bogdan passed?" Ozera presumed.

"Oh, heavens no," he countered. *"I am the second successor to Father Bogdan. The old Father passed away after a crossing into the early 1300's. He was, I believe, 73. The next Abbot was his protégée, Father Dorin, who served until the 1600's. During Father Dorin's time I left the Monastery ... and then returned."*

"You left?" Ozera asked, startled. *"How did you get back in?"*

"I was 25 and still hadn't taken final vows. This is a mystical place, Domnule Ozera, but it is also a small place." He smiled. *"We would stay a year or two after each crossing before we crossed again. In that time we would plant and harvest crops, breed cattle, and re-affiliate with the people in*

the area. They all knew about us and the Monastery, that we would leave, and come again, and again, every generation or so. All were asked to preserve the Monastery secret. And for over a millennium they have done so."

"People would come and go after a crossing. One of our women would leave on a heritage mission to assess the latest invader occupying the area. One or two new people might enter the Monastery – perhaps an orphan, a young woman seeking a life with God, or maybe a young farm boy aspiring to be a guard and soldier. And one or two people would leave. Anyone could leave or enter at any time."

"And you left?" Ozera asked.

"Yes," the old Abbot replied. *"I sought life, a life outside the Monastery."*

"And you found one?"

He nodded. *"The year was 1351. The Black Death had just ravaged most of Europe, though by God's grace it circumvented this area. I married a local woman and we raised four children."* He paused, reflecting. *"For 34 years, I was a husband, father, farmer, a church deacon, even mayor of Breaza. I traveled widely throughout the area – Wallachia, Moldova, the Balkans, Macedonia, and Hungary."*

"But through all that time I remembered the Monastery. Before I left I had already crossed a dozen times, and those are experiences like no other – being able to see what mankind has done with the last 30 or 40 years. My wife and children never knew. So when my wife died, the children already grown and gone, I returned. I sold my farm and moved back to this area. And on a summer night in 1385, the Monastery returned."

"I re-entered and learned that nothing had changed inside, except me. I was 57; I had learned the ways of the world. I had lived and loved. Father Dorin warmly welcomed me

*back, and later he embraced me as his protégé. For four
years I studied and learned under him. Then one day, after
crossing from 1429, arriving in 1465, he died. I became
Abbot and since then, I have led our crossings ... 14 of them."*

Ozera sat quietly for a while, absorbing this incredible story.
There was one question he had to ask – a question that stuck
in his mind like a burr, since the Colonel first briefed him
about the Monastery.

"Can you go back in time?" he asked the old Abbot
sheepishly.

"No." The response was quick. *"Father Bogdan was insistent
and adamant on that. He'd say: 'Time goes only one way,
forward, and so do we. It is the way God made the world and
the gift, and we follow His will.' He dismissed any further
discussion."*

Ozera thought a moment about the Pennsylvania Monastery.
What did happen there? The Monastery on their mountaintop
disappeared overnight – it was not demolished or removed.
Was it a crossing? Clearly the Romanians were involved, if
not responsible. They, too, apparently all disappeared.

"Father Radu, could crossings happen somewhere else?"

The old priest considered it. *"I don't know. Many factors are
involved. Is the location here, on this mountain, one of them?
It certainly needs to be a holy place, one touched by God.
But isn't God everywhere? A leader with the gift is needed,
one who has experienced crossings. He must inspire and
astound the others."*

"Inspire and astound?" he asked.

*"It helps for participants to remember and relive the threat of
assault we have so often faced. That dread, as it was with
Father Bogdan that first time, forced our people to face their
mortality, their death. The participants must also believe that*

they can with God's grace be saved and achieve salvation. These are emotions deep within the soul of all of us, and they must be present for the crossing to occur."

He added: *"Most importantly, though, you need people with the gift – at least a dozen of them."*

"A dozen? Is that how many are needed to cross ... this whole place?" Ozera asked, his hands and arms indicating the whole surrounding structure.

"It can be done with no less than twelve," Father Radu said. *"We have tried with five, seven, even ten. It does not work. Even Christ needed twelve apostles."*

"Did Daciana know this?"

Father Radu thought a minute. *"Yes,"* he answered, nodding.

"And the leader ... needs to be a priest?" Ozera asked.

"I don't know," the old man replied, *"But for all the generations we have crossed, our Abbot, a priest, has presided."*

"Could a woman preside and successfully cross?" he asked bluntly.

The old priest looked up at him and, after a moment, his furrowed face reformed into a smile. *"Daciana Lupescu,"* he said, in typical fashion – asking a question with a statement.

Ozera nodded, *"Yes."*

"Domnule, or should I call you Căpitan, Ozera?" He did not expect an answer. He already knew. But how? The gift? Could he read minds? What else did he know?

"Daciana left us after we crossed to 1968," the old Abbot told him. *"She was just 17, but she was wiser and more mature*

than most women much older." Ozera pictured Dacey as a vivacious 17-year-old. So, she left the Monastery in 1968. That explains why all the Colonel's intelligence resources could dig up no trace of her before then.

"Where did you meet her?" Father Radu asked, *"Is she well?"*

"We met in America, about a year ago," Ozera said. *"She was in her late 30's, maybe 40 – when I last saw her, several months ago. She is the most seductive woman I have ever met."* Ozera paused, then added: *"I miss her terribly."* He looked up at Father Radu, into his aged face, and wondered whether he was saying too much. Father Radu had been very honest and open with him and he felt it only fair, in return, to confide in him.

"She left you, and now there is much distance between you," the old priest said, *"And you fear she may be gone forever?"*

"Yes," Ozera replied, dejectedly.

"Căpitan, forever is a long, long time," he told him. *"Daciana was born in 1429, the third and youngest daughter of ... a woman I loved."* Ozera raised an eyebrow. *"Yes, her mother was Ilinca, the woman I told you about, that night of the first crossing."*

"So in this place," Ozera said, *"Only 17 years passed from 1429, when Daciana was born, to 1968, when she left?"*

Father Radu nodded. *"And in that time Daciana took part in a dozen crossings. She became her mother's student, and she was her mother's daughter – sultry, seductive. You no doubt found that yourself years later, Căpitan, no?"* Ozera just smiled and nodded in agreement.

"Daciana, too? She was in the heritage mission?" Ozera asked.

"Yes," the old Abbot told him, sensing that they had been lovers. He knew, too, this was a subject Căpitan Ozera might find disconcerting.

"It was in her blood. Daciana was herself a child of the heritage mission. Her mother bore her after returning with the seed of an Agha of the Ottoman Turks. Daciana became like a granddaughter to me. She was still just an infant when Father Dorin died and I became Abbot. We remained very close as she grew up and into adolescence."

"She was very smart and quickly learned the ways of the Monastery ... and crossings. In her 17 years here she took part in many crossings. She wanted to know everything, and often asked about the gift and crossing. And I answered her questions. Then, when she was 15, rather than take her vows as a monk, she decided instead to enter into training for the heritage mission."

"Then we crossed, from 1914 to 1941, and found a new invader had encamped throughout the area: Germans, Nazis, who were massing to invade Russia. Although she was just 16, Daciana volunteered to undertake the next heritage mission. And in the fall of 1941, she bravely left."

"About that time her mother, Ilinca, began having health problems. In the cold of February 1942, my beloved Ilinca died. We hadn't heard from Daciana, but that's the way it often was. Half the women sent out on heritage missions never returned. Ilinca was the exception; she went out and came back, successfully impregnated, three times."

"Daciana returned that summer. She was already four months pregnant – impregnated by a German general named Paulus. The Nazis had since moved on. We all could see that she had been through a lot, and she reacted without emotion to the passing of her mother. Then, on Christmas Day, 1942, Daciana Lupescu bore a male child – Sandu, short for Alexandru."

Ozera took it all in. It was like listening to a fairy tale, about a remarkable woman who had witnessed 500 years of human history ... before she was even 17 years old. Dacey had given him some details about her past. It didn't make much sense at the time, but now all the pieces fit.

"With the next crossing we arrived in 1968," Father Radu continued. *"Afterwards, Daciana came to me and asked to leave the Monastery. She didn't need my approval, but she sought it, and I gave it. She agreed to leave her son, so that his blood would eventually be assimilated within our people. Daciana left, and as she left, I saw myself leaving, so many years before."*

"I cannot see the future," he went on, *"and perhaps that is a good thing. I only have feelings. I feel that Daciana is alive ... in some place and time. But my feeling on the day that Daciana left has not changed – that I shall never see her again. And that grieves me deeply."* The old man sat back, and Ozera thought he saw tears in those dark, deepset eyes.

Ozera sat quietly a moment, then stood up. *"Father,"* he said respectfully, *"Thank you for your time ... and your memories. I, too, doubt I will ever see Daciana again. And that is a future that I don't look forward to."* With that he turned and walked out.

"Never again? Don't be so sure, Căpitan," the old Abbot said to an empty room.

* _ * _ *

XIII: Monastic Life

Ozera didn't get to see Father Radu again for over a week. He spotted the old Abbot here and there, busily meeting with aides and conducting service in the great hall. But the opportunity to sit and talk face to face with him didn't present itself.

In the meantime he made himself quite at home, taking the time to explore and examine every nook of the ancient structure. He observed and mingled with every aspect of life in the Monastery. He estimated that there were about two dozen occupants of the Monastery, plus a handful of children. A young woman named Martina was charged with the children's care, feeding and welfare.

One of them was Sandu, Daciana's son. He was about two and a half, blond and blue-eyed – likely resembling the father more than the mother, Ozera surmised. Alexandru Lupescu. It was the same last name as Dacey, but Ozera learned that Lupescu was the name given to all children born in the Monastery. These were usually children of the heritage mission and had no formal fathers. Lupescu – of the wolf – the ancient symbol of Dacia.

Dimitrie became Ozera's near-constant companion, performing the roles of escort, valet, advisor, guard and guide. Ozera took note of a very attractive and sultry woman – about Dacey's age, who even resembled his beloved Daciana. He asked Dimitrie about her and learned she was Angelina, the oldest daughter of Ilinca. So, Ozera thought to himself, she was Dacey's oldest sister, which explained the physical similarity.

It turned out Angelina ran the Monastery's heritage mission and had two young ladies in training. Like Dacey, she too was the product of a heritage mission – her mother's first. That was 40 years ago, as time is reckoned inside the Monastery – but more than a thousand years to the outside world, Ozera calculated.

Every now and then the captain of the guard, Căpitan Bălan, would catch up with Ozera, sit and commiserate. But it was not exactly idle banter. The two captains talked tactics, weapons, training and defense strategies. Bălan asked, and Ozera offered his assessment: The Monastery can readily be seen by spy satellites. It was indefensible against a determined force with today's weapons. Indeed, even a relatively small force, platoon size, could surround the structure and, in very little time, penetrate and assail the Monastery.

An escape plan was sorely needed, Ozera pointed out. Căpitan Bălan understood and nodded. They looked at each other. Neither said it, but both knew the occupants of the Monastery **did** have an escape plan.

"How will we know they are coming?" Bălan bluntly asked him. Clearly he and Father Radu had been discussing what may be coming.

"First there will be reconnaissance," Ozera knowledgably replied. *"Probably a plane – a fast plane with cameras, followed by a recon on the ground. That will be a patrol – several scouts, lightly armed."*

"And then?" Bălan asked.

"Troops, probably by helicopter," Ozera told him, succinctly. It was the transport the Russians used for years to get to and from their research facility down the mountain. And it was almost certainly how they would bring troops to this remote plateau high in the Carpathians.

The big question in Ozera's mind: Which superpower with spy satellites would notice the Monastery first, follow up and check it out? Ozera tried to explain to the Căpitan that it could be America, which he viewed as unlikely given

Romanian sovereignty, or Russia, which would be suicidal to launch an operation in Romania just now.

But Bălan had no preconceived notions of East versus West, and he didn't care. If they threatened the Monastery – the last bastion of the Dacian way of life – they were the enemy.

"Where did you get the AK-47s?" Ozera asked.

"Are they out of date?"

"No, no," Ozera said, assuring him that the AK-47 was still, in 1991, one of the best and most prevalent weapons in the world.

Bălan explained how, after a crossing, he would dispatch two of his best men with some gold and jewelry, to retrieve whatever they could bring back about recent military developments. After arriving in 1968 they returned in a week with materials on the weapons and tactics of Vietnam – and four Romanian-made AK-47 rifles, plus ammo.

"My men borrowed them from a Russian guard post late one night, after first leaving them a few bottles of vodka," Bălan told him with a smile. *"A big improvement over the bolt-action German Mausers we acquired back in 1941."*

It was a near impossible task for Bălan, Ozera pondered, trying to stay abreast of military developments, in jumps of 25 or 30 years at a time. What would he find in 25 or 30 years hence? He couldn't even imagine. But the thought intrigued him.

A few days later Ozera and Căpitan Bălan were walking outside, around the Monastery – early morning on a clear sunny day, warm for mid-November. They both heard it and looked skyward. From time to time a high-flying jet would be seen passing over, barely audible but with a telltale vapor trail. But this was different.

This was a jet, but flying slow. It was too high for Ozera to identify. It was clearly visible; he estimated 10,000 feet over this remote corner of the Carpathians. They caught the glint of the plane, a reflection from the sun – not just once, but several times. It was circling and making several passes, directly over them.

The two men had realized earlier that they both had the gift. But it wsn't until now that they actually used it. They looked at each other. Not a word was spoken, but Ozera clearly heard the Căpitan asking: 'Is that them?'

And Ozera reflexively replied, 'Yes, probably.' He said nothing, but he knew that his answer was received and understood.

Căpitan Bălan nodded, turned and ran off, at a jogging pace, back to the entrance. He was going to update Father Radu. Ozera just ... knew it.

*_*_*

XIII: Preparation

When Ozera returned to the front gate he saw that Dimitrie was there, waiting for him. He took Ozera to Rather Radu's office. The old Abbot was seated at his desk; Căpitan Bălan standing before him. Seeing Ozera, Father Radu waved him in.

"For a thousand years our Monastery has remained hidden, a secret," he said to Ozera. *"An enemy had to track and follow one of our people back here, or a scout team would find us by happenstance. Now, I'm told our adversaries have eyes high in the sky and can look down on us from the heavens."* Ozera looked at him and tacitly nodded. *"Căpitan Bălan says we have been spotted, and soldiers may be coming. Not even two weeks since we arrived here. It is as you said."*

They talked, as if planning a military operation. The Abbot, a man of God, was clearly in command. He accepted that role; it went with the job. And he had many questions for Ozera: What are the enemy's likely actions? What would happen next? How many would they send? What could they do?

They developed a plan of action, largely following Ozera's recommendations: Maintain alert observation, and at night, listening posts. Expect a scouting party – three to six men – very covert, camouflaged and able to move silently. One of them will be a radio operator. One, in charge, will be an officer.

Bălan knew what to do: Quietly take them out, one at a time if possible. The others would follow, to find their missing man and see what happened.

Ozera added: *"Don't let any of them escape. Don't let them report back by radio."* Bălan nodded.

"What do they want?" the Abbot asked Ozera. It was a clear question – thrusting into the heart of the matter.

"*They want to know about the gift. They want to know about crossing,*" he said. "*They want to know if they can do it, how they can use it to their advantage. They suspect, but they don't know.*" Ozera thought a minute, then added: "*You should keep everybody nearby, close at hand, and be ready to assemble your people on short notice.*"

"*Thank you, Căpitan,*" the old Abbot said, "*Could you leave us now, please?*" Ozera turned and was about to walk out, when Father Radu interrupted. "*No, Căpitan Ozera, please stay.*" Ozera looked over at Bălan, who clearly was caught off guard. He quickly recovered, bowed ever so slightly to the old priest, turned around and walked out, notably avoiding Ozera's view.

"*Căpitan, we may not have time for this conversation again,*" Father Radu told him. "*At the first sign of assault you must leave. Get out of the Monastery. Otherwise you will go ... with us, where we go.*" Ozera understood and nodded.

"*Father,*" he told him, "*I cannot go back. I face arrest, prison, maybe worse – not for what I've done, but for what I know. I would like to stay here, and go forward with you.*"

"*I see,*" Father Radu replied. "*But be sure you know what you are asking for. There is no return. All that you know outside of this place will be left behind us, in the past, forever.*"

"*I understand,*" Ozera said, with resignation. He had thought it over. What would it be like? Who would still be there? Dacey? His family? The Colonel? Then Ozera had a thought.

"*Father, how many people do you expect will take part in the next crossing?*"

The old Abbot thought about it and tallied them in his mind. "*Thirteen. With you then, fourteen,*" he replied.

"Would it be possible to perform the next crossing with just twelve?"

"Yes, we can do it with twelve," he replied. *"I told you that. But why? We could cross further with everyone participating."*

"I have a reason – to me a very important reason."

"We'll see," the old priest told him. An ambiguous answer, leaving the matter open. Ozera nodded, then stood and turned to go.

"Căpitan Ozera," the Abbot called to him. *"One other thing. You will find, in time, that the gift opens your world to you, and you to your world. In time, if you follow your hunches and feelings, you will be served by them."* Ozera, a bit confused, just nodded. Was he describing precognition – knowing, or sensing, what is to come?

"I have a feeling about you," he continued, *" I sense we – you and I – will meet again, not just here and now but at some distant time to come."* Ozera did not respond. What was he trying to say?

"If it is inevitable that you will return here someday, and I feel it is, please consider joining us, even, if it is God's will, as my successor. You have the life experience, the temperament, the insight." Ozera was taken aback. It was a suggestion he never could have foreseen. And it was a future he could not now envision. He had his mind on the here and now.

Ozera smiled at the old Abbot. *"We'll see,"* he tersely responded, intentionally repeating his words back to him. With that he turned and left.

* - * - *

"Sir. Domnule Ozera," the voice said, waking Ozera from a sound sleep. He felt someone gently tapping his shoulder. He opened his eyes and saw Dimitrie.

"You need to come with me, now," he told him. *"Please, dress quickly. No robe."*

Dimitrie was wearing a dark overcoat. No robe. Ozera got up and dressed, leaving his robe, and grabbing his overcoat. He checked his watch: 2:30 am. The two scurried along the now-familiar pathway to the great hall and then through the tunnel to the front gate. One gate was ajar. The two of them slipped through.

The night was pitch dark, not even stars shining. Cloudy and overcast, Ozera reasoned, and likely a new moon. Dimitrie led him out over the field to the stone stairway. The ground was wet from a recent rain. By the time they reached the edge of the open field their eyes had adjusted to the darkness. Ozera sensed there might be danger ahead. He reached into his deep hip pocket and found his gun. He popped the clip, saw it was full, and snapped it back in. Dimitrie heard the noise and looked back, as Ozera pulled the barrel slide and chambered a round.

At the top of the steps they looked down and saw figures at the bottom. Dimitrie signaled Ozera to follow him as he descended. Near the clearing at the bottom Ozera could make out two figures lying on the ground, one standing. Ozera stepped onto the clearing and saw it was Căpitan Bălan standing over the bodies of two men, both clad in hiking jackets and boots. One had a arrow through the chest. The other had a slit throat.

"Dressed like hikers with backpacks, but no wallets or identification," Bălan said quietly but distinctly. *"Here is what they were packing,"* he said, gesturing off to the side, where the contents were laid out. Quite an assortment: night-vision binoculars, short-stock AK-47s with scopes, a map, a handheld radio and spare battery, banana clips of ammo, an

automatic handgun with silencer, compass, a fancy camera with night scope, survival knives and plastic canteens.

"Ready for a fight, but no food," Ozera remarked. *"They weren't planning on staying long."*

"Two of the scouts you predicted," Bălan said. *"But in the middle of the night?"*

"Those are night-vision scopes," Ozera told him. *"They make it look like daytime. I'll show you how to use them. And it is the dark of the new moon, and cloudy – perfect conditions for a scouting mission. There is at least one more, the leader, that's not here."*

"Two more," Bălan said. *"In the hotel in Bobeica. They arrived yesterday."* Ozera was impressed with his intelligence. *"Two of my men are down below. One will run back and notify us if there is any more activity."*

"There will be, but not tonight. They'll wait til morning for these two to show up. They will come up in the morning looking for them."

Ozera went over and examined the dead men's gear. Professionals, he thought. No markings on the weapons. The rest of it – radio, knives, canteens, clothing and boots – could have been bought anywhere in Europe. No way of telling which side these two men worked for.

"I'll clean up here," Bălan said to Ozera. *"Please go brief Father Radu. He would want you there anyway if I reported."* Ozera couldn't tell if there was resentment in the captain's remark, or if he was just being pragmatic. In either case, he acknowledged and returned with Dimitrie, taking much of the scouts' gear, back to the Monastery.

"More will come," Ozera told the Abbot. *"Căpitan Bălan's men may get the other two, but they will send more."*

Father Radu sat listening intently, elbows on his desk, the chin of his furrowed face resting on his hands.

"Will it be another scout patrol, or will they come in force?" he asked him.

Ozera shook his head. *"I don't know,"* he told him candidly.

"We will begin preparation for the crossing. I do not want to lose people if we are attacked," he solemnly pronounced. *"Tell me, Căpitan, do we have four more days?"*

"Maybe. Maybe not," he replied, *"Can't we go sooner if we have to?"*

"Two of our senior people – our historian and librarian – are conducting research in Vatra Dornei. They have until Tuesday to return. And Căpitan," the old Abbot added: *"they are two of our gifted participants."*

* - * - *

"Căpitan!" the guardsman yelled from the top of the stone staircase. He came running across the field to Ozera and Bălan, who were just inside the open front gate. He arrived in a minute nearly out of breath.

"The two other enemy scouts were coming; they have been killed," he announced, panting.

As he caught his breath he related what happened: He and another guard were in their camouflaged positions, some 50 feet apart, when the two came slowly and quietly through the woods. They were dressed like the other scouts and had their automatic weapons at the ready. The first one passed and the guardsman shot him square through the back with an arrow. The other saw him fall and turned and ran back the other way. Both guards gave chase – one with handgun and silencer, the other with knife and AK-47. They found him behind a tree and shot him. But, the guard reported, he was talking on the radio.

Ozera and Bălan looked at each other. The last enemy scout was probably the leader, and he likely reported back that they had been attacked.

"Was he speaking our language?" Bălan asked.

"No, it was a foreign language I didn't recognize." Could it have been Russian, or English, or maybe German? The guardsman didn't know, and so they still had no idea who was behind the transgressors. One thing was clear, though, more of them would be on the way.

"We have a couple days, at most," Ozera told Father Radu. *"It will take that long to put together an assault team and operation. They still don't know our strength, but since their advance team has been eliminated they will come ... with more men and better armed."* The old man nodded. He understood.

"The congregation will assemble for a crossing at midnight Tuesday," the old Abbot pronounced. It was a commitment, and it would not change. Just two days away. Father Radu was leaving as much time as he could for the researchers he had sent out to get back.

Căpitan Bălan and Ozera huddled and discussed strategy. The next incursion would likely be by helicopter. They reasoned it could arrive at the old Russian landing zone down the mountain, and they would sneak up from there. Or they could land right on the Monastery's plateau, if a frontal assault was their plan. No surprise then. Beyond that they could only conjecture.

Neither Father Radu nor Bălan particularly cared who this newest invader was. But Ozera did. He did not think the U.S., or its local surrogates, would intentionally risk destroying the Monastery. Rather, he supposed they would want to get inside, study it, and interrogate the occupants to learn what is going on. And he could only speculate what the Russians knew and wanted, or how they would conduct an assault.

Two guard posts were established. One would be positioned on a cliff overlooking the old landing zone. The other would be atop the stone staircase. Both would scamper back quickly to the Monastery if and when the enemy showed up. Anyone still outside the Monastery would be repatriated. And first thing in the morning all livestock, tools and supplies would be moved back inside.

By the next afternoon there was still no sign of intruders – or the two missing researchers. Clearly Father Radu felt responsible for their remote assignment, and grief-stricken at the prospect of leaving on a crossing without them. Before dinner Ozera checked the guard posts. The guardsmen, on six-hour shifts, were present and alert, and attuned for helicopters.

Tuesday morning came without incident, except that the aroma of the stables was again beginning to permeate Ozera's room. His companion, guide and valet – Dimitrie – was nowhere to be seen, so he got washed and dressed and headed down to the dining hall for coffee. He passed the great hall and saw most of the Monastery's occupants seated in pews, as Brother Constantin, the corpulent and very uninteresting assistant abbot, conducted a communion service.

Ozera got a coffee and headed through the vaulted tunnel to the front gate. One of the massive wooden doors was open and two figures entered, walking towards him: Father Radu and Căpitan Bălan. The old Abbot walked right up to Ozera. He was clearly agitated.

"Căpitan Ozera," he said. *"You may yet have your wish. There may be just 12 of us tonight, and you are heartily invited to be one of them."* He turned and strode off angrily down the entrance tunnel.

Bălan walked up to him: "*We've still no sign of or word from our two missing researchers, and that bothers him a lot,*" he explained. "*Father said he knew they were alright, at least for now, but he feared – he had a feeling – they would not make it back in time to be with us tonight.*"

"*Any sign of trouble?*" Ozera asked.

"*No, not yet,*" Bălan replied. "*I just posted fresh guards. They're on duty until sundown. And I just dispatched my sergeant to check Bobeica. He'll be back this afternoon.*"

"*And we are going tonight, no matter what?*"

"*No matter what,*" Bălan iterated, nodding.

Throughout the day the two commanders continually checked the guard posts and other preparations. Ozera and Bălan were both out by the front gate when the sergeant returned from the village below. He ran across the field from the stone steps to Bălan and, breathing heavily, made his report: No sign of the missing researchers, and no sign of any enemy or even strange activity. Bălan thanked and dismissed him.

"*It's quiet now,*" Bălan said, turning and looking Ozera in the eye. "*But I have a feeling...*"

"*... They **are** coming,*" both said in unison, nodding.

- * - * - *

XIII: Assault

The afternoon passed uneventfully. It was uncharacteristically quiet at dinner, although the dining hall was full. All knew that, at midnight, the Monastery and all within it would be crossing. They were like passengers waiting for a train – looking forward to getting aboard, but understandably reticent about not knowing the destination.

After dinner Ozera went to the great hall and settled into the last row of pews. Several acolytes sat praying on the front bench by the altar stone. A rotund Brother Constantin stood behind the altar, droning on in Latin. As time passed more of the congregation came and sat down, filling in around the altar, and the activity level gradually heightened. Then Father Radu emerged, stepping behind the altar. Brother Constatin, not skipping a syllable in Latin, picked up his prayerbook and moved back, yielding the central spot to the old Abbot.

Almost unnoticed, Căpitan Bălan entered near the back and passed through the great hall with one of his men, exiting into the entrance tunnel. Ozera got up and followed. Near the open front gate was piled the equipment taken from the earlier enemy scouts – rifles, pistol with silencer, night vision goggles. He picked up the goggles and stepped out.

Bălan was dispatching his man to retrieve the others who were still out on guard duty. Bălan and Ozera waited uneasily outside the main gate. It was a clear, cold November night, and on this isolated mountain plateau the stars shone brightly.

One of the guardsmen came running back, rifle in one hand, rucksack and binoculars in the other. He was the furthest guard, perched on a ledge overlooking the valley, the old Russian research site and the clearing that was the helicopter landing zone. No sign of any activity, he reported to Bălan, who thanked him and sent him in.

They waited. Ozera showed Bălan how to wear and turn on the night vision goggles. He was impressed and looking up, down and all around.

"It's like daytime with these," Bălan said.

"They work by amplifying ambient light, like the stars or moon," Ozera explained. *"You need very little light for them to work. They have changed the face of night operations."* Bălan continued his admiration of the goggles.

Ozera, though, began to wonder where the last two men were, and asked Bălan.

"They should be at the guard post by the stone staircase, right over there," Bălan said, gesturing to the spot across the field. *"We'd better go see what's keeping them."* Ozera agreed.

They stepped inside the gate, pulled off their robes and grabbed two of the AK-47's.

"Bring the goggles," Ozera added.

The two men started off across the field, Bălan with the night-vision goggles around his neck. They were half way when they heard a burst of machinegun fire up ahead.

"Get down!" Ozera instinctively yelled. They hit the ground, just as another burst ripped. *"AK-47,"* he uttered. They saw no flashes in the dark; it had to be coming from down the stone staircase. Bălan started to get up, heading for the stairway. Ozera reached out and forcefully grabbed his arm, stopping him.

"We need to go back," Ozera said, *"If something happens to either of us, no one will get out of here. The whole Monastery will be lost."*

"What do you mean!?" Bălan asked. He didn't know. Father Radu apparently didn't tell him, that at least 12 participants with the gift were required for a crossing.

"I can't explain it now. But you and I must be there for the crossing."

"You go back!" Bălan told Ozera, looking him in the eye. *"They are **my** men! I need to know what happened to them!"* A situation in the Iraqi desert flashed through Ozera's mind. He capitulated and let go of him. Both men got up and pulled the bolt on their assault rifles, ready to fire automatic. Bălan put on the night-vision goggles and turned them on. The two soldiers advanced, running in a crouched position.

They neared the top of the staircase and saw a body lying, lifeless. It was the man Bălan had just sent out to retrieve the guards. Ozera checked him. Several chest wounds. He was gone.

Ozera crawled up to the staircase, peeked over stealthily and looked down. There was activity on the clearing down below, but it was too dark to make out. Bălan crawled up next to Ozera and looked down. He saw three bodies – one was his guard, the others ... looked like the two researchers Father Radu was waiting to return.

"That's how they got here," Bălan whispered to him, *"No helicopters. They intercepted our researchers and forced them to show them the way back here – and then killed them."*

A dozen or so night-vision-goggled, black-ops soldiers were down on the clearing, probably more were down below behind them. They knew the gunfire would alert whoever was up above, and two of the soldiers started climbing up the stone staircase. Without thinking Bălan pointed his AK-47 and fired full automatic, dropping the two on the stairs and wounding a handful of the others. The others scrambled for cover, but there was none: The clearing was a killing zone. Their position compromised and the element of surprise gone,

Ozera fired too. Maybe they'd think there were more than just the two of them.

"Okay, let's get out of here!" Ozera hollered, *"Your men are gone! We've got to get back!"* Bălan reluctantly nodded. They backed up, got up and headed for the Monastery in a dead run – some hundred yards to cover.

They hadn't gone 30 feet when two grenade rounds impacted the stone at the top of the steps, almost knocking them off their feet. It was proper procedure for assaulting a sniper, Ozera appreciated, firing to keep his head down ... while soldiers moved into position to assault. But it would be a minute or two before they reached the top. Self-preservation – a human attribute that no amount of training could overrule – would slow them down.

Almost there, the yellow torchlight beaming out like a beacon through the open, heavy-wooden gate. There was just a hundred feet to go when the first machinegun burst sounded behind them. A couple rounds ricocheted off rocks just to their right

"Who the fuck **are** those guys?" Ozera muttered between gasps.

Another blast from behind, and a split-second later rounds hit the ground right at their feet. They arrived at the open gate just as another machinegun blast ripped. Ozera dashed inside to safety. Bălan was right behind him, almost in, when a round caught his leg. He went down inside the tunnel, finally safely inside. Ozera, still gasping for breath, ran to him. A shot through the thigh, apparently right through, but a lot of bleeding.

Two guards, just inside, didn't know what to do. Ozera yelled that no one else would be coming, so close up and bar the doors! They looked at each other, concerned, for a moment; two of their comrades were still out there.

"They are dead," Bălan yelled, *"Close up, damn it!"* He was holding his leg and also still trying to catch his breath. Ozera grabbed a nearby equipment belt, found one of their robes and ripped off a strip of cloth. Bălan was bleeding profusely. Ozera folded the cloth and pressed it on the wound, then fixed the belt around his leg and tightened it. Bălan groaned involuntarily.

"Can you get up?" Ozera asked him. *"We need to participate in the crossing."* Bălan nodded and Ozera helped him up. The guardsmen closed and barred the massive wooden gate doors. Ozera told the two guards to get rifles loaded and ready and get back near the end of the tunnel, under cover. They immediately complied.

With Ozera propping him up, Bălan hobbled through the tunnel and into the great hall. It was brightly lit – hundreds of candles supplemented the usual wall sconces. It seemed everyone in the Monastery was there – most were seated on the benches and pews, some robed men and women, including Father Radu, stood solemnly around the ancient altar stone. All eyes were on the two of them. It was dead quiet.

"Down to the altar," Bălan told Ozera. They walked gingerly, Ozera with his arm around him. The others standing around the altar moved aside to make room for them.

"Just us!" Ozera emphatically told the old Abbot. *"The others are gone. Please proceed, Father, quickly."* Father Radu turned his gaze to Bălan. They exchanged looks and, in a moment, both nodded in tacit understanding and concurrence.

- * - * -

XIII: Crossing

Ozera glanced around the altar, counting heads. Ten robed figures standing, plus him and Bălan.

Father Radu was concentrating, in prayer, his head bowed. The other robed figures did the same, and so did Bălan. Ozera didn't know what to do so he followed Bălan's lead.

The old Abbot then raised his head and slowly gazed about the sanctuary – his white hair, furrowed face, deep-set dark eyes – an ancient persona – but radiating anticipation, confidence.

"It is time," Father Radu said. He raised his hands – his thoughts, his will, encompassing the congregation. He gazed upwards, his arms outstretched.

"Almighty God," he began, *"For millennia you have watched over us. Since the time of the beginning they have come. Macedonians. Celts. Romans. Goths. Huns. Byzantines. Kitigars. Avars. Slavs. Bulgars. Magyars. Pechenegs.... "*

Ozera felt Bălan slip, almost collapsing. His face showed pain. He wrapped his now aching arm around him tighter.

"... Saxons. Turks. Russians. Hungarians. Nazis. Communists," Father Radu finished the incredibly long litany of invaders and conquerors. So many oppressors, Ozera thought, for so long.. How these people have endured truly is a miracle.

The old Abbot continued, *"For millennia we have faced the invaders, and yet, through all the centuries, You have given us the ways and the wisdom to survive – our people and our way of life. On this night, we again beseech you."*

He turned to those around the altar stone. *"Lower your cowls; look me in the eyes,"* he commanded. They did.

Just then two explosions in rapid succession, emanating from the entrance tunnel, rocked the great hall. Ozera recognized the sound – grenade shells. They – whoever they were – were looking to penetrate the main gate doors. And in short order they would. He knew what was coming next. With holes in the massive wooden doors, they would spray the entrance tunnel with automatic weapons fire, to clear it of nearby defenders.

Father Radu was clearly shaken by the unexpected explosions, but nevertheless continued: *"Brethren, understand that your faith, the belief of every one of us here, is crucial to our salvation. A mortal enemy is upon us, and you should be filled with fear."* He paused, and then added: *"But know this, too. Deliverance is at hand."*

"We have been infused over the many centuries with the will to survive, and the means," he continued. *"God has plans for us. And to fulfill our destiny, His will, we must survive."* He scanned the group, pausing to look each in the eye. They weighed every word he spoke.

"Take each other's' hand," the old priest commanded. *"Each of you must believe we can survive. "Death is at the front gate, but know in your heart and mind that we can survive, that we can have a future in this world. Believe it. Pray for it. And concentrate on your prayer."*

Ozera looked at Bălan, whose face had turned pale. He was staring at Father Radu, deeply engaged. Ozera then turned his attention to the Abbot, too, and when their eyes met, he felt it. It was something pulling inside him. He knew it wasn't malevolent, and he knew he had to yield to it. He let himself go.

The sound of machinegun fire then reverberated from out in the tunnel.

Father Radu again raised his head and arms, his voice bellowed: *"Almighty God, we beseech you. You are the*

Creator, you are life eternal. Our time in your service is but the blink of an eye. Yet we are yours forever."

He continued: *"We, your faithful, whom you have blessed, pray for deliverance. We pray to live on ... to see our future!"* he paused, then added, in a much subdued voice: *"Thy will be done."*

Ozera knew it was over. It was quiet again in the entrance tunnel. They must have crossed. He looked over at Father Radu, who was standing uneasily, his arms on the altar supporting him, his head hanging. He seemed exhausted.

"Oh, no!" he heard someone wail. It was a robed woman on the other side of Bălan, who had been holding his hand. He looked at Bălan; his head was hanging limply. He carried him over and laid him on the first-row bench, then saw the huge puddle of blood by the altar where he was standing. Ozera looked down at his leg and a blood-drenched pant leg. The bullet wound, near his groin, had nicked the femoral artery. He tenderly cradled his head. He was gone.

Ozera looked over at Father Radu, who looked back at him across the altar stone, expressionless. Then the old Abbot nodded – a nod of understanding. He knew. He knew Bălan was dying, but he continued anyway. Bălan had told him, in the unspoken way they communicated, that he could make it through the crossing rite. And he did. It was the last thing he did.

_ * _ * _

XIII: Afterthoughts

The morning sunbeam touched his face and in a moment he awoke. He looked around the small living room and, like most mornings recently, a sense of melancholy and loneliness came over him.

He felt he didn't belong here, in this time. It had been over a year since he returned from Europe. The only person from the world he knew was his brother, Pat. And to Pat he was a ghost from the past. He tried to sense if Pat, too, might have inherited the gift. He did not. Everyone else from his world – his parents, the Colonel, Mrs. Griffiths – all were gone.

Ozera sighed. He still had no plan, no goals. But he knew from his military experience that staying in shape, and staying clean and mentally sharp, would help him accomplish whatever he did eventually set his mind to. For now it would be a brisk, two-mile run down and back the canal path along the Delaware River.

As he jogged his thoughts proliferated. Dacey and her countrymen. Where were they now? Was she alive? Would he ever see her again?

The Monastery in Romania. Where were **they** now? Others with the gift lived in the area. Did they cross again? Father Radu asked him to return, but Ozera didn't seriously consider it. He did not expect to ever again see that remote mountain plateau in the Carpathians. But Father Radu apparently thought he would. Maybe the old Abbot knew something he didn't. Premonition, it seems, was a part of the gift for some.

What actually happened to him in that Monastery in Romania? And was it the same thing that happened there on the Pennsylvania mountaintop? Was the gift simply the result of genetic evolution? How rare was it? All the Romanians who came to Pennsylvania with the Colonel, including Dacey, had it, it seems. And so did he. Apparently not all people with the gift have the same powers and capabilities to the same extent.

How much of crossing was the power of prayer? Ozera was not religious, not even spiritual, and yet he was integral to the crossing he took part in. How much of crossing was the Monastery itself – its shape, location, construction – the altar and guardian stones? Or might it be, as Dacey insisted, some combination of some or all of these things?

But if it was a one-in-a-million, one-time combination of all these things, how could it also have happened on a mountaintop in Pennsylvania – 5,000 miles away, in a version of the Monastery just built in 1990? Of course, Dacey did make sure the Monastery in Pennsylvania was … exactly as it needed to be.

Dacey – the woman he loved. Her confidence, her incredible sexuality and passion. Her unspoken wisdom, knowledge of him, of the past. She must have sensed and maybe knew it was possible, that everything needed to achieve a crossing was there in and around the Pennsylvania Monastery and mountaintop – including a dozen 'gifted' Romanians who she knew well, and who would do whatever she said. Had Dacey planned it all along?

Too many questions and too few answers, Ozera thought after finishing about a mile of his run. He would clear his mind and enjoy the scenery instead – the sluggish canal on one side of the running path, frozen around the edges, and the cold rippling Delaware on the other.

Most broadleaf trees had shed their leaves, although a few stubborn ones hung on, delivering autumn's final tinge of color. It was a cold Sunday morning and the scattered patches of ice confirmed it was still below freezing. Ozera's rapid breathing still exuded short-lived puffs of chilled vapor as he ran. He finished, his lungs now sore from the cold air. He crossed over the footbridge back to the highway and headed back up the road to his small house.

"Home again, home again," he uttered to an empty house, throwing his front-door key on the table. The morning sun now drenched the modest living room in light. Watching dust particles dance in the sunbeams, a feeling came over him. It was just a feeling, but he sensed that somehow, today would be something special. It was like he learned back in Romania, the feelings he would share with others who had the gift. He would be meeting someone else soon with the gift. It was a premonition. He felt it.

He had concluded that no one within a hundred miles had the gift, not even his brother. Since his return he suspected a few times that someone he met might have it – a man here, a woman there, someone with dark-haired, high-cheekbone features or with a Romanian-sounding name. But all attempts to communicate – to plant a harmless mental suggestion and have them respond, like Father Radu taught him – so far failed.

Still only 8:30 am, according to the digital clock on the coffeemaker. It was his usual morning routine: after his run he'd shower and shave while the coffeemaker hissed and gurgled. Then he'd figure how to best spend the rest of the day.

Cleaned up, clad in sweatshirt, jeans and sneakers and with a steaming black coffee in hand, Ozera plopped into the armchair at his desk.

"Computer!" Ozera announced. "Status!" The computer activated and immediately began checking its sub-routines.

"Good morning, Brad. There have been 18 motion-sensor alerts since you last checked," the synthesized female voice replied.

It was a high number of incidents – an uncommonly high number. "Computer! What times were they?" he ordered.

"Starting at 0431 this morning, then 0630 and then every five minutes since 0655," she replied, emotionless. The program was set to record any motion-sensor disturbance and snap a picture of it, but no more than once every five minutes. That gave roaming animals a chance to move out of the field of vision before the next check five minutes later.

"Computer! Show me the first alert."

"This was taken at 0431 this morning," the synthesized voice said, while at the same time displaying a picture on the large, high resolution display screen. It showed a night-vision shot of the mountaintop with a raccoon looking right in the camera's lens. Ozera chuckled.

"Computer! Show me the next alert!" he said.

"This was taken at 0630 this morning," the voice said, and a picture displayed of a bright, incoherent mess. He'd seen this before, at dawn. The camera faced towards the southeast. And if the rising sun shone into the camera lens while it was still set for night-vision, this would be the result. The blinding sun and early morning shadows would trip the motion detector.

"Computer! Show me the next one!"

"This was taken at 0655 this morning," and an updated picture flashed on the screen.

"Holy shit," Ozera muttered. He plopped his coffee mug on the table, much of it splashing out, and stood up. In a few seconds he had grabbed an overcoat and charged out the front door, slamming it shut behind him.

The picture on the screen showed two robed figures who had walked into the camera's field of vision, tripping the motion detector and camera. Behind them was a massive structure that wasn't there before – well, not for a long, long time.

He pulled off the roadway by the blocked off entrance and parked. He jumped out, slamming the hybrid-car's door behind him, and took off running up the gravel drive. Halfway up he saw a robed figure coming down. It was the cook's assistant, looking the same as when he last saw him. He looked up and saw another coming down – it was Maria the cook.

"Good morning, Captain!" she exclaimed as she bounced along in the bright morning sun. He stopped to catch his breath and nodded in recognition to her. She, too, looked the same – as if she'd made him breakfast in the dining hall just yesterday.

"Is everybody okay?" he called to her.

"Just fine," she yelled back, and continued on down the path.

Up at the parking lot were the others – all in their robes, all in good spirits and health, some pausing to exchange greetings with him. But there was no Dacey. He ran the remaining way up the pathway to the top, stopping just outside the Monastery, the large wooden gates were both wide open.

As he labored to catch his breath a figure emerged from the entrance. It was Dacey. She looked tired, drained. She looked over and, seeing him, started crying. He went to her, arms open.

"Oh, Brad," she said, sobbing, as they embraced. "I hoped, I felt you'd be here. But I expected … a much older you."

"I am a little older," he said with a smile, "But a lot wiser. It's a long story, Dacey. God, I'm glad to see you."

She smiled up at him. She looked frail. He put his arm around her as they walked away from the Monastery, down the path together. She stepped unsteadily and they stopped a moment.

"We have to walk all the way down to the entrance," he told her. "Can you make it?" She looked at him hopefully and nodded. He looked into her eyes – and it came to him.

"You're pregnant. We are going to have a child," he said quietly, contemplating the thought.

She nodded. "A son," she said and smiled slightly.

* _ * _ *

The horses whinnied as they approached the gate, alerting the guard. He turned and yelled inside.

"*Go tell the sergeant! They're back from Bobeica with supplies.*"

Two men led the heavily laden horses to just outside the gate. The horses snorted disrespectfully.

"*So what's happening down below? Is the village still there?*" the guard asked facetiously.

"*It's there, but a lot of things have changed,*" the older one replied, a serious tone in his voice.

Two robed men exited from the gateway – a wiry young man with jet-black wavy hair, and a taller, broad-chested man in his late 20's, with a ruggedly handsome face, wearing a Special Forces Green Beret. The guard hastily unshouldered his rifle and snapped to attention.

"*They just got back, Captain,*" the guard said. The captain nodded and went over to the older man.

"*How'd it go, Iulian?*" he asked him.

"Fine, sir," he replied, *"We told them we were from the Monastery. They looked puzzled and took us to the new owner. But he seemed to be expecting us. He gave us everything we asked for, and he wouldn't take any payment."*

The Captain nodded approvingly. Iulian was one of his best men. He was keenly aware of everything happening around him. He could accurately assess the situation and report concisely.

"Is there any reason we shouldn't send our people out?" the Captain asked him directly.

"No, sir. No danger down in the village that we saw. But there's some strange new things our people need to know before they go out."

"Okay. Good job," the Captain said. *"Go report to the Prior and tell him whatever you learned."* He nodded and ran inside.

Iulian knocked on the open door and an aging, 50-ish Ozera looked up. *"Brother Iulian. Welcome back,"* he said.

"Your son sent me to report to you, sir."

"Just a moment," Ozera said, standing up. *"Let me get the Abbess."* He walked to the door behind him and knocked. A female voice asked him to enter.

There, behind an old wooden desk sat Dacey, her long white hair pulled back in a ponytail. In Ozera's eyes she was, and would always be, the most beautiful woman he'd ever known.

"Dacey, my love," he said softly. "Iulian is back and ready to report. Let's hear what he has to say."

She looked up at him lovingly, and gave him a wink.

###

www.ingramcontent.com/pod-product-compliance
Lightning Source LLC
Chambersburg PA
CBHW030752260626
47169CB00001B/13